A
Peculiar
Courtship

A
Peculiar
Courtship

Laura Beers

MORE ROMANCE BY LAURA BEERS

ENGLAND, 1813

"Papa, I pray that you are safe," Lady Hannah whispered, as her hands circled around her waist tightly in a vain attempt to comfort herself, and also to ward off the chill. Her borrowed, tattered, wool dress did little to keep her warm on these cold spring mornings.

She moved to the small window, looking out onto the green rolling hills that she had grown accustomed to seeing for these past weeks. The tip of the sun began to emerge over the field, illuminating the low-hanging, translucent mist. Not so long ago, she would have been fast asleep in her soft featherbed, but now she was on a farm and had chores to do. Just this morning, she had awoken before dawn and had already fed and milked the cow.

A movement caught her attention. She saw a group of smelly, four-legged sheep walking in the gated pasture, forming a tight circle. She rested her forehead against the cold, glass pane, and started giggling at the thought of Lucy spending her morning coaxing the flock of sheep into a circle. Hannah had no experience with sheep prior to her stay with the Dawsons, but she had grown to love these long-wooled, silver animals.

"Hannah, you up there?" Lucy's loud voice came from the bottom of the ladder.

"I am. I will be down shortly," Hannah shouted. An image floated through her mind of her former governess shaking her head at her lack of decorum.

"Don't bother. I'm coming up." Within a few moments, Lucy climbed up the ladder and joined her by the window. Her blonde hair was pulled tightly into a bun at the base of her neck, highlighting her slender face and blue eyes. "Are you thinking about your father again?"

Hannah lifted her head off the window pane and turned to face her dear friend. "Yes. I pray that he is safe." A light sheen of moisture clouded her eyes as she willed herself to blink the tears away. "What if he is dead?"

With a kind smile, Lucy replied, "And what if your father is in his study, smoking cigars, drinking champagne, and has his feet propped up on his insanely expensive, utterly priceless, sofa?" Her smile then turned mischievous. "Or he could be riding around his lands while wearing diamonds woven into his greatcoat, all while he is enjoying delicious pastries."

Hannah chuckled softly. "I believe you might be a little confused about how the gentry make use of their time, or spend their money."

Lucy hugged her tightly, then leaned back. "Your father could be back at your castle, desperately trying to find you. Just be patient. We will get a note to Lord Beckett, then all will be well."

Comforted by her friend's kind words, Hannah acknowledged, "You are right, of course." She sat down on the edge of her straw bed with a smile on her lips. "Just so you know, I do not live in a castle."

"No?" Lucy smiled. "Palace then."

Hannah ran her fingers over the fleece sheets on her bed. "Do you truly believe Samuel will make the journey to deliver the note for me? After all, I do not know exactly where Lord Beckett's estate is."

Lucy tilted her chin up, leveled a stare at her, and said in all seriousness, "He will do as I ask of him." For a moment, no one spoke, then she broke into a fit of giggles.

Hannah laughed loudly at her friend's mischievousness. "I cannot wait to be properly introduced to Samuel today. I feel as if I am already acquainted with him, since you have regaled me with story after story about your betrothed."

Lucy gave her a mock pout. "I do not talk about him *all* the time."

"You do, but I am not complaining," Hannah said as she grabbed her friend's hand, yanking her down to sit next to her on the bed.

"Samuel is such a hard worker, you know." Lucy's eyes gleamed with joy. "He bought the livery stable in the village over a year ago, and as soon as he acquires three horses of his own, we will be married. Right now, he only has two."

Hannah could not help but tease her friend. "Just two?" She tapped a finger against her lips, pretending to be in deep thought. "What if we brought Samuel your largest sheep, Horace. He is the size of a pony. Would that be permissible?"

"Don't tease me about Horace," Lucy said, as a giggle escaped her lips. "He enjoys parading after me."

"Like Samuel," Hannah quipped.

She knew she had said the right thing, because Lucy's eyes glazed over for a moment before turning her attention back to the conversation. "I just love him so much. I think about him all the time. I even dream about him at night."

Hannah's lips twitched slightly. "Samuel, or Horace?"

Rolling her eyes, Lucy said, "Samuel, silly." She glanced at the opening in the floor before she leaned closer. "He kissed me last time we were in town. I'm hoping he will kiss me again today."

"He kissed you?"

"Yes. He snuck in a kiss at his livery stable when he showed me his new horse." Lucy's eyes looked dreamy. "I really enjoyed kissing him."

"You should refrain from kissing Samuel until you are married. If anyone caught you kissing, then…"

"Then what? He will be forced to marry me?" Lucy laughed. "That is what I want more than anything else in the world."

Smiling, Hannah replied, "I keep forgetting how different our worlds are. Among the ton, or High Society, being caught in a compromising position, like kissing, is scandalous and brings shame to you and your families."

"Have you never been kissed?"

Hannah shook her head in response. "I have never had a suitor, either."

"Oh, a suitor," Lucy said mockingly. "You had better not marry a suitor unless you love him." She lifted an eyebrow. "Or does your father pick a groom for you?"

Hannah smiled in amusement at Lucy's mock disapproval. "My father defied his family when he married my mother, who was a Spaniard. I believe my father will let me follow my heart, as he did with his own."

"When you do marry, can I come to your wedding?"

Hannah gave her a surprised look. "Of course, you may come to my wedding, but only if I can come to yours."

Lucy looked sheepishly at the ground. "My wedding won't be anything special. We will probably just post the banns and get married at the parish." Lucy started smoothing out her thin, weathered dress, a sign that she was upset. "We don't have any extra money for another dress and you are currently borrowing my spare one."

Hannah sighed and wished she could help Lucy with funds, but she couldn't do that until she was reunited with her father. "It does not matter what you get married in. It is more important to *whom* you get married."

Lucy offered a weak smile, seeming unconvinced. "I hope you are right."

"Besides, I promised you that I would find a way to provide your family with extra funds as soon as I am reunited with my father. If not for your immediate care, I would have died in that ravine."

"You owe us nothing." Lucy turned and rested her back against the wall. "We got the best of that bargain. Since you recovered, you have been helping me with my chores."

Laughing, Hannah retorted, "I am afraid I am more of a hindrance than help."

"Well, my mother has enjoyed having another woman around," Lucy conceded with a smile.

Hannah's lips pressed into a tight line because she never seemed to win this argument. The Dawson family had been nothing but kind and nurturing these past few weeks, welcoming her into their small one-bedroom home with a loft, and using their meager supplies to help her. She was aware that their funds were extremely limited, and yet they never complained that she was another mouth to feed. Even though she helped with chores, she could never repay them in hard labor.

"Girls, stop chatting and come down for breakfast. We need to hurry if we want to get on the road soon," Mrs. Dawson's cheerful voice called from the main floor.

"You heard Ma," Lucy said, jumping off the bed and scurrying down the ladder.

With a heavy heart, Hannah glanced out the window, watching the sun slowly work its way up past the green hills. Her hand clutched her father's last letter in her pocket. The letter told her what to do if she encountered any danger. The instructions were explicit: *Trust no one, except Lord Beckett.*

Once they arrived at the village, she would need to persuade

Samuel to get a note to Lord Beckett. Until then, Hannah was going to bask in the love that the Dawsons showered freely upon her, knowing she was blessed to have been saved by such a kind, loving family.

"HANNAH, YOU NEED TO PUT MORE DIRT ON YOUR FACE," MR. Dawson said, holding up a pile of dirt in his hands. "Your skin is still too white."

"But I already rubbed dirt on my face and the bonnet hides my black hair," Hannah complained. She did not want to rub any more dirt on her person.

Mrs. Dawson came up to her, gently placing an arm around her dusty shoulder. "Dear, what Mr. Dawson is attempting to say, but is not bold enough, is that you are still too clean. We don't want anyone to take a good look at you, since the daughter of an earl would never be as filthy as you are."

Sighing, she held out her hands. "Just a little then." Mr. Dawson dropped the dirt into her awaiting hands. She hesitated as the dirt billowed around her fingers, attempting to reason with them one more time. "There is a chance that no one will be searching for me in this area."

Mr. Dawson shook his head. "I don't want to take that risk. You have very distinctive features and we do not want anyone to take note of you."

Hannah knew that he was referring to her long, straight, black hair and porcelain skin that was so much like her mother's. "I disappeared from my estate almost six weeks ago. Plus, we are at least a two-day ride from my home. Those men might have given up trying to find me."

"And your steward?" Mr. Dawson pressed. "Would he have given up trying to locate you?"

Shaking her head, Hannah replied, "Most likely not. I would imagine that he is anxious to find me. He wouldn't want me to inform anyone of his involvement in my attempted abduction."

Annoyed, Lucy shouted from the wagon, "Just put the dirt on your face, Hannah. The longer we are on the side of the road, the less time I get to spend with Samuel."

Mrs. Dawson's lips curled into a smile. "Well, I believe that the mistress has spoken."

Hannah knew that she was outnumbered and started rubbing dirt on her face and neck. "Is this sufficient, Mrs. Dawson?"

"Aunt Maggie," Mrs. Dawson corrected kindly. "You must remember to call me Aunt Maggie when we arrive at the village."

"Yes, Aunt Maggie," Hannah said with a smile, as she wiped her hands off on her dress. Unfortunately, she was not sure which was dirtier, her hands or her dress. "Uncle Phillip?" She noticed that he was looking at something in the dirt road near the horses. She sucked in her breath when she realized what had drawn his attention. "No! Absolutely not!"

Looking apologetic, Mr. Dawson said, "If we smear dung on your dress then no one would even approach you, much less talk to you."

Hannah whipped her head around to the wagon. "Please, Mrs. Dawson," she pleaded.

Mrs. Dawson winced as she looked down at the smelly pile. "Phillip, do we really need to use horse dung to keep people away from her? If we keep Hannah by us then no one will get close enough to talk to her."

"Besides, if Hannah has dung on her then I refuse to let her be around me and Samuel." Lucy huffed.

Laughing, Hannah could not resist teasing her friend. "You just want Samuel to kiss you again."

Lucy's face turned bright red as she stuttered, "I... uh... that is..." She gave up and dropped her gaze to her lap.

"One kiss every six weeks sounds like a proper courtship to me," Mr. Dawson commented as he assisted his wife into the wagon. He winked at Hannah as he helped her into the back of the wagon. "Besides, we raised ourselves a right, proper girl who knows what we expect from Samuel."

"Yes, Pa," Lucy said with her gaze still firmly on her lap.

The wagon dipped as Mr. Dawson seated himself in the front and reached for the reins. As he flicked them, the horse started methodically walking along the dirt road. In every direction, Hannah noticed lush green fields rising and falling, eventually mingling with towering trees.

Mr. Dawson's voice broke up the silence that had descended over the family. "I am sure hoping that Samuel will recognize Lucy. After all, it has been six weeks and a lot can change in the appearance of a young woman during that time," he teased. "Maybe Samuel found a more agreeable young lady that does her chores without complaining."

"Ma, will you please ask Pa to stop teasing me," Lucy said through clenched teeth.

Smiling, Mrs. Dawson said, "Phillip, will you please stop teasing Lucy."

"What do you think, Hannah? Should I stop teasing Lucy about Samuel?" Mr. Dawson asked, glancing over his shoulder.

Lucy shot her a pleading glance and Hannah decided to take pity on her friend. "I do believe that we have teased Lucy enough for the day," she replied.

Thank you, Lucy mouthed.

"Please tell me about the inn where we are staying tonight," Hannah said, deliberately bringing up a new topic.

"The inn is near the edge of the village and is a respectable place," Mrs. Dawson answered.

"And the beef stew." Mr. Dawson's approving whistle was

soft. "The inn boasts comfortable beds, and it is a real treat to rest my head there when we ride into town every six weeks."

Hannah was curious. "Why not sell the fleece, or buy supplies, then drive the wagon back home? Would that not save you the expense of sleeping at the inn overnight?"

Mr. Dawson faced straight ahead as he answered her question. "As you may have noticed, it takes almost three hours to bring the wagon into the village, especially when it is loaded down with the fleece we hope to sell." Shifting the reins into his one hand, he reached over and affectionately patted Mrs. Dawson's leg. "And my poor wife could not endure six hours in a wagon, and I dare not leave her alone at our farm, so we plan for this extravagance every time we come into town."

Lucy leaned forward, with her hand at the side of her mouth. "Besides, I get to spend more time with Samuel if we stay overnight."

"If you look over that rise, you will see the village. Just a few more minutes now," Mrs. Dawson said, pointing at the rising smoke coming from the chimneys.

Mr. Dawson tilted his head back towards her. "Remember, you are our niece and are visiting from the north. Don't speak to anyone, and keep your head down. We will talk to Samuel and ask him to leave immediately."

Once again, Hannah was grateful that the Dawson family was willing to help her. "I have funds with me to pay Samuel for his journey." Her father's instructions insisted that she carried twenty pounds with her everywhere she went. The money was to ensure her passage to Lord Beckett.

"You will have to discuss that with Samuel after we guarantee his cooperation. He will charge you a fair price, that I am sure," Mr. Dawson said, nodding. He turned back to focus on the team.

The wagon slowly rolled onto the worn cobblestone streets of the village as it made its way towards the center. Careful to keep her head down, Hannah could not help but glance at the shops. Beautiful ribbons and lace were displayed to the public through glass windows. Delicious aromas of meat and freshly baked bread made her stomach growl, reminding her that she had not eaten since breakfast.

Lucy must have heard the offending noise, because she gave her a knowing smile. "Don't fret. It will only take a brief time for Pa to conclude his business, then we can go to the inn for some beef stew."

The wagon lurched to a stop in front of a plain, stone building with a thatched roof. A worn sign reading *Mercantile* hung over the door. Mr. Dawson locked the brake on the wagon and jumped off. He came around to the other side and helped Mrs. Dawson climb down.

Mr. Dawson placed his hand on the side of the wagon, and lowered his voice as he said, "We will attend to our business and head right back." He waited until Hannah looked directly at him. "Keep your head down and do not speak to anyone." She nodded and watched them stroll into the building.

"Lucy!" a deep, male voice shouted over all the noise of the village. "Lucy!"

Lucy jumped up, causing the wagon to rock back and forth, and started waving. "Samuel!"

A few moments later, a tall, broad-shouldered man assisted Lucy out of the wagon. Once her feet were on the ground, he immediately pulled her into a tight embrace. "I have missed you, Lucy," Samuel said, clearly not caring a bit if anyone could overhear him.

Hannah risked a peek at her friend and was rewarded to see joy etched on Lucy's face. It was apparent by their joint reactions that these two loved each other. What must it feel like to love a man and to have that love returned wholeheartedly? For the briefest moment, Hannah felt a twinge of jealousy towards her dear friend.

Samuel glanced in her direction and she dropped her gaze back down to her lap. "And who do we have here?" he asked.

With a wave of her hand, Lucy replied, "Oh, that is just my cousin from up north."

"Does your cousin have a name?" Samuel pressed.

"Of course, she has a name. It is Ha…, uh… Harriet," Lucy said, recovering nicely.

"Hello, Harriet," Samuel said to her weathered, faded bonnet. When she failed to respond, he asked, "Is she mute?"

"Oh no, Harriet is very shy," Lucy attempted to explain. "She doesn't talk to strangers at all, so you should stop trying to talk to her. It is making her feel uncomfortable."

"All right," Samuel stated, turning back to give Lucy his full attention. "The most amazing thing happened. When I was in the woods a few weeks ago, I came across a beautiful white horse with black socks. It had a fancy side-saddle attached, but no rider."

Hannah gasped. *Samuel was talking about her horse, Pirata.*

Leaning closer to the wagon, Lucy asked in concern, "Harriet, are you feeling well?"

"He is talking about my horse," she said in a hushed tone.

Samuel continued his story, unaware of her turmoil. "I was able to rope the horse and board it at the livery stable. Do you know what that means, Lucy?" His voice was filled with excitement. "I finally have three horses. We can be married!"

An awkward silence filled the air for a few moments. "Maybe you should attempt to locate the owner of the horse," Lucy suggested.

An incredulous huff escaped his lips before Samuel replied, "I did. I spent over an hour looking for the rider. It was obvious that the horse had been wandering for some time in the woods. It was skittish, so it took me days before I could properly tend to it. I made some inquiries, but no one has come forward." Hannah could hear Samuel shuffle his feet. "I thought you would be pleased that we could finally be married."

"I am!" Lucy exclaimed quickly.

"Then what is it?" he prodded gently.

Hesitantly, Lucy ventured, "I think I may know the owner of the horse."

Hannah slightly raised her head to watch the interaction between Lucy and Samuel. He ran his hand through his hair and it was obvious that Lucy's revelation frustrated him. "How could you possibly know who owns that horse, Lucy?" he asked in apparent disbelief.

She lowered her voice. "I believe the horse belongs to Lady Hannah, the daughter of Lord Pembrooke."

Samuel laughed loudly. "You are teasing me, right? How would you even know Lady Hannah? The whole village has been talking about her disappearance six weeks ago. There's a reward of fifty pounds for her return. Can you imagine that much money?"

"Who is offering the reward?" Lucy asked as she smoothed out her dress.

"Two men came into town about a month ago and announced the reward. Rumor has it that the steward of Lord Pembrooke is putting up his own money for her safe return."

Hannah closed her eyes, suddenly feeling nauseous, remembering the betrayal of Mr. Walker, her family's steward. She had trusted him! Her father had trusted him!

Lucy's voice broke into her thoughts. "I've heard that Lord Pembrooke's steward is a bad man. You need to stay away from those men, especially if they are associating with the steward."

"Where did you hear that? The steward is trying to return Lady Hannah back to her home," Samuel insisted.

"Maybe he sent those two men to abduct her in the first place," Lucy countered.

Samuel furrowed his brow. "I must be missing something

here. I did not realize you knew so much about Lady Hannah and her situation. How did you hear about it on the farm? I'm certain news doesn't travel that fast out that far."

Nervously, Lucy glanced over her shoulder. "Uh... someone stopped to rest at the farm a few weeks ago and told us about it. I just want you to avoid those men."

"You are not making any sense," Samuel said, clearly frustrated by the direction of the conversation.

At that precise moment, Mr. Dawson came out of the building with a huge smile on his face. "Mr. Rosen said he will buy all the fleece. I'm going to bring the wagon around back to unload."

Samuel placed a hand on Lucy's arm. "Do you mind if I keep Lucy with me for a few moments, sir?"

Nodding, Mr. Dawson said, "Don't mind at all, my boy. Hannah can stay with me while we unload the wagon."

"Hannah? I thought your cousin's name was Harriet," Samuel inquired.

Flustered, Lucy attempted to explain, "Her name is Harriet Hannah but she prefers being called Harriet."

Hannah dropped her gaze firmly to her lap, refusing to acknowledge the silence around her. Suddenly, she found herself being picked up by the waist and placed on the ground next to the wagon. She kept her focus on the ground, but realized they did not give Samuel enough credit, as he obviously saw through their ruse.

Samuel huffed as he stood in front of her. "I think only Harriet Hannah can answer my questions."

"Samuel, please. This is not the time or the place for this," Lucy whispered urgently.

Hannah heard Samuel blow out a long breath. He gently grabbed her upper arm and guided her into an alleyway. She could hear Mr. Dawson and Lucy following closely behind. Once deep into the narrow passage, Samuel dropped her arm.

"Are you Lady Hannah?" Samuel asked directly.

Hannah shook her head and kept her gaze fixed to the ground. The smells in the alley made her question what kind of liquid was sitting stagnant on the ground. She wished for a rose-scented handkerchief so she could put it up to her nose at this moment.

Samuel growled. "Look at me, Lady Hannah. I'm not a simpleton."

Hannah tilted her head to look at Lucy and Mr. Dawson. They both nodded their encouragement. She squared her shoulders, straightened her spine, and lifted her eyes to meet Samuel's intense gaze.

🐿 2 🐿

HANNAH GOT HER FIRST GOOD LOOK AT SAMUEL. HE HAD DARK blond, curly hair, with an unruly lock curling low on his forehead and dark green eyes. His face was square, and a hint of stubble shadowed his jaw. She could see how Lucy found him attractive. Even though his green eyes were blazing and his arms were crossed tightly in front of him, she did not fear him.

"Lucy, can you explain to me why you are masquerading Lady Hannah around as your cousin?" Samuel's jaw was clenched so tightly that she worried he might crack a tooth.

"Well, you see…" Lucy's voice trailed off as Samuel latched his gaze onto her. "We found her and… uh…"

"You found her, so you kept her?" Samuel asked in disbelief.

Placing his hands in front of him, Mr. Dawson said, "Samuel, you need to calm down. We have a rational explanation and we don't want to draw attention to ourselves." He glanced over his shoulder. "Why don't you walk the girls over to the livery stable to discuss this matter? As soon as Mrs. Dawson and I finish our business, we will join you at the inn."

Samuel nodded his head and put his hand out indicating the ladies should walk out of the alleyway ahead of him. Upon reaching the crowded street, he offered his arms to them. They started walking and Samuel leaned over, whispering to Hannah, "Just follow my lead. Don't look up or your disguise will be useless."

They walked a few blocks until horse dung gave off a pungent, repellent stench, an unfortunate sign that the livery stable was nearby. As they entered, the sounds of the horses reached Hannah's ears. She looked up to see her horse in one of the stalls and broke into a run.

"Pirata!" Upon reaching her beloved friend, she wrapped her arms around his neck and breathed in the familiar scent. After a moment, she released her grip and slowly stroked her horse's neck, speaking in a reassuring tone.

Samuel leaned against the stall, smiling knowingly. "I take it this is your steed?"

"Yes, we became separated when I fell off," Hannah confirmed, refusing to take her eyes off her horse.

"Why is your horse named Pirata?" Lucy asked as she stood close to Samuel.

"Pirata is the Spanish word for pirate," she revealed. "I named my horse after my mother shared a book about Piratas."

Samuel shook his head, putting one finger to his lips and pointing to a small office in one corner of the stable with the other hand. "Follow me. We need to talk openly and this is not the place to accomplish that."

Hannah begrudgingly left her horse and followed Samuel and Lucy into a small office. Samuel closed the door behind him, then moved to sit behind a small, crude desk. He pointed to two old wooden chairs facing the desk. "Please sit and start explaining what is going on."

Hannah sat as rigidly as she could in the wobbly chair, clasping her hands in her lap. "Mr…" her voice trailing off as she frowned. "Oh dear, I am afraid I do not know how to address you, since we have not been formally introduced."

"Call me Samuel." He smirked and added, "After all, you will be my cousin when Lucy and I are married."

Hannah cleared her throat, attempting to gain some control over this conversation. "I believe we all underestimated your ability to see through my disguise."

Samuel guffawed, then attempted to stifle it. "Dirt on your face is not a disguise. Any fool could see your black hair, which is not at all common around here."

Smiling playfully at her, Lucy said, "We should have let Pa use the dung."

"What?" Samuel exclaimed in disbelief.

"Pa wanted to put horse dung on Hannah's dress so no one would approach her," Lucy informed him.

Wiping a hand slowly over his face, Samuel asked, "Lucy, what have you got yourself into?"

"What have I gotten myself into?" Lucy repeated back. "Am I a child that needs to be looked after? Is that the way you think of me?"

Samuel frowned. "No, that is not what I think. Can someone please just tell me what is going on?"

As Hannah met Samuel's gaze, she knew it was time to tell him the truth. "About six weeks ago, Mr. Walker, the steward at my father's estate, betrayed my family. He sent two men to abduct me when I was out for a morning ride. My horse is incredibly fast, which allowed me to lose them in the woods near my home. Unfortunately, I rode so far into the woods that I lost my way. I wandered around for days until Pirata stumbled and I was thrown. Next thing I knew, I was at the Dawsons' home, and I have been staying there ever since."

Lucy piped up, "We found Hannah when we were out looking for truffles. She had a nasty bruise on her head and a fever when we found her. We took her home and cared for her."

In an irritated tone, Samuel said, "Lady Hannah is not a stray animal. You can't just take her home and keep her."

Lucy furrowed her brows as she stared at her betrothed. "Didn't you hear the part where I said she had a fever? She spent almost two weeks in bed recovering."

"What did she do the rest of the time?" Samuel asked.

"I learned how to milk a cow," Hannah announced proudly.

"Congratulations, it took you four weeks to learn how to milk a cow," Samuel said dryly.

Defensively, Hannah replied, "No, I also learned how to feed the chickens, and I helped Lucy with her other chores."

Samuel placed his arms onto the desk, and leaned forward. "You put Lucy at risk by being at her farm."

Lucy sat forward in her chair, causing it to wobble. "Samuel, you are being ridiculous. Why would anyone suspect Lady Hannah was living on a sheep farm?"

Samuel eyed Hannah suspiciously. "And you did not think to alert the magistrate?"

"Pray tell, how would we have traveled to see the magistrate?" Lucy said, raising her voice. "You know we only can afford to come to town every six weeks to trade and get supplies."

"Besides, I was told only to trust Lord Beckett," Hannah asserted.

Samuel reluctantly removed his gaze from Lucy to acknowledge Hannah's claim. "Who told you to trust Lord Beckett?"

Hannah's hand slipped into her pocket and clutched the note there. "My father sent me a note explaining that my life could be in danger and to seek out only Lord Beckett. I was hoping that you might deliver a note to him for me?"

Sighing loudly, Samuel asked, "Where might I find this Lord Beckett?"

Hannah gave him a nervous look as she explained, "I do not know. I am not familiar with his family."

"Don't all of your families mingle during the Season?" Samuel asked incredulously.

"I have spent most of my life in Bath at our country estate and I have not been introduced into Society yet," Hannah informed him.

Samuel looked up at the rafters for a moment. "Assuming I can find Lord Beckett, what will you tell him in the note?"

"I can only imagine that Lord Beckett is aware of the pending threat on my life and would welcome the news of my whereabouts," Hannah said, hoping her statement was even remotely true.

Samuel observed her for a moment before he ventured, "Lady Hannah, I am unable to close the livery stable for a week to do your bidding. I apologize, but..."

Hannah spoke over him, "I can pay you. How much do you require?" He had to deliver the note. There was no other way.

Samuel started shaking his head and pushed away from the desk. He walked to the other side of the room, which was only a few feet. "My answer is no."

Lucy rose from her chair, walked over to him, and placed her hands on his chest. "Please, Samuel. I have grown to care for Hannah like a sister. Her life may be at stake. Can you please help her?"

Samuel gazed at Lucy for a long moment before he brought his hand up to tenderly embrace hers. "You do not understand. If I close the livery, then it will be even longer before we can be married."

Lucy's eyes pleaded with him. "I do understand, but Hannah needs our help. I would not want to get married sooner at the cost of her safety."

Samuel's eyes flickered towards Hannah. She could tell he was not pleased at this development, but his eyes softened as he focused back on his betrothed. "When you look at me like that, I would do anything you ask of me."

Lucy threw her arms around Samuel's neck. "Thank you, Samuel. I love you so much."

Without releasing his hold on Lucy, he said, "Well, it appears that tomorrow I will ride out to find Lord Beckett, wherever he may be."

Hannah gave Samuel a relieved smile. "Thank you, Samuel. I will pay you whatever you think is fair."

Samuel acknowledged her comment by nodding his head. "Ladies, let me escort you to the inn, while I attempt to find someone to fill in for me here."

Hannah strolled out of the office and moved towards her horse's stall. As she walked closer, two men stepped out of the shadows. Her eyes grew wide as she recognized them. Both times she had only seen them from afar, but there was no mistaking their profiles. One of the men was tall and lanky, whereas the other man was short and stout. She quickly froze, lowered her head, and took a few steps backward, attempting to put more space between them.

Samuel's booming voice echoed in the stable. "Can I help you two?"

The two men were edging closer and panic swelled inside of her. Should she run? Samuel came to stand next to her, stopping her retreat.

Lucy must have sensed her alarm because she slipped her arm around Hannah's shoulders. "Come on, cousin. Let's wait in the office until Samuel concludes his business, then we will be on our way."

"Before you go, we were wondering if either of you have seen Lady Hannah around town?" The man's voice was grizzly.

Samuel placed his hand on the small of her back, reassuring her that everything would be all right. "No, but we will watch for her. I would not mind the reward money." He chuckled. "Gentlemen, I am going to walk these ladies out, but I will be back to assist you."

One of the men stepped closer towards her. His worn brown boots were only a few feet away, and it was all she could do not to squeak. "Do you mind if I ask this little lady if she has seen anything?"

Samuel stepped forward, slightly blocking her view from the repulsive man. "Actually, I do mind. My cousin is extremely shy and does not wish to talk to strangers." He extended his arm and Hannah eagerly latched onto it.

Together, they quickly walked along the street towards the inn. "Are they following us?" Hannah asked quietly after a few moments.

Glancing over her shoulder, Lucy confirmed, "No, but they are ogling us. They are both extremely unfortunate-looking. I think the constable should arrest them just because their ugliness offends me."

Hannah laughed at her friend's antics. Lucy could always make her laugh, even when the situation was dire. "I think most criminals are required to be unfortunate-looking."

Samuel did not look amused by their humor. "We need to devise a new plan. I'm surprised they did not try to stop us, but the people milling outside the livery must have given them pause. It was obvious they did not believe you are my cousin," he pointed out.

Hannah dropped her head in defeat. "I am sorry. First, I put you and your parents at risk. Now, I am putting Samuel at risk, too."

Samuel stopped walking and turned her to face him. He put his hands on her forearms, waiting for her eyes to meet his. "Don't give up. We will figure this out." He waited until she nodded, then he dropped his hands. "We will find this Lord Beckett and he will keep you safe. I promise."

Tears came to Hannah's eyes and one trailed down her face. "Thank you, Samuel." She wiped her face and hoped that no harm would come to these good people.

3

Lord Jonathon Beckett saw the lights of a village up ahead. He urged his horse into a run. For almost six weeks, he had been searching for Lady Hannah, only going home to replenish his clothing and supplies.

His uncle, Lord Charles Beckett, had tasked him with retrieving Lady Hannah from her country home and protecting her until she was turned over to his uncle's care. Unfortunately, Lady Hannah seemed to have disappeared on her morning ride and no one, not even her housekeeper or steward, had any idea where she might have run off to.

It was vital that Lady Hannah be placed under protection. Her father, Lord Pembrooke, claimed to have proof of Lord Camden's failed assassination plot against Prinny, the Prince Regent. If Lady Hannah fell prey to Lord Camden, a known French spy, then all would be lost. He would use her as a pawn in his game of treachery.

No, I will find Lady Hannah and keep her safe, Jonathon thought, as he rode hard towards the village. Ever since he had been given this assignment, he felt it was vitally important, almost personal. He shrugged off the feeling, knowing that was a ridiculous notion. This was his job as an agent of the Crown, and protecting Lady Hannah was just another assignment.

Jonathon slowed his horse as he rode into the village. Most of the shops were preparing to close as the sun started setting, casting a dark haze over the village. No one acknowledged his presence as he made his way through town, looking for the livery stable. He noted the inn and heard loud laughter floating through the open windows.

Jonathon pulled up near the livery stable and tied his horse to a post out front. He walked in and saw a man pacing back and forth, mumbling incoherently.

"I was hoping to board my horse for the evening," Jonathan announced.

The man stopped pacing and looked at him, apparently just noticing he had a customer. "I'm sorry, but it appears that I will be closing the livery for a few days while I am forced to deal with a pressing matter."

"By chance does this village have two livery stables?"

"No. However, the inn does have a stable in the back, but you will have to groom and feed your horse yourself," the man informed him.

Jonathon nodded. "Thank you for your time."

Turning to leave, a flash of white caught his eyes. He walked closer to the stall that housed the white horse and leaned over to see if it had black markings along its feet. His breath hitched. This was Lady Hannah's horse! He turned back to the man and asked, "Do you know where the owner of this horse is?"

Shaking his head, the man answered, "No, sir. I found the horse in the woods when I was riding. It appeared that the rider, a woman by the side-saddle, must have let her horse loose."

Jonathon walked closer to the man. "Will you take me to where you found the horse?"

The man rubbed his chin with his hand. "Sir, I told you that I have something that I need to do. I don't have time to take a ride into the woods."

Jonathon restrained his retort. This was the closest he'd come to discovering Lady Hannah's whereabouts. Attempting to reason with him, he explained, "I have been searching for Lady Hannah for these past six weeks. I have been tasked to keep her safe by her father, Lord Pembrooke. If her horse was found nearby, then there is a chance she could be in the vicinity. It is of utmost importance that I find her before anyone else does."

The man walked closer to Jonathon, appearing to size him up, then crossed his arms in a show of strength. "Two men were here earlier and they were also looking for Lady Hannah. They claim to have the support of Lord Pembrooke's steward."

"That may be true, but I have a direct order from Lord Pembrooke, and the Crown, to locate and protect Lady Hannah," Jonathon said in a commanding voice.

The man's eyebrows shot up. "You work for the Crown?"

"Yes." Normally, he did not announce that he worked as an agent for the Crown, but he needed this man's cooperation.

The man tilted his head and studied him for a long time. "Maybe I can help you, but only if you help me first." He paused. "Do you by chance know a Lord Beckett?"

"Why?" Jonathon asked warily.

"I have to deliver a note to him, but I don't know where his estate is. I planned to ride to London but it will take a couple of weeks to get there and back."

"What is in the note?" Jonathon pressed.

"It is between Lord Beckett and myself."

"Would it help if I told you that I am Lord Jonathon Beckett?"

"That would be convenient," the man said with a laugh.

Jonathon's clothes were dusty from the long trail ride, but he held his head up high. "I truly am Lord Jonathon Beckett, second son of the Duke of Remington."

Suspicion crept into the man's eyes. "Can you prove that you are Lord Beckett?"

Jonathon pulled off his signet ring and extended it to the man. "This is the Beckett Family crest."

The man studied the ring, but shook his head. "I'm sorry, but I am not familiar with the Beckett crest." He seemed reluctant when he handed the ring back. It appeared that this man was disappointed the ring did not confirm his identity.

Jonathon was confident that this man knew more than he was letting on about Lady Hannah's whereabouts. "I have the letter that Lord Pembrooke wrote to my uncle, Lord Charles Beckett."

The man's eyes lit up. "That should be proof enough. Can I see it?"

Jonathon raced out to his saddle bags, secured the note, brought it back, then handed it over and waited while the man read the letter. "What do you think?"

With a nod, the man refolded the letter and handed it back. "I believe you, Lord Beckett. Please call me Samuel."

"What note were you planning to send to my residence?"

Samuel's face broke into a huge smile. "I know where Lady Hannah is." The shock must have registered on his face, because Samuel started laughing. "Lucy, my intended, showed up in town today with Lady Hannah, attempting to pass her off as a cousin. The moment I saw Lady Hannah, I had no doubt of her identity. Her father wrote to her and told her to only trust Lord Beckett, but she didn't know where I could find him."

"Can you take me to her?" Jonathon was anxious to see Lady Hannah.

"Yes. You should be aware that the two men who originally tried to abduct her have tracked her down. They are at the inn right now and are just waiting for a chance to grab her," Samuel admitted.

Jonathon heard the word inn and started walking towards the

stable doors. Samuel followed closely behind him. "What is the plan?"

As they drew closer to the inn, Jonathon whirled around to face Samuel. "We need to extract Lady Hannah from the inn."

Samuel stared at him curiously for a moment. "How do you propose we do that?"

Glancing back at the livery, Jonathon said, "Go retrieve my horse, then saddle Lady Hannah's horse and leave them by the cluster of trees behind the inn." Jonathon pointed to the trees he'd mentioned. "Also, can your intended... Lucy, was it?" He waited for Samuel to nod. "Can she ride?"

Samuel crossed his arms. "I don't want Lucy to be in any danger."

Putting his hands up in front of him, Jonathon attempted to reassure Samuel. "Lady Hannah and I will ride south. I just want you and Lucy to ride north on the main road, then circle back after a few hours. The two men will eventually realize that they were tricked, but it will give us a decent head start."

Samuel's lips tightened and slowly curled downward. Jonathon could see that he was not pleased with this plan. Slowly, Samuel dropped his hands and said, "Fair enough, my lord. Lucy has become quite attached to Lady Hannah and I would hate for anything to happen to her."

Jonathon held Samuel's gaze, determined to show him how serious he was. "Do not worry, Samuel. I will protect Lady Hannah with my life."

Samuel dropped his gaze and walked back towards the livery. Jonathon entered the inn, grateful he would finally meet Lady Hannah.

"DEAR, YOU REALLY NEED TO EAT SOMETHING," MRS. DAWSON cooed by her ear. "You must keep up your strength. All will be well."

Hannah sighed loudly, feeling as if all was lost. "How can all be well? Those two horrible men have been staring at me for the past hour, and Samuel is not leaving until tomorrow."

Smiling, Lucy appeared dreamy-eyed. "Don't worry, Samuel will fix this. He will find a way to keep you safe. I know it."

Hannah refrained from rolling her eyes at her innocent friend. The two men sitting in the corner of the room had pistols sticking out of the front of their filthy trousers. The tall, lanky man had greasy, thinning hair and his clothing appeared to hold more dirt than the road leading into the village. The short, stout man had slightly cleaner clothes, but his face was oily and he had a long, bushy mustache and beard. The tall man caught her looking back and winked.

Hannah turned away and stared at the beef stew in front of her. The churning in her stomach was not from her hunger, but from the dread she was feeling. What was she going to do? She had to find a way to leave undetected, without putting Lucy and her parents at risk. She could ask Samuel to saddle her horse and she could ride all night. Someone had to know where the Becketts' estate was, or at the very least, point her in the general direction.

Hannah closed her eyes and attempted to calm her breathing. If she fled into the night alone, she would have no protection. She would be at the mercy of those two men, if they caught up to her, or any highway robber that she came across. Tears welled up in her eyes, one escaping and rolling down her face. "I let you down, Father," she mumbled under her breath.

"How did you let your father down?" A rich, baritone voice said close to her.

Opening her eyes, she turned her head to see who was speaking to her. An extremely handsome man with a square jaw, dark brown hair, and piercing green eyes was gazing back at her. His eyes were filled with warmth, which seemed to contradict his rugged appearance. He was straddling the bench, drawing her attention to his fine linen shirt, which gaped slightly open, revealing a well-defined, muscular chest.

She realized his mouth had stopped moving and he was just looking at her, smiling. *Oh no, he had asked her another question.* "Would you mind repeating the question?"

His smile broadened to show a set of perfect white teeth, and he looked amused. "I asked, twice now, may I add, 'How did you let your father down?'"

Hannah blushed. She glanced down at her clasped hands. "I was not addressing you, sir, when I was speaking."

"No? And who were you speaking to?"

"If you must know, I was talking to myself," she confessed.

One side of his mouth curled up. "You are mad then?"

Hannah huffed. "No, I am not mad. Now will you please leave us?"

"*Us*? Oh no, you truly are mad," he said mockingly.

"Yes, us. As you can see..." She stopped speaking when she noticed that Lucy, her parents, and Samuel were now sitting at the opposite end of the table, enjoying their bowls of beef stew. When had they moved? "It appears that I need to join my group, if you will excuse me."

As she started to rise, the man put his hand on her arm, and leaned in. "Lady Hannah, I insist. I must speak to you. It is most urgent."

Hannah sat back down and lowered her voice. "How do you know my name?"

The man dropped his hand from her arm. "I am here to help."

Hannah shifted her gaze from his face. "I'm afraid no one can help me now, save it be one man."

"And if I am that man?"

Hannah shook her head. "Thank you for your inquiry, sir, but I must decline your assistance."

He ran his hand through his hair as he kept his gaze trained on her. "That is not an option," he said firmly.

Her eyes widened at his insistence. "And why not?"

"I was sent to help you." His eyes roamed her dirt-covered face and neck.

She bit her lower lip as she debated how to reply to his request. Ironically, she felt safe and protected in this stranger's presence. But it mattered not, because her father told her to trust only one man. She squared her shoulders. "There is only one man that I can trust, and it is most assuredly not you."

The handsome stranger chuckled. "I was not informed that you were so incredibly stubborn."

"I will not sit here and be insulted by a stranger."

He leaned close, too close to be considered proper. "Allow me to correct that situation immediately." His warm breath reached her cheek and she shuddered involuntarily. "I am Lord Jonathon Beckett." He sat back with a knowing smile.

Hannah arched an eyebrow in disbelief. "Impossible. You are too…"

"Handsome?" He smirked, humor lighting his eyes.

She shook her head even though she had a similar thought. *He was much too handsome for his own good.* "No, I was going to say…"

"Charming?"

"Young," she blurted. "You are much too young. My father informed me that Lord Beckett is a trusted friend, so I naturally must assume they are of similar age."

Lord Jonathon nodded his understanding. "Lord Charles Beckett, my uncle," he said deliberately, "sent me to retrieve you from your country home and place you under his protection. I work for the Crown."

Hannah's eyes roamed his face. She desperately wanted to

believe him, but she needed one more piece of information to verify his identity. "What is the code?"

His face grew solemn as he leaned forward. "I hope I say this correctly." He hesitated before saying, "*El tiempo lo cura todo.*" Jonathon's eyes held a glimmer of uncertainty.

She was amused at his pathetic attempt at Spanish, but he knew the code. "Time heals all wounds," she said softly. "My mother used to say that to me."

Jonathon leaned back and glanced over his shoulder. "It would appear your admirers are still watching you."

Hannah did not need to turn around to confirm his statement. "They are horrid men. The stench alone from that tall man should render him unconscious."

Jonathon's lips twitched. "The stench?"

Hannah gave him a haughty smile and nodded. "When he stood in front of me in the livery stable, the smell of horse dung was a pleasant distraction from the smell emanating from his person."

Jonathon casually rested his arm on the table. "Well, let's try to avoid them and their stench."

She waved her hand, dismissing his comment. "The shorter one did not have a repugnant smell, just the tall one," she informed him.

"Ah. Well, this conversation has become quite informative, but may I suggest we get back to the matter at hand?" he said with a smile.

Hannah shrugged her shoulder, enjoying the banter. "All right. I am open to discussing the matter."

"In a few minutes, Lucy will walk over here and inform you that she is retiring to her room for the evening. You will agree to go with her. Once inside your room, you will use the rope that is hanging out your window to climb down. I will be waiting for you, and we will run into the woods, then ride all night."

"I see. You want me to climb out the window in a dress and you will be waiting for me," she repeated back, pursing her lips.

"Yes."

"And leave Lucy in danger?" Hannah started shaking her head. "I will not place Lucy in harm's way."

"Do not fret. Lucy will also climb out the window and will be joined by Samuel. Together, they will ride in the opposite direction to give us a much-needed lead."

Hannah smiled graciously. "I am amenable to the plan."

"Excellent." Jonathon's eyes roamed her simple, threadbare wool dress. "Why don't you take a few moments and change into another dress before climbing out the window?"

Her eyes narrowed slightly, hoping that this man would not offend her friends over their tattered clothing. "I do not have another dress, nor did Lucy bring another dress to change into." She stared at him defiantly, daring him to say something else about the condition of her borrowed dress.

Jonathon acknowledged her statement with a wave of his hand. "That is of no consequence. We will order you a new wardrobe when we arrive at Uncle Charles' estate."

Hannah noticed that Lucy was glancing their way and it appeared she was getting ready for the farce. She turned back to Jonathon. "Before Lucy comes over, I was hoping to discuss finances with you."

"Do you require funds?" he asked curiously.

Hannah bit her lower lip as she realized how bold she was about to be. "My father instructed me to carry money with me wherever I went, in case I needed funds to travel to safety. I have not used any of it and I was hoping to give it to the Dawsons for all their generosity. I know it is a tidy sum and it would help them greatly."

"How much money do you have?"

"Twenty pounds."

Jonathon rubbed his hand over his scruffy chin. "By all means, give them the money. I have sufficient for our needs."

Hannah felt a huge burden lifted off her shoulders. She nodded gratefully. "Thank you. I trust that my father will reimburse you for any expenses that I incur."

Before Jonathon replied to her, Lucy joined them and announced loudly, "I am exhausted and would like to retire for the evening. Would you be so kind as to join me?"

Hannah nodded her consent and rose from her seat, noting the way Jonathon perused her figure as she stood up. How ironic that a handsome man was finally looking at her, and she was dressed in a battered, shapeless dress. Lucy looped her arm in Hannah's and they began their escape.

4

"THAT SHOULD DO IT," HANNAH ANNOUNCED AS SHE LATCHED the flimsy lock on the worn, wooden door.

Lucy peered out the window and saw a rope hanging down, secured to a small desk leg just as Jonathon had described. "Do you want to go first?" Lucy asked as she picked up the rope.

"Either way, but first I want to give you something." Hannah reached into the pocket of her borrowed dress and pulled out a small bag of coins, extending it towards Lucy. "I already spoke to Lord Jonathon, and we decided that you should have this money."

Shaking her head, Lucy refused to accept it. "No, you might still need it."

Hannah walked over and pressed the small bag into Lucy's hand. "I can never repay your family for all the kindness and love that you have shown to me these past weeks, especially since you saved my life, but I can attempt to start repaying my debt. If your parents refuse to take the money, give it to Samuel and use it to fulfill his dream of owning a stud farm."

"I don't know what to say, but thank you," Lucy said humbly.

"Consider it payment for teaching me how to milk a cow." Hannah laughed.

Lucy smiled. "It has been fun to pretend to have a sister, even for a few weeks."

Jonathon's head popped up through the open window. "Will you two exit the window? I should have emphasized that time is of the essence."

Lucy waited until Jonathon was back on the ground before she started her descent. As soon as her feet touched the earth, Hannah grabbed the rope. She had just eased herself over the edge of the window sill when she heard banging on the door, accompanied by muffled shouting. As she neared the ground, she jumped the remainder of the way.

Jonathon grabbed her bonnet off her head and tossed it to Lucy, who placed it on her own. Samuel helped Lucy onto her horse before he mounted. Lucy glanced at Hannah with an expression of worry before she kicked her horse into a run.

Grabbing her arm, Jonathon pulled her tight against the stone wall, using the shadows to cloak them in darkness. Hannah could hear her door being forcibly opened. The men cursed as they realized their prey was gone. As the men's voices faded away, Jonathon grabbed her hand and led her towards a cluster of trees. Running further into the woods, they saw the outlines of two horses tied to a tree.

When moonlight broke through the trees, Hannah recognized Pirata. Jonathon grabbed her waist and effortlessly placed her onto the saddle. Within moments, they were racing their horses away from the inn, using only the moon to light the way.

As the sun hit directly above, Jonathon knew it was time to take a break from the saddle. They had pushed hard, but the horses, and Hannah, needed a break. They were avoiding the main roads, which made it easier to find a small stream near a thicket of trees.

"Shall we rest?" He looked back to watch Lady Hannah nod, bring her horse to a halt, and slide off before he could even dismount.

She slowly made her way to the stream and repeatedly splashed water onto her face and neck. As she turned to face him, he was rendered speechless. Now that her face was clean from all the dirt, her skin was as flawless as white jade, and strands of her black hair were breaking free from the bun at the back of her neck. Her brilliant, dark-blue eyes latched onto his, and he found himself unable to utter a coherent sentence. How had he not noticed how beautiful she was before now?

Lady Hannah gave him a curious look and he realized he had been staring. He dropped his gaze as his horse whinnied. He patted the animal's neck and remarked, "We have been pushing the horses hard. We do not want them to go lame."

"All right. I would not mind a longer rest." Hannah lowered herself down to the ground, leaning back against the trunk of a birch tree.

Jonathon secured the horses and joined Hannah. He sat beside her, noting how good it felt to sit on solid ground. Glancing over, her shallow breathing told him that she had drifted to sleep. He studied her face. The way her dark lashes fanned out over her pale cheeks fascinated him. His eyes moved towards the loose strands of black hair that hung around her face. Her hair was straight, appearing as fine as silk threads, but he did not dare touch it for fear of waking her.

After a sufficient rest for the horses, he placed his hand on Hannah's shoulder and nudged her awake. She opened her eyes and gave him a brief smile.

"Time to go," he said as he took a moment to stretch his back.

For the next few hours, they rode hard, alternating between galloping and trotting. Fearing the horses needed another break, he slowed his horse to a fast walk and Pirata matched his speed. Glancing over at Hannah, Jonathon noted that although she was sitting erect and square in her saddle, the dark circles under her eyes betrayed her fatigue.

He was curious about Hannah's life these past few weeks. Did she truly work on the farm, or did she just help with the cooking and housekeeping? Both were beneath her, but cooking and housekeeping was easier than working outside. "You said you worked on a farm. What were your chores?"

Hannah pressed her lips together into a tight line before she answered. "Anything that was required of me, but I mainly helped Lucy with her jobs."

"Which were?" Jonathon prodded.

"I would rather not say," Hannah said as she gripped her reins tighter.

He noticed her rigid posture, but pressed anyway. "May I ask why?"

Hannah huffed, but maintained eye contact. "I was not going to sit around the farm and not render assistance to the Dawsons. They offered to let me stay inside the farmhouse and rest, but I wanted to help them, truly help them, for saving my life."

"I think that is admirable," he said honestly, attempting to understand her hostility.

"Oh," she replied softly. "However, it has taken a toll on my hands and now they are calloused." She held up her hands to show him.

"So, you are embarrassed by the callouses on your hands?"

"No. I am afraid of what you will think when I tell you about life on a farm."

"Why would you care what I think?" He was not sure if he should be offended by her comment.

Hannah rolled her eyes. "Well, not *you* specifically. I have grown up hearing stories about the ton and how they refused to accept my mother because she was a Spaniard. If anyone from the ton heard I milked a cow, I can only imagine how quickly I would be labeled an outcast."

Jonathon understood her concern. "The ton is full of critical, entitled dandies and gossipy biddies, but they are mingled with kind and loving people. Like everything in society, you have to look for the good and avoid the bad."

"And do you avoid the bad?" Her eyes roamed his face, searching for an answer.

"Like the plague." He softened his words with a big smile. "Now, if you would be so kind as to elaborate on what chores you performed?"

"I will answer your question, only if you will answer one of mine," she said, her eyes suddenly full of mischief.

He shrugged. "I suppose that is only fair, but you first."

Hannah visibly relaxed in the saddle as they continued their fast pace. "I learned how to milk a cow, but I only just became proficient at it." She glanced over and smiled. "I helped shear the sheep."

"Impressive," he said with a tip of his head.

"Thank you." Hannah smiled. "I must confess that these past few weeks have been wonderful." Jonathon's doubtful expression must have showed on his face, because she rushed to say, "I am not talking about the farm experience, but how the Dawson family welcomed me into their home. It was nice to have a mother again, if only briefly." She gave him a sad smile at that admission. "Plus, I have never had a sister before."

"I have two sisters. You are not missing much," Jonathon teased, as he tightened his hands on the reins.

"Now it is your turn," she said, turning to him. "My father

sent me a letter a few weeks ago stating my life could be in danger, but provided me with no explanation. In fact, the letter was worded very cryptically, and not his normal writing style. What I would like to…"

Jonathon assumed he knew why and cut her off. "Did you keep the letter?"

"I did. My father told me to present the letter to Lord Beckett, so I thought it must be important. But in all the confusion, I forgot to hand over the note to you." Hannah slipped her hand into a pocket and pulled out a small, neatly folded piece of paper.

Jonathon reached for the letter and carefully opened it.

My dearest Hannah,

Your life is in peril. Trust no one, except Lord Beckett. Remove twenty pounds from safe. Keep it with you always. If threats appear, use money to travel to Lord Beckett.

Remember, trust no one, except Lord Beckett. Give him this letter for his records. As you do not know Lord Beckett, he will relay a code phrase. This will prove that he was in communication with me. The code is what Mother always used to say.

Your Loving Father

Jonathon folded the letter and placed it into his pocket, then turned to Hannah. "Your intuition was correct. This is a coded message."

Hannah furrowed her eyebrows. "What does it say?"

"I am unable to decipher codes on sight, but I know someone who can." Jonathon's sister, Eliza, could crack this code in mere minutes, but Hannah could never know of his sister's involvement. "My uncle has a code book at his estate. I am familiar with this code, but it will require some time."

Hannah nodded and seemed satisfied by his response. "I knew something was strange about that letter and now it makes sense." She glanced ahead, before turning her attention to him. "Now, back to my question. Why is my life in peril?"

Jonathon winced. What could he say that might appease her curiosity, without fully revealing the truth?

"You better not be trying to find a way to lie to me," Hannah said, annoyed, searching his face. "I want the truth. That was the agreement, remember?"

He adjusted the reins in his hands before he answered. "It is not that I do not want to answer your question, but I am unable to. It is in your best interest to not know the truth." He gave her a dashing smile to soften his words. "Do not fear, though. You are in my protection."

"What makes you think it is in my best interest not to know the truth?" Hannah asked, her eyes narrowing.

"In my experience, women have delicate constitutions, and the dangers of..."

"Don't be daft!"

Jonathon swiveled his head around, wary of her condescending tone. "I beg your pardon?"

Hannah stiffened, as if preparing for battle. "I have spent the last few weeks living on a farm because my steward betrayed me. Two men chased me into the forest and I would have died if not for Lucy and her family. My father's last note informed me that my life was in peril and I have no idea if he is dead or alive, but you are trying to pacify me by saying I have nothing to fear. So logically, I must assume that you are daft."

Jonathon sighed. "Lady Hannah, I am trying to protect you..."

Hannah kicked Pirata and started galloping away from him.

He urged his horse to catch up to hers. For a split second, he was impressed with her horsemanship, but that was replaced by his growing frustration that she was attempting to flee from him.

Hannah glanced back and saw him gaining on her so she urged her horse to run faster. Jonathon leaned low and pushed his horse until he was riding parallel with Hannah, then reached for the reins. Grasping the reins, he gently eased their horses to a stop. He didn't relinquish the hold on her horse, and narrowed his eyes at Hannah. "What possessed you to do something so foolish?"

In response, she turned her fiery glare towards him. "How dare you! I am not a weak-willed woman that will sit back and allow you to dictate my emotions."

"I did no such thing," he said, confused.

"You lied to me. How can I trust you if you lie to me?"

"I did not lie to you."

"You asked me a question and I answered honestly. When I asked you a question, you refused to tell me the truth."

"I do not want to upset you…"

Hannah slid off her horse and started walking away… rather, *stomping* away. Jonathon stared at her retreating figure, not knowing why she was so upset. He wished his sister, Eliza, was here so she could tell him what he had done wrong.

Jonathon looked up at the grey sky in frustration. He dismounted, leading the horses to where Hannah stood with her rigid back to him, mumbling to herself. It sounded like she was speaking in Spanish. Her black hair blew around haphazardly in the wind, making her appear young and vulnerable as she stood alone in a large field.

"Lady Hannah, I have no idea why you are so upset," he ventured calmly.

She turned to face him, her eyes filled with moisture. "For weeks, I have been in fear for my life, for my father's life and I have no idea why." A tear slid down her cheek and she quickly wiped it away with her hand. "I kept telling myself that once I met with Lord Beckett, he would tell me why someone is trying to kill me, but now you stand here, knowing all the answers, yet you refuse to tell me."

Jonathon's heart wrenched open at her vulnerability and he knew he needed to tell her the truth, at least some of it. He took a step closer to her. "Believe it or not, I really am attempting to protect you."

"From what?" she shouted, throwing her hands in the air.

Jonathon glanced nervously at the darkening sky, knowing they needed to ride out or they would be caught in the storm. Frustrated, he sighed and turned his attention back to Hannah. "I will tell you some of what you seek, but there are some things I am unable to divulge."

"I can accept that," she said, wiping the tears off her face.

He studied her for a moment then conceded. "Fair enough."

"Thank you, Lord Jonathon."

"I will answer your questions, but not here. We need to ride to an inn that I scouted on the way here, hopefully before the storm hits," he said, his tone curt. This detour was taking far too long.

As Hannah walked closer to her horse, he placed his hands on her waist and gently raised her onto the side-saddle. His hands lingered on her waist, surprised at how small it was under the ill-fitting dress. She shifted into position, and reached for her reins.

Frowning, he asked, "You are not scheming to go on another run without me, are you?"

"No, I think we have come to an understanding," she said, grinning.

Dumbfounded, Jonathon stared at her, attempting to understand how quickly her temperament changed. He patted her horse's neck and walked around to mount his own. "Let's ride," he said as he urged his horse on.

AFTER TROTTING FOR A FEW HOURS, THEY SLOWED TO WALK THE horses. Hannah recognized this as a perfect opportunity to ask her questions. She glanced at Jonathon. "Why is my life in peril?"

Jonathon clenched his jaw and continued to look straight ahead. After a few moments, he said, "Your father was given documents that prove someone had orchestrated an assassination attempt against Prinny."

"The man implicated in the documents must be quite influential for my father, and the Crown, to take this matter seriously."

His eyes scanned the trees around them, looking for danger, no doubt. "He is," Jonathon admitted as he glanced over with a faint smile playing on his lips. "Now, is it my turn for a question?"

She huffed. "My question has not been sufficiently answered. I still do not know the identity of the man hunting my family."

"Lord Camden," he said, almost as if the name was an expletive.

"Lord Camden? I am not familiar with his name."

Jonathon threw his head back and laughed. "Are you familiar

with any of the ton? You were not familiar with my father, the Duke of Remington, or the Beckett family line, and we are quite influential."

Shrugging, Hannah said, "My mother and I enjoyed the serenity of our country house. Besides, my father forbade us to travel to London without him and he was never home."

"Why did your father forbid you to travel?"

"I do not know, but in the end, he was right."

Jonathon's eyes continuously scanned the horizon, but she knew he was listening intently to her. "What do you mean?"

"My mother wrote to my father and asked for permission to travel with my uncle, the earl, and the countess and my cousin, Jennifer, but he denied her request." Her voice hitched. "My cousin was a few years older than me and wanted to have her first Season. My mother just wanted to go to London to shop the latest fashions." She glanced down at her hands as her eyes filled with tears.

Jonathon studied her as she spoke. "What happened?"

Hannah blinked away her tears, since crying never seemed to accomplish anything. "My mother went against my father's wishes, and there was a horrible carriage accident. The magistrate informed us that a cart had lost a wheel and was abandoned in the road. My uncle's carriage was going too fast to stop, causing the carriage to roll multiple times. By the time someone came across the scene of the accident, they were all dead."

She didn't want to see the pity in Jonathon's eyes, or the polite, vague words that always accompanied the sharing of her story. Hannah had learned to avoid the subject of her loved ones' deaths. How could she convey the crushing blow of losing her mother, aunt, uncle, and cousin, in the same accident? She tightened her hands around the reins, and urged her horse forward.

"Hannah," he said compassionately.

She refused to look his way as she kept her shoulders rigid, even though she could see from the corner of her eyes that he kept glancing at her.

After her uncle died, her father became the new Earl of Pembrooke, and retired from his commission in the Navy. Suddenly, she became Lady Hannah. Now a titled lady, she received invitations to all types of social gatherings, but she refused to attend. No one wanted her as Miss Hannah, but it would appear she was desirable as Lady Hannah. If the gentry were so fickle in Bath, she knew she would loathe a Season in London.

Jonathon's voice broke through her thoughts. "How old were you when your mother died?"

"Sixteen," she answered wiping a lone tear off her cheek.

"I am curious about one thing. When I went to your country home, you lived only with your household staff. Why did you not live with your relations while Lord Pembrooke was serving as an Ambassador?"

Frowning, she explained, "My mother's family disowned her when she married my father, and I have no other relations on my father's side."

"Why did your father not take you to Spain with him?"

"I pleaded to go with him, but my father did not want to uproot me from the only home that I have known. He left me in the capable hands of my governess. I have not seen my father in four years. He left the day after the funeral for Spain."

"Your father abandoned you at sixteen?"

"I do not think it was his intention to abandon me, but he had spent years in the Navy. I have to believe he was unsure about how to raise me."

"You were hardly a girl at sixteen," Jonathon pointed out.

"No," she murmured her agreement, "but, I look just like my mother and that must have caused him great pain."

"Your mother must have been very beautiful," he stated.

"I always thought so," Hannah said sadly as she tilted her

head to look up at Jonathon. "It is my turn for a question," she said with a tight smile. "Tell me about your family."

JONATHON GAVE HER A SIDEWAYS GLANCE, HOPING HE COULD BE as vague as possible. His family was a topic he tended to avoid, especially with an inquisitive young lady who seemed to deduce everything. "Well, I have an older brother and two sisters."

"Are any of them married?"

"Yes, Kate married Lord Camden almost four years ago." *And is miserable*, he thought to himself.

Hannah whipped her head around with her mouth agape. "Wait, the same Lord Camden who tried to assassinate Prinny and is trying to hurt my family?"

"Yes. He is my brother-in-law." Hannah's face paled and he rushed to clarify. "I just learned of his involvement a few weeks ago, but my uncle has been aware of his treasonous acts for some time now."

"Why is Lord Camden not in Newgate?"

Jonathon gave her a tight frown, knowing he posed the same question to his uncle. "You cannot arrest an earl with circumstantial evidence. No court would convict him. That is why the documents your father carries are so vital to the case."

"Why can't *you* just kill him?" Hannah asked with an arched eyebrow.

Jonathon chuckled. "Now you are starting to sound like..." His voice trailed off. He could not tell her that his sister, Eliza, often asked that same question.

"Like who?"

He gave her a smug smile. "Now you are starting to sound like me."

Hannah smiled wide, her eyes twinkling with mischief. "Is your other sister married to a traitor, or do you have a one traitor per family rule?

Jonathon's lips twisted in amusement. "Eliza married Lord Sinclair two weeks ago at his estate. In fact, I encouraged my uncle to partner them together..." He stopped. He could not tell Hannah that Eliza and Lord Sinclair worked as agents for the Crown, or that Eliza's code name was *Shadow*.

Hannah's voice broke through his thoughts. "You encouraged your uncle to partner them together at what?"

"As dance partners," he said, recovering nicely. "They met at a ball and it was love at first sight." That was partially true.

"Ah. That sounds romantic." Hannah glanced up at the sky. "Is your older brother married?"

"No, Luke is in Scotland managing the family estates and holdings. He also has a thriving horse stud farm."

"And your father and mother?" she asked, glancing at him.

He took a deep breath and decided to tell her the truth. "My father lives with his long-time mistress, Lady Anne, and my mother and I are not very close."

"I apologize for the intrusion into your family situation. I can tell you do not like to talk about them," she said, her eyes betraying her concern.

"I am quite fond of my siblings, but I tend to avoid discussing my mother. She is a cruel, conniving woman who tends to hurt whomever is in her path," he said bitterly. Hannah gasped, and he realized how he must have sounded. "I apologize for my bluntness, but not for what I said. My mother, the Duchess of Remington, kicked Eliza out of the abbey when she was ten years old because of her intellect."

Hannah's eyes grew wide. "How could a mother be so cruel to abandon her daughter so young?"

"The duchess had no love for Eliza and seemed to delight in creating new ways to torment her," he said as he clenched his jaw tight. "I was at Eton when she was sent to live with my uncle."

"She did not live with your father?" Hannah asked, surprised.

"No, that would have created a scandal. A titled young lady being raised by her father and his long-time mistress..." He let the accusation hang, even though they recently discovered that Lady Anne was Eliza's real mother.

"Poor Eliza."

"Eliza is one of my greatest friends. I trust her with my life." In fact, Eliza had saved his life many times as his partner.

Hannah arched an eyebrow. "What an odd thing to say."

"What? That my sister is one of my greatest friends?"

"No, that sounds plausible. I am referring to the fact that you trust your sister with your life." Hannah seemed to study him. "She must be a remarkable lady."

Chuckling, he said, "Eliza is one of a kind. Even though she is stubborn, she is extremely loyal and will defend you to the end."

"I would like to meet..." Hannah's voice stalled with the sound of horses approaching fast.

Jonathon quickly put his finger to his mouth and they slowly backed their horses into the thicket. He dismounted and reached for Hannah's reins.

The pounding of hooves became louder and two riders appeared before them. They were bent over their horses, urging them to run faster. Their beady eyes were roaming the trees surrounding the road but seemed to scan right over them.

As they disappeared down the road, he turned to Hannah. "It appears that our diversion did not work as well as we intended." He slapped his leg in frustration and hissed an expletive under his breath. After a moment, he looked up at her with his usual charm and said, "Do not fear. The inn I scouted is off a side road and will be discreet."

Hannah glanced up at the dark clouds that had started to grow in density. "How much longer until we reach the inn?"

"A few hours if we ride hard, barring any unforeseen circumstances." Jonathon mounted his horse and veered them towards a deer trail, parallel to the main road. He urged his horse into a trot.

Every so often, he would look back to watch Hannah trailing close behind, her black hair flowing around her shoulders and her cheeks pink from the wind. She was incredibly beautiful.

Hannah met his gaze and smiled, causing her entire face to light up with radiance. Briefly, Jonathon imagined what it would be like to court Hannah. No, he did not have time to be distracted from his mission.

As he turned to face forward, he felt the first drop of rain hit his head.

6

LADY HANNAH WAS COLD, EXHAUSTED, AND TIRED OF THIS drenching rainstorm. Her dress was plastered against her as water ran unrepentantly down the length of her body. She shivered, but kept her line of sight on the silhouette of Jonathon's horse. The rain was coming down at such an angle that she could barely see ahead of her.

As they crested a hill, she saw a slight sliver of light. Kicking her horse into a run, she used that light as a beacon. Jonathon also raced his horse towards the light and they rode until the outline of two buildings loomed before them.

This must be the inn that Jonathon had scouted out. It was a small, but tidy wooden building, with a thatched roof and a detached stable. As they pulled their horses to a stop in front of the inn, the street was flooded with water.

Jonathon dismounted and looked back expectantly at Hannah. Normally she would have slid off her horse, but she did not have the energy to dismount. He walked over and put his hands on her waist. "How are you faring?" he asked, his voice filled with concern.

Hannah placed her hands onto Jonathon's shoulders, grateful for his assistance. "About as well as you, I imagine."

Jonathon slowly slid her down the length of his body, not relinquishing his hold when she was on the ground, which was good, because her legs were weak from the long ride. "I believe it will be for the best if we pretend to be married," he said, gauging her reaction.

Hannah's whole body was soaking wet and she would have agreed to anything at this moment to get warm. "As you wish."

His eyes roamed over her face. Slowly, he reached up and tucked her plastered hair behind her ears. "All right. Let's get you warm and into bed, my wife."

Her face burned with embarrassment, but she felt it was important to clarify. "You do realize that we are *not* actually married and you have no marital rights?"

Jonathon gave her a crooked smile in response and reached for the reins to her horse. He started walking towards the stable, as he said over his shoulder, "Typically, I would ask a lady to wait for me inside, but I do not want you out of my sight. Would you mind coming with me to put away the horses?"

Hannah wrapped her arms around her soaking wet dress and followed Jonathon into the stable. The familiar scents of hay and animal noises met her once she stepped inside. Jonathon made quick work of settling the horses in for the night. Once the horses were secure, he reached out his hand and said, "Should we make a run for it?"

Hannah grabbed his hand and together they sprinted towards the main door of the inn. Jonathon arrived first, quickly opening the door and stood aside as she entered.

An older, burly man, with kind eyes, met them by the front door, as the lights and boisterous noise spilled from the main hall. He looked them both up and down before he spoke, "Come in and warm yourselves. My name is Mr. Ross and this is my inn. Can I get ye a room?"

Jonathon nodded. "Yes, and a hot meal."

Running his eyes over Hannah's dripping frame, the innkeeper asked, "Would yer lady also like a warm bath? It would cost ye more coins, but I could bring up a tub with hot water to your room."

Hannah's eyes went wide with pleasure at the thought of a bath. Before she could communicate her thoughts on the matter, Jonathon replied, "Yes, my wife would appreciate a bath. Furthermore, bring two plates of food up to our room. We wish to retire early for the evening."

Jonathon walked closer to the man and pulled out a handful of coins. The innkeeper's eyes lit up at the sight of them. He bowed his head at Jonathon and said, "As you wish, sir." He reached his hand into his pocket and pulled out a key. "If ye will follow me, I will take ye to your room."

Jonathon offered her his arm as they followed the innkeeper. They turned the corner and were led into the main hall. Long wooden tables were evenly spaced throughout the room and men of all sizes and ages were sitting down. Two serving maids were carrying trays and delivering drinks to the men. At the far end of the room, stood a rickety staircase leading up to the second floor.

As they kept to the wall, the innkeeper pushed the men out of their way. Hannah tightened her grip on Jonathon's arm and edged closer to him. He must have felt her discomfort, because he patted her hand, but his eyes remained fixed on the rowdy-looking men in the room.

Hannah glanced around and noticed a man gawking at her. He had a round, dirty face with an unkempt beard and his eyes lewdly perused her body. As she quickly averted her eyes, she noticed the man stand and start to approach her. He grabbed her arm, causing her to release her hold on Jonathon, and flung her around to face him. "This wench is not yer wife. When ye are done with her, I want a turn at pleasuring her."

Hannah gasped, and her free hand flew up to slap him. How dare he speak to her like that?

The man was quicker and grabbed her hand and used it to propel her into him. "Ye are a feisty one," he said with a laugh, revealing a mouth full of rotting, discolored teeth. She attempted to look away from his pudgy face. His rancid, inebriated breath on her cheek was making her stomach churn.

"Leave my wife alone," Jonathon growled behind her.

The man tightened his hold on her arms and did not bother to glance at Jonathon. "It is obvious this strumpet is not yer wife. She is a working girl and I aim to show her a good…"

Before Hannah even blinked, Jonathon threw the man against the wall. He tried in vain to remove Jonathon's forearm, which was pressed tightly against his throat. His pudgy face was turning red as he struggled to breathe.

Jonathon leaned closer, causing the man's eyes to fill with fear. "If you ever speak to a lady like that again, I will gut your stomach and disembowel you without a second thought." He growled out his words, leaving no doubt of the validity of his claim.

The man's face became blotchy and his efforts to remove Jonathon's forearm grew weaker. Mr. Ross stepped closer and said firmly, "I think ye sufficiently made your point."

Dropping his arm, Jonathon stepped back, allowing the man to crumple to the floor. His concerned eyes roamed up and down Hannah's body, as if searching her for injuries. He grabbed her hand tightly. "Come, let us get you upstairs."

Hannah stayed close behind until the innkeeper opened the door to their room. Jonathon gently nudged her into the room and he closed the door, leaving her alone. She could hear muffled voices from the other side, and it sounded like Jonathon was voicing his opinion of the clientele of the inn.

The muffled noise stopped, and Jonathon entered the sparsely furnished room. A small bed was in the corner with a nightstand next to it, housing a wash basin. There was a fireplace, but no heat radiated from the cold ash, and a lone, armless chair sat near the door.

Jonathon stood staring at her for a long moment. He sighed and ran his hand through his wet hair. "Lady Hannah, I cannot begin to apologize for the behavior of that uncivilized oaf. Did he hurt you?"

She stood mesmerized by the compassion in his eyes and in his tone. Jonathon was truly worried about her and it warmed her heart. "He did not hurt me, thanks to you, Lord Jonathon."

"Jonathon," he said hoarsely. "I would like you to call me Jonathon."

Hannah knew the impropriety of using his given name, but nothing about this situation was proper. "All right, but you must call me Hannah."

"I would like that very much," he said, taking a step forward.

Hannah's eyes watched his handsome face, noticing his dark green eyes and his charming demeanor. "Thank you for protecting me, Jonathon," she said sincerely.

Jonathon took another step closer and ran his hand through his hair again. "I apologize for my outburst back there, but I do not think I have ever been so afraid..." His voice trailed off.

Hannah boldly threw her arms around his waist, having an intense desire to be comforted by him. At first, his body stiffened, but his arms slowly came around to encompass her. She relaxed into his touch, enjoying the physical contact. Although her dress and hair were wet, she started to warm up by his touch, his presence.

"That man was revolting..." She stopped, not daring to voice her trepidations about what just occurred. "Thank you."

Jonathon's arms tightened around her. "It is my duty to keep you safe."

Hannah stiffened, immediately dropping her arms and took a step back. *What a fool she was*! His job was to protect her, nothing more! Yet she had thrown herself into his arms. "Yes, well, thank you." Her tone was forced as she stepped back. She took a moment to compose herself. "My father will be most appreciative."

Jonathon gave her a puzzled look. "Hannah, did I do…" His voice trailed off as someone pounded on the door. "Yes?" he shouted, without taking his eyes off her.

"We have a bath for ye," came the booming reply.

Jonathon's mouth opened, as if he wanted to say something, but instead he turned and opened the door. Two men shuffled in with a big basin and proceeded to fill it with water. Once they were finished, Jonathon started to close the door, but was stopped by a little girl with soot on her cheeks coming into the room. Without a word, she stepped to the fireplace and started a fire in the hearth.

Hannah wrapped her hands around her waist. Jonathon watched her as if he was afraid she would bolt out of the room. She lowered her eyes to the tub and hoped the water was at least warm. How she wished for a nightgown or a new dress to put on after her bath.

Jonathon cleared his throat. "I'm sure you'll want some privacy while you bathe." He opened the door and procured a key from his pocket. "I will lock the door from the outside to ensure your protection."

Hannah gave him a tight smile. "Thank you."

He nodded his head in response and closed the door behind him. True to his word, she heard the door being locked from the outside.

Hannah stood and walked over to the bath, placing her fingers into the water. It was warm! She smiled and quickly removed her wet, soiled dress, placing it near the fireplace to dry. Slowly, she eased into the tub, enjoying the warmth of the water.

For a moment, she thought back to how being in Jonathon's arms had felt so natural and reassuring. Leaning the back of her head against the base of the tub, she sighed in disgust at her behavior. "His duty is to protect you, nothing more," Hannah mumbled under her breath.

Now if only she could convince her treacherous heart to follow her lead.

JONATHON MARCHED DOWN THE STAIRS IN SEARCH OF THE innkeeper. At the base of the stairs, he stopped and glanced back up towards their room. What had just happened up there?

He had almost killed a man tonight with his bare hands, because he laid his hand on Hannah... his Hannah. No, she was not his, and he needed to remind himself of that. He could not lay claim to her simply because he saw her first. His assignment was to deliver her to Uncle Charles, where she would be placed under his protection until Lord Pembrooke arrived safely back on English soil.

A flicker of Hannah's enchanting face came into his mind, and instead of dismissing the thought, he found himself remembering the feel of her body pressed against him. Her wide, expressive blue eyes gave him a glimpse into her soul, allowing him to see an intelligent, brave young woman.

Jonathon had never known a lady like her. So far, she had not complained, even when the rain had descended upon them. He smiled as he remembered her attempt to outrun him. No woman had ever tried to intentionally flee from him. Normally, the women flocked to him because of his title and connections.

Jonathon's eyes roamed around the room in search of the innkeeper. He saw him eating bread in a corner. Quickly walking over, he sat across from him. The innkeeper nodded his head in acknowledgement and finished chewing. "What can I help ye with?" he asked while wiping crumbs off his hands.

"I was hoping Mrs. Ross might have an extra nightgown? My wife and I are packing light and she left one behind."

Mr. Ross gave him a disapproving stare. "This is a respectable inn, and I do not look kindly on ye taking advantage of that young lady in your room." He shook his head. "That young woman is not your wife, so ye can drop the act," he said bluntly as his eyes roamed the main hall.

It was abundantly clear what this man thought of him, but Jonathon needed to say something to smooth the way. He needed the innkeeper's help and he would not get it if he repulsed the man.

Jonathon glanced around as he leaned forward. "You are correct in your assessment. That young lady is not my wife, but there is more to the story than that." The innkeeper leaned forward to hear his hushed voice. "I work for the Crown and I am tasked with her protection for now. My job is to deliver her into the protection of a very influential lord, who will keep her safe until her father can claim her." Jonathon hoped that his earnestness would convince the innkeeper of his honest intentions. He sat back on the bench and waited for Mr. Ross to respond.

"I believe ye. That makes more sense than her being yer wife," he said with a bob of his head.

Jonathon didn't know if he should laugh or be insulted by the innkeeper's comments. "I beg your pardon?"

Mr. Ross laughed. "Yer eyes track her wherever she goes."

Jonathon furrowed his eyebrows. "I have to keep watch on her because I am protecting her," he explained.

The innkeeper laughed again as he stood up. "I will go see about finding ye a nightgown for yer wife."

Jonathon kept his eyes fixed on the door to their room, and leaned back against the wall while waiting for the innkeeper's return. To his surprise, the man came back with a short, plump woman next to him, and she was carrying a small bundle draped over her arm. Her white hair was pulled back into a low bun, and she had a friendly countenance about her.

As they approached, Jonathon stood up and bowed respectfully. "Ma'am."

The cheery woman smiled at him. "Aren't you a gentleman? I heard that your wife," she paused, giving him a conspiratorial smile, "has no nightgown, and I assume, no undergarments or a brush?"

Jonathon instantly felt at ease around this woman. "You are indeed correct."

The woman patted his arm, as if he were a little child. "I will go upstairs and see to yer wife's needs."

"Thank you, ma'am. It is most appreciated."

She gave him a gracious smile and climbed up the stairs. When she reached the door, she knocked, then pulled a key out of her pocket. Jonathon watched as she stepped inside the room and shut the door.

"Don't ye fret none. My wife will lock the door from the inside. She is a smart one, she is."

It took Jonathon a few moments before he tore his eyes away from the door upstairs, and he found the innkeeper looking at him with an amused grin. He ignored the man's expression and said, "We will need to leave at first light tomorrow. Would you see that our horses are fed and saddled first thing in the morning?"

The innkeeper nodded. "Aye. I can do that."

"Also, two men are in pursuit of Hann...," he corrected himself, "my wife."

Mr. Ross gave him his full attention. "Can you describe them?"

"One is tall and lanky, and his companion is short and stout, complete opposites. My wife said that the tall one has a very strong odor and both are extremely unpleasant to look at."

His comments earned a small chuckle from the innkeeper. "Ye have our protection. I will let ye know if anyone comes and asks about you, or your pretty little wife."

Before Jonathon could respond, Mrs. Ross walked out of the room. She waved him up. "Yer wife is ready for a quick supper, then to bed. I will send up some bread and cheese." She started to walk past him but stopped. "I will also send up extra blankets, so you can bed in the corner. I would offer you another room," she put her hand up when Jonathon shook his head, "but I know you would refuse."

"Thank you, ma'am," Jonathon said with tenderness. It had been a long time since a stranger had shown such kindness.

She smiled up at him. "Off with you now. Protect that pretty little wife of yours."

Jonathon started to open the door, but stopped. He knocked and waited for Hannah's voice to allow him entry. After all, it was the only proper thing about this whole situation.

7

Hannah threw open the door, assuming it was the dinner that Mrs. Ross promised. Instead of food, she saw Jonathon leaning against the door frame. "Oh, I apologize, I was expecting our supper."

Jonathon glanced back over his shoulder, watching Mrs. Ross glide down the stairs. "You must be famished if you are so elated at the thought of food."

Hannah stepped back further into the room to allow Jonathon access. He walked in, locking the door behind him. Suddenly, the room seemed very small. She went over to the bed and slowly sat down, carefully braiding her hair into a long braid.

Once she could no longer pretend to braid her hair, she turned her attention to the crackling of the low fire and pulled the oversized nightgown tighter against her body. She scanned the small room, noting the old floral wallpaper was worn and faded, but the room was clean. The rain pelted against the small window on the north side.

For the past few weeks, she had been sharing a bed with Lucy, but now she was sharing a room with Lord Jonathon. What if her father found out? Would he understand? After all, she was told to trust Lord Beckett, and he sent his nephew to protect her.

"Hannah? What is the matter?" Jonathon asked from his side of the room.

Turning to face him, she replied honestly, "I just realized that we would be sharing a room for the entire night, and the impropriety of the situation."

He looked apologetic. "I cannot risk leaving you alone. It is for your own safety."

"I understand."

"Mrs. Ross is sending up a blanket and I will be sleeping by the fire, fully clothed, if that helps you." Her eyes must have betrayed her relief at his words, because he asked, "Did you think we were going to share a bed?"

Hannah nodded.

Jonathon chuckled. "Is that why your face looks as if you had a fright?"

Shrugging, she said, "I was unsure about the sleeping arrangement."

Jonathon leaned back against the wall, looking entirely pleased with himself. "Well, if you are agreeable to share the bed then I would not object."

Hannah huffed. "I am not agreeable."

His eyes twinkled with amusement as he crossed his arms over his chest. "Your virtue is safe with me, Hannah."

She gasped and whispered forcefully, "You must not speak of those things."

"You have nothing to fear from me."

Hannah met his gaze and knew that no truer words had ever been said to her. She did not fear Jonathon physically. Quite the opposite in fact, she felt safe in his presence.

A loud knock caused Jonathon to glance away. He reached for the pistol tucked in the front of his trousers. "Yes?"

"We have yer dinner, sir, and an extra blanket," a muffled

voice said from behind the door. "And to take the tub, if yer wife is finished."

Jonathon unlocked the door and cracked it open. He must have determined it was safe, because he opened the door and reached for the tray. Two lanky young men walked into the room and picked up the tub. After they left, Jonathon locked the door and laid the tray down next to her on the bed. "Considering we do not have a table, would you mind if I sat on the bed while we shared a meal?"

Hannah's lips curled up into a thin smile. "I think that is a fine idea, my lord."

Jonathon sat down and leaned back against the wall. "Well, it appears for dinner we have a choice of bread, dried meat, and cheese."

Hannah plopped a piece of cheese into her mouth. "Sounds delicious. I am famished."

Jonathon smirked at her. "Yes, I remember the way you almost ravaged me when you thought I was food."

Hannah's mouth fell open. "I did no such thing."

Jonathon winked at her as he reached for the bread and tore it into two pieces, handing her a piece. "I must admit that you look better without all that dirt on your face. When I first met you, I had no idea what color your skin was."

Hannah smiled. "Mr. Dawson kept making me put dirt on my face and neck. He thought it enhanced my disguise."

Jonathon shook his head. "I do not think it did anything to disguise your appearance other than to confirm you needed a bath."

Hannah relaxed against the wall before she spoke. "Mr. Dawson wanted to put horse dung on my dress in hopes that no one would approach me."

Jonathon shuddered. "What happened?"

"Lucy stopped him because she did not want Samuel to be repulsed by the smell."

"Smart girl."

"Lucy became like a sister to me. When I see my father again, I want to help Lucy and her parents. They saved my life, in many ways," she said, brushing the bread crumbs off her nightgown.

Jonathon rolled his head against the wall to face her. "What do you mean?"

Hannah reached for a piece of meat. After she finished chewing, she explained, "Well, for starters, they found me in the woods and nursed me back to life, but they also made me feel a part of their family. Mrs. Dawson hugged me just as freely as she hugged Lucy. Often, I was clumsy as I completed my chores, but Mr. Dawson would just smile and offer words of encouragement."

"It sounds like a perfect haven," Jonathon stated, watching her closely.

"For the past few years, I have been in a constant state of grief, but the Dawson family helped me restore my passion for life. It took almost dying to remember that I am still alive, and I have so much to be grateful for."

Jonathon stretched his back and it drew her attention to his muscular shoulders and arms. Hannah had never been around a man in such a state of dress before, and she found her eyes uncooperative as she attempted to look away. Finally, her eyes moved up and she noticed that Jonathon was watching her as she stared blatantly at his chest.

She ducked her head as her cheeks grew extremely warm. Thankfully, Jonathon's voice reached her ears. "I am grateful to the Dawson family for keeping you safe, even though it was nearly impossible to find you."

"I am sorry. How long have you been looking for me?" Hannah asked, reaching for another piece of cheese.

"Almost six weeks now. I arrived at your country estate only days after you disappeared."

Her hand stopped with the piece of cheese halfway to her mouth. "Oh my, I had no idea anyone was searching for me," Hannah said honestly. "I mean, I hoped your uncle would have helped me when I eventually contacted him, but I thought I was on my own until then."

"No, I was dispatched almost immediately after my uncle received the letter from Lord Pembrooke," Jonathon said, putting his hands behind his head.

"You have been looking for me this entire time?" Hannah asked in amazement.

Jonathon smiled. "Yes, off and on. In between searching for you, I did help to bring down a powerful merchant who was selling English women to brothels across the world."

Hannah's eyes grew wide. "Oh my, how horrible for those women."

After a few moments of silence, Jonathon turned so he was facing her with his shoulder resting against the wall. "How did you escape, Hannah?" His tone was light, but Hannah sensed it was important for him to find out what happened.

She picked up the empty tray and placed it under the bed. "Mr. Walker, our steward, betrayed me," she said with a sad smile. "I was out on my morning ride and Mr. Walker rode up to me."

"Did you take any footmen with you?"

Hannah shook her head slowly. "I ride alone, assuming I stay within view of the estate."

Jonathon gave her a knowing look. "Did you stay within view of the estate?"

She averted her eyes from his disapproving stare. "No, I often ride to see the ruins of an old medieval castle. It is about an hour's ride from the estate."

"Was Mr. Walker aware that you rode to the ruins?"

Hannah bit her lower lip. "He was the one who first told me about them."

"Ah," Jonathon replied.

She rested her shoulder against the wall, turning towards Jonathon. "I was almost to the ruins when Mr. Walker rode up to me. I sensed something was wrong, because he seemed nervous and his face was blotchy. At first, I thought his wife had died, since her health had been declining, but then he grabbed my reins. He told me that he was sorry, but he needed the money for his wife's medicine. To make matters worse, Mr. Walker told me it would be best if I went along willingly."

"Was he alone?"

"No." Hannah leaned the side of her head against the wall. "That is when I saw two riders approaching in the distance, one tall, lanky man and one short, stout man, and I noticed the stark contrast right away. An overwhelming impression of danger came over me and I knew I had to escape. I jerked my reins back and raced my horse into the thicket, as if the hounds of hell were chasing me, and in my case, they were."

"I cannot believe you outrode them." He sounded impressed.

Hannah rolled her eyes, fighting back her annoyance. "Why, because I'm a lady?"

Jonathon seemed amused by her response. "No, because it is extremely difficult to navigate between trees."

She shrugged her shoulders. "True, but I had no choice."

"At some point, you fell off your horse," he reminded her.

"That was long after I lost the men in the woods." Hannah glanced at the low burning fire before continuing. "I rode for hours in various directions until I was completely turned around. I started climbing along a trail, parallel to a deep, narrow gorge with rushing water, and my horse started slipping." She tugged at the long sleeves of her nightgown. "I do not remember much after that."

"Is that when the Dawsons found you?"

She nodded. "My next memory was waking up in the Dawsons' house. My fever had just broken and Lucy was sitting next to the bed, chattering about Samuel and his horses. They were so happy to see me awake, and insisted I stay in bed until I fully recovered."

"Did you confide in them?"

Hannah yawned and quickly brought her hand up to cover her mouth. "Yes. Apparently when I was feverish, I started screaming about how the men were coming to get me. Once I woke up and told them the truth, they believed me without hesitation."

Jonathon arose. "You should get some sleep. We will need to leave at first light." He reached for the spare blanket and tossed it on the floor near the fireplace. As he laid down, he removed the pistol from the front of his trousers and set it next to him.

Hannah slipped under the blanket and laid her head down on the pillow, turning towards Jonathon. It had a weird odor and was lumpy, but at least she had a pillow. "Goodnight, Jonathon."

Jonathon smiled. "Goodnight, Hannah."

She rolled over to face the wall. Hannah was exhausted and wanted to sleep. If she faced Jonathon, she would be too tempted to stare at him, dreaming of him holding her again.

My goodness, she was acting like a love-crazed fool.

JONATHON WAS ALERT, PISTOL IN HAND, BEFORE THE SECOND soft knock on the door. He glanced at Hannah, confirming she was safe and still tucked into bed. The soft glow of the embers in the fireplace allowed him to see her curled into a ball, facing the wall.

In two strides, he was at the door, his instincts alerting him that this was friend rather than foe on the other side of the door.

The soft knock indicated that the person did not want to arouse attention. "Who's there?" he asked in a hushed voice.

"Mr. Ross," came the muffled reply.

Jonathon opened the door, pointing the pistol at Mr. Ross' chest and poked his head out to survey the small, dark corridor for a potential threat. He stepped back, lowered the pistol, and ushered the innkeeper into the room. "What time is it?"

"Early." Mr. Ross glanced at the ruffled blanket on the floor, nodding his head with approval. He turned back to Jonathon and said, "Two men have been asking about ye and yer wife. One was tall and one was short, and the tall one had a powerful stench to him, just as yer wife said."

Jonathon tucked the pistol in the front of his trousers. "When did they arrive?"

"About two hours ago. They rented a room down the hall, but there is more," Mr. Ross announced. He glanced at Hannah's sleeping form and lowered his voice. "They told me quite the tale. They said Lord Beckett abducted their sister with the intention of ruining her. Is there any truth to that?"

Jonathon did not know where to begin since it was all a lie, except about his identity. Hannah's soft voice joined their conversation. "They are lying. Those men have tried on multiple occasions to abduct me. Lord Jonathon is helping me flee to safety." Hannah pulled her knees up to her chest and wrapped her arms around her legs. "Please, Mr. Ross, do not hand me over to them."

Jonathon could hear the fear in her voice and he longed to comfort her, as he did last night. "You have nothing to fear, Lady Hannah. I have no doubt that Mr. Ross saw right through their story." Jonathon lifted an eyebrow towards the innkeeper, daring him to deny it.

Mr. Ross gave Hannah a warm smile before addressing Jonathon. "The only part of the story I believed was that ye were a lord. That was an easy thing to see."

Jonathon nodded his approval. "Thank you for the warning. We will hurry and depart before the sun comes up."

The innkeeper stepped forward, concern etched on his face. "After their second drink, I heard the men grumbling. It appears that they posted guards on the main road towards London. Ye weren't planning on going that way, were ye?"

Jonathon rubbed his hand over his stiff neck. "My uncle lives a few hours out of London, and I had planned to place Lady Hannah under his protection." He glanced down at her and expected to see disappointment lining her features, but instead, he saw trust in her eyes. How was he going to keep her safe?

"Ye could stay here for a few days, my lord," the innkeeper offered.

Suddenly an idea popped into his head. He would take Hannah to a place that he would not fear for her safety. He withdrew some coins from his pocket, handing them to the innkeeper. "If you would be kind enough to saddle our horses, we will depart as soon as they are ready."

Accepting the coins, Mr. Ross nodded. "Take care of yer pretty wife." Before he opened the door, he said over his shoulder, "I will have my wife wrap up some breakfast for ye to eat on the road."

As the innkeeper left, Jonathon locked the door behind him. "I apologize for the early morning, but we have a long ride ahead of us."

Hannah rose from the bed and neatly folded the blanket. "Where are we going?"

Jonathon leveled his gaze at her. "The safest place that I know."

🦋 8 🦋

HANNAH AND JONATHON REINED IN THEIR HORSES ON TOP OF A large hill, overlooking a wide, expansive valley divided into farmland and cow pastures. "This is a marvelous view," she said, wishing she could paint this lovely scenery.

"It is," Jonathon agreed, leaning forward in the saddle. "Shall we proceed?"

"Now will you tell me where we are going?" Hannah inquired, urging her horse forward.

"We are heading to Eliza's estate, Chatswich Manor. In fact, we have been on their land for over two hours now."

Hannah's eyes widened as she looked at him. "You are taking me to Eliza's estate? Was she not just married two weeks ago?"

"Yes," he confirmed.

"Why are they not on their wedding tour?"

Jonathon kept his gaze straight ahead. "Lord Lansdowne is on his deathbed and they did not want to leave him so near the end."

"Wait, Lord Lansdowne, as in the Marquess of Lansdowne?"

Jonathon quirked a brow. "You have heard of the Marquess

of Lansdowne, but not of my father, the Duke of Remington?" he drawled.

She waved a hand, dismissing his teasing. "Everyone has heard of Lord Lansdowne." Jonathon eyed her warily, so she rushed to add, "Rumor has it that he is the richest man in England."

Shrugging, Jonathon said, "That would not surprise me.

Hannah's stomach rumbled loudly. She pressed her hand to her belly, hoping that Jonathon hadn't heard, and asked, "How much farther?"

"In a mile, the road splits. The right road leads to a moderately-sized village. The left leads to Eliza's estate. May I suggest we…"

Hannah kicked her horse into a run, shouting over her shoulder, "I will race you there."

She heard Jonathon's laughter as his horse caught up to hers, riding side by side until a large estate loomed in front of them. She slowed her approach, gawking at the sheer size of the imposing building. In fact, it was longer in length than her entire village back home.

The lavish, three-level, stately structure was set on a hill, causing it to appear even larger than life. The wide, evenly spaced, embellished columns were accented by gold-leafed window frames. Two towers extended high above the flat roof, but the carved stonework above the main door commanded her attention.

The estate was backed by wooded, rocky hills, and a large river flowed away towards the valley. The cobblestone road leading up to the estate ran through a well-maintained garden. As the road widened, Hannah saw a large, wooden stable to the right, and multiple corrals with horses grazing complacently.

A circular, cobblestone drive led upwards to the main entry where two groomsmen rushed to assist them with their horses. Jonathon dismounted and walked over to her horse. Hannah knew he was waiting to help her dismount, but the estate was too majestic to look away.

"Lady Hannah?" he prompted her.

She glanced down at him. "I cannot go in there," she said nervously, as she ran a hand over her threadbare dress, "wearing this."

"That is ridiculous. My sister will not care what you are wearing. I am quite certain she will relish the fact that she can take another lady shopping."

Hannah bit her lip. "Perhaps I should go through the servant's quarters?"

Jonathon frowned. "You are worrying needlessly."

Hannah winced as she looked at the estate. Could she hold her head high and walk into the Marquess of Lansdowne's home wearing a farm work dress?

Jonathon sighed. He flicked his wrist back towards the groomsman, and took the reins in his hand. He mounted his horse. "Let's go to the village. I am sure we can stay at the inn until a dress can be made for you."

Hannah's resistance melted as her eyes tracked him. She knew how her body ached from riding all morning, but he was willing to get back in the saddle to help her feel more at ease. What an incredible act of kindness. "No, Jonathon. I think we have been in the saddle long enough today. I just hope your sister is as kind and gracious as you have led me to believe."

Jonathon's lips twitched, appearing as if he was suppressing a smile. "As you wish, my lady," he agreed as he dismounted and walked back over to assist her.

Hannah placed her ungloved hands on his shoulders, feeling his taut muscles under the shirt. "Thank you, my lord," she answered playfully.

Jonathon tucked her hand into his elbow, and she found herself relaxing against him as they strolled towards a large, black door with bracketing columns. Her thin, worn boots allowed her to feel the curvature of the cobblestones and her feet ached with fatigue. She glanced at Jonathon.

"It was very kind of you to offer to take me to the village for a new dress."

His free hand came up to rest on hers. "I'm just glad you did not insist that we go." A wide smile lit his face. "If you had, I would have dragged you off your horse and thrown you over my shoulder."

Hannah stopped and attempted to pull her hand out of Jonathon's. He wouldn't release his hold on her hand, but she didn't try very hard to escape. "You tricked me?"

He chuckled. "I did, and my ruse worked splendidly, do you not agree?"

Hannah's lips tightened into a thin line, feigning disapproval of his plan, but in all honesty, she was too tired to ride in the saddle anymore. Furthermore, the thought of food and a warm bath made her giddy with excitement. "If you were not already my hero, I would be very disappointed in you," she admonished him.

Jonathon turned to face her, keeping her hand enclosed in his. "You think I'm your hero?" he asked as he seemed to gauge her sincerity.

She smiled at him. "You saved me from a terrifying ordeal. How could I not think of you that way?"

His eyes turned stormy, as if he were fighting an internal battle. A moment later, his eyes cleared, and his gaze roamed her face, repeatedly lingering on her lips. "I am flattered that you think so highly of me, Hannah." His voice seemed low and husky.

The way he said her name made her look first at his lips and then his eyes. She couldn't decide which one should hold her interest, considering they both commanded her attention.

As their eyes met, Jonathon's lips parted, and he stepped closer. "I am not worthy of your esteem."

Hannah resisted the urge to place her hand on his chest. "I will be the judge of that, Jonathon."

For a moment, neither of them spoke as they gazed into each other's eyes. Hannah was afraid to speak, or move, for fear of breaking the connection that she felt towards him.

"Lord Jonathon," a loud voice boomed from behind.

Hannah jumped, startled. Jonathon chuckled at her reaction.

"Mr. Larson," Jonathon answered back in a cheerful tone. "It is good to see you." He led her towards the large, six-paneled entry door where Mr. Larson was standing.

He was a tall, older man with salt and pepper hair, wearing a white shirt with tan trousers. As Mr. Larson's gaze rested on her, she could see that his eloquent eyes encompassed warmth and tranquility, which immediately set her at ease. "You found her, I see," he said with a smile.

Standing aside, Mr. Larson let them enter. Once they were inside, Hannah tried not to gape at the extravagance of the rectangular-shaped entrance hall. It was two levels high, with carved, wooden paneling bracketing the lower level. A massive marble fireplace stood directly across from the main door, and a round, plastered ceiling with an amazing quadratura painting gave the illusion that it extended up to yet another level. A grand staircase dominated the left side of the hall.

Jonathon cleared his throat to get her attention. "Mr. Larson, may I present the elusive Lady Hannah, daughter of the Earl of Pembrooke," he said, properly introducing her.

Mr. Larson bowed. "It is a pleasure to finally meet you. I know Jonathon has been searching for you quite vigorously these past few weeks." He smiled at Jonathon and added, "And I had no doubt that he would find you."

Jonathon returned his smile. "Thank you. Although, I had my doubts."

Mr. Larson briefly glanced down at her clothing, and a frown tugged at his lips. "Are you well, Lady Hannah?" he asked, his eyes betraying his concern for her well-being. She knew he was asking about more than her immediate health.

Hannah's gaze flickered to Jonathon before saying, "I am. I thank you for your concern, Mr. Larson." She had been shown more compassion in the last six weeks than she had received since that horrible carriage accident over four years ago.

His face softened as he studied her but then turned to Jonathon. "I saw you ride up and dismount, then mount again, and dismount again…" his voice exaggerated the story, "and I was wondering if that was a new tradition amongst the ton."

Chuckling, Jonathon said, "I was attempting to convince Lady Hannah to come inside, because she is under the impression that her dress is not the height of fashion."

Mr. Larson wisely did not comment on the condition of her dress, but instead stated, "I'm sure that Lady Lansdowne will be ecstatic to take you shopping tomorrow. She has discovered that the dressmaker in town carries exquisite fabric and ribbons, and is quite adept with a needle." He winked at her. "Her words, not mine."

"Are Eliza and Benedict not home?" Jonathon asked, glancing around the entry hall.

"They are in the red parlor…" Mr. Larson stopped, and lowered his voice. "You must have not heard that Lord Lansdowne passed away a few days after the wedding. Benedict is now the Marquess of Lansdowne."

"How is he handling the death of his father and the new title?" Jonathon asked with a solemn face.

Mr. Larson rubbed his hand over his chin. "Your sister has been a tremendous help, but he is struggling with being thrust into his new role. It is a huge responsibility."

"Mr. Larson," a condescending voice admonished him from the opposite side of the entry hall. A tall, heavy-set, middle-aged man marched towards them with a look of disdain on his face. "May I remind you, *again*, that the steward does not open the door for Lord and Lady Lansdowne's guests, nor should he speak so openly about the lord of the house."

Hannah tightened her hold on Jonathon's arm as he said, "Mr. Harvey, it is good to see you again." From Jonathon's tone, it was apparent he did not care for Mr. Harvey's reprimand of Mr. Larson.

Mr. Harvey stopped short of them and bowed respectfully. "It is good to see you again as well, Lord Jonathon." His gaze roamed to Hannah's face and then slowly perused her tattered dress and boots. He lifted an eyebrow at Jonathon, as if waiting for him to explain why a street urchin was in a marquess's home.

"May I present Lady Hannah," Jonathon informed Mr. Harvey.

Hannah tipped her head towards the butler. "Please excuse my attire, Mr. Harvey, but I have been on a farm," she said, ducking her head in embarrassment. She glanced at Jonathon and he had the nerve to act amused by her explanation.

"It is not my business to criticize how you are dressed, Lady Hannah," Mr. Harvey said, although his eyes told her that was exactly what he was doing.

"Right, then," Mr. Larson said as he broke up the awkward silence, "may I escort you to the red parlor, Lady Hannah and Lord Jonathon." He extended his palm outward indicating the direction of the red parlor.

As they followed Mr. Larson through an expansive hall with green, floral wallpaper, Hannah couldn't help but look at the family portraits adorning the walls. Towards the end of the hall, Mr. Larson stopped in front of a door and knocked loudly.

He glanced at them as he waited for an answer. "It only takes once walking in on them," Mr. Larson remarked, shaking his head.

Stifling a groan, Jonathon complained, "I thought marriage would have curbed their blatant affection towards each other."

Hannah threw him an inquisitive look. "Is it not a good thing for a married couple to be in love?"

Jonathon shook his head. "You will see what I mean."

"Enter," a muffled shout came from inside the room.

JONATHON WALKED INTO THE ROOM WITH HANNAH ON HIS ARM and Mr. Larson trailing behind. His first glance of the room showed Benedict, his close friend and brother-in-law, putting on his black waistcoat. His hair was tousled, and it was evident that they had interrupted an intimate moment.

Eliza was smoothing out her mourning dress when she looked up. "Jonathon!" When her eyes tracked to Hannah, they grew wide. "Is this who I think it is?"

"Lady Hannah, may I present Lord and Lady Lansdowne," Jonathon said.

Eliza walked closer and stopped short of Hannah. "We do not stand on formalities here. Please call me Eliza."

Benedict moved to stand next to his wife and put his arm around her waist. "And please call me Benedict. After all, if you call me Lord Lansdowne, it might take me a few moments to even recognize that you are addressing me."

Hannah smiled widely. "Then you must call me Hannah." Her grip on Jonathon's arm relaxed, and it appeared she was at ease again.

Jonathon glanced over his shoulder. "I noticed that Mr. Harvey is still employed as the butler."

Benedict shrugged. "He came with the house."

"He reprimanded Mr. Larson and frightened Lady Hannah," Jonathon informed them.

"Oh, dear." Eliza shook her head. "We are letting time pass before we implement any changes to the household staff. Jane has been most helpful during this time, but she is still grieving the loss of her husband."

Jonathon noticed that his sister glowed, and it warmed his heart to see her so content. "You look happy, Eliza," he said as he gave her a hug.

"I am. Benedict sees to my happiness," she said as he released her.

Eliza moved to an ivory sofa and extended her hand for everyone to sit. Jonathon escorted Hannah to an adjacent sofa and waited for her to sit down. Eliza lifted an eyebrow at him as he claimed the seat next to her and he shot her a warning look. Mr. Larson sat on an upholstered chair with rounded arms.

Jonathon glanced around the room, noting red vertical wallpaper and red paintings on the walls. "I see why this is called the red parlor," he said mockingly.

Eliza ignored his comment and addressed Hannah. "Benedict and I are relieved that Jonathon finally found you. May I ask where you have been?"

Hannah glanced at Jonathon, as if asking permission to speak. Understanding her hesitation, he turned to face her and lowered his voice. "You are free to speak openly with them. They will guard your secrets as well as I do."

Giving him a grateful smile, Hannah turned her attention back to the group. "I apologize for not trusting you, but my father told me to only trust Lord Beckett."

"Which one?" Benedict asked.

"Well, my letter was not clear on that point, but Lord Jonathon knew the code phrase when he found me," Hannah explained.

"That reminds me. Hannah kept the letter from her father and it looked like a coded message to me. Would you mind looking at it?" Jonathon asked as he handed the letter to Eliza.

She opened it, quickly absorbing the contents. Eliza stood and crossed to a small desk, retrieving paper and a quill. After a few minutes, she returned with the letter and a new piece of paper. Handing the letter back to Hannah, Eliza sat down.

"Basically, the letter states everything that we already know. It confirms that Lord Pembrooke is on a ship with *Hawk*, and he should arrive any day now. He stated he would contact Lord B, which we can reasonably presume is our uncle. Lastly, he implied that his documents would have great significance to the Crown."

Hannah's eyes grew wide. "You found all that information in the short letter I received?" she asked in awe.

Eliza smiled her understanding. "If you must know, the code read, *Hawk on ship. Six. Contact Lord B. Papers vital.* I have read enough codes to fill in the lines."

Jonathon nudged Hannah. "My sister has been deciphering codes since she was ten." He glanced at Mr. Larson. "Will you send a message to Uncle Charles and let him know what we uncovered? Also, please inform him that Hannah is under my protection for the time being."

Mr. Larson nodded. "I will send someone straight away."

Smiling at Hannah, Eliza asked, "I am curious. Where have you been for the last six weeks?"

"On a farm," she said, smoothing out her tattered dress.

"A farm?" Eliza repeated.

"Yes, a sheep farm," she clarified, "but there was also a cow, two goats and lots of chickens."

Benedict spoke from his seat next to Eliza. "Lord Beckett mentioned that Lord Pembrooke might have given you instructions in case you were faced with danger. Did the plan actually include living on a sheep farm?"

Hannah shook her head good-naturedly. "No, the plan was for me to take our fastest carriage to Lord Beckett's estate the moment it appeared that I was in any danger."

"Then what happened?" Benedict asked, leaning forward.

Hannah pursed her lips. "Our steward betrayed me, and I fled for my life," she said sadly.

Jonathon placed his hand over her fisted hands to remind her that she was not alone. "You have nothing to fear, Hannah. You are safe."

Hannah smiled at him, her eyes filled with trust. "Well, I should probably start at the beginning, then..."

Jonathon removed his hand and sat back while Hannah shared every detail of the past six weeks. He interjected comments if he thought they were of value.

When Hannah finished, she leaned back in her seat and glanced at him. Jonathon was so proud of Hannah for sharing her story. Although, she had left out one important fact that he couldn't resist teasing her about. "You failed to mention that you learned how to milk a cow."

Hannah's eyes narrowed, but before she could respond, Eliza gushed, "You learned how to milk a cow? How extraordinary."

Hannah gave her a puzzled look. "I did not think any ladies of the ton would find it 'extraordinary'."

Eliza laughed. "You are correct. Ladies of the ton would give you the direct cut if they learned you milked a cow like a common farmhand, so you must keep that between us. But," she smirked, "I do things all the time that would scandalize the ton."

"You do? What sorts of things?" Hannah asked curiously.

Benedict tapped his chin with his finger. "Just today, my lovely wife wore men's clothing as she practiced archery with her longbow."

"Yesterday, Mr. Harvey almost fainted when he saw Eliza and I fencing in the exterior courtyard," Mr. Larson added.

Hannah looked at Eliza in amazement. "You can fence?"

"I can," Eliza confirmed. "Would you like to learn?"

Hannah radiated excitement as she nodded enthusiastically. "I would love to."

"We can start tomorrow." Eliza then glanced at her dress. "But first, we need to go to the village and acquire new clothes for you."

Jonathon smiled at Eliza. "I had hoped that you would say that. Would you mind if I stay back with Benedict, assuming Mr. Larson will be joining the ladies?"

Mr. Larson nodded. "I will bring four footmen for additional security."

Eliza smiled at Hannah. "Benedict hired Mr. Larson as my personal steward for a wedding present."

"At double the salary of the estate's current steward," Benedict grumbled.

Jonathon laughed at Benedict's mock grousing. "Mr. Larson came with Eliza. If you had not hired him, he would have just loitered around the estate to ensure Eliza's safety anyway."

"If Eliza can fence and shoot the longbow, it sounds to me like she can defend herself," Hannah mused.

Benedict affectionately gazed at his wife. "I know she can protect herself, but I will always worry about her safety. Mr. Larson is a sound investment, in my opinion."

Eliza leaned forward and kissed Benedict on his lips, lingering for a few moments. Jonathon glanced at Hannah for her reaction and noticed a pink hue to her cheeks. He leaned close and whispered, "I warned you."

"I think it is admirable," she offered, her eyes twinkling.

"Thank you, Hannah." Eliza rose from the sofa, causing all the men to stand. "If it is all right with you gentlemen, I would like to take Hannah upstairs for a long bath and a rest before the dinner bell."

Jonathon arose, offering his hand to Hannah.

"I would be delighted," Hannah said, not even attempting to hide her joy.

"I believe we can also borrow one of Jane's dresses for you

to wear to dinner tonight," Eliza said as she started walking towards the door.

Hannah almost skipped behind her, but stopped as she reached the door. She turned to Jonathon and asked, "You will be here for dinner, won't you?"

He smiled and bowed. "I will be here." She gave him a shy smile and turned to follow Eliza.

Jonathon watched Hannah depart, his eyes lingering on the open door. He turned to find Benedict and Mr. Larson watching him with smug smiles on their faces. "What are you two looking at?"

Benedict glanced at Mr. Larson. "The interaction between you and Lady Hannah was quite telling," he said, smirking.

Mr. Larson crossed his arms. "It appears that Lord Jonathon is smitten with the beautiful Lady Hannah."

He was too fatigued to argue with their teasing. "I will be in my usual guest room," he said as he walked towards the door.

Benedict laughed. "You mean the guest room that you used for two days before the wedding?"

"Yes, and I will need use of your valet," Jonathon said over his shoulder as he walked into the hall, ignoring the sound of snickering behind him.

9

HANNAH TRAILED BEHIND ELIZA AS THEY MADE THEIR WAY UP the stairs and down a long hall. Eliza glanced behind her, saying, "I am going to place you in the guest room next to my bedchamber."

"Is that not Lord Lansdowne's bedchamber?"

"Benedict," she corrected, "and, no. We actually share a room." Eliza's hand swiped through the air. "I know the ton would disapprove, but I enjoy sleeping next to my husband."

Hannah smiled approvingly. "My mother and father shared a bedchamber until her death. In fact, they used to kiss each other in front of me frequently." Her hand went over her heart. "I have always wanted a marriage like that."

Eliza stopped in front of a door that was surrounded by intricate wood carvings. "I had given up on the thought of marriage, believing that men were incapable of fidelity and love, but Benedict convinced me to trust him with my heart." She smiled, her eyes conveying her happiness. "I believe true love is always worth the risk."

Hannah absorbed what she said and nodded. "I hope to have a great love story like you and Benedict have."

Eliza opened the door. "Your love story has just begun."

Eliza's words took Hannah aback. Was her affection for Jonathon that obvious?

However, all her worries flew out of her head when she stepped into a large bedchamber with embellished windows, a small fireplace, and large four-poster bed. She noted the blue wallpaper, sofa, and a large floral carpet running length-wise across the room. Lastly, her eyes fell onto the bathing tub near the fireplace and a pretty, blonde servant who was testing the water.

"This is beautiful," Hannah stated.

Eliza glided into the room and smiled at the servant. "Martha, you are a godsend. Would you mind assisting Lady Hannah with her personal care today?"

"I would be delighted, my lady." Martha curtsied towards Hannah. "I happened to overhear Mr. Harvey mentioning Lord Jonathon brought home a stray." Her lips twitched in amusement, then gave way to a full smile. "Lady Eliza has mentioned, on more than one occasion, that Lord Jonathon was searching for you, so it was a reasonable conclusion that he found you."

Eliza laughed at Martha's comment. "Lady Hannah is the most beautiful stray I have ever seen," she said good-naturedly. "Why don't you take a nice, long bath while I go and see about acquiring a dress for you for this evening?" She turned to leave, then stopped. "I will ask the housekeeper to send someone up to act as your lady's maid while you are here."

Within a few minutes, Hannah was relaxing in a bath and leaning her head back against the metal tub. The warm water felt amazing against her skin, and the smell of rosewater reached her nose. Her eyes gently closed, and the next thing she knew there was a knock at her door.

Martha bustled in with a handful of white garments and laid them on the sofa. "I see that you are finally awake. You looked so peaceful in the bath that I let you sleep."

"Thank you, but I believe I would like to get out now," Hannah said as she lifted herself up. Martha placed a large robe over her and assisted her out of the bath.

"The dowager marchioness had a new set of undergarments for you to use," Martha said.

As Hannah placed on the undergarments, she relished the feeling of the silk material against her body. "Oh, I must thank her," she said.

"Thank me for what, dear?" A handsome older woman with brown hair pinned into a chignon, wearing a silk black dress, walked into the room, and closed the door. She had a dark green dress draped over her arm.

Hannah curtsied, but it seemed silly since she was in her undergarments. "I wanted to thank you for the use of your clothes, Lady Lansdowne. It has been weeks since I have worn proper clothing."

The dowager marchioness walked up to her and patted her cheek. "Eliza told me you were a beautiful lady, but that does not do you justice. You are exquisite, my dear."

"Thank you," Hannah softly replied. Her heart warmed at the kindness shown by this family towards a virtual stranger.

"Eliza told me about all that you have endured these past few weeks," she said, shaking her head. "You are a remarkable girl with an inner strength that most ladies could not even imagine. You should be proud of yourself."

Hannah's eyes filled with tears at the older woman's astounding comments. "You are most kind, Lady Lansdowne," she managed to say after a few moments.

"Please call me Jane, and I think we will be fast friends," she said as she laid the dress on the bed. "I'm afraid I do not have any white dresses for you to wear, but Eliza suggested you might like this one."

Hannah fingered the high-waisted, green muslin dress with puffy sleeves. "It is beautiful."

Martha motioned to a chair at the dressing table. "Lady Hannah, may I suggest we start with your hair?"

Smiling, Jane said, "I shall see you at dinner tonight, child." She quickly exited the room, closing the door behind her.

Hannah sat down in front of Martha at the dressing table. "You have the most unusual black coloring in your hair," Martha stated as she brushed it.

"My mother was a Spaniard. I was told that I look just like her," she said.

"Then your mother must have been beautiful," Martha commented.

Hannah wistfully smiled. "I always thought she was the most beautiful person I knew, but she was judged harshly because of her looks. Most of the English gentry ostracized her because of her lineage, never mind that she descended from royalty." She frowned. "My mother chose to ignore the whispers about her appearance, but I know it hurt her. Which is why she relished her time at our country home in Bath."

Martha's hand stilled. "I have no doubt the whispers were born of jealousy. Many gentlemen prefer the classic blonde hair and fair skin, but your black hair and porcelain skin makes all the other women look drab in comparison."

Hannah turned around in her chair. "Thank you, Martha. Your kind words have touched me."

Martha smiled in response and reached for the pins. "I have the perfect idea for your hair."

A short while later, Hannah looked in the mirror. Her black hair was piled high on top of her head and small curls framed her face. Martha had even woven ribbons throughout. "Well done, Martha," Hannah said in admiration.

Martha fetched the dress and approached her. "And now the dress," she said. Martha fastened the buttons on the back, then stood aside and inspected the fit. "It's as if it were made for you."

Hannah looked in the mirror and gasped. The dress did fit perfectly, and was only enhanced by her elaborate hairstyle.

As she admired herself in the mirror, Eliza walked in and stopped. "You look beautiful."

"Thank you, Eliza," Hannah replied as Martha walked up and handed her matching green kid gloves. While she was putting them on, she thought about what Jonathon would think when he saw her, and she smiled.

"What are you smiling about?" Eliza asked.

Hannah looked up and blushed. "I was just wondering what Jonathon will think when he sees me. Ever since he found me, I have been covered in dirt and grime, and my hair has been impossible to tame into a braid. Furthermore, my borrowed dress was tattered and hung limp around my body."

Eliza exchanged a look with Martha before saying, "I have no doubt that your beauty will render him speechless."

Hannah shook her head. "I did not mean to imply that he might find me attractive. I was just musing..." Her voice trailed off as her hands covered her warm cheeks.

"We would have to be blind to not notice the way you two look at each other." Eliza laughed.

Hannah watched her hands as they smoothed down her dress. "I have only known Jonathon for a few days now."

Eliza reached for her hand. "I did not mean to embarrass you, but I am speaking the truth. Jonathon is very protective of you."

"Well, of course he is. He has been tasked with keeping me safe, and he takes his duty very seriously," Hannah stated matter-of-factly.

Eliza's eyes twinkled in amusement. "Yes, very seriously," she teased as she looped their arms together.

Jane floated into the room, nodding her approval at Hannah. "Shall we go down and join the men? They are waiting for us in the drawing room."

As they neared the drawing room, Benedict's voice could be

heard echoing down the hall. "Lady Hannah will stay as Eliza's guest until Lord Pembrooke can come and collect her."

Jonathon's grumbling voice now could be heard. "I do not understand why I cannot stay here."

"You must think of Lady Hannah's reputation. You spent two nights together with no chaperone. You shared a room at an inn. If anyone were to find out, she would be ruined, and..."

As the women entered the room, Benedict closed his mouth and looked away. Jonathon sat on the sofa, facing away. He obviously hadn't noticed them enter. "That is ridiculous. Hannah is like a little sister to me, nothing more."

Benedict cleared his throat, his eyes nervously cutting towards Jonathon. "Ladies."

Jonathon immediately arose and turned around, his eyes filled with remorse.

Hannah felt warmth creep into her face and she knew it must be flushed red with embarrassment. She had dressed with painstaking care for Jonathon, but all he felt for her was brotherly affection. Now, she needed to escape for a moment and collect her thoughts.

Benedict moved to kiss his wife's cheek, effectively cutting off Hannah's quick retreat. To exit, she would have to walk around her hosts.

Smiling, Benedict stated, "You are looking well, Hannah."

Hannah gave him a faint smile. "Your wife has ensured that I have been treated with the utmost hospitality, and I am most thankful for your graciousness."

"You are most welcome here," Benedict said, his kind eyes reaffirming his message.

Eliza looped arms with her. "Most welcome," her voice said a little too enthusiastically.

Hannah's eyes moved of their own accord to Jonathon who seemed rooted to his spot near the sofa. He was dressed in a black coat with tails, a white vest and cravat, and shiny black shoes. His dark brown hair was styled fashionably, but was slightly longer, which lent a sense of danger to his image.

Jonathon was a ruggedly handsome gentleman and she was a fool to think he would ever see her as anything but a country bumpkin. It did not matter that she was the daughter of an earl, because a man like Jonathon would always be unavailable to her. He was tasked with protecting her, nothing more. Yet her treasonous heart had fallen for him.

"Does Hannah not look beautiful this evening, Jonathon?" Jane asked with a polite smile.

"Yes, she does." Jonathon's eyes had not wavered from her since she walked into the room. Now, he stood with eyes that gleamed with pity. She did not want his pity. She needed to collect herself.

She removed her arm from Eliza's and mustered all the dignity she could find as she tilted her chin. "Please excuse me for a moment. I fear I left my handkerchief in my bedchamber."

As she turned to leave, Jonathon stepped around the sofa. "Hannah, please wait," he said uncertainly.

Hannah pretended she had not heard him and walked out of the room. As soon as she was in the safety of the hall, she picked up her skirt and ran for the security of her bedchamber.

ELIZA'S EYEBROW LIFTED, BUT SHE DID NOT SAY ANYTHING. HER expression told him that he just made a serious mistake with Hannah, but he already knew that.

Benedict glanced towards the open door and back at him. "You should go after her."

"And say what?" Jonathon asked as he wiped a hand over his

freshly-shaved chin. "I just announced that I think of her as a sister."

"And do you?" Jane questioned.

"Hell, no," Jonathon yelled. "She is the most beautiful woman I have ever met. I have grown to care for her, although it sounds ridiculous since I have only known her for a few days."

Benedict and Eliza exchanged amused glances as he put his arm around her. "Then go after her. We can postpone dinner for a few moments," Eliza said with a smile.

Frowning, Jonathon admitted, "I do not think she returns my feelings."

Benedict coughed, which sounded more like a laugh. "I think Lady Hannah will be receptive to whatever you say."

Jonathon looked to Eliza and Jane and they each offered him an encouraging nod. He turned and walked out of the room and looked towards the stairs. At the top, he saw a flash of green moving quickly towards the guest rooms.

He took the stairs three at a time, but still didn't catch her. He stood in front of the door to her bedchamber and hesitated for a moment before he lightly knocked.

"Come in," Hannah said in a faint voice.

Slowly, he turned the handle and opened the door. Lady Hannah was sitting on the settee, staring absently at the low-burning fire, occasionally wiping at her face. The only light came from the fire, and he assumed she was crying.

"Hannah," he said softly, not wanting to alarm her by his presence.

"Oh, Jonathon, you startled me. I thought you were Martha," she said, as she turned away from him and wiped her face. Holding her head erect, she stood and walked to the dressing table. "I will be down shortly. I seemed to have misplaced my handkerchief." Her voice sounded quivery and she kept her rigid back to him.

He took a step closer. "I would like to apologize for what I said in the drawing room. I want you to know that…"

She cut him off. "You do not need to explain anything. You said nothing wrong." She slowly turned and offered him a weak smile. "I believe I am more fatigued than I led myself to believe. I think it would be best if I retired for the evening." Diverting her eyes from his gaze, she added, "Would you please give my regards to everyone?"

"That would be a pity, since you have already dressed so elegantly for dinner." Jonathon allowed his eyes to peruse her body. "I would beg you to reconsider. You will no doubt add sparkling conversation to the dinner table."

Hannah met his gaze, but her eyes were guarded. "I appreciate what you are attempting to do, but I feel that it is best if I retire for the evening."

"Best for whom?" Jonathon took a tentative step forward. As he came closer, he saw that her eyes were red and swollen, and her bottom lip quivered, as if she held back more tears. "How can I make this right?"

A tear escaped her eye and she quickly wiped it away. "You did nothing wrong. I am just fatigued from our journey."

"You are a terrible liar, my dear," he said, with a lift of his eyebrow.

She lowered her gaze to the floor. "I beg you to leave," she said dejectedly.

"No," he said. In two long strides, he stood in front of her. He placed his finger under her chin and raised her head to look at him. "You are in distress."

She attempted to lower her gaze, but his finger held firm. "It is nothing. A good night's sleep is all that is needed."

Jonathon slowly brought his hand up to cup her cheek. "No, you are wrong. I do not believe I will sleep well knowing that you are down the hall from my chambers."

Hannah looked perplexed. "I assure you that I am perfectly safe at Chatswich Manor."

His free hand slowly came up and rested on her other cheek. "I found that I enjoyed sleeping near you at the inn," he said as his eyes searched hers.

She blushed and averted her eyes. "You must not speak of that night again."

"Hannah," he said, suddenly breathless. Her eyes latched onto his and he felt as if he could stay in this moment... forever. A pucker at Hannah's brow reminded him that he needed to gain control of his thoughts. "As you are aware, we have only known each other for a few days," he ventured, but stopped when a frown formed on her lips.

She took a step back, but he took a step forward, and her eyes grew wide. "As I was saying," he said, with a crooked smile, "we have only known each other for a few days, but I find myself unable to stop thinking about you."

Hannah placed her hands on his forearms. "Truly?"

"Truly." Jonathon chuckled. "I find myself intrigued by a beautiful young woman with black hair, who somehow has beguiled me."

A small smile grew at the corners of her mouth. "I did no such thing."

His thumbs slowly caressed her cheeks. "I believe it may have started after you removed all the dirt off your face."

Hannah allowed a soft laugh to escape. "I must have looked a fright."

"Or it could have been when you attempted to flee from my presence."

"That was of your own making," she said with a smile.

He grew serious. "Regardless, my assignment is to protect you, not seduce you, and as a gentleman, it is inappropriate for me to make any advances towards you."

Hannah bit her lower lip, her cheeks bright pink. "Yet, you have not seduced me."

"But you have seduced me," he said hoarsely, his thumb moving to caress her bottom lip. "Dare I hope that you hold some regard for me?"

Hannah's eyes held vulnerability and he knew it must be difficult for her to divulge her feelings. Slowly, she nodded. Her lips parted as her eyes darted towards his lips.

Jonathon needed no further invitation as he slowly lowered his head, ensuring Hannah had time to resist, if she so desired. He kissed one corner of her lips and then the other corner. Then his lips descended onto hers, gently pressing their lips together, enjoying the soft fullness of her mouth.

Being mindful that they were in her bedchamber, he broke the kiss and leaned his forehead against hers. "I apologize. I had no right to do that."

Hannah's eyes never left his lips. "I was not opposed to it."

Jonathon's hands wrapped around her waist. "I can make no promises to you."

"Nor would I ask you to."

He marveled at how perfectly she fit in his arms. "I am not at liberty to even attempt to pursue you until you are out of my protection and residing with your father."

Hannah nodded, her eyes filled with compassion. "I understand." She rose onto her tiptoes and kissed his cheek. "I trust you," she whispered sweetly in his ear.

Jonathon's breath wavered at Hannah's comments. For some reason, the unfounded trust that she placed in him made him feel like a hero, but he knew he was far from it. Would he still hold her affection when she learned more about him? For now, he would not dwell on that since all he wanted to do was learn everything he could about Hannah.

Reluctantly, he dropped his arms and took a step back. He offered her his arm. "Shall we go to dinner, my lady?"

She laid her arm on his and glanced up. "Do you think I should freshen up first?"

Jonathon's eyes slowly roamed all over her face, taking a ridiculously long time. He noticed that she blushed at his blatant perusal. "I do not think you have ever looked more beautiful."

Hannah rewarded him with a brilliant smile, and his knees suddenly felt weak. *Good gracious, she was stunning!* He made a vow with himself that he would do whatever it took to have Hannah gift him with another all-encompassing smile as quickly as possible.

10

HANNAH WOKE UP TO A STREAM OF LIGHT HITTING HER FACE AS the drapes were yanked open. She curled into a ball and slowly opened her eyes.

A thin, young woman, close to her age, stood next to the bed. She smiled shyly. "Good morning, Lady Hannah. My name is Maggie. I thank thee for the opportunity to assist thee in dressing."

Hannah found Maggie's attitude contagious and she smiled back, slowly sitting up on the bed. "Is this your first time acting as a lady's maid?"

"Oh yes, my lady." She executed a deep curtsy.

Hannah immediately felt at ease with her. "Well good, because I have never had a lady's maid before."

Maggie opened her mouth in astonishment. "But you are a lady."

Smiling, Hannah confessed, "True, but I never employed a lady's maid. At my father's estate, the upstairs maids rotated helping me dress and arrange my hair."

Maggie sat on the bed. "We can learn together then." Her

eyes grew wide and she jumped off the bed. "Sorry, I shouldn't have done that."

Hannah stood and walked over to her wash basin. She splashed water on her face and reached for a towel. Suddenly, she remembered she had no dresses to wear. "Maggie, do you know what happened to the dress that I wore when I arrived?"

Maggie giggled. "I do. It was burned."

Hannah's face fell. "Oh no, I have nothing to wear."

Maggie nodded her understanding. "Lady Lansdowne, the dowager marchioness, sent over another dress that I pressed this morning." She glanced at the sofa where the dress was neatly positioned.

"Thank you," Hannah said as relief washed over her. She had no desire to wear that threadbare dress, but she had not dared impose on her hostesses again. "Can you arrange hair, Maggie?" she asked as she sat down at the dressing table.

"Oh yes, ma'am. I arrange my sisters' hair all the time," Maggie said, striding over to stand behind her. As she reached for a brush, she added, "Although, I have never brushed such purty black hair before."

Hannah found that she really enjoyed chatting with Maggie and lingered in conversation while she pinned her hair up. It wasn't as fancy as the way Martha styled it, but it was still beyond what she could accomplish.

Maggie scooped up the rich blue, high-waisted dress and helped her into it. "Lady Lansdowne asked for you to join her in the dining room when you are ready," Maggie said, smiling as she stepped back.

Hannah glanced in the mirror and hoped that Jonathon would be joining them for breakfast. As she reached the doorway, she spun around. "You are a natural lady's maid, Maggie."

Maggie dropped into a low curtsy again. "Thank you, my lady."

Hannah quickly descended the stairs, but suddenly realized

she had no idea where the dining room was. Jonathon had given her the tour of the house after dinner, escorted by Eliza and Benedict, but she had paid more attention to his lips than the tour. She glanced into each room she came to and she found multiple dining rooms, but none of them were being used to serve breakfast.

Well, she would just have to wait until a servant came by and she could ask for directions. As she sat down on a chair in the hall, a rich, baritone laugh floated to her ears. She looked up and saw Jonathon, dressed in a white shirt, dark grey waistcoat, and cravat, approaching her. Her heart skipped a beat at the sight of him.

"Eliza thought you might be lost and sent me in search of you." Jonathon smirked.

Hannah genuinely smiled up at him. "I have counted three dining rooms so far, but I have failed to locate the dining room that is serving breakfast."

"That is because Eliza uses the dining room off the kitchen for breakfast," he said, looking amused by the information he shared. He offered his arm. "Come, I will escort you to the informal dining room where your breakfast awaits."

"Thank you. My plan was to wait until a servant could give me directions."

"Ingenious," he said, smiling down at her. "If I remember correctly, I did give you a tour of the estate last night and pointed out all the dining rooms."

"True, but I'm afraid I was distracted during the tour," she admitted as Jonathon stopped in front of an open door. She turned to face him, her eyes dropping to his lips. She watched him slowly swallow. After a moment, she adverted her eyes and walked into the dining room.

"Hannah, it is good to see you. I was afraid you might have lost your way, so I sent Jonathon to find you," Eliza said, picking up her teacup.

Hannah took a plate and dished herself some food from the buffet before she sat down next to Eliza. "I was lost, but Jonathon helped me find the informal dining room." She glanced back towards the door. "But I am afraid he has disappeared."

"Do not be absurd," Jonathan said, striding into the room. "I was just momentarily distracted."

Benedict entered behind him, dressed in similar attire, and bent to kiss his wife on the cheek. "Ah, my beautiful wife. What are your plans today?"

Eliza, dressed in a black crepe, high-waisted dress, glanced towards her. "If it is all right with you, I was hoping we could go to the village. We need to buy you a few things and see the dress-maker. Jane's dresses are beautiful, but they are not practical for a debutante. You will need dresses in white and pale colors."

Hannah took a sip of her tea. "I am afraid I do not have any funds available to me. Jane's borrowed dresses will be fine, if she does not mind."

Eliza smiled at her. "Do not be ridiculous. I have needed to order additional mourning gowns, and Benedict will not mind buying a few dresses for a new friend."

Benedict glanced up from his food and smiled indulgently at his wife. "You may buy anything you so desire." He then looked at Hannah. "Please accept our hospitality and let Eliza buy you whatever she deems fit."

"I cannot thank you enough for your kindness towards me, a stranger no less." Hannah's voice showed her genuine gratitude.

Benedict wiped his mouth with his napkin, and returned it back to his lap. He gave her his full attention as he said, "Lord Pembrooke is a great man, and I consider it a privilege to have you as our guest."

Hannah put down her fork, surprised by Benedict's words. "You know my father?"

"No, but his reputation precedes him as a man of great integrity." Benedict glanced towards Jonathon, before continuing, "He has served admirably as the Ambassador to Spain these past few years."

"Thank you," she cooed. "I appreciate your kind words."

"Eliza, are you really teaching Hannah to fence later today?" Jonathon asked.

Hannah turned her body towards Eliza. "Oh, I hope so."

Eliza placed her napkin on her plate. "That is the plan, but first we need to go to the village." She rose gracefully, causing the men to rise, as well. Turning to Hannah, she asked, "Are you ready?"

Hannah jumped up, eager for the day to continue. "I am."

AFTER BEING POKED AND PRODDED FOR WHAT SEEMED LIKE AN enormous amount of time, Hannah was finally free of the dressmaker's clutches. Eliza had taken it upon herself to order her three afternoon dresses, a velvet riding habit, a nightgown, undergarments, and she commissioned a ball gown for her. Hannah had to admit that she was excited for her new wardrobe to arrive. The dressmaker assured her that most of the items would arrive at Chatswich Manor by the next day, but the ball gown would take two weeks due to the amount of stitching required.

Hannah walked along the cobblestone street with Eliza, arm in arm, as they received well-wishes from almost everyone who greeted them. It became apparent that Eliza knew many of the villagers, and was loved in return.

She glanced back at Mr. Larson and the footmen guarding the carriage. Mr. Larson noticed her watching him and smiled. It seemed odd to her that Benedict insisted that his wife must be so well protected. Mr. Larson always stayed behind them, but his eyes seemed alert to any possible threat, which seemed silly because this quaint village couldn't possibly hold any danger for a marchioness.

The entrance to the village was lined with tiny cottages, and young children darted in between them, laughing with their friends. Hannah stopped to admire the cordwainer's shop and heard the clanking coming from the blacksmith's open-air work-shop. The rest of the village held an inn, the merchant shop, a pub, the dressmaker's shop, and a livery stable. A well-kept parsonage sat back on a hill overlooking the village.

An older woman approached and informed Eliza that her grandson had died in the war. Eliza's hand flew to her mouth and she quickly put her arm around the woman's shoulder, providing what comfort she could.

Hannah took a step back, not wanting to intrude. The merchant shop's display of brightly colored ribbons in the window caught her eye. "May I go into the shop?" she asked quietly.

Eliza waved her hand indicating she could go into the store. Hannah heard the bell chiming above her head as she walked in. A friendly older man looked up from assisting another customer, greeting her before putting his head back down.

Hannah looked at a display of ribbons and gently fingered the material. She heard the door's bell chime again, and assumed it was Eliza. As she started to turn around, the tip of a knife's blade stroked her throat. A man reached around her waist and pulled her against him. His offensive body stench gave away his identity before he even opened his mouth. "It is good to see you, Lady Hannah."

The man jerked Hannah away from the table and she noticed that his shorter partner was pointing a pistol at the shopkeeper and the young woman. "Where is your back entrance?" he growled.

The shopkeeper looked helplessly at her and pointed towards the rear. Her assailant kept the knife at her throat and forcefully pushed her towards the back door. After they exited, he grabbed her forearm tightly and yanked her to face him. His eyes narrowed, spewing hatred towards her. "If you scream, I will slit your throat." She nodded, hoping the man would loosen his grip on her arm. He lowered his face to hers and looked at her in disgust. "Do you know how much time I have wasted looking for you?"

The short man glanced nervously at her. "Slim, we got to go."

"The only thing I'm looking forward to is what I'm going to do to you before we turn you over," Slim said menacingly.

Hannah shrank in fear, but Slim held her with his crushing grip on her forearm. He started leading her away from the village, and with every step Hannah grew more terrified that he would kill her.

"Gentlemen, I must ask you to release my friend." Eliza's cheery voice drifted from behind her, but she had to be imagining things. Her friend would never attempt to approach men with weapons. *Oh no, Eliza did not know they were armed.*

Slim stopped and turned around, taking Hannah with him. He placed the knife to her throat, pulling her tight against him. "Lady, this be none of your business."

The shorter man kept his pistol trained on Eliza, but it was faltering. "What do you want, lady?"

Eliza smiled apologetically at them and said, "It appears that you are attempting to abduct my friend, and I cannot possibly allow that to happen."

Slim was pressing the knife into the flesh of her throat, and she could feel a trickle of blood running down her neck. "If you don't go away now, I will kill her, and you," he growled, his voice filled with hatred.

Drooping her shoulders, a pout formed on Eliza's lips. "I just became friends with her and I absolutely cannot part with her. I have loads of money. Could I possibly buy her back from you?"

The shorter man glanced at Slim and asked, "What do ye think?"

"Give us your money and we can talk trade," Slim demanded.

Hannah felt relieved as the knife slightly lifted off her flesh. Eliza flashed a smile and reached for the reticule hanging around her right wrist. She opened it and made a show of placing her hand inside. The short man leaned slightly closer to see what she pulled out.

Before Hannah even took another breath, Eliza held a small pistol pointed towards Slim in her left hand. Her cheery demeanor was gone and she looked confident... almost lethal. "I have changed my mind. You will release Lady Hannah immediately, or you will die." Hannah heard her cock the pistol.

Laughing, Slim did not relinquish his grip nor did he remove the knife. "Lady, go home before Don shoots you."

Don's hand started wavering and he brought his free hand up to help support the pistol. "Please lady, just go home. I don't want to have to kill you."

"Gentlemen, I believe we are at an impasse," Eliza said, her voice unwavering. "I will not leave here without Lady Hannah, but I guarantee you will."

"Just shoot her," Slim snarled.

Before Hannah could tell Eliza to run, Eliza threw a dagger into Don's hand, causing the pistol to tumble to the ground. Don dropped to his knees, clutching his hand, cursed, and howled in pain.

Eliza placed the pistol into her right hand and said, "Now it is your turn."

Slim lowered his head and used Hannah as a shield. His hand started shaking as he continued to press the knife against her throat. "I am going to back out of here, or I'm going to kill her."

The sound of another pistol cocking floated in the air. "I'm afraid we cannot let that happen." Mr. Larson's voice came from behind her.

Before Hannah could scream, Slim pierced the knife into her neck and she feared her death was imminent. Suddenly, the pressure around her throat lifted and the knife dropped to the ground. Slim's hands released her and she heard a loud thud. Hannah glanced behind her and saw he was on the ground, unconscious. She ran towards Eliza's open arms, noting that she wasn't holding her pistol anymore.

After a few moments, she felt composed enough to step away. "Thank you, Eliza." She turned around to see the footmen had tied up Don and Slim while Mr. Larson held a pistol pointed towards them. Feeling moisture, she gingerly touched her throat. Pulling it back, she saw her hand was stained with blood.

"Are you all right, Lady Hannah?" Mr. Larson asked, his eyes watching her carefully.

Hannah nodded, but her eyes strayed back to her blood-stained hand. Suddenly, the world started spinning and the darkness overtook her.

11

JONATHON SAT NEXT TO HANNAH'S BED AND WATCHED THE RISE and fall of her chest, assuring himself that she still lived. The doctor had come and gone, but he stayed long enough to stitch up her throat and administer laudanum for the pain. As he left the bottle of medicine by her bed, he reassured them the dark bruising on her forearm was superficial.

A white bandage was tied around her neck, but the sutures were still visible. Hannah had been seconds away from having her throat slit. No, he did not want to dwell on that. He couldn't dwell on that.

How could he have left Hannah in Eliza's care? She was his responsibility, yet he stayed behind to avoid going to the dressmaker. He dropped his head into his hands. *I almost lost her.*

A thin, young woman walked in humming and carrying a bundle of clothing in her arms. When she saw Jonathon at Hannah's bedside, she curtsied deeply, which under normal circumstances would have made him smile. "Pardon the interruption, Lord Jonathon. The dressmaker sent over a few of Lady Hannah's new clothes."

"What is your name?" he asked.

"Maggie, my lord. I am acting as Lady Hannah's maid while she's at Chatswich Manor."

Jonathon stood up and reached for Hannah's hand, not wanting to leave her. "I need to speak to Lady Lansdowne, but I do not want Lady Hannah to be left alone."

"I will sit next to her," Maggie said, draping the clothing over the back of the sofa.

Jonathon leaned forward, boldly kissing Hannah's forehead. "Thank you, Maggie. Please alert me if Lady Hannah awakes, or if there are any changes to her health."

Maggie stepped closer to the bed. "The doctor gave her laudanum and informed Lady Lansdowne that she should sleep until tomorrow."

"And you will stay close all night?"

Maggie's eyes softened as she watched Hannah sleep. "Ye can rest assured that she will want for nothing."

He reluctantly released her hand and stepped back. Murmuring his thanks, he walked swiftly out of the room. He needed to know what had gone wrong at the village today, for his sanity's sake.

He found Eliza, Benedict, and Mr. Larson in the red parlor and their faces seemed to mirror his mood. As he walked into the room, Eliza glanced up from her seat on the sofa. "How is Hannah?"

Approaching the drink cart, Jonathon reached for the brandy decanter, removed the stopper, poured himself a drink, and quickly threw it back into his throat. "She is resting. The doctor had to put four sutures where the man attempted to slit her throat," he growled. Pouring himself another drink, he drained it just as fast.

Benedict walked over and took the decanter out of his hand. "Becoming inebriated will not help the situation." He put his hand on Jonathon's shoulder, nudging him towards a chair. "Come sit down so we can talk about this."

Jonathon untied his cravat and plopped down on the proffered chair, across from Eliza and Benedict. Mr. Larson sat on an adjacent armchair with a drink resting in his hand.

"Maybe someone can explain to me how Hannah almost got her throat slashed on a trip to the village?" Jonathon snarled.

Eliza frowned. "She had gone into the merchant shop to look at ribbons while Mr. Larson and I remained outside."

"Let me get this straight." Jonathon jumped out of his seat and pointed a finger at Eliza. "You willingly left her alone, knowing that Lord Camden will stop at nothing to abduct her."

Sighing, Eliza continued despite his outburst. "The two men were waiting in an alley and followed her into the store. We immediately recognized the threat and acted accordingly. We saw that they were going out the back entrance and followed them. I provided a distraction as Mr. Larson blocked their retreat."

"The man started slashing her throat," Jonathon accused. "She almost died."

Mr. Larson interjected, "That was my fault. I assumed that the man would drop the knife since I had a cocked pistol to his head. Once I realized his intent, I rendered him unconscious."

Jonathon glared at Mr. Larson incredulously. "His intent? You mean, slashing Hannah's throat?"

"Lord Camden wants Lady Hannah alive, because she is useless to him dead. We," Eliza glanced at Mr. Larson, "did not think his thugs would try to kill her."

Jonathon paced. He felt angry, but realized he was more upset at himself for not being there for Hannah. Why did he not go to the village with her?

"You need to calm down and take a seat," Benedict ordered. "Eliza and Mr. Larson will explain everything. I am sure you will agree that they did an admirable job of protecting Hannah."

Jonathon stopped pacing and flopped down on an armless chair. He raked his hand through his already mussed-up hair. He wanted to know every minute detail of the attempted abduction.

Eliza recounted the events of the incident with Mr. Larson interjecting only to clarify a point. When she finished, Benedict placed his arm around her shoulder, pulling her against him. "I am proud of you, Eliza. You and Mr. Larson saved Hannah," he said, giving her a quick kiss on the head. "I'm sure Jonathon recognizes now that your quick thinking saved her life." His tone brooked no argument.

Jonathon tipped his head back to look at the ceiling. He knew Benedict was correct. Eliza and Mr. Larson had saved Hannah from an abduction and death. When did this assignment get so complicated? His job was to retrieve Hannah from her country home and protect her until he turned her over to his uncle.

In his defense, he was unprepared to protect a beautiful young woman, with black hair that shines in the moonlight, and who possessed the uncanny ability to match him wit-for-wit. After he kissed Hannah, he knew his feelings ran deep, but he could not act upon them until she was no longer under his protection.

First, he needed to apologize to Eliza and Mr. Larson. "I am sorry, Eliza," he said, meeting her gaze. She nodded her forgiveness, and he turned to Mr. Larson. "And I apologize to you, as well." He rose from his chair, walked to the window sill, turned, and leaned back on it. "I realize *now* that I overreacted."

"It is difficult to watch someone you care about suffer," Eliza conceded.

After a moment, Jonathon spoke again. "I believe it would be best if I take Lady Hannah to Father's estate until Uncle Charles provides me with further instruction."

Benedict pulled his arm away from Eliza and sat forward in his seat. "Lord Beckett sent over a missive while you were in Lady Hannah's room." His tone held censure.

Jonathon frowned. "Surely, you did not expect me…"

Benedict raised his hand to stop him. "This is my home and Lady Hannah is now my responsibility," he said sternly.

"Like hell, she is," Jonathon said, crossing his arms.

Benedict humphed before continuing, "Lord Pembrooke is residing at your townhouse in London and *Hawk* is with him. No one is aware of Lord Pembrooke's location, and your Uncle requests that you return to town immediately."

"How did Uncle know I was here?" Turning to address Mr. Larson, he asked, "Did your messengers ride through the night to deliver the missive?"

Mr. Larson shook his head. "No, the messengers should deliver your note to Lord Beckett today, informing him that Lady Hannah has been safely retrieved."

"Lord Beckett assumed you would check in with Eliza," Benedict explained. "He has requested your presence in London to help with your unexpected houseguests."

Jonathon grimaced as he took a moment to digest the information. "We will depart as soon as Hannah is recovered. We may have to take it slow but we could arrive by the end of the week, assuming we can borrow a carriage."

Benedict glanced at Eliza knowingly. "No. Hannah will remain here under our protection."

"Absolutely not," Jonathon shouted as he jumped up from the window sill. "Hannah is my responsibility and will remain under my protection."

Benedict arose, walked over to the drink cart, and poured himself a drink. "Putting aside all the other improper situations that arose from retrieving Hannah, you cannot travel with an unchaperoned lady, in an enclosed carriage, for three days and spend two nights at an inn. It is just not done." He sipped his drink. "You would ruin her reputation and yours."

"Then I will marry her," Jonathon concluded.

Benedict started choking on his drink. "You cannot marry her. You just met her!"

"You and Eliza fell in love quickly," Jonathon pointed out.

Benedict glanced helplessly at Eliza, before asking, "Are you saying you are in love with Hannah?"

He shook his head. "No... maybe..." His voice trailed off. "I will let Uncle Charles know that I will not be coming to London. I am not going to leave Hannah."

"Your assignment was to retrieve Lady Hannah and place her under protection. You will leave her here at Chatswich Manor and we will ensure her safety," Eliza stated.

"Like you did today?" Jonathon retorted.

"Careful, Jonathon. You are speaking to my wife," Benedict growled a warning.

Eliza's eyes narrowed. "I know that you have suffered a shock today, but so have I." She put her hands on her hips and her eyes were fiery. "You have a job to do, and if you ever want a chance to court Hannah properly, then you need to go to London and find the proof we need to have Lord Camden arrested."

"Uncle Charles does not need me in London. He has an office full of agents at his disposal," Jonathon said, attempting to rein in his temper.

Eliza sighed and pointed out, "Lord Camden is our brother-in-law, and we have unique access to him that the other agents lack."

Jonathon decided to point out the obvious. "Benedict is now related to Lord Camden by his marriage to you. Why did Uncle Charles not request his presence in London?"

Benedict put his drink down on the tray with a loud clank. "I'll go with you."

Eliza stood and moved to face Benedict. "Why would you go?"

Her husband placed his hand on her forearm. "Jonathon

makes an excellent point. Besides being related to Lord Camden, I am also the Marquess of Lansdowne now. Which means we have unparalleled access to him and we can bring him down that much faster."

Eliza took his hand. "We have only been married for two weeks. It is still technically our honeymoon."

"This is not our honeymoon." Benedict chuckled. "As soon as Lord Camden has a noose around his neck, we will take a real wedding tour." He looked at Jonathon, then leaned closer to whisper to his wife, "Without Jonathon."

"I can hear you Benedict," Jonathon said, a teasing lilt in his voice.

"Didn't we retire from the spy business?" Eliza asked, gazing into her husband's eyes.

Benedict smiled warmly as he gently cupped her cheek. "I am worried that Jonathon will fail to make a good impression on his future father-in-law. If I do not help him, then who will?"

Eliza bit her lower lip as if contemplating Benedict's words carefully. "I see your point."

Jonathon rolled his eyes. "I wish you two would stop talking about me as if I were not in the room."

Benedict stepped closer to Eliza. "I also have a more personal reason to see Lord Camden arrested for treason as soon as possible."

"And why is that?" Eliza asked.

"I would like to retrieve Kate. She appeared dejected at our wedding, and every time Lord Camden approached her, she cowered," Benedict stated.

"Do you think Lord Camden beats her?" Jonathon asked, his hands balling into fists. He hadn't seen much of his sister since her wedding to Lord Camden, but he hadn't considered that her husband might be abusing her.

"I did not see any bruises, or I would have called him out right there," Benedict explained, "but I want to get Kate far away from Lord Camden before the Crown starts officially investigating him. We have no idea how he is going to react under the pressure, and I do not want him to flee with Kate, or worse." By the look on Benedict's face, Jonathon knew he, too, was worried that Lord Camden might kill Kate rather than set her free.

"Thank you," Eliza said, pulling him into a hug. "I love you."

Mr. Larson stood and interjected, "I am glad we could come to a consensus. Jonathon and Benedict, you will depart tomorrow at first light, and Eliza and I will stay behind and guard Lady Hannah." He bowed to them. "I will see to the security protocols with the staff."

Jonathon turned to find Eliza and Benedict in an embrace. Benedict glanced at him, a smile forming on his lips. "You will be dining alone tonight. We will request a tray to be sent to our room." He scooped Eliza up into his arms, causing her to squeal in delight. "I want to give her ample time to thank me for my service."

Jonathon's mouth gaped open in surprise as he watched Benedict carry Eliza out of the room.

HANNAH FELT GROGGY AND COULDN'T SEEM TO OPEN HER EYES. She tried turning her head, hoping her eyes would open. With a mighty effort, she finally succeeded. Although the drapes were still closed, the light filtering in told her the sun was high in the sky. Her mouth felt as if she'd had cotton in it all night. She tried to lick her lips, but her tongue was dry, too.

"Let me help you," Maggie said, suddenly appearing next to her.

She placed the cup to her lips and enjoyed the cool water moistening her mouth. Then she swallowed. "Ow!" It was more whispered than voiced, however. Raising her hand to her neck, she felt a large bandage. With a jolt, the events of the previous day came flooding back. Tears welled in her eyes and she allowed them to flow freely.

"Oh dear," Maggie said before she fled the room.

Hannah could feel the sutures under the bandage. The words of the doctor came to her mind, 'You are a lucky one. If this had been any deeper, you would have died.' If it were not for Mr. Larson and Eliza... she shuddered and refused to finish the thought.

From the moment she discovered her steward's betrayal, all she had done was run and hide, hoping someone would protect her. And what had that gotten her? Nearly killed.

Luckily, Eliza had come to her rescue, standing her ground against two men. There was no hesitation in her eyes as she leveled her pistol at the two abductors, nor when she threw her dagger at Don. In fact, Eliza appeared to be completely at ease with her weapons. Maybe she should ask Eliza to teach her how to defend herself in case danger reared its ugly head again?

Hannah swallowed again, but thankfully, the pain was not as intense. First, she had to get out of this bed and find Eliza. As she tried to sit up, a wave of nausea rushed over her and she laid back again. *New plan*, she thought, *I'm going to feel better, then seek out Eliza.*

Jonathon practically ran into the room, with Maggie not far behind. He sat on the edge of the bed. "You are awake," he said.

"I am," Hannah croaked. Maggie adjusted the pillows so she could lean back against them. "How bad does my throat look?" Her fingers felt the bandage again, lingering over the sutures.

Jonathon reached for her hand, tenderly encompassing it with his. "You should avoid touching your neck. We do not want to risk infection."

"I need to thank Eliza and Mr. Larson," Hannah said, refusing to take her eyes off him.

Jonathon glanced towards the door, then returned his compassionate gaze to her. "You should know that there has been a change of plans."

He seemed to be hesitating. "A change of plans?" she prodded, curious.

His grip on her hand tightened. "I have been called to London by my uncle. He has a new assignment for me."

Hannah's eyes widened at his announcement. "You are leaving me?"

Jonathon shook his head. "Your father reached English soil and is hiding out at my townhouse. No one is aware of his location, and my uncle has entrusted me with continuing the investigation against Lord Camden in London."

She nibbled on her lower lip, trying to find the courage to ask her next question. "Since my father is hiding at your townhouse, may I go with you?"

Jonathon smiled weakly. "You will stay here. Eliza and Mr. Larson will see to your protection until I return."

Suddenly, it occurred to Hannah that this would give her a chance to train with Eliza. She could learn the basics of fencing, throwing daggers and firing pistols. With Jonathon gone, she would have plenty of time to practice. That thought was exciting.

Her excitement must have shown on her face because Jonathon raised an eyebrow. "Are you pleased to see me go?" The vulnerability reflected in his eyes betrayed his calm demeanor.

Hannah rushed to explain. "No, not at all. I will miss you dreadfully."

Jonathon smiled, and she continued, "I hoped that your sister would teach me how to fence, shoot a pistol, and throw a dagger. This will give me the opportunity to learn."

His eyes grew guarded. "Whatever for?"

"Ever since we met, I have had to turn to you or Eliza for protection. I want to learn to protect myself."

Jonathon shook his head, brushing her comment aside. "I will protect you. You do not need to concern yourself with using weapons."

"And why is that?" she asked, irritated.

He patted her hand, trying to reassure her. "Because you are a lady."

"Eliza is a lady."

"But you are not Eliza," he reasoned.

Hannah pursed her lips. "Well, of course not. I did not mean to imply that, but she can show me the basics. Surely no harm will come from that."

He patted her hand again, as if he were pacifying a child. "True, but would you not rather spend your time excelling at ladylike pursuits... such as, embroidery, singing, or playing the pianoforte?"

"I abhor needlework and I cannot sing."

"Chatswich Manor has a lovely pianoforte. I have no doubt that Eliza will be willing to let you practice on it while you recover from your injury." Jonathon smiled, ignoring her comment.

"Why don't you want me to learn how to defend myself?" she asked, attempting to raise her raspy voice.

He raked his hand through his groomed hair, thoroughly ruffling it. "It is not necessary." His voice raised a notch. "A lady does not shoot pistols."

Her eyes narrowed. He had almost fooled her into thinking he truly cared about her, but it seemed he only wanted a lady he could control. "A lady also does not milk cows or work as a farmhand," she argued.

His eyes darted toward Maggie who was sitting in the corner, polishing Hannah's ankle boots. "You had no choice," he said, lowering his voice.

"A lady does not share a room at the inn with a gentleman that is not her husband," she added, emphasizing her words.

Jonathon leaned closer. "You cannot speak that way in front of the servants. It might damage your reputation," he said in a hushed tone.

"I would like you to leave," Hannah directed. Jonathon reached for her hand, but she withdrew it.

He looked puzzled. "I apologize if my words offended you. That was not my intent."

"Then what *was* your intent?"

Jonathon blinked at the bluntness of her question, then, as he recovered, his eyes grew wary. "I was attempting to help you see how foolhardy it is for you to fence, throw daggers, or shoot pistols." He glanced at her neck then back at her face. "Besides, I would like to be the one who protects you from now on."

"And if you are not around? What then?"

"Then Eliza can protect you," Jonathon said simply.

"I want to protect myself, Lord Jonathon."

His eyes widened at the use of his title. "You do not understand what you are asking for," he said sharply.

"I know perfectly well what I am asking for. If Eliza will teach me, then I want to learn how to defend myself," she replied.

"Teach you what?" Eliza asked, gliding into the room.

Hannah turned her head to look at Eliza, hoping she wouldn't laugh at her request. "When my neck heals properly, would you be willing to teach me how to fence, and shoot a pistol, and throw a dagger like I saw you do yesterday?"

Eliza's face lit up. "I would love to."

"Eliza," Jonathon growled, turning in his seat to face her. "I do not think it is proper to teach Hannah how to do those things."

"Nonsense. I think learning how to defend oneself is a useful tool," Eliza said, coming to her defense. "Although, you should know that I have been throwing daggers since I was a child. It takes a lot of practice to hit your target."

Hannah nodded her understanding. "I have plenty of time to practice."

Jonathon grunted but they both ignored him. "Benedict sent me to tell you that he is ready to depart, and to stop wooing Hannah. Also, he wanted me to confirm that you two are being properly chaperoned." Eliza's expression showed her amusement.

"Hannah's lady's maid is acting as a chaperone," Jonathon said, tilting his head towards Maggie.

Approaching the bed, Eliza's tone was playful. "His exact words were, 'like bloody hell he will be in Hannah's room without a chaperone, since he refused to leave us alone when I was proposing.' He is still holding onto some resentment about that, so watch out." Eliza laughed as she placed a hand on her brother's shoulder.

Jonathon shrugged. "If you remember correctly, I did leave you two alone while I went down to fetch Father."

"Oh, I know, but you know Benedict," Eliza teased. She glanced between the two of them and her smile faltered. She looked back at Jonathon. "I will stall Benedict for five more minutes, so choose your next few words to Hannah *wisely*."

Jonathon watched her leave before turning back to Hannah. "We will continue this conversation when I get back."

"I would prefer not."

Jonathon started to interject, but she shook her head to stop him.

"You seem to be under the impression that I am weak-willed and you can mold me into something I am not."

Jonathon sat back, his expression giving away nothing. "I am doing no such thing."

"You are, by denying me the one thing that I wish," she said.

"Proper ladies…"

"Do not finish that sentence." She glared at him.

Searching her face, his brows furrowed. "I fear recent events may have muddled your thinking. Once you have recovered, I have no doubt that you will begin to see reason."

Hannah's mouth gaped open in shock and outrage. Did he just say that? How could a highly intelligent, handsome man be so profoundly ignorant?

He must have taken her silence as proof of the truthfulness of his words, because he playfully tapped the end of her nose with his finger.

As she prepared to unleash her fury, she was interrupted by Benedict's deep voice coming from the doorway. "Hannah's chambers are forbidden to you."

Jonathon's eyes did not leave Hannah's face and he remained seated on the bed. "I came to check on her."

Benedict was not amused as he leaned against the doorway, his arms crossed. He glanced at Maggie in the corner, before saying, "Next time, I will insist that Mr. Larson act as chaperone."

He walked forward into the room. "Eliza distracted me long enough to buy you a few more minutes, but we need to ride hard if we are to arrive at the first inn by nightfall."

Jonathon nodded. "I'm ready."

Standing, he said softly, "Take care of yourself, Hannah."

That's what I'm trying to do, she thought as she watched him go. She felt as if her heart left with him, which was foolish. When Jonathon came back after his mission, would he still care for her? Did she want him to care for her? Whether Jonathon approved or not, she was going to have Eliza teach her to protect herself.

What if he objected and demanded that she stop? She set her chin in defiance. He could try, but she would not stop. They were not betrothed and she was free to fill her time as she saw fit. If

Jonathon didn't like the person she wanted to become, then so be it.

The doctor said to stay in bed for the next few days, but as soon as it was expedient, she would start her training. She would learn to defend herself. Just the thought of that freedom elated her.

❧ 12 ❧

AFTER RIDING FOR TWO DAYS STRAIGHT, ONLY STOPPING TO SWAP out their horses and to catch a few hours of sleep at the inn, they arrived in front of Jonathon's townhouse on Grosvenor Street.

A footman appeared, waited for them to dismount, and accepted the reins. As Jonathon and Benedict ascended the stairs, the main door opened wide and Mr. Wilde stood aside to allow them to enter. "It is good to see you, Lord Jonathon and Lord Lansdowne." He bowed respectfully as they walked into the entry hall.

Jonathon removed his riding gloves and cape, handing them to Mr. Wilde. As Benedict followed suit, Jonathon asked gruffly, "I am under the impression that I have guests in my home."

"You do, my lord. Lord Pembrooke and Mr. Adrien Stanton are in your study," he confirmed.

Jonathon frowned. It couldn't be the same Adrien Stanton... could it? "When did they arrive?"

"They arrived three days ago with Lord Beckett, who instructed me not to disclose their location," Mr. Wilde said while he organized the clothing.

"Good, good," Jonathon mumbled. "Please continue to see to

their comfort, but use discretion, even around the household staff." He knew how servants conversed with each other and he didn't want his servants to unintentionally inform servants of other households that Lord Pembrooke was back in town.

Mr. Wilde nodded. "Business as usual then," he said, with a hint of a smile.

Chuckling, Jonathon repeated, "Yes, business as usual."

He glanced at Benedict. "Shall we?" He led the way to his study at the rear of his townhouse.

As they drew closer to the open door, voices drifted out to greet them. Benedict grabbed Jonathon's forearm, and in a hushed tone warned, "Remember, this may be your future father-in-law. You need to make a good first impression."

Jonathon arched an eyebrow. "Meaning?"

"Just don't..." he hesitated, then smirked, "just don't be *you*."

"I have no idea what you are referring to." Jonathon glared.

Benedict started chuckling, but turned it into a cough. "You are serious then?"

Jonathon frowned. "Enough. Let's get this over with." Entering the room, he acknowledged the two men sitting on his brown leather sofa, facing the fireplace. "Lord Pembrooke. Mr. Stanton."

As the two men stood, turning to face him, Jonathon focused on Lord Pembrooke. He was a tall man with wide shoulders, appearing to be in his late forties. His brown hair was neatly groomed. His dark-blue eyes, so like his daughter's, seemed to assess everything about him.

Jonathon bowed courteously. "Allow me to introduce myself. I am Lord Jonathon Beckett."

"It is a pleasure to finally meet our host." Lord Pembrooke's voice showed his disapproval.

Jonathon ignored Lord Pembrooke's comment and observed the man standing next to him with a measure of surprise. It *was* him...the same Adrien Stanton. He and Mr. Stanton had met before, in a clandestine meeting in an alley four years ago in Florence. At the time, he'd had long, brown hair, a scruffy beard, and tattered clothes, remnants from his last undercover assignment. Now, Mr. Stanton stood before him looking every bit the gentleman that he was. His hair was cut short with long sideburns, his clothing was the finest quality, and his tall, muscular frame gave him an air of danger.

"Lord Jonathon," Mr. Stanton said, bowing.

Jonathon stepped forward, still surprised at his drastic change of appearance. "Mr. Stanton, I barely recognized you. You look very different from the last time we met."

Mr. Stanton smiled knowingly. "I believe the last time I saw you, I was also extremely vocal about my new assignment."

Jonathon laughed and slapped him on the shoulder. "Yes, I believe you were." He turned to Benedict, including him in the conversation. "Mr. Stanton was not pleased at the thought of impersonating a French Naval officer."

He turned back to his guest. "Did you infiltrate the war ship?"

Mr. Stanton shook his head. "My undercover assignment took me on a different course. After two years serving on various frigates, I had the opportunity to serve as the under-secretary to Admiral Pierre Dominique Garnier."

Benedict whistled. "Admiral Garnier is rumored to be the most decorated Admiral in Napoleon's Navy."

Mr. Stanton nodded. "He is. He is also extremely irritating."

Jonathon huffed. "Aren't all the French?" After a moment, he motioned towards Benedict. "Lord Pembrooke and Mr. Stanton, may I introduce you to Lord Lansdowne."

Lord Pembrooke kept glancing at the door as if he were looking for someone. "Is my daughter with you, Lord Jonathon?"

Jonathon shook his head. "No. I had planned to take her to

my Uncle's estate, but we found it necessary to divert to Lord Lansdowne's estate."

"I was led to believe that you were protecting my daughter, but you left her unattended at an estate that is at least two days ride from here?" Lord Pembrooke's voice took on an edge.

Jonathon clenched his jaw tightly. "I resent the accusation. I did not leave her unprotected."

"I suggested we leave Lady Hannah with my wife, Lady Lansdowne and Mr. Larson, a former agent," Benedict said as he moved closer.

Lord Pembrooke's eyebrows flew up, now directing his ire at Benedict. "You left my daughter's protection to your young wife and an old, retired agent?"

Jonathon forced his voice to remain calm as he tried reasoning with Lord Pembrooke. "You must trust us that my sister, Eliza, is extremely capable of guarding your daughter."

"Wait, your sister, as in the beautiful young enchantress that wields daggers in alleyways?" Mr. Stanton interrupted.

Narrowing his eyes, Benedict growled, "That enchantress is now my wife."

Mr. Stanton put up his hands in defeat. "You are a lucky man. That is all I'm adding."

Lord Pembrooke stormed towards the door. "If you do not go get my daughter right now, then I will."

"No one is going anywhere." Jonathon's voice was firm. "I can assure you that your daughter is safe. My sister is trained in multiple weapons and will guard Hannah with her life." It was on the tip of his tongue to tell Lord Pembrooke that Eliza had killed more men than Jonathon and Benedict combined.

Lord Pembrooke grabbed the door handle, glaring back at him. "If it was your daughter, would you leave her in Lady Lansdowne's hands?"

Without hesitation, Jonathon confirmed, "I would."

Before Lord Pembrooke could reply, the door opened and

Lord Charles Beckett appeared with files in his hand. "Arthur, do sit down. I can assure you that my niece, Eliza, is more than capable of protecting Lady Hannah."

Lord Pembrooke's gaze shifted between Jonathon and Lord Beckett, his eyes sparking with fury. "She is a woman! A marchioness, no less! What does she know about defense? This is my daughter's life. I have already lost my wife, my brother and his wife, and my niece. I cannot lose my daughter." His voice cracked with a mixture of rage and grief.

Lord Beckett placed his hand on Lord Pembrooke's shoulder. "I understand, which is why I tasked my finest agent, *Shadow*, to go and protect your daughter."

Smiling gratefully at him, Lord Pembrooke looked relieved. "Thank you. Now I know that she will be safe." He sat down on a red armchair adjacent to the sofa.

Jonathon sat on the sofa, focusing on Lord Pembrooke. "I was told that you have documents that prove Lord Camden is responsible for the failed assassination attempt on Prinny."

Lord Pembrooke glanced up, his eyes now clear and focused. "*Hawk...* I mean, Mr. Stanton, brought me the papers from Admiral Garnier's desk, blowing his cover and risking his own life."

Mr. Stanton sat down next to Jonathon. "The documents are coded, but I was able to decipher one of the pages. It was in a common code used among the French officers. However, the other page is in a code that I have not seen before."

"What do you believe is on that document, Mr. Stanton?" Benedict asked, standing near the fireplace.

Mr. Stanton leaned back on the sofa. "I cannot fathom. If the paper hadn't been filed with the coded missive from Lord Camden, I would have dismissed it."

"How did you know the letter was from Lord Camden?" Jonathon asked, curiously.

"The envelope containing the missive was sealed with Lord Camden's signet ring," Mr. Stanton explained.

"How did you ever recognize the seal?" Benedict asked in amazement.

Frowning, Mr. Stanton interlaced his fingers. "Lord Camden is my cousin."

He stood and walked towards the window directly behind the desk. "Which is why I recognized the seal. We used to play with the wax and seal when we were younger."

Jonathon clapped his hands onto his thighs, his eyes taking everyone in. "It seems Lord Pembrooke is the only one here not related to Lord Camden. I say we just kill the treasonous bastard and be done with it."

"Jonathon…" his uncle warned. "Lord Camden is still an earl."

"I believe there is something more going on than an assassination attempt on Prinny," Mr. Stanton said.

Lord Beckett nodded. "I agree. Lord Camden must be reporting to someone on English soil, and we need to find out whom."

He turned to Jonathon. "Since *Shadow* is busy guarding Lady Hannah, I am tasking you with finding another agent that can decode those French documents."

Jonathon glanced towards Benedict. Without saying it aloud, Uncle Charles had asked him to summon Eliza to review the French documents. "As you wish," he confirmed.

Lord Beckett stood and the others followed his lead. "I have other issues that I must address, but I am leaving Lord Jonathon and Lord Lansdowne in charge of this mission. Once the agent has deciphered the enemy code, inform me at once."

He then turned to directly address Lord Pembrooke and Mr. Stanton. "Gentlemen, you are safe at Lord Jonathon's townhouse. I have agents guarding it around the clock. Do not do anything foolish that could possibly jeopardize the entire mission." He then excused himself from the room.

Lord Pembrooke and Mr. Stanton sat back down, resigned to their confinement.

Jonathon leveled his gaze at Benedict and tipped his head towards the door. They excused themselves and walked out into the hall, closing the door behind them. Being conscious that they were not alone, Jonathon lowered his voice. "I will send a note asking *the agent* to come to town. I was thinking they could stay at Beaumont Castle."

Benedict nodded his approval. "My thoughts exactly."

"If we take the documents to *the agent* then they have no reason to be in London…"

"Which means, they will be safe from Lord Camden's prying hands," Benedict finished his thought.

Jonathon nodded. "I will send a messenger immediately."

13

F ROM THE DRAWING ROOM WINDOW, ELIZA WATCHED HANNAH, who was dressed in a pair of boy trousers and white shirt, practicing throwing a dagger. She had spent the last three days teaching Hannah the art of fencing and dagger tossing. She was pleasantly surprised that Hannah was already proficient with the longbow.

Hannah had been a delight. She really wanted to learn how to defend herself, and her positive attitude was quite contagious. Besides being clever, it was obvious what Jonathon saw in Hannah; her inner strength, intellect, and her incomparable beauty.

"Is she still practicing?" Mr. Larson asked, walking into the room and glancing over Eliza's shoulder.

Not taking her eyes off Hannah, Eliza answered, "She is getting better. It only took her fifty attempts to hit the mark."

"That is an improvement. Yesterday, it was almost sixty-five attempts." Mr. Larson chuckled. "I saw you gave her a dagger from your collection."

"I did. It can be placed in the pockets that Maggie sewed in her dresses," Eliza informed him.

"Did you teach her how to sharpen it?"

Before Eliza stepped away from the window, she confirmed that the eight footmen she'd assigned were still standing guard around Hannah. "I spent the entire breakfast going over the proper care of a dagger, much to Mr. Harvey's dismay," Eliza joked.

"A note was delivered from Lord Lansdowne," Mr. Larson said after a moment, handing her the paper.

Eliza read quickly. "It appears that my presence has been requested by Uncle Charles. One of the documents that Lord Pembrooke smuggled out of Spain is coded and he wants me to attempt to decipher it."

"What about Lady Hannah?" Mr. Larson asked.

"Jonathon wants us to bring Hannah and stay at Beaumont Castle," Eliza reiterated, suddenly becoming concerned. "Oh no, does Beaumont Castle still maintain guards and household staff?"

Nodding, Mr. Larson confirmed, "Lord Lansdowne asked me to keep it fully staffed for circumstances such as these."

A loud cheering noise came from outside. Eliza and Mr. Larson ran to the window to witness Hannah laughing as she ran to the tree, where her dagger stuck out of the center of the knot-hole she'd been using as a target.

"She is a determined young woman, is she not?" Mr. Larson observed, amused.

"She is a delight. I hope Jonathon does not ruin it," Eliza said, shaking her head. "He can be so serious."

"I prefer the term 'dedicated'," Mr. Larson quipped.

Eliza frowned. "Hannah is a clever girl and I have no doubt she will learn that I work for the Crown."

"You technically do not work for the Crown, and if you did, then your status would be retired," Mr. Larson pointed out.

"I just fear Hannah will think of espionage as exciting."

Mr. Larson smirked. "Like you did when you started?"

"Exactly, and we know how that ended," she said, smoothing her mourning dress.

Mr. Larson chuckled. "You brought down an entire slavery ring, killing Mr. Wade and saving hundreds of girls, and that was just your last mission."

Eliza shook her head as she glided to the door. "You can make anything sound exciting, but I am off to ask Martha to pack for our departure. At least I will not have to wear mourning gowns when we are at Beaumont Castle."

"And I will inform Mr. Harvey of our upcoming trip, then go collect our delightful dagger thrower," Mr. Larson said.

FOUR DAYS LATER, JONATHON AND BENEDICT, SIMILARLY dressed in white shirts, buckskin breeches, and knee-high riding boots, raced their horses toward Beaumont Castle. A groomsman came out to relieve them of their horses and they quickly strode towards the main door. A loud screeching noise stopped them.

"Well, it is a relief that the portcullis was down," Jonathon joked, raising his voice so he could be heard above the clatter.

Once the noise stopped, the door swung open and Mr. Larson greeted them. "Come in, my lords." He ushered them in.

They stepped into the two-level stone- and wood-paneled entry, and waited until the portcullis was lowered before Jonathon asked, "Where is Lady Hannah?"

Mr. Larson smiled, almost as if he were anticipating the question. "Follow me, Lord Jonathon," he said, proceeding towards the interior courtyard. "The ladies are both in a fencing lesson."

Jonathon's feet faltered. "Fencing lessons?"

Benedict slapped him on the back. "Come along. I want to see my wife."

The classic sounds of sword fighting increased until they stepped outside into the interior courtyard. Eliza was dressed in her standard fencing attire of trousers, white shirt, and black boots, with padding encompassing her body. Her hair was tied tightly into a bun, and she was wearing a wire mesh mask. Her sparring partner helped to demonstrate her incredible skill and precision.

Jonathon's eyes gravitated towards another set of fencers. He recognized Hannah's black tresses pulled into a bun at the base of her neck, but wisps of hair escaped, cascading down her back. Her white shirt was damp and clung to her back while her tan trousers shaped her lower half remarkably well.

Hannah defended herself well against her fencing partner, but her swipes weren't fluid. She lacked the confidence of a seasoned fencer, but her skill went beyond beginner. Without thinking, he approached Hannah and her partner. "May I?" he asked, pointing at the long, thin sword. The man handed it over and bowed out.

Jonathon slid into standing position and gave Hannah a salute with the sword, then loudly announced, *"En garde."* He slowly advanced towards her. At first, she tentatively blocked his thrusts and remained in a defensive stance, but as her confidence rose, she switched to an offensive tactic.

Jonathon found himself enjoying the fencing battle. Hannah was mindful that he was lacking the protective padding, and avoided bringing the sword too close to his body. Even though she lacked strength, her sword placement had a strategic advantage that compensated.

"Halt!"

Jonathon and Hannah stopped and swiped down their swords. He turned to see who had halted the match. Eliza and Benedict stood arm in arm watching them, smiling widely.

Mr. Larson stood next to them and his lips were twitching. "If you two are finished, the cook has prepared a fine breakfast, and it is waiting to be served in the dining room." His smile widened as he excused himself.

"How long were we sparring?" Jonathon asked Eliza.

"About thirty minutes. My lesson ended some time ago, so we stayed and watched your sparring match with Lady Hannah."

Turning to face Hannah, Jonathon watched as she removed her mask, revealing bright red cheeks and matted black hair across her face. *She even looks beautiful after a fencing lesson.*

"You show remarkable skill for a beginner," Jonathon commented.

"Thank you," Hannah said, wiping her hair back from her face. "Eliza has been very patient with me. Today was the first day I was given a lesson from another instructor." She beamed at him.

A footman came to relieve her of her fencing equipment and she thanked him as she handed him the padding from her chest and arms. As Hannah turned to face Jonathon, the white bandage on her neck caught his eye.

Of all the stupid things Eliza could have done, she allowed Hannah to fence while still injured. "Eliza!" His shout echoed throughout the interior courtyard. Hannah's eyes widened at his loud voice and she took a step back. He inwardly cursed himself for scaring her.

"Whatever is the matter, Jonathon?" Eliza asked, reappearing from inside the castle.

Jonathon turned to face his sister. "You let Hannah fence while she was still injured?"

Eliza's eyes flashed with irritation. "I did no such thing. The doctor removed the sutures and changed her dressing before we left Chatswich Manor."

"She is still injured and should not be exerting herself," Jonathon said slowly.

Eliza's eyes flickered to Hannah before saying, "Hannah is stronger than she looks, Jonathon. I would have…"

"No, Hannah needs rest for her body to heal," he said, cutting Eliza off.

"Enough!" Hannah shouted next to him. "You do not have the right to decide what I can and cannot do!"

She stepped in front of him. "If I want to spend hours fencing, then I will. If I want to throw daggers, I will. And if I want to tell a lunatic to stop ordering me around, I WILL!" She spun around and stormed into the castle.

Once Hannah was out of sight, Jonathon stepped closer to Eliza. "What have you done to Hannah?"

Eliza laughed loudly. "I have done nothing to Hannah but listen to her and help her." Her eyes captured his attention. "A woman does not like to be told what to do."

"Hannah is still injured and someone needs to protect her," Jonathon stated what he thought should be obvious.

Eliza shook her head, dejectedly. "If you continue in this attitude, you will lose her, and that would be a pity, because I think I like her more than I like you." She turned and sauntered back inside.

Jonathon's hand balled into a fist as he started pacing. He had a duty to protect Hannah and he was failing. Why didn't she want his protection? When she had called him her hero, her eyes held unfailing trust in him and immense gratitude. Why couldn't she look at him like that again?

He wanted her to look at him like that again. What was he doing wrong?

14

FROM THE SAFETY OF HER ROOM, HANNAH WATCHED JONATHON pace back and forth in the courtyard. He appeared to be muttering to himself. Why did he have to be so infuriating? He seemed to enjoy the sparring match, but his mood soured when he saw the bandage around her neck.

Maggie bustled into the room with the wash basin. "I got you some more water, and I have pressed the white cotton dress."

Hannah walked away from the window and removed her soiled clothing before she turned to the wash basin to splash cool water over her face. She dressed and sat down at the dressing table.

While Maggie was arranging her hair, she said, "Thank you for coming with me. I know the carriage ride was hard for you."

Maggie's face blanched. "I don't like riding in a carriage. I can't believe a person can ever get used to all that rocking."

Hannah glanced up at Maggie, who was quickly becoming a friend. "I believe no one enjoys riding in a carriage, but learns to accept it for the mode of transportation that it is."

Eliza glided into the room. "Oh good, you are almost ready. I wanted to escort you down to breakfast."

When Maggie finished with the last pin in her chignon, Hannah stood. "I am famished."

Eliza started to say something, but changed her mind. As they strolled down the hall, Eliza stopped her at the top of the stairs and whispered, "My brother is being a tyrant, but he means well. Please be patient with him."

Hannah tried to stifle a laugh, but failed. "Do not fret, I can handle his Lord Grumpiness."

Eliza started to laugh and covered her mouth with her hand. "Lord Grumpiness. I like it."

"Ladies, are you going to join us to break our fast, or continue to giggle like debutantes at a ball?" Benedict called from the bottom of the stairs.

Hannah laughed once more before she gained her composure. "Shall we?"

Eliza's smile widened. "Yes, let us go break our fast with the gentlemen."

At the bottom of the stairs, Benedict waited for them, his eyes twinkling in amusement. "My dear, I do not think I have seen you laugh that hard at anything I have ever said. I'm afraid my ego is bruised."

Eliza released her hold on Hannah's arm and chasséd over to whisper something in Benedict's ear. His eyes grew round, and Hannah swore she saw Benedict blush before he escorted his wife into the dining room.

Hannah stood back, feeling like an interloper. Jonathon's breath drew near her ear. "I warned you about their displays of affection."

She kept her face straight, enjoying Jonathon's masculine scent. "I still think it is sweet."

Jonathon looked contrite. "About my behavior out there, I apologize."

Tilting her head, Hannah asked, "What exactly are you sorry for?"

"I need a reason to apologize?" he asked, taken aback by her question.

"Typically, you apologize for something specific, so yes," she answered.

Jonathon deliberated for a moment. "I apologize for raising my voice around you."

"Wrong," Hannah said, brushing past him towards the dining room.

Jonathon reached for her arm, stalling her. "You cannot expect me to apologize for trying to prevent you from reinjuring yourself. That is preposterous."

Sighing, she slowly turned to face him. "I am not a child. I am a grown woman who has a will of her own."

Jonathon looked disapproving. "If you overexert yourself, you might cause your wound to open, and an infection could set in."

Hannah pursed her lips in frustration, but she needed to say a few things to him. "Jonathon, I want you to know how grateful I am that you rescued me and brought me to safety," she hesitated, "but I no longer require your protection."

Jonathon reared back as if she had struck him. "You do not want my protection?" he asked, confused.

Hannah took a step closer to him, looking into his eyes. "Being under your protection means I have to bend to your will and do what *you* find acceptable," she said, attempting to make him understand her frustration.

Cautiously, Jonathon placed his hands on her shoulders, and with a gentle voice asked, "And what if I don't want to stop protecting you?"

"Then you need to stop ordering me around." Hannah's voice was firm.

"But what if it is in your best interest?" he pressed.

"I will be the one who decides that." She tried to focus on her words and not his inviting lips.

For a few moments, Jonathon's eyes roamed her face, then he nodded. "I will stop ordering you around, if you agree to take better care of yourself."

So close, she thought. She shook her head and walked towards the dining room, telling herself she did not care in the least if Jonathon followed her.

JONATHON SAT BACK, WATCHING HANNAH EAT HER BREAKFAST. She looked stunning in her white dress, which enhanced her wide, dark blue eyes. Strands of black hair were already breaking from her coifed hair. He desperately wanted to run his fingers through its silkiness.

He could not believe that she had the audacity to ask him to stop protecting her. He would rather die! Was Hannah not aware of how much she meant to him? Maybe he should step back and let her continue thinking she could protect herself. Once she realized it was an impossible feat, she would come running back to him. He would welcome her back with open arms. Perhaps she would let him kiss her once more.

"Jonathon," Eliza sternly said, interrupting his thoughts. "Do refrain from brooding at Hannah."

He met Eliza's gaze and frowned. "I am not brooding."

"Glaring, then," she said, issuing him an unspoken warning. "You are making my guest feel uncomfortable." Eliza reached over, briefly placing her hand over Hannah's in a show of support.

Hannah withdrew her hand and reached for her teacup. "His glaring is of no consequence to me." As she took a sip, her teacup partially hid a hint of a smile.

Why was she smiling? Could she not tell how upset he was? Jonathon opened his mouth to say something, but caught himself when he noticed Benedict deliberately shaking his head, warning him to keep his mouth shut.

Eliza wiped her mouth with her white linen napkin before asking, "Are those the documents you asked me to review?"

Jonathon picked up the two sheets of paper next to him on the table. "They are," he confirmed, extending them towards Eliza.

She accepted the papers and started perusing the first document. After a few moments, she looked up with a furrowed brow. "This first page uses a code commonly used among French Naval officers a few years back. That code hasn't been used for a couple of years, probably because it was too easy to decipher. That dates this document to be at least two years old."

"Mr. Stanton was able to confirm that missive was about the assassination attempt against Prinny," Jonathon said.

Eliza lowered the documents, glancing up in confusion. "Who is Mr. Stanton?"

"Mr. Stanton's code name is *Hawk*. He has been undercover as Admiral Garnier's under-secretary and smuggled these documents to Lord Pembrooke in Spain," Jonathon informed her.

"I see," Eliza said as she picked up the pages again.

"What about the second page? Do you recognize the code used in that missive?" Benedict asked.

Eliza studied the document carefully. She looked up and sighed, obviously frustrated. She dropped the pages onto the table. "I do not recognize this code. It appears to be Latin-based, but it could be an ancient dialect. I just don't know at this point."

"Were you able to meet with my father? Is he well?" Hannah interrupted, her eyes hungering for information.

Jonathon nodded. "I did. Lord Pembrooke and Mr. Stanton are staying at my London townhouse. Your father is well and inquired about your safety."

Hannah nibbled on her bottom lip. "Would it be possible to go to my father?"

Jonathon sat back in his seat, his forearm resting on the table. "It is not safe for you to travel into London."

"Can he come to Beaumont Castle?" Hannah asked, turning her hopeful gaze to Eliza.

Eliza placed her napkin on the table, giving her an apologetic look. "Unfortunately, that is not an option. Beaumont Castle is a heavily guarded secret, and only a few people are even aware of its existence."

"But my father and Mr. Stanton both risked their lives to bring the coded messages to Lord Beckett. Surely, they can be trusted with the location," she suggested, confusion evident in her voice.

"It is not just about the location," Eliza said slowly, seeming to choose her next words carefully. "Because of my skills with codes, I consult for the Crown on occasion, and it is of utmost importance that my contribution goes unnoticed."

"I see," Hannah said softly. "May I be permitted to write a note to my father, assuring him of my safety?"

Nodding, Jonathon confirmed, "That's a good plan."

Eliza rose from the table with the documents in her hand. "If you will excuse me, I will be in the library trying to decipher this code." She quickly walked out of the room, her dress swaying as she walked.

Pushing back his chair, Jonathon said, "I'm going to report to Uncle Charles and see if his agents uncovered anything else pertaining to Lord Camden."

He looked at Benedict. "Are you coming back to London with me?"

"No. I am staying here with my wife," Benedict said as he followed her out of the room.

As Hannah rose from her chair, she asked, "Would you mind waiting while I write the note to my father?"

"It would be my pleasure."

"Thank you."

He stood until she exited the room, then sat down again. He wanted to fix his relationship with Hannah, but how? Maybe he should abduct her and take her on another journey? No, kidnapping her was not the answer. Somehow, he had to convince her that he truly cared about her, while pretending he wasn't protecting her.

❦ 15 ❦

TWO DAYS LATER, JONATHON WAS WALKING TOWARDS ELIZA'S drawing room when he heard Hannah's laughter drifting through the corridor. He quickened his stride until he walked through the door, but then came to an abrupt stop.

Hannah and Benedict were sitting opposite of each other at a small table engaged in a game of chess. By his observation, they were well-matched and neither noticed his arrival.

Benedict placed his finger on his queen and Hannah started tsking. "That is a risky move."

A wide smile graced Benedict's face as he moved his queen. "Not risky at all, since I'm two moves from checkmate."

Jonathon noticed the twinkle in Hannah's eyes. "I fear the only way to recover from that move is to…" She smiled as she moved her own queen. "Checkmate."

Benedict's jaw dropped in astonishment. "Checkmate?" he asked in disbelief as his eyes scanned the chess board.

"I believe I have won four times now," Hannah teased.

Benedict chuckled. "Now you sound like Eliza." He leaned back in his chair and crossed his arms. "I would like to remind you that I have won a total of three times."

Deciding he needed to make his presence known, Jonathon cleared his throat.

Glancing his way, Hannah's eyes lit up and a bright smile graced her lips. "Jonathon, I didn't hear you come in."

Hannah's smile always rendered him speechless. Her hair was piled high on her head, with soft curls running down the side of her face, and her red, full lips drew his complete attention. It had been too long since he had last seen her. He reminded himself that he still hadn't said anything. "I did not want to announce myself and interrupt your chess match."

She smiled as she placed her hand next to her mouth, shielding it from Benedict's view. "It was not really a chess match. It was more of a massacre," she said with a teasing lilt in her voice.

"Two moves. I was two moves away from checkmate," Benedict argued, pretending to pout as he arose and adjusted his waistcoat.

Jonathon offered Hannah his hand. She arose, her eyes twinkling. "Eliza warned me that he was not a very nice loser."

Benedict dramatically placed a hand over his heart, feigning disappointment. "You have damaged my pride enough for one day, Hannah. I am going to check on my wife." He gave them a mock salute.

Jonathon forced his attention away from Hannah to focus on Benedict. "Before you go, has Eliza come any closer to deciphering the code?"

"No. She has been in the library for the last two days." He rubbed his neck with his hand. "We ended up falling asleep on the sofa in the library last night."

"Uncle Charles sent me to check on her progress," Jonathon told him.

Benedict looked knowingly at Hannah. "What a burden that must be for you," he said wryly. "If you will excuse me, I will be in the library."

As he walked into the hall, he shouted over his shoulder, "I am sending in Mr. Larson to chaperone."

Jonathon turned back to Hannah, his hand outstretched. "Come with me. I want to show you something."

Hannah looked puzzled. "What?"

Jonathon wiggled the fingers on his outstretched hand. "Trust me."

Hannah reached for his hand, and gasped a little when he pulled her close. "Let's go before Mr. Larson finds us."

Hannah's eyes held a question, but she nodded.

His hand tightly encompassed hers while they slipped out the back entrance of Beaumont Castle. A passing guard tipped his head towards them as they began to run towards a cluster of birch trees. "We are almost there," he said, glancing over his shoulder.

Hannah held tightly to his hand as they ran. As the sounds of rushing water greeted them, Jonathon slowed to a walk. Hannah's eyes lingered on the trees they passed. A babbling brook ran through the north side of Eliza's property, and she had insisted on having a bench moved to this location. He had since learned that this was a place of solitude for her.

Jonathon led Hannah to the bench and sat down beside her. "It is beautiful," Hannah exclaimed, her eyes bright and full of excitement.

Jonathon kept his eyes focused on her. "It is." He watched Hannah as her eyes found a small brown bird perched low in the trees, watching it as the bird took flight.

"Thank you for showing me this place," she said, finally looking at him.

Jonathon tore his eyes away from her to look at their surroundings. "This is Eliza's favorite place to come and meditate."

"I can see why. It is so peaceful here."

Turning his body to face her, Jonathon wanted to ask if she

had missed him, but opted for a safer question. "How are you faring?"

Hannah's face broke into a huge smile, radiating happiness. "I have had the most wonderful time at Beaumont Castle. In the mornings, I practice with my dagger until we break our fast, then I rotate through archery and fencing lessons."

Jonathon groaned inwardly at the thought of Hannah spending so much time learning weapons of war. Although archery was a popular pastime amongst the ton. "I see," he said, attempting to keep the criticism out of his voice.

He must have failed, because Hannah's face fell flat. "Why are you so against me learning how to defend myself?"

"Defend yourself from whom?"

Hannah angrily jumped to her feet, staring down at him with narrowed eyes. "From anyone that intends to do me harm."

Frowning, he knew she was mistaken if she thought she could thwart a man's attack. "You could no more stop a man intent on hurting you than you could outrun a bull."

Hannah placed a hand on her hip. "Not right now, but eventually I hope to."

Jonathon deliberately rose to stand in front of her. Hannah's chin tilted and her head lifted so she could glare into his eyes. "You think this is a game?" he asked harshly.

Her chest heaved with fury. "No, but this is my life now."

Jonathon grabbed her wrist, wrenching it behind her back before she cried out in protest. Hannah attempted to squirm out of his hold, but he held her back tightly against him. He leaned down and whispered, "You have no idea what you are up against." He held on for a moment longer, then dropped her hand, stepping back.

Hannah kept her back towards him, not uttering a word. She rubbed the wrist that he had twisted behind her back. After what seemed like hours, but was probably only a few minutes, she turned to face him. He saw raw pain etched on her face. Her voice choked when she said, "Thank you for pointing out my deficiencies."

His heart lurched at the sadness behind her words. What had he done? At the time, he felt a demonstration was prudent, but now he felt like a cad. Why did he feel the need to prove to her that she could not defend herself? He took a step towards her, but she stepped back, shattering his heart in the process.

"Hannah... I am so sorry," he attempted.

She smiled weakly. "If you will excuse me, I would like to lie down." She curtsied politely, then spun around and ran towards the castle.

"Hannah, wait," he pleaded, but she did not stop. He raced to intercept her before she left the cluster of trees, stopping in front of her. "Please, do not go. I would like a chance to apologize."

"You made your point and you were right." Resignation filled her voice.

Jonathon winced knowing that he had, until a few moments ago, longed to hear those words. Now, they sounded cheap and petty to his ears. He gently placed his hands on her shoulders. "I do not want to lose you over this," he said.

Hannah shook her head, her chin stubbornly lifted, her bottom lip trembling. "You cannot lose something that you never possessed."

Her words made him feel like he had been punched in the gut. His pride had won. His pride had pushed Hannah away. Instead of encouraging her, he railed on her and embarrassed her. Why was he so against her trying to protect herself? Regardless, Jonathon was not going to give up. She was worth fighting for! He needed to woo her and put aside his silly aversion to her learning weaponry. How could he make this right?

Jonathon let go of her shoulders, reaching for her hands. He brought them up to his lips. "You once led me to believe that you were fond of me." His eyes searched hers, hoping to convey how much he cared for her.

She did not pull her hands away, which was a good sign. "I did, but so much has changed since that day," she said with a sad smile.

Jonathon again winced at her words, knowing she spoke the truth. "Nothing has changed for me," he said firmly.

Hannah's lips tightened to a straight line. "How can that be?" She glanced over his shoulder, her expression pained. "You are not the man I thought you were."

Jonathon's heart sank even lower at her words. "What am I doing wrong?" he asked humbly.

Her gaze found his, her blue eyes moist with tears. "You are trying to control me. You refuse to let me choose for myself."

He decided to ask the one question he should have asked from the beginning. "Why are you so adamant about learning how to defend yourself?"

She huffed and started to pull her hands away, but he held firm. "I really would like to know this time," he said without a hint of guile.

"You do?" She eyed him suspiciously.

"Yes. I know the question may have come too late, but I am ready to listen," he admitted.

Hannah's face softened a little. She led him towards the bench and sat back down.

Jonathon sat down on the bench next to her, giving her a wide berth. He ran a hand through his hair. "Did I hurt you?" he asked, his eyes searching her wrist.

She shook her head. "No."

"I am so sorry." Jonathon looked pained and he sighed

loudly. "I should never have touched you in that manner." Hannah turned her head to watch him, attempting to gauge the sincerity of his words. "Please forgive me?" he asked, humbled.

She gazed into his dark green eyes and saw vulnerability, unmasked. Immediately, she knew he was truly asking her forgiveness. "I forgive you."

Jonathon's face relaxed, but his gaze did not waver. "I am ready to listen, to understand."

Hannah's eyes roamed the trees, then centered her gaze on the stream, frowning. "For these past few months, I have felt weak and vulnerable. As if I had no control over my life. I have been betrayed, chased, forced to hide out on a farm, and almost had my throat slashed."

"Oh, Hannah." His words soft.

"In all that time, I felt as if I did not have a choice in the matter. I constantly depended on others to protect me, to help me."

She turned her gaze back towards Jonathon. "Then I saw Eliza stand up to those men. She did not run or hide, but she faced them as a woman. I want to stand up to my attackers."

Jonathon shook his head. "No, that is too dangerous."

She rolled her eyes deliberately. "Don't be daft. I have no intention of starting a fight, but I want to be able to defend myself if it comes to that."

"Hannah," he said with a furrowed brow. "Eliza is not just a consultant to the Crown. She is…" His voice trailed off.

Hannah placed her finger on his lips, stalling his attempt at words. It had not escaped her notice that Eliza had more guards than Prinny himself. Eliza also had a talent for deciphering enemy codes, and she possessed skills like fencing, throwing daggers, and shooting pistols. It was apparent that Eliza was an agent for the Crown, not just a consultant as she pretended to be. Regardless of Hannah's intuition, she would never dare say anything, because she valued Eliza's friendship and safety.

"I know you have not told me Eliza's full story," Hannah removed her finger from his lips, "but I don't need to know."

"It is not my story to tell," Jonathon said, as he took her hand into his own.

"I know, nor am I asking you. Either way, my loyalty resides with you and Eliza."

She enjoyed the feeling of Jonathon's hand encompassing hers. "Eliza appears to be a strong-willed, confident woman. You could no more control her than teach a babbling brook to play the pianoforte."

Jonathon's lips twitched. "At times, Eliza can be stubborn."

"True," Hannah agreed, "but she also is a formidable woman."

"That is a true statement." Jonathon glanced at the castle, before asking, "Is that your wish, to be like Eliza?"

Hannah smiled a little, knowing it must have pained Jonathon to ask that question. "No, I do not wish that."

He breathed a sigh of relief. "Then what do you wish for?"

"When the time comes, I want to be able to stand my ground and defend myself."

Jonathon raised an eyebrow. "Are you sure? I could pull some strings and make you a consultant," he teased.

Hannah's spirits lifted at his teasing words. *Finally! This was the Jonathon she had grown to care for.* "No, that is not necessary."

Jonathon gave her a crooked smile. "To recap, you just want to know how to throw a dagger, fence, and shoot a pistol, in case you need to defend yourself?"

She nodded. Finally, he was beginning to see reason.

Jonathon rubbed his chin as if deep in thought. "Since you already are learning how to throw a dagger and fence, would you like me to show you how to shoot a pistol?"

Her eyes widened in surprise and her voice rose with excitement. "Would you? Right now? Eliza has not had time to show me and I noticed you are carrying one in your…" she trailed off, glancing down at the pistol tucked into his trousers.

Jonathon stared at her for a minute then shook his head, with a smile on his lips. "Not now. If I discharge my pistol *now*, then guards would descend upon us before I even hit my mark."

Hannah reached into the pocket of her dress. She retrieved the dagger and slowly pulled it out of its sheath. "We could practice throwing my dagger," she suggested.

"Eliza gave you one of her daggers?" His face showed surprise.

"Yes," Hannah said proudly, handing the small dagger to him for his inspection. "She let me pick one out of her collection."

Jonathon leaned back and looked at her dress. "And you were carrying this dagger in your dress?"

Hannah reached in and pulled out the pocket of the dress. "I had Maggie sew in a pocket so I could retrieve my dagger quickly."

Jonathon's eyebrow rose. "You carry a dagger in your pocket?"

It's fun to rile him! Hannah thought.

"Is that a problem?" Her own raised eyebrow dared him to challenge her.

His brow relaxed, his tone softened. "No. It is your choice, but I urge you to use caution."

"It is sheathed when I'm not using it," she informed him. "It is not a large dagger, but I could use it in case of an emergency."

Jonathon inspected the hilt and frowned. "You are correct that this is a small dagger, but to carry it in your pocket? Well, I guess it is better than being strapped to your thigh."

Hannah smiled. "That is what I thought when I saw Eliza's dagger. Although, she mentioned she had placed slits in her dress, which makes it more accessible." When Eliza confided to her that a dagger on your thigh is not the easiest to get to in times of danger, Hannah knew that Eliza had experienced that first hand.

Jonathon handed the weapon back and pointed towards the closest tree. "Impress me with your dagger throwing skills," he challenged, looking amused.

Hannah stood and turned to face the tree he pointed out. She planted her feet and started reviewing Eliza's instructions. *Plant your feet. Focus on the target. Bring the dagger back. Throw the dagger as you step forward.* As she released the dagger, it sailed past the tree that she was aiming for, clinking off an adjacent tree.

"Last time it took me fifty attempts to hit the mark," she said, hurrying to retrieve the weapon.

She came back to the same place and repeated Eliza's directions in her head. She released the dagger and was pleased to see it hit the tree she picked, but nowhere near her intended mark.

Over and over, she tried as Jonathon offered encouragement. On her thirty-fourth attempt, she finally embedded the dagger into her chosen target. She started squealing as she skipped to retrieve it. "Did you see that?"

Jonathon rolled his eyes mockingly. "Yes, I saw that you hit the tree."

"I am getting better. It only took me thirty-four times to hit my mark," she said proudly as she pulled the dagger out.

Jonathon smirked. "Well, if you ever threaten to throw a dagger at me, I know I have a fair chance of getting out of the way."

Hannah sheathed her dagger and placed it back into her pocket. "Can you throw a dagger?" she asked.

"No, but I carry one in my left boot," he said, pulling out the knife to show her.

"You carry a knife in your boot?" she asked, surprised.

Jonathon dropped it back into its place, and pulled a small pistol from his right boot. "This boot carries my spare pistol."

"May I see the pistol?" She stepped closer and held her hand out.

Jonathon hesitated, then reluctantly handed her the small weapon. "Be careful with that."

Hannah turned the pistol over and ran her fingers across the metal. It was so dainty. "Can I have a pistol like this?"

Jonathon's eyes seemed haunted for a moment. "Carrying weapons must seem exciting to you, but it is a necessity for my work. I have no joy in dispatching my weapons."

"I understand," she said, handing the pistol back to him. "When will you teach me how to shoot?"

She saw indecision playing in his eyes, but after a moment he responded, "I will teach you tomorrow, assuming Mr. Larson will give his approval."

Hannah could not contain her giddiness, and she boldly placed her hand on his chest. "Thank you, Jonathon."

Her smile was unrestrained as she gazed at him. "Thank you for understanding how much this means to me."

Jonathon's gaze roamed her face, as he delved deeper into her eyes. Hannah found herself lost in his green eyes and was unable to break the spell that he cast over her, nor did she want to. His head lowered, until his lips teased over her mouth. "My dear Hannah," he whispered against her lips.

"What is going on here?" Eliza said from behind them.

Hannah jumped, dropping her hand from his chest. "Jonathon has agreed to teach me how to shoot a pistol," she said, recovering quickly.

Eliza lifted an eyebrow. "Did he now?"

She glanced at the pistol that was still in Jonathon's hand. "Are you instructing her now?"

Jonathon appeared flustered as he quickly tucked his gun back into his boot. "No, I was just showing her my spare pistol."

Eliza glanced between them, smiling knowingly. "Mr. Larson

told me that you two were down near the stream and I came to fetch you."

She focused on Jonathon. "I want to show you what I discovered in the library."

As they walked back towards the castle, Eliza waved to someone in the tower facing them. Hannah glanced up and saw only a shape of a man. "Who are you waving to?"

Eliza chuckled. "Mr. Larson. He has been watching you the whole time through a looking glass."

Jonathon tilted his head to look up at Mr. Larson, and raised his hand in acknowledgement. "To be honest, I'm not surprised in the least."

❧ 16 ❧

HANNAH TRAILED BEHIND JONATHON AND ELIZA AS THEY quickly ascended the stairs and entered the library. Along one wall of the large, rectangular room were shelves, from floor to ceiling, haphazardly filled with books of every size. A large window overlooked the fields leading up to Beaumont Castle, and a brick fireplace dominated the wall on the opposite side of the room. Two velvet sofas near the fireplace flanked a low table, which was currently covered in open books. Large floral carpets ran the length of the room, and each corner held a round table adjacent to a side chair.

Benedict stood at the mantle of the fireplace and slowly turned as they entered. "Did you find them?"

"I did. Although, I interrupted Jonathon showing Hannah the pistol he carries in his boot," Eliza teased.

Benedict placed his arms around her waist, pulling her close. "I did not attempt that tactic when I was courting you."

Laughing, Eliza leaned into him. "That is a relief."

Hannah stifled a small sigh. Obviously, Eliza and Benedict were a love-match. They only had eyes for each other. She longed to find a love so true, to be loved so unconditionally.

"Shall we join them?" Jonathon whispered to her as he offered his arm.

"I'm sure we could sneak out of here and they would not notice," she observed as Eliza blushed in reaction to Benedict's whispered comment.

Jonathon whispered conspiratorially, "They are both spies, but they are distracted. We have ten minutes. What do you have in mind?"

Hannah tapped her lips gently, pretending to consider her answer. "Look for secret rooms?" she suggested, her eyes twinkling.

Jonathon shared a crooked smile. "This is a medieval castle. I imagine there are many secret tunnels."

Hannah tightened her grip on Jonathon's arm. "Where should we begin?" she asked, eagerly.

Before Jonathon could reply, Eliza's voice interrupted their whispered plans. "There are many secret passageways throughout Beaumont Castle, mainly designed for servants. There is one tunnel that extends about two hundred yards away from the castle. The exit is on the north side. However, before I take you on a tour, I need to speak to Jonathon."

"So close," Jonathon muttered under his breath. Hannah stifled a giggle.

Jonathon started to lead her towards the sofa, but she planted her feet and detached her arm from his. "I believe Eliza wanted to speak with you alone."

"Come join us," Eliza invited as she gracefully sat down. Jonathon escorted Hannah to the empty sofa facing his sister and claimed the seat beside her.

As Benedict sat near Eliza, she picked up a sheet of paper from the table. "I have completely decoded the first page. As Mr. Stanton said, the missive does reveal specific details about the assassination attempt against Prinny. However, even though the envelope contained Lord Camden's wax seal, there is nothing else to indicate Lord Camden's involvement."

"But the French had a missive with Lord Camden's seal. Does that not prove he is involved?" Hannah asked.

Jonathon shook his head. "Any decent barrister could have that evidence thrown out of court."

Reaching for the paper in Eliza's hand, he read the decoded message aloud. *"Attempt thwarted by Shadow. German caught, killed. Revealed nothing. New plan in motion. Remain alert. -M."*

He looked at Eliza, his eyebrow raised. "It is signed M."

"I have never decoded a message from M before." Eliza frowned.

"They hung the German within days of the assassination attempt, but the fact that *Shadow* saved Prinny from a mercenary was reported almost immediately," Benedict added.

Jonathon glanced down at the paper again. "Whoever wrote this had knowledge of the investigation, because they discovered that the German revealed nothing under direct torture. Who had access to the case?"

"I can ask Uncle Charles to compile a list, but it might be long," Eliza said, looking displeased. "If you remember, Prinny delivered a joint address to both Houses of Parliament. He told them of the assassination attempt and praised *Shadow* as a hero of the English people."

Hannah remembered reading in the newspaper how *Shadow* scaled three levels on the outside of the building to save the Prince Regent. "How did *Shadow* learn of the attempted assassination?"

Eliza flickered a glance at Jonathon. "According to reports, *Shadow* overheard two German men speaking about the scheme during the ball at my mother's abbey and intervened before Prinny was in any real danger."

"Did Prinny reveal any information about the investigation in the joint address?" Benedict asked.

Jonathon nodded. "We all know how Prinny loves to embellish, but he did state that the accomplices were still at large and would be hunted down."

"And were they?" Hannah asked Jonathon.

He shifted in his seat. "No, they were not."

"Oh," Hannah said softly. "What happened?"

He rubbed the back of his neck. "Our investigation uncovered a scullery maid who was the leak at the ball. She must have passed along information to the German men about where Prinny's guest room was, and then left the window unlocked for them. On the night of the ball, she disappeared, along with the other German assailant."

Hannah turned back to Eliza. "I assume you were at the ball. That must have frightened you."

Smiling brightly, Eliza admitted, "It was not frightening at all. In fact, I found it exhilarating."

Benedict encompassed her hand in his own. "You must excuse my wife. She tends to find the oddest things exciting," he said with a teasing grin.

Eliza smiled tenderly at Benedict, then turned back to Jonathon. "The second document is using a code I have never seen before. I have not been able to establish a pattern."

Curious, Hannah asked, "How does one decipher a code?"

Eliza's eyes lit up and her hands came alive as she started talking. "That is an excellent question. Typically, I review the document and try to establish a pattern within the text. Many times, the coded message is hidden within the text. Sometimes, the codes are based on thousands of numbers or they could be based on a specific piece of literature."

Amazed, Hannah stared. "How are you able to recall the pieces of literature?"

Leaning closer, Jonathon whispered, "My sister has a perfect memory."

"What does that mean?" Hannah whispered back.

Eliza laughed. "Once I read a book, it becomes permanently etched into my mind. Since I love to read, I read a book once and can remember its contents even years later."

"That is amazing. How I envy you!" Hannah commended her.

Eliza's smile dimmed a little. "Not everyone feels the same as you."

"Well, they should," Hannah said adamantly. "After all, you are helping to defeat Napoléon."

Eliza's smile brightened again before turning her attention to the second paper. "Regardless, I cannot find a pattern in this code. I can't tell if the code is hidden in the message or if there is an external key. I also confirmed that no invisible ink was used."

Sitting forward in his seat, Jonathon tried to encourage her by saying, "You just need more time."

Eliza shook her head. "I fear I might not be able to decrypt this one. I see no pattern." She released the paper from her hand and watched it float back to the table. "It is very frustrating."

"If you make an additional copy, I can take it to Uncle Charles. He can send it to the home office for their review," Jonathon offered.

Benedict frowned. "If a code needs deciphering, Eliza is the best in England. If she cannot decrypt it, then I have little faith in the home office."

"I disagree. The home office has created a team led by Sir George Scovell to decipher the French codes. In fact, two years ago, Sir Scovell deciphered the Army of Portugal Code. I understand it was based on a combination of one hundred and fifty numbers," Jonathon commented.

"Maybe Eliza and Sir Scovell could work together to decipher this code?" Hannah suggested.

"No," Benedict said. "No one knows that Eliza works as an age... um... consultant."

"Can you guess who the letter is from or who it is intended for?" Jonathon asked.

Eliza shook her head. "No, but my instinct tells me that this is related to Lord Camden in some way. After all, the first page was sent with Lord Camden's seal, and he has been sending confidential information from Parliament to the French."

That revelation shocked Hannah. "Why is Lord Camden not in Newgate if he is selling state secrets?"

"Uncle Charles intercepted most of the letters Lord Camden sent, but they have not discovered his contact," Jonathon replied.

Eliza sat on the end of the sofa, turning towards Benedict. "I believe a thorough search of Lord Camden's study is in order."

"His London townhouse or his country home?" Benedict asked casually.

Eliza tapped her mouth with her finger. "Let's start with his country home."

"I will go with Benedict," Jonathon stated quickly. Eliza raised her eyebrows and opened her mouth, ready to debate the decision, but her brother continued. "It makes more sense if I go. If we get caught, Lord Camden will not know of your involvement."

Hannah watched as Eliza squared her shoulders and tilted her chin defiantly, ticking off each point on her fingers. "I have broken into more offices than the two of you combined, I know what to look for, and most importantly, I can absorb any documents we find without removing them from Lord Camden's office."

Benedict reached for Eliza's hands, quieting them. "If you feel so strongly about it then I will go with you."

"Blazes," Jonathon muttered under his breath. "What will be your excuse if you are caught? Camden is a French spy, not just a horrible relation."

Eliza's eyes narrowed. "Let us assume that I will not be caught."

"Maybe I should go with you," Jonathon suggested.

"No. Eliza is my wife, my partner," Benedict spoke firmly, his hard gaze brooking no argument.

Jonathon muttered another expletive under his breath as his eyes flickered to Eliza. "Do you plan to leave Hannah unprotected?"

Eliza rolled her eyes. "Hannah is safe at Beaumont Castle, especially with Mr. Larson to watch over her. However, if you are so worried about her safety, then you may remain overnight to ensure her protection."

"You will stay in a guest room," Benedict clarified.

Jonathon smirked. "Why bother? You did not stay in a guest room when you remained overnight."

Benedict clenched his jaw tightly, and a muscle twitched below his ear. "That was different and you know it."

Hannah glanced between Jonathon and Benedict. Neither seemed willing to back down. She placed her hand on Jonathon's arm to get his attention. He glanced at her and some of the tension drained from his shoulders. He covered her hand with his. "Fair enough. I will stay at Beaumont Castle tonight, while you two break into Camden's study."

Benedict's eyes focused on their combined hands. His voice was firm. "And Jonathon will stay in a *separate* guest room?"

Jonathon's grip on her hand tightened. "I am a gentleman, am I not?" he growled.

Eliza leaned over and whispered into Benedict's ear. His face softened as he looked at her, then glanced back at them. "My wife has informed me that Mr. Larson will be chaperoning this evening, so I have nothing to fear."

Benedict stood up. "I believe I will go find him now and inform him of our plans."

Eliza's eyes followed him as he left the room, then she

looked back at them. "You need to stop baiting Benedict," she told Jonathon with a quick head shake. "Now he will ensure Mr. Larson will sleep outside of Hannah's room all night."

Jonathon arose, then offered Hannah his hand. "Would you like to take a tour of the gardens until dinner?"

Hannah eyed him suspiciously. "I believe we still have hours until dinner.

Jonathon winked. "I know. We will walk slowly."

❧ 17 ❧

NIGHTTIME ENGULFED ELIZA AND BENEDICT AS THEY JOGGED towards the rear of Lord Camden's darkened country home. They were dressed in black, with pistols tucked into their waistbands. Eliza added a cloth cap to conceal her hair. Her dagger was strapped to her left thigh on the outside of her trousers.

She led the way towards the study window in the rear left corner of the house. A large, multi-paned glass window loomed in front of them. Carefully removing one of the panes, she handed it to Benedict, who placed it on the ground. Eliza reached in, unlocked the window, and climbed inside. Before she pulled her feet in, she brushed off the bottom of her boots to remove any excess dirt.

The curtains were draped open, and she could see a large mahogany desk near the window, a settee sitting opposite, and shelves lined with books, spanning one length of the room. The other side held a small, marble fireplace and the interior door. Above the sofa, a large, gaudy painting dominated the room. In it, Lord Camden, dressed in his white finery, sat on top of a black stallion, looking arrogant and highly self-important.

After her husband climbed in the window, Eliza began to pull open the desk drawers. Benedict positioned himself near the door while Eliza searched the desk. The room was dark except for the moonlight streaming into the room. She saw a candle on top of the desk and decided to light it. It was risky, but she needed to see what was in the desk.

As she opened the large drawers, she found files containing ledgers, expense reports, and documents on agriculture, but nothing that could help decipher the code, or prove Lord Camden was a traitor. After closing all the drawers, she moved to the bookshelves. Her eyes skimmed every book, looking for one that looked out of place or overly worn. She did find Aristotle's books, but that proved nothing, except that he had exceptional reading taste. Eliza sighed inwardly. *This was a wasted trip*!

As Eliza turned to face Benedict, she saw the door handle slowly dip downward. Someone was opening the door! With his pistol in hand, Benedict leaned back against the wall, ready to intercept the threat. Eliza quickly ducked behind the desk, blew out the candle, and drew her pistol.

The door opened slowly and a lone candle illuminated the room momentarily before it was blown out. Eliza heard a soft, muffled cry. She came out from under the desk and saw Benedict's hand covering the mouth of a petite, blonde woman. When the moonlight shone on her face, Eliza gasped. It was her sister, Kate. Her eyes were wide and fearful. Rather, her right eye was opened wide. Her left eye was bruised and swollen almost shut.

As Eliza approached her sister, Kate relaxed when she recognized her. Mouthing, "Kate," to Benedict, he dropped his hand from Kate's mouth.

Glancing at Eliza's clothes, Kate asked in a hushed tone, "What are you wearing?"

"I will explain later," Eliza said, noticing that Kate's lip was cut, as well.

"I apologize for my behavior," Benedict said, stepping out

from behind her. His eyes narrowed when he saw her face. "What happened to you?"

"Matthew," Kate said bitterly.

Throwing her arms around her sister, Eliza whispered, "Oh, Kate."

Kate clung to Eliza. "I am running away. I cannot endure another moment in his presence. I was preparing to flee when I saw the light under the door."

Eliza pulled back. "You must come home with us." She glanced at Benedict, who nodded, confirming what she already knew. His eyes were filled with anger.

"Why are you breaking into Matthew's study?" Kate asked, sitting down on the settee.

Benedict crouched down in front of her, keeping his voice low. "Your husband is a traitor and has been aiding the French."

Wincing, Kate confessed, "That does not surprise me."

"We have been searching the study for a key that will help decode a French message that was intercepted by the Navy," Eliza added. "So far, we have found nothing."

"Did you check in his iron chest?" Kate asked.

Eliza's eyes skirted the room. "Where is that?"

"Behind that ghastly painting of Matthew," she said, rising. "And the key is in the fireplace near the damper." Walking over to the marble fireplace, she placed her hand in the flue and produced a small metal key.

Eliza and Benedict both lifted Lord Camden's enormous painting off the hooks and leaned it against the shelving. A wooden box, bound with iron hoops, was set into the wall.

Benedict stood on the settee and carefully pulled out the iron chest. He placed it on the ground in front of Eliza as Kate handed her the key. Dropping to her knees, Eliza inserted the key and tilted up the lid, allowing access to a large stack of papers stuffed inside.

Pulling out the documents, she rifled through them. Most

dealt with deeds and investments, but three pages gave her pause. Two pages were written in the same code as the one she had back at Beaumont Castle. The third appeared to be the key. However, she could not be certain until she tried it out.

Folding the pages, she placed them into the pockets of her trousers. Benedict glanced over and asked, "What are you doing? Camden will know that we were here if you take those pages."

Shrugging, Eliza replied, "He will know someone was here anyway, since his wife will have disappeared."

Nodding, Benedict returned the iron chest to the recess of the wall before they rehung the painting.

Eliza turned towards her sister. "Are you sure you want to sneak away with us?"

Kate tilted her chin. "I have never been so certain of anything in my life."

Within a few moments, Benedict had hopped out the window and assisted Kate. Once Eliza exited the window, she replaced the pane of glass while Benedict shuffled the dirt around the window to hide the multiple footprints.

Reaching for Kate's arm, Eliza whispered, "Now we run."

They used trees to shield themselves from any patrolling guards, but they only met silence. Arriving at the carriage, they relaxed a little, and were glad to be on their way back to Beaumont Castle.

Eliza was sitting next to Kate with her arm around her shoulder. "Did Camden do this to you?"

Kate's eyes welled with tears. "Two nights ago, I told him that I was carrying his babe. He flew into a rage. At some point, I must have passed out."

Benedict muttered expletives under his breath. When Kate stopped speaking, he looked up. "My apologies, Kate, but I plan to kill your husband."

"You have my permission," Kate said, stifling a sob.

Eliza's arm tightened around her shoulder. "And the babe?"

"I lost the baby today," Kate confirmed. As tears flowed down her face, she wiped them away angrily. "You must understand, I had to leave or he would have eventually killed me."

Eliza closed her eyes tightly, fighting back her own tears. Her poor sister had endured so much, and now this. She'd see that Lord Camden paid for this.

18

HANNAH AWOKE TO A LOUD, CONTINUOUS METAL SCREECHING from the portcullis. Opening one of her eyes, she noticed that it was still dark outside. She pulled a pillow over her head and thought about trying to fall back to sleep. She had been dreaming about Jonathon, and he was leaning in to kiss her when she was so rudely awakened.

She could hear a commotion and muffled shouting. Something must be going on. She rolled out of bed and reached for her wrap. Her hair was braided loosely and hung over one shoulder. She knew she wasn't dressed decently, but she only intended to peek around the corner.

Opening her door, she heard Jonathon exclaim, "What happened to you?"

Oh, no! Eliza must have been hurt on the mission. Without a second thought, Hannah rushed down the staircase, but stopped when she saw Benedict holding a petite, blonde woman in a dark blue traveling gown. As the woman peered up at her, Hannah noticed the swollen eye and cut lip, but also noted that they did not hide her beauty at all. Who was this beautiful woman in Benedict's arms and where was Eliza? Was she all right?

As she descended the stairs, she noticed Mr. Larson and Eliza loitering nearby. "Oh, Eliza. I was worried that you might have been hurt," Hannah confessed, her hand covering her heart.

Jonathon ran up the few stairs to escort her down. "Lady Hannah, may I present my sister Kate, also known as Lady…"

"No! I do not ever want to be called that again," Kate demanded, tears welling up in her eyes.

Hannah heard the raw anguish in Kate's voice. What happened to this woman? "It is a pleasure to meet you Kate. You must call me Hannah."

Kate glanced at Jonathon in confusion. "You're married?"

Jonathon's face paled slightly. "No, I…why would you think that?"

Frowning at his reaction, Hannah decided to take pity on him under the circumstances. "What Jonathon is so eloquently attempting to say, is that we are not married. I am under his protection because…" she glanced nervously at Jonathon, "… your husband is trying to abduct me."

"Of course, he is." Kate's eyes were filled with regret. "I am sorry Matthew is causing you such pain."

"It appears that he has caused you pain, as well," Hannah said softly, hoping she could help ease Kate's pain, if only a little.

Forcing a smile, Kate replied, "I hope that is now in the past." She looked up at Benedict. "You may put me down now."

Instead, Benedict walked her into the drawing room and gently sat her down on the settee, as everyone followed.

Eliza sat next to Kate. "I asked the cook to bring in some tea and sandwiches. I thought you might be hungry."

Kate stifled a yawn. "I apologize for being such a burden. After all, I practically forced you to take me with you."

Benedict smiled kindly at his sister-in-law. "You are always welcome in our home."

Kate glanced around the drawing room. "And this is home?"

Eliza gently covered Kate's hand with her own. "Yes, this is Beaumont Castle. From now on, you will live with us. Matthew will never hurt you again."

Kate smiled weakly, wiping away fresh tears. "I belong to Matthew. He will not give me up without a fight. I do not want any harm to come to you for harboring me."

Eliza placed her arm around Kate's shoulder. "Do not fear for us. Besides, no one knows about Beaumont Castle. You are safe here."

"How can no one know about this place?" Kate sounded doubtful.

At that moment, Mr. Larson walked into the room with a tray of tea and sandwiches. "Mrs. Dobbs asked me to bring in the tray because she did not want to wake up the maids yet."

Eliza took the tray from Mr. Larson, placing it on a round table. "Thank you, Mr. Larson. Please join us. We will be asking Kate some questions and I think you might be interested in the answers."

Mr. Larson hesitated, then chose a chair near the door.

Turning to Kate, Eliza explained, "Mr. Larson is responsible for the security at Beaumont Castle. No one comes near here without his consent."

"He also doubles as an effective chaperone," Jonathon joked.

Mr. Larson chuckled. "Yes, first Eliza and now Hannah. I am too old to play chaperone."

Hannah smiled tenderly at him. "I think you do a spectacular job, Mr. Larson."

"Thank you, Lady Hannah," he replied, returning her smile.

Eliza poured a cup of tea and handed it to Kate. "Do you mind explaining what happened before Matthew attacked you?"

Kate accepted the teacup with a shaky hand, and took a lingering sip. "A few months ago, the beatings intensified when Matthew came home after a night of drinking. He forced his way into my bedchamber and roughly…"

Her voice cracked. Trembling, she placed her cup on the table. "Afterwards, he raved like a lunatic about how he married into a family of spies. He even accused me of being a spy. Mostly, what he shouted was in French, which is his preferred language when he is inebriated."

Jonathon leaned forward in his chair. "What else did he say?"

"Matthew was furious that you and Eliza spoke to a man named LeBlanc, I believe." Kate put her hand to her temple. "Yes, Monsieur LeBlanc. Also, he seems to believe that Eliza is working for the Crown, which is ridiculous, of course."

Jonathon exchanged a look with Eliza. "Did he say anything else?"

Kate shook her head. "No, he passed out shortly after."

"What else can you remember?" Eliza asked.

Kate glanced nervously at her sister. "Matthew seems to loathe you. He enjoyed tormenting me by calling you a strumpet and other vile names."

"Well, it should please you that I return the sentiment. I abhor him," Eliza said.

Kate's eyes grew wide. "You must be careful of Matthew. He has a cruel temper and no qualms about hurting a lady."

Benedict chuckled. "My wife has no qualms about killing an earl."

"Lady Camden..." Mr. Larson interjected.

"Kate, if you will," she said, lifting her chin.

"Have you witnessed any interactions between the duchess and Lord Camden?" Mr. Larson asked, leaning forward.

Kate stiffened and clasped her hands together. She closed her eyes for a moment. "Yes. Mother would come over every few months and they would lock themselves in his study. Once, I made the mistake of opening the door, and caught them in an... intimate position," she said, lowering her voice.

Jonathon jumped up from his seat and strode over to the drink cart. He poured himself a generous helping of brandy and gulped it. Refilling it, he muttered, "Of all the despicable things Mother could have done…"

He stopped speaking and took another swallow.

"Did Mother or Matthew see you?" Eliza asked, concerned.

Kate shook her head. "No. They were too busy to notice me. However, last month, Matthew stayed at the country home, and Mother began visiting him weekly. I overheard them yelling about Mr. Wade being a failure. As I turned away, I heard Mother mention Jonathon's name."

Jonathon brought over an armless chair and placed it next to Kate. Sitting down, he asked, "What did you overhear?"

"I heard that Mr. Wade was killed by *Shadow*. Mother and Matthew were discussing the possibility that you might be *Shadow*."

She hesitated, studying his face, then asked, "Are you *Shadow*?"

Jonathon glanced briefly at Eliza, then returned his attention to Kate. "No, I am not *Shadow*."

Kate's hand went to a round, gold locket around her neck. "Then you are in grave danger, Jonathon."

He gave her a tentative smile. "Do not fear for me, but I need to know if anything else was said."

Kate winced as her tongue brushed over the cut on her lip. "They discussed an upcoming vote in the House of Lords, regarding the bill to end the war against France. I apologize I did not hear more, but I dared not linger. Matthew would not have been kind if he found me listening at the door."

"Smart girl," Benedict complimented her. "What was Lord Camden's reason for your recent beating?"

Touching her bruised eye, she winced again. "Two nights ago, Matthew came home inebriated, smelling of another woman's perfume. I told him I was with child. That news enraged him, and he started hitting me, specifically in my stomach."

Hannah gasped. "Why would he want to hurt the baby?"

Kate's eyes filled with tears. "He muttered over and over that he did not want an English bastard."

"That does not make sense." Eliza frowned.

"I know, but nothing seems to please him. I have always believed that he never really wanted me as his wife."

"Then why did he and Mother insist on a betrothal agreement?" Jonathon asked, irritated.

"I do not know. But he has never exhibited any real affection towards me since our wedding tour. After that, I was banished to our country home." Kate's voice was soft.

A somber silence hovered over the group.

After a few moments, Mr. Larson spoke quietly. "Kate, if I may suggest, we should have a doctor attend to your wounds."

Jonathon looked surprised. "Can we risk bringing a doctor to Beaumont Castle?"

Mr. Larson rubbed his chin. "Sir Dixon was an army surgeon and is a good friend of mine. I could send Roger into London to ask if he is willing to make the trip."

Eliza nodded. "Please send Roger at his earliest convenience." She turned back to Kate. "And we should put you to bed."

"Would you like me to carry you upstairs?" Benedict offered.

Kate smiled faintly. "No, but I thank you kindly." Eliza looped her arm through Kate's. They climbed the stairs slowly with Benedict trailing behind.

Hannah stood and glanced at Jonathon, who was sitting with his elbows on his knees, leaning forward. His sad, resigned look tore at Hannah's heart. Crouching in front of him, she took his hands in her own. "How are you faring?"

Jonathon raised his head slowly. "Did you see Kate's face?"

"I did." She leaned closer. "She is safe now."

"Have you ever hated someone so much that you schemed to kill them?"

Shaking her head, she replied honestly, "No, I have not."

Jonathon's brief laugh was humorless. "Of course not. You are too kind to ever have that hatred stir inside of you."

Hannah cupped his cheek with her hand. "What Lord Camden did to your sister is unforgivable, but Kate needs you to be strong. You need to be brave and beat him at his own game. If you kill him outright, then you will end up in Newgate."

"No. I would make it look like an accident." Jonathon's voice was firm and she had no doubt he meant it.

"It would destroy you," she said softly.

Jonathon's eyes were filled with sorrow. "I have killed men before."

"Were they killed in your line of duty?"

"Yes."

Hannah cupped both cheeks in her hands, holding his face gently, her eyes pleading with him to understand. "You are a good man, Jonathon Beckett. I have no doubt that you have saved many lives in your work and brought many evil men to justice. But you must bring in Lord Camden the right way. You do not want his death on your conscience."

As she closed the tiny distance between them, she whispered, "You will always be my hero," before she brushed her lips against his. For a moment, their lips were pressed together, but when he did not return her kiss, she pulled back and dropped her hands, her face burning with embarrassment.

Jonathon placed his finger under her chin and lifted her face to look at him. "You kissed me," he said, with surprise in his voice.

Hannah felt as if her face might literally catch on fire if she did not escape from this room. "If you will excuse me…"

"No, I will not excuse you," Jonathon said with a crooked smile. Hannah watched him as he leaned closer, stopping until he hovered over her lips. "I cannot believe you kissed me."

"It will not happen again," Hannah assured him, although she desperately hoped she was wrong.

"Now, that would be a pity. I give you leave to kiss me whenever you so desire," Jonathon whispered, his breath lingering on her mouth.

Was he toying with her? Hannah did not know if he was flirting or teasing her. As she opened her mouth to ask, his lips melted into her own. She tingled from her lips down to the tips of her toes. Tenderly, he deepened the kiss, keeping it achingly slow, and wonderful. With her hands on his shoulders, she pulled him closer to her.

Jonathon broke the kiss and leaned his forehead against hers. "Thank you, Hannah. I needed that."

"You needed to be kissed?" she teased.

His eyes filled with emotion. "No, I needed you."

With her heart swelling from Jonathon's praise, she confessed, "I need you, too."

"You should probably go back to bed," he said.

They slowly walked towards the stairs, hand in hand. "Early tomorrow, I will need to return to my townhouse," Jonathon told her. "Uncle Charles will want a status update. I assume Lord Camden will show up asking about Kate."

Stopping outside her bedchamber, Hannah's smile was teasing. "Be safe and try not to kill Lord Camden."

Jonathon raised her hand to his lips. "Good night, my dear."

As Hannah gazed into his eyes, she melted towards him. His eyes drew her in and she longed to stay with him. How she wished she could remain side by side, always. "Good night," she whispered, reluctantly entering her room.

As she heard Jonathon's footsteps fade down the hall, she prayed that he would be safe.

❧ 19 ❦

A FEW HOURS LATER, JONATHON ENTERED THE LIBRARY, DRESSED in buckskin breeches, white shirt, and knee-length riding boots. He saw Eliza at the table, writing. "I assumed you would be here already," he said, crossing the room to her.

Eliza put down her feather quill and stretched her shoulders. "I couldn't sleep after putting Kate to bed. I decided to decode this message before you left."

Jonathon dropped onto the sofa across from her. "You deciphered the code?" he said, surprised.

Eliza smiled, adjusting her wrap. "No, but in all the excitement of last night, I failed to mention we found the key to the code in Camden's iron chest."

"Ah," he said, leaning back. "What does the document reveal?"

"It is a cryptic message. *Plan progressing. Players performing. No one suspects.*" Eliza tucked a piece of hair behind her ear. "What is Matthew planning?"

"We know that Wade supplied Camden with secrets. Maybe that note was sent prior to Wade's death," Jonathon suggested.

Eliza picked up the paper, flipping it over. "Perhaps. There is no date on the missive, nor is it signed."

"I haven't decoded the second paper I saw, but I should have it in a few hours. My eyes are tired, and I fear I need to sleep before I undertake that one."

Jonathon glanced around, half expecting to see his brother-in-law. "Where is Benedict?"

Eliza tucked her feet under her wrap. "He went to fetch some tea. He fell asleep on the sofa and woke up about half an hour ago."

Jonathon took a long look at his sister. He could see she was tired, but she appeared agitated, too. "What has you so upset?"

Eliza bit her lower lip, a sure indicator of her inner turmoil. "I'm angry on many levels. I cannot believe what Kate has endured these past four years at the hands of her husband."

Jonathon frowned. "I understand. I plan to contact Father about Kate's dilemma. He will be furious at how Matthew has treated her."

Eliza looked depressed, almost defeated, which was not like her. "For these past few years, I have been saving girls from slavery, but I did not help my own sister."

Jonathon moved over to sit next to Eliza. "I blame myself for allowing the marriage to happen in the first place."

Eliza shook her head. "You could not have stopped the wedding. Mother was adamant about Kate marrying Camden."

Jonathon rubbed his eyes. "Well, Camden's reign of terror ends now. We will keep Kate safe."

"Are you concerned that he believes you are *Shadow*?"

"No, we planned it that way."

"But…"

"No buts," Jonathon replied, cutting her off. "We covered our tracks, but Mother betrayed us by reading Father's correspondences from Uncle Charles and informing Camden. Let us allow him to think he knows who *Shadow* is. It will work to our advantage, I'm sure."

Eliza hugged her arms tightly around her wrap. "I would feel more comfortable if you would let Mr. Larson protect you."

"I do not need a nursemaid, Eliza," Jonathon said. "Besides, I have two agents at my townhouse. I believe it is time to utilize their skills."

"Would you at least ride with Roger when he retrieves Sir Dixon?" Eliza asked, still concerned.

"If that will comfort you." Jonathon smiled faintly. "I do ask one favor, though."

Eliza looked knowingly up at him. "Let me guess. Protect Hannah and stop teaching her defensive weapons?" she teased.

He chuckled. "Protect Hannah, yes. But I must admit, I have grown very fond of watching her throwing daggers and fencing in trousers."

Eliza playfully narrowed her eyes. "Careful, it almost sounds as if you approve."

He put up his hands in surrender. "I am beginning to see the merit of Hannah learning to defend herself. Besides, it makes her happy and I find I would do anything to see her smile."

"I like Hannah. We will keep her safe."

"Who likes Hannah?" Benedict asked as he walked in carrying a tray. "Did Jonathon declare his intentions to Hannah yet?"

Jonathon smirked. "Do you not employ any servants at Beaumont Castle?"

"Eliza employs the basic few for security reasons, you know that." Benedict placed the tray on the table, carefully avoiding all of the books, then poured a cup of tea.

Jonathon stood, laughing. "If being a marquess does not suit you, then you might consider working as a scullery maid."

Benedict handed the cup of tea to Eliza then poured another

cup. "Why are you bothering me so early? Normally, I require a few more hours of sleep before I can endure your prattle."

Benedict offered the tea to Jonathon but he declined. "I wanted to ride out early to try and catch Uncle at his office," Jonathon said.

Benedict took a sip of tea and placed the cup back on the saucer. "I can ride with you."

Jonathon shook his head. "No, that is not necessary. Eliza has already made me promise to ride out with Roger."

Benedict nodded his head in approval. "Good. You need to be on high alert, since Camden suspects you are *Shadow*."

Jonathon picked up a piece of paper from the table. "Is this a copy of what you decoded?"

Eliza took another sip. "Yes, please take that to Uncle Charles."

Jonathon tucked it into his pocket, nodded to each of them and walked out. He stopped in front of Hannah's door, raised his hand to knock, then hesitated. She was probably still asleep and would not welcome the intrusion. They had said good-bye the night before, and he did not want to become a nuisance.

He leaned against her door. Last night, he'd been shocked when she kissed him. She had never initiated contact between them, yet it seemed so natural, so perfect. Would it be too soon to propose marriage? No, she was still under his protection. This was not the time to court her.

He pushed away from the door and descended the stairs. He must stop Lord Camden before he'd be free to court Hannah.

Jonathon strode into the study at his townhouse, annoyed that Uncle Charles was not in his office yet. He left a message with his uncle's private secretary asking to see him today. Walking over to his desk, he sank down into his chair, noting a large pile of correspondence that Mr. Wilde had neatly organized. He pulled the pistol out of his waistband and placed it in the top drawer of the desk.

As he reached for the top page of the pile, Mr. Stanton strode into the room. "Good, you are back. What did you find out?"

Trailing closely behind, Lord Pembrooke asked, "How is Hannah?"

Jonathon decided to push aside the pile of correspondences as the two men sat down. "First, Lady Hannah is doing well and sent you another note." He took the note out of his pocket and handed it to Lord Pembrooke, then turned to Mr. Stanton. "Second, the agent confirmed your initial assessment of the first document. It was about the assassination attempt against Prinny."

Mr. Stanton nodded his approval. "Did the page implicate Lord Camden?"

Shaking his head, Jonathon replied, "Sadly, no. The only evidence is his signet seal on the envelope, and that is purely circumstantial, certainly not enough to arrest an earl for treason."

"And the second document?" Mr. Stanton asked.

Jonathon leaned forward in his seat and intertwined his fingers, resting them on his desk. "The agent found the key to the code in Lord Camden's iron chest and decoded it this morning."

He shared the message contents, then added, "I went to report my findings to my uncle this morning, but he was not in his office yet. Once I speak to him, I have no doubt his office will pursue this new lead."

Lord Pembrooke frowned. "As long as Lord Camden is free, then my Hannah will be in danger."

"And your two lives," Jonathon added, pointing to each of them.

Obviously frustrated, Mr. Stanton jumped up from his chair. "I do not understand. What is my cousin trying to gain from this? When we were younger, Matthew was frail and unable to attend Eton and Cambridge with me. He was tutored at home and was decent to all the servants. This does not sound like the cousin I remember."

Lord Pembrooke remained seated but looked stern. "I am not going to hide any longer. I will take Hannah home with me and hire as many guards as it takes to keep her safe."

Jonathon did not like that option. As of now, he only had to travel forty minutes to see Hannah, but her country home was days away. He held his hands up. "My uncle should be here shortly and we can discuss our options before we act in haste."

A loud commotion from the entry hall drew their attention. Jonathon removed his pistol from the top drawer and slowly rose.

Lord Camden stomped into the room. In other circumstances, his attire and mannerisms would have been comical, with his white pantaloons, white shirt with matching cravat, and a purple waistcoat. But even in this situation, the enraged expression on his face nearly made Jonathon laugh.

As Camden drew closer to Mr. Stanton, Jonathon could see the familial resemblance, both were tall with brown hair, the same facial structure, similar eyes, and wide shoulders.

Lord Camden's eyes were narrowed and filled with hate as he glared at Jonathon. "My wife is missing. You would not know anything about that, would you?"

Jonathon could not help himself. He started tsking in mock disapproval. "You misplaced your wife?"

Mr. Stanton chuckled but turned it into a cough when Lord Camden turned towards him. "And who are you?"

Jonathon was taken aback. Lord Camden did not recognize

his own cousin? Did people normally need to be introduced to their own relations? "It appears that you are confused..."

"I apologize, my lord," Mr. Stanton cut in. "My name is Mr. Dixon, and this is my father." He pointed at Lord Pembrooke. "We are Lord Jonathon's solicitors."

Lord Camden flicked his hand at them. "You are dismissed. I need to speak to Lord Jonathon about a private family matter." Mr. Stanton and Lord Pembrooke bowed to Lord Camden and exited the room quickly.

Jonathon politely indicated he should sit, but Lord Camden waved him off. "I want my wife," he commanded.

"No," Jonathon stated flatly, then sat down and placed his pistol on the desk.

Lord Camden narrowed his eyes and took a step forward. "She is my wife. My property."

Jonathon rested his hands on his desk and tapped his thumbs together. "Kate ran away from you because you assaulted her."

"Kate and I had an unfortunate argument, and she is angry with me."

"Beating your wife until she lost your unborn baby is not an unfortunate argument," Jonathon growled.

"She was not really with child," Lord Camden said calmly as he took a seat. "She has desired a baby for so long that she convinced herself that she truly was with child."

Jonathon continued to tap his thumbs together, pretending to mull over what Lord Camden was saying. He was trying to rein in his temper before he shot his brother-in-law. Finally, he felt in control of his emotions. "You are a liar, and Kate will never be returned to you."

Lord Camden slammed his hands onto the desk. "Then I will go to the magistrate."

Jonathon smiled smugly. "Excellent. After Kate has been examined by a doctor, we would like to show the magistrate her injuries, sustained at the hand of her husband."

"Those injuries occurred when she accidentally fell down the stairs." Camden dismissed the accusation with no hint of shame.

Jonathon huffed. "I have sent a message to my father and he will be here shortly. You may discuss it with him."

Lord Camden appeared to be shaken that the Duke of Remington was taking an interest in Kate. "I would like to speak to my wife," he paused, "to encourage her to see reason."

"Kate does not ever want to see you again, and she is somewhere you will never find her." Jonathon's voice was unyielding.

Lord Camden pursed his lips. "We shall see."

Standing, Jonathon pointed to the door. "If you will excuse me…"

Lord Camden arose and pulled at the arms of his waistcoat. "I want my wife back, and I will retrieve her by any means. She belongs to me."

Jonathon rose, placing his hands on the desk and leaning forward. "Not for long. Kate will be seeking a divorce."

Camden jerked back. "Impossible. On what grounds?"

"Adultery and attempted murder," Jonathon said slowly.

Lord Camden threw his head back and laughed. "That is ludicrous. No one will believe her."

"Kate's father, the Duke of Remington, and her brother-in-law, the Marquess of Lansdowne, will both be supporting the divorce. You are just a lowly earl, with no friends. Whom do you believe the courts will side with?"

"You would not dare." Lord Camden glowered viciously at Jonathon for a long, tense moment, then his eyes darted to the pistol on the desk. "Fine, keep the strumpet," he spat.

Jonathon moved around the desk and stepped closer to his brother-in-law. "My sister is not a strumpet and I strongly suggest you refrain from making such lewd comments in the future."

Lord Camden did not try to hide the fury on his face. "There will come a day that you will be begging me for my favor."

"I do not believe that day will ever come," Jonathon replied with contempt.

Lord Camden took a step forward, now standing toe-to-toe with him. "We both know that you and your precious family have nothing on me. If you did, then I would not be here."

Jonathon clenched his jaw. "I would not get too comfortable, if I were you."

Lord Camden's sneer was cruel, cold, and mocking. "You should know that I never wanted Kate in the first place. I really wanted Eliza. Do you think she would be as feisty in bed as she is in person?"

Without conscious thought, Jonathon pulled back and delivered a crushing blow to his face, feeling immense gratification as he made solid contact with his left eye.

Lord Camden's head flew back, but he quickly recovered, grabbing Jonathon's shoulders. Pulling him forward, he kneed him in the stomach.

Trying to catch his breath, Jonathon was not prepared for Lord Camden's fist to slam into his face. He fell backwards into a chair. Jumping up, he plowed his own fist into Lord Camden's stomach, throwing him against the wall. Without hesitation, his hands wrapped around Lord Camden's throat.

Jonathon tightened his hold, knowing that enough pressure would kill him. He would finally be done with this traitorous bastard, but Hannah might never forgive him. He loosened his grip as he pictured Hannah's disappointment.

No, he would honor his promise and would not kill Lord Camden... today, at least. He dropped his hands, stepped back, and watched as Lord Camden massaged his throat. "Get out," he ordered. Jonathon knew better than to turn his back on the enemy. He stood still, watching, breathing hard.

Lord Camden glared at him. He straightened slowly, warily. "I will enjoy watching you die."

There was no humor in Jonathon's laugh. "I feel the same way about you."

Lord Camden eyed him as he moved to the door, then he was gone. Jonathon righted the chair and looked up when Mr. Stanton and Lord Pembrooke appeared in the doorway. "How much did you hear?"

Mr. Stanton walked fully into the room. "Almost everything up until you two went to blows. What set you off?"

Shaking his head, Jonathon answered, "It does not matter. I wanted to hit him before he even walked in the room. He just gave me a good enough reason."

Mr. Stanton poured himself a drink, then announced, "That man was not my cousin."

Jonathon smiled sadly. He understood his reluctance to claim Lord Camden as family. "I would not claim him as a relation either."

"No, that man is *not* my cousin," Stanton repeated himself. "He is an imposter."

Jonathon shook his head. "That is impossible."

Mr. Stanton leaned against the wall facing Jonathon with a drink in his hand. "My parents died when I was eight. I went to live with my aunt and uncle in the town of Alnwick in Northumberland. Matthew and I were raised as brothers," he pointed at the door, "and that man was not Matthew!"

Frowning, Jonathon said, "I am not saying I do not believe you, but how could someone pose as an earl? That does not make sense."

"It does, and I know how," Lord Pembrooke's shaky voice interjected.

❧ 20 ❧

ASCENDING THE STAIRS, ELIZA PICKED UP THE SKIRT OF HER pink-floral, high-waisted gown. Mr. Larson informed her that Jonathon had requested her presence in the library. She pushed in a strand of hair that always seemed to escape her chignon, no matter how skillfully Martha pinned it.

Gliding down the hall, she stopped near the door. She heard voices she did not recognize filtering out of the room. Placing her hand in the slit of her dress, she fingered the hilt of her dagger and prepared herself for battle. Then she heard Jonathon's laugh, followed by Benedict's, a sure sign the strangers were friends, not foes.

Eliza squared her shoulders and walked in, keeping her hand inside the folds of her dress, but stopped short. Jonathon and Benedict were sitting in two chairs with their backs to the door. The two men, whom she did not recognize, arose and bowed as she entered. Benedict and Jonathon immediately followed suit, and Benedict walked swiftly to greet her.

He leaned close, whispering, "You are safe. You do not need your dagger."

Eliza frowned slightly and whispered back, "What is going

on? Who are these men, and why are they here?"

Jonathon joined them and she noticed his swollen eye. "What happened to you?" Eliza asked as she gingerly reached up and touched his eye, causing him to wince.

"Lord Camden and I had a heart-to-heart," Jonathon said, gently removing her hand. "But that is not why I am here." He turned to face the two men. "Lord Pembrooke and Mr. Stanton, I would like to introduce you to my sister, Lady Lansdowne."

Eliza politely curtsied, suppressing the fuming turmoil inside of her and plastered on a smile for her unexpected guests. "If you will excuse me gentlemen, I need to have a word with my brother." She quickly exited the room, with Benedict and Jonathon trailing her.

She spun around, preparing to voice her disapproval, but Jonathon had his hands up in front of him. "We discovered something big today. I would never have brought them to Beaumont Castle if they could not be trusted, and you need to hear them out."

Benedict placed his hand on the small of her back. "I do not know Mr. Stanton, but I can vouch for Lord Pembrooke. He was a remarkable field agent."

Eliza crossed her arms over her chest. "And what did you tell them about me?"

Jonathon rubbed the back of his neck with his hand. "Nothing, yet. I thought we could tell them you are fluent in several languages and interpret missives when requested, assuming it comes up."

"Does Uncle Charles know that they are here?"

Shaking his head, Jonathon replied, "No, but we need to act on this information fast."

Eliza pursed her lips together. "I do not like this, Jonathon. I do not have control of this situation, and it is unnerving."

Jonathon sighed. "Trust me. Please."

"Fine." Eliza dropped her arms. As she walked back into the

room, she assessed the gentlemen before her. Lord Pembrooke was an older, distinguished gentleman with a strong jaw and pleasant features. "Lord Pembrooke," she said with a polite smile.

As she turned to address Mr. Stanton, he stepped forward. "Eliza?" he asked in disbelief.

Eliza's smile faltered. "Have we met before?"

Mr. Stanton walked closer, watching her intently. "I was in the alley with Jonathon in Florence when you killed that man with your fancy dagger."

Eliza's smile grew genuine. "It is good to finally be properly introduced. Jonathon," she said, glancing over her shoulder at him, "refused to introduce me to you that night."

Benedict stepped up and placed his hand on her waist, pulling her close. Eliza's gaze took in Mr. Stanton's trimmed hair, clean-shaved face, and nicely tailored clothes. "Cleanliness looks good on you, Mr. Stanton."

His eyes roamed her face before saying, "And you look even more beautiful than I remember." Benedict cleared his throat loudly, but Mr. Stanton continued. "And you must call me Adrien."

Smiling, Eliza replied, "Then you must call me Eliza." Benedict's grip around her waist tightened, and she looked up at him affectionately. It appeared that her husband was jealous of Mr. Stanton, which was ridiculous, because Benedict was the most handsome man she had ever known.

Lord Pembrooke approached Eliza. "I understand that Hannah is staying here, and *Shadow* is protecting her."

Eliza could see the distress in Lord Pembrooke's eyes over the care of his daughter. "Only a handful of people are aware of Beaumont Castle's existence, and it is heavily guarded at all times. *Shadow* is coordinating the protection of Lady Hannah, so please do not worry for her safety."

Benedict escorted her to the sofa. After she was seated, the men sat, as well.

Jonathon looked at Eliza. "When Lord Camden came to attempt to retrieve Kate, he failed to notice his cousin, Mr. Stanton, who was standing in the same room. In fact, he showed no signs of recognition."

"The man claiming to be Lord Camden is an imposter," Adrien announced.

Eliza gasped. "Are you certain?"

"Yes, without a doubt," he confirmed.

Jonathon turned towards Lord Pembrooke. "Now, would you mind telling Eliza and Benedict what you told us earlier?"

Nodding, Lord Pembrooke said, "When I first started working as an agent, my mission was to infiltrate the French army, in hopes I could gain favor and become a double agent. I was assigned to the 57e Ligne, often referred to as *Le Terrible*, and witnessed horrible atrocities committed in the name of war. Years later, due to my skill with languages, I was trained for a special mission under the direction of Admiral Garnier. He seemed to believe that his plot could collapse the English government from within."

"How long were you there?" Eliza asked, curiously.

"Over ten years." Lord Pembrooke sighed before he continued. "About five years ago, I had a rendezvous with a man that had an uncanny resemblance to my brother, the Earl of Pembrooke. We met near the border of Scotland in a village called Rockcliffe. From the beginning, the man seemed to trust me, revealing specifics of the mission, boasting of our good fortune. The plan was for him to assume the role of Lord Pembrooke, my brother, who had not been seen in London for many years due to his wife's failing health. The ironic part was that my role was to impersonate myself, the long-lost brother, whom people assumed was dead, lost at sea."

"Did you tell your family that you were serving in the Navy?" Benedict asked.

Lord Pembrooke nodded. "It was safer that way, or at least I thought it was." He stood and walked to the window, peering out. "As the man laid out the plan, I thought I would have time to save my brother, his wife, his daughter, and my family, but..." His voice cracked with emotion.

"But, then the man said the family had already been dispatched. In fact, we were to leave in a few hours so he could lay down near the wreckage and assume his new identity."

Lord Pembrooke turned to face them. "They were planning to remove my brother's body and bury it along the trail. By killing off my entire family, no one would contest the imposter's new identity as Lord Pembrooke."

"Wouldn't the household staff recognize the imposter?" Jonathon asked.

Taking a moment to rein in his emotions, Lord Pembrooke shook his head. "A new country home near London was bought under Lord Pembrooke's name, and included a new household staff. That was where I was supposed to meet up with the imposter to assume my role as his brother."

Tears welled in Eliza's eyes for Lord Pembrooke as he returned to his chair. He continued, his voice tight and controlled. "At that point, rage overcame me and I killed everyone associated with the mission. I spared no one. By ending their lives, I had ended the scheme."

Lord Pembrooke glanced at Mr. Stanton. "At least, I thought I had." His eyes held unspeakable sadness. "I raced towards the location of the supposed carriage accident, but I was too late. The carriage had rolled over and they were all dead."

"But Hannah was not in the carriage. Why did you abandon her and go to Spain so soon after the accident?" Jonathon felt he had to ask.

Lord Pembrooke appeared to take no offence from the disapproval in Jonathon's tone. "I was worried that the French would try to kill me and Hannah, so I agreed to be an Ambassador to

Spain. I thought I could protect her if I held a prominent position and stayed away from her. I thought someone from the 57e Ligne might come looking for me."

"Did you learn what they intended to accomplish by impersonating an earl?" Benedict asked.

Lord Pembrooke shook his head. "No, we only received additional information after specific milestones were met. By killing the group, I severed ties with those who were giving further directions. If I had been thinking like an agent at the time, I would have been more careful, but I was overcome with grief." He put a hand across his face and closed his eyes.

A silence descended upon the room. Eliza tapped her finger on Benedict's hand. "Based upon what you just said, if Lord Camden is an imposter, then he was replaced right before the death of your brother, Lord Pembrooke. Kate married Camden almost five years ago. That must have been right after the imposter took the real Lord Camden's place."

She stood and walked over to the table. "This code is starting to make sense now." She picked up a paper and handed it to Adrien. "Do those names look familiar to you?"

Adrien perused the page. "Yes, these are my relations with their birth and death dates."

"And how did your aunt and uncle die?" Eliza inquired.

Adrien's eyes grew wide. "Their carriage ran into an abandoned cart in the middle of the road."

Giving her full attention to Adrien, Eliza said, "It appears that your death date is listed on that document, which means the imposter Lord Camden does not even realize that he has a living cousin."

"We need to find out everything about what Lord Camden has been doing these past few years. I know that he is a leader among the Whigs in the House of Lords. But what is his mission?" Jonathon shifted in his seat.

Benedict focused on Adrien and Lord Pembrooke. "Both of

your lives are at risk if Camden discovers your true identities. Lord Pembrooke can testify of the scheme and Mr. Stanton can identify the imposter."

Eliza gave Lord Pembrooke and Adrien a tentative smile. "I believe you would be safest if you remained at Beaumont Castle as our guests. Although, I should warn you that we have a light staff and have learned to make do on our own."

The sound of a pistol discharged in the distance. They all rushed to the window that overlooked the grounds in front of the castle. For a few moments, no one spoke as they all scanned the horizon. Then a lone rider emerged from the trees and raced towards the castle.

"Would Hannah be practicing her shooting right now?" Jonathon asked curiously.

Eliza shook her head. "No, last I saw her, she was sparring in the interior courtyard."

Lord Pembrooke's eyebrow raised nearly to his hairline. "Are you referring to my daughter? When did she learn to shoot and fence?"

Smiling, Eliza replied, "Hannah has a natural talent for fencing, and Jonathon taught her how to shoot a pistol."

Before anyone could respond, Mr. Larson swiftly entered the room, breathing heavily. "All is well. The perimeter was breached, but the threat has been eliminated."

Eliza walked closer to Mr. Larson. "What happened?"

Mr. Larson eyed the men in the room. "It would appear someone followed Lord Jonathon and his guests, but stayed behind the tree line. A rider on patrol saw him and approached. Unfortunately, the man attempted to retrieve his pistol and was killed instantly."

"Was there anyone else with the rider?" Benedict asked, moving to stand next to Eliza.

"No, the man was alone," Mr. Larson confirmed.

Eliza had known the day would come when someone tried to

approach Beaumont Castle. "Thank you, Mr. Larson." He nodded and bowed, turning to leave. "Before you go, Lord Pembrooke and Mr. Stanton will be staying as our guests until further notice."

Mr. Larson's jaw dropped but he recovered quickly. "As you wish, Lady Lansdowne."

As Eliza walked out of the room, Benedict picked up the books off the table and started placing them back on the shelves. Jonathon could not resist teasing him. "Have you considered hiring more help?"

Benedict chuckled. "I employ over two hundred people at Chatswich Manor, but good help is hard to find for a medieval castle in the woods."

Laughing, Jonathon retrieved some books to help Benedict with his trivial task. "I can only imagine."

Adrien leaned against one of the shelves near Jonathon. "Is Lady Lansdowne an agent?" Curiosity filled his voice.

"No," Jonathon and Benedict said in unison.

Crossing his arms over his chest, Adrien pressed his point, stubbornly. "Then what is her role within the agency?"

Benedict turned to address him. "That is none of your concern," he said firmly.

That seemed only to fuel Adrien's curiosity. "I know she can decipher codes, throw daggers, is well-read," he said, motioning to the books, "and apparently teaches ladies to fence."

Benedict clenched his jaw so tightly that a muscle ticked under his ear. "You will stay away from my wife," he said, stepping closer to Adrien.

Jonathon put his hand up to Benedict's chest, stopping him, before addressing Adrien. "I did not bring you here to speculate on Eliza's role within the agency. She has a talent for languages and Lord Beckett uses her on a case-by-case basis. That is all you need to know." His glare was hostile as he warned, "Do not make me regret my decision to bring you here."

Adrien tilted his head, appearing contrite. "I apologize. I just find Lady Lansdowne's situation to be quite extraordinary, and I'm not one to leave a puzzle unresolved."

"There is no puzzle," Benedict growled as he slammed the last book onto the table. Without glancing back, he stormed out of the room.

Jonathon lips curled into a disapproving frown. "You do realize Lord Lansdowne is a former agent and can discharge his pistol accurately up to twenty yards. I would not try to aggravate him, because he is extremely protective of his wife," he stated, looking pointedly at Adrien.

Adrien straightened his back and nodded. "I understand. I will stop speculating aloud."

"See that you do." Jonathon's tone was icy. He turned to see Lord Pembrooke staring out the window, his eyes drooped in sadness. "Lord Pembrooke, would you like me to take you to see your daughter?"

Lord Pembrooke turned to face him, the sadness transformed by his smile. "I would like that very much."

Walking down the stairs, the three men could hear the classic sounds of fencing echoing throughout the main hall. He led them to the interior courtyard until they could see Hannah, dressed in her men's clothing with protective padding, sparring with her partner.

As he watched, Jonathon was impressed that Hannah's skill had vastly improved in such little time. She was holding her own against her instructor. The sparring match was invigorating to watch, more like a competition than a lesson. Occasionally, the teacher would stop and provide instruction, then would ask Hannah to demonstrate.

Jonathon wanted to step in and spar with her, but stopped himself. He did not know how Lord Pembrooke would react if he took over the lesson. Glancing at Hannah's father, he saw nothing but pride radiating from him, and a sheen of moisture covering his eyes.

The instructor ended the lesson by saluting to Hannah, and she saluted him in return. She removed her wire mask and a footman collected her sword and padding. She turned, and her eyes lit up when she saw Jonathon. Then she glanced at Lord Pembrooke and her eyes widened further. "Papa!" she shouted, running into his arms.

"*Mi hermosa hija*," Lord Pembrooke murmured in her hair as he embraced her. "*Te amo.*"

After a few moments, Hannah leaned back to look at her father's face. "I cannot believe you are here. I have missed you."

Pulling her back into an embrace, her father whispered, "I have missed you dearly."

Jonathon heard Hannah say, "I love you, Papa."

Lord Pembrooke broke the embrace and placed his arm over her shoulder, keeping her tucked close to his side. "I cannot believe how much you look like your mother."

Hannah glanced at Jonathon, smiling so brilliantly that he was rendered speechless. Her eyes shone with gratitude and trust, and it reminded him of the look she gave him when he first rescued her. "Thank you for bringing my father to me."

Jonathon wanted to say, *To see you smile like that, I would bring you anything your heart desires*, but instead, he just nodded his response.

Noticing his swollen eye, Hannah furrowed her brow. "What happened to your eye, Lord Jonathon?"

Jonathon frowned in response to Hannah using his title, and hoped it was simply because her father was present. "Lord

Camden and I had a disagreement," he said with a slight shrug of his shoulder.

"Oh no," she said, her eyes growing wide, this time with fear.

Jonathon winked at her, attempting to reassure her that he was unharmed. "I took care of him the same way I took care of the man at the inn."

Hannah drew a relieved breath. "Good. I have no doubt he deserved it," she replied with a private smile that was reserved just for him. She turned back to her father and they walked into the castle, completely absorbed with each other.

"That was Lady Hannah?" Adrien asked.

Jonathon blinked a few times at the retreating figures of Hannah and her father. He'd forgotten about Adrien. His answer was short. "Yes."

"She is an exceptionally beautiful woman," he said.

Jonathon frowned. "She is mine," he growled.

Adrien's eyes twinkled with humor. "Does she know that you have claimed her?"

"I have not made my intentions known, but we have an unspoken understanding," Jonathon said calmly, hoping it was true.

Adrien shook his head, laughing under his breath. "Well, I would not wait too long to make your intentions clear, because I would never want to lose a woman like Lady Hannah."

Standing alone in the courtyard, Jonathon realized he wanted to do everything in his power to claim Hannah as his own, but did she want to be his wife? He had stared down some of the cruelest, vilest men in all of England and never flinched. But the thought of asking Hannah to marry him absolutely petrified him. The thought of losing Hannah caused his heart to be momentarily torn from the depths of his soul. No, he could not, would not, lose her!

21

HANNAH WENT TO HER ROOM TO DRESS FOR DINNER WITH A grateful heart. She had enjoyed walking around Eliza's gardens with her father. He seemed less guarded than she remembered. He eagerly listened as she shared what she had endured since the attempted abduction. She avoided talking about the time she spent alone with Jonathon, but praised him for coming to her rescue.

A smile touched her lips as she recalled those tender moments with him. She missed spending so much time alone with him and wondered if he felt the same. She loved his rugged exterior, which covered his tender, kind heart.

Nearing Kate's room, she noticed the door was ajar and she could hear Eliza's elegant voice. She peeked in. Kate, clad in her nightgown, was sitting up in the large four-poster bed, covered in white blankets. Eliza was throwing open the window drapes, letting in the last glorious rays of the sunset.

Eliza was obviously attempting to convince Kate to come down to dinner. "Please Kate, you must get dressed."

Kate smoothed the blankets with her hands. "My eye looks

even more wretched today and I have nothing to wear except the traveling dress that I wore last night."

Pushing the door open, Hannah offered, "You can borrow one of my dresses. I am taller than you, but Maggie should be able to sew up the hem so it will not drag on the ground."

Kate smiled gratefully, but it did not reach her eyes. "I am afraid my temperament is not fit for guests."

Hannah smiled her most encouraging smile. "Please come to dinner and we will cheer you up. Besides, you and Jonathon have matching swollen eyes," she jested.

Kate gasped. "What happened to Jonathon?"

"Jonathon had a heartfelt discussion with Matthew," Eliza informed her as she sat on the edge of the bed.

Kate's hand flew to her mouth. "Oh no, is he all right?"

"Matthew or Jonathon?" Eliza teased.

Kate stiffened. "I do not care about Matthew. I am concerned about Jonathon, since I have been on the other side of Matthew's blows."

Hannah felt her eyes prick with tears at Kate's admission. She did not know what to say, but managed to murmur, "You poor thing."

"I am so sorry," Eliza said, her voice wavering with emotion. "I should have helped you."

Shaking her head, Kate reassured her sister, "You would have helped me if you had known, but Matthew kept me locked away from my family. It was not your fault. I should have tried to flee as soon as I discovered I was with child, but I truly thought it would please him."

Hannah sat on a chair near the bed. "What did the doctor say?"

Kate tilted her head back to rest against the wall. "He confirmed I lost the baby, most likely from Matthew's beating." Tears welled up in her eyes and rolled down her face. "He took the only thing that was good in my life, as if he enjoys tormenting me."

Eliza patted her hand. "The doctor also made note of all the bruises and scars that prove Matthew was abusing you. Father and Benedict will support your petition for divorce."

"Can a woman even petition for divorce?" Hannah asked in surprise.

Eliza nodded. "Benedict's barrister informed us that Parliament will listen to Kate's case if she can prove adultery and an imminent, life-threatening situation. He truly believes attempted murder, coupled with a pattern of abuse, will prove cause for a divorce."

Kate huffed. "Proving Matthew's infidelity will be easy enough. He tried to force his intentions on every female employee at our country home. The poor women shrink from his presence, and I have helped more than one girl escape his clutches."

Hannah shook her head in disgust. "That is horrible. I cannot begin to imagine what you have had to endure."

Kate's face paled as she kept her gaze down. "Please do not insist that I go down for dinner. I really would prefer to be alone, hidden away to avoid the pitying looks."

Hannah leaned closer to the bed, rushing to explain. "Oh, I am so sorry. I meant no offense."

Kate's eyes flickered to hers and they looked tired, withdrawn. "You did not offend me, but I would really appreciate being alone tonight."

Hannah smiled faintly. "May I check on you tomorrow?"

"I would like that," she answered.

Eliza stood. "I will not pressure you anymore, but I insist you get dressed tomorrow," she said, her voice gentle but firm.

Kate slid down so her head was resting on her pillow. "Thank you for understanding."

"Would you like a tray sent up?" Eliza asked as she moved to close the drapes, cloaking the room in darkness once more.

"No, I prefer to sleep," Kate said, her voice resigned.

Eliza returned to the bed and placed her hand on her sister's cheek. "I love you, Kate. Tomorrow you must be strong, but for tonight, you can rest from your pain." She turned and walked out the door.

Hannah followed her, closing the door behind them. Eliza stood in the hall, wringing her hands, her eyes filled with worry. Hannah reached for Eliza's hands, stilling them with her own. "Kate will recover. You just need to give her time."

Eliza bit her lower lip and nodded. "I should dress for dinner."

Hannah withdrew her hands. "As should I. I will ask Maggie to alter one of my new dresses so Kate has something to wear tomorrow."

"I should go into town and order her a new wardrobe." Eliza sighed.

"All shall be well, you will see." Hannah knew she was trying to convince herself, as well.

Eliza smiled up at her. "I am truly grateful that you are my friend, Hannah."

Returning her smile, Hannah admitted, "I am glad, too. I do not have very many friends."

Eliza's eyes dimmed for a moment, but she blinked it away. "Nor do I."

Spontaneously, Hannah reached out and embraced Eliza. "We should hurry and dress for dinner. We do not want to keep the men waiting," she laughed softly, trying to lighten the mood.

HANNAH LOOKED INTO HER DRESSING ROOM MIRROR AND admired her new dinner dress. It was a sheer, pale purple, high-waisted dress, with white embroidery net overlay, short sleeves, and the skirt was slightly gathered along the front. Maggie had piled her hair high, placing small ringlets at her forehead and weaving small purple flowers through it, giving her a regal appearance.

She heard a quiet knock at her door and turned away from the mirror. She reached for her gloves and walked towards the door, assuming Eliza had come to escort her down to dinner. Throwing open the door, she came face-to-face with Jonathon.

His eyes widened as they roamed her hair and face, then lowered to her dress. "You look beautiful," he said in a low, awestruck voice.

Hannah felt herself blush as she, in turn, admired his tailored black jacket, which enhanced his muscular build. Her eyes took in his crisp white shirt with its stiffened collar, noticing that his white cravat was slightly askew. She reached up and straightened it, then boldly rested her hand on his chest. "Perfect," she said softly.

His gloved hand encompassed hers. "I snuck up to escort you down to dinner."

"I am so glad that you did, Jonathon."

He graced her with the crooked smile she so loved. "I see that I am back to Jonathon."

She smiled flirtatiously up at him. "I could not very well call you by your given name in front of my father, now could I?"

"No, I suppose not, but I do enjoy hearing my name on your lips."

"Jonathon," she said coyly. "Jonathon, Jonathon..."

Without warning, his lips pressed firmly against hers, cutting off her words. After a moment, he stepped back, but did not drop his hand from hers. "You do not know what you do to me," he said hoarsely. "It appears that I lose all rational thought when I am around you."

Hannah's heart swelled. "I am not complaining, Jonathon," she whispered.

His eyes darted to her lips again and she slowly licked them in anticipation of another kiss. He groaned. "I need to take you down to dinner before I pull you into a room and kiss the impertinence out of you."

As Jonathon took her hand from his chest and wrapped it around his arm, Hannah said, "I find your idea has merit." She met his gaze, thrilled that his eyes were molten with passion.

Clearing his throat, he led her down the hall. After a moment, Jonathon seemed to compose himself, because his next words were, "What am I going to do with you?"

Before she could think of a response, they had descended the stairs and were entering the drawing room. Hannah noticed her father, Eliza, Benedict, and another man engaged in conversation.

"Who is that man near my father?" she whispered.

Jonathon tapped her hand playfully. "Come, I will introduce you." As they approached the group, Mr. Stanton broke off to greet them. She felt Jonathan tense for some reason when he made the introductions. "Mr. Stanton, I would like to introduce you to Lady Hannah."

Mr. Stanton, dressed in a high-waisted, dark green waistcoat, tan trousers and a white shirt, coupled with a white cravat, bowed respectfully towards her. "Lady Hannah, it is an honor to meet you." He accepted her outstretched hand, bringing it to his lips. "Although, I am certain we will become dear friends soon enough."

Jonathon tightened his hold on her hand still draped in the crook of his arm. Glancing up at him, she saw his jaw clenched tightly.

Turning back to Mr. Stanton, she nodded politely. "I understand you helped my father journey back to England in safety. I commend you for your bravery and thank you for your service to our family."

Mr. Stanton puffed up at her praise. "Your father was more than capable of finding his way home, but it allowed me a chance to practice my Spanish."

Her father walked over and greeted her with a kiss on the cheek before saying, "Mr. Stanton is a fine young man. He risked his life to bring me those documents and kept an old man company on a fishing vessel for over a month."

Eliza and Benedict joined them. "Is that how you escaped from Spain, aboard a fishing vessel?" Eliza asked curiously.

Lord Pembrooke nodded his response. "Mr. Stanton was shot as he departed my townhouse in Spain, and we pulled him back in before he was shot again. We were unable to book passage on any ships, since we needed to depart immediately and did not want to leave a trail. Fortunately, my footman had a cousin who was the captain of a fishing boat that was departing the following morning. We snuck onboard in the dead of the night, hiding in the cargo hold until the ship was at sea."

Mr. Stanton interjected, "Since the captain was unable to alter his course for a few weeks, we helped the crew with various tasks."

Hannah's eyes lit up with amusement. "Did you catch any fish?"

Amused, her father replied, "No, I was assigned to the galley."

"You were?" Hannah asked, with wide eyes.

Lord Pembrooke's eyes twinkled as he leaned forward slightly. "I can peel potatoes faster than Mr. Stanton."

Mr. Stanton chuckled. "I did not know it was a competition or I would have peeled faster."

"Everything is a competition, my dear boy," her father said light-heartedly, throwing his hands up in the air.

Benedict extended his hand to Eliza. "And on that note, may I escort you in to dinner, my lady?"

Eliza laid her hand on his. "I would be honored."

Jonathon kept his grip on Hannah's hand and followed Eliza and Benedict. As they stepped into the dining room, Mr. Larson approached the group with a large file in one hand and a small note in the other. "Lord Beckett sent over a missive."

Jonathon dropped her hand and reached for the letter. He reviewed it, then informed the group, "Uncle plans to bring Mother in for questioning tomorrow. He believes there is sufficient evidence for an arrest. They will arrive at my townhouse at noon."

Jonathon met Eliza's gaze. "He wants both of us there when he questions her."

Eliza's face paled. "I do not know how I could benefit the conversation."

Benedict put his arm over her shoulder and pulled her close. "It is time to face her and show her who you truly are. You are not a scared little girl anymore. You can do this."

His words seemed to bolster Eliza's courage. "All right. We will face the devil herself tomorrow." With her lips twitching, she said, "But I am wearing my dagger."

Benedict chuckled. "Of course, you are, my dear. I would expect nothing less of you."

Mr. Larson handed the file, overflowing with pages, to Jonathon. "Lord Beckett sent word that this is everything his agents have compiled on Lord Camden and the duchess."

Jonathon glanced towards the dining table and sighed. "Well, I suppose we had better rush through dinner if we want to get through all of this information before tomorrow morning."

He looked at Hannah with regret. "It appears our evening will be cut short."

22

JONATHON SAT IN THE STUDY AS LORD PEMBROOKE, ADRIEN, Mr. Larson, Benedict, and Eliza all pored through the documents regarding Lord Camden and the duchess.

Eliza finished absorbing the last page of her pile and reached for another piece of paper. "We need to establish a timeline."

She focused on Adrien, sitting across from her on the opposite sofa. "Start at the beginning, if you will. Let's narrow down when an imposter could have come into play."

Adrien looked up from reading the paper in his hand. "I went to live at my uncle's estate in Northumberland, near the Scottish border, after my parents died from influenza. I was almost eight years old. My ten-year-old cousin Matthew was stricken, as well, but lived, although his heart was weakened. My Aunt Caroline feared for him and refused to send him to school with me. When I came home on holiday, Matthew and I were inseparable." Adrien's voice hitched, and he worked to compose himself. "He was like a brother to me."

Lord Pembrooke placed his hand on Adrien's shoulder. "I am sorry that you lost your family in this way."

Adrien's eyes were sad, almost mournful as he looked at

Lord Pembrooke. "I had not even considered that. Since we discovered that man is an imposter, I have not taken so much as a moment to mourn the loss of my family. I fear I have too much hate inside."

Lord Pembrooke nodded. "I understand the anger, but do not give in to it as I did. It only makes you regret the time you have wasted."

Eliza tapped the quill feather against her lip. "Lord and Lady Camden died in a carriage accident and the title was passed down to Matthew. A few weeks later, Lord Camden bought the country home he resides in, and retained the current household staff from the previous owner."

Jonathon pulled out a page from his current pile. "In this document, it states that Lord Camden fired all of the staff from Pratt Hall through a new solicitor. He did not provide any of them references, but did ensure they were all well paid."

Adrien jumped up, sending papers cascading to the floor. "He did not provide them references?" he shouted. "Those poor people." He turned to Jonathon. "What about at his London townhouse?"

Jonathon perused the page. "He fired them, too, without references. He did buy a new townhouse in Portman Square."

"You do realize that you are the rightful Earl of Camden? The title passes to you, since your cousin is dead," Benedict commented.

Adrien leaned down and picked up the pages off the floor. "I do, and when this is over, I will right the wrongs this imposter did to my uncle's staff."

Mr. Larson held up a page. "According to this report, Matthew was thrown from the carriage and sustained minor injuries. Maybe the accident altered his brain and made him change?"

Adrien sat down with the pages. "No, he is an imposter. I have no doubt."

Eliza sighed heavily after reading the pages, dropping them on the table. "There is nothing suspect about his business."

Benedict leaned forward in his seat. "I propose we assume that the imposter was working with a group that helped implement the carriage accident, switching the imposter for Lord Camden and burying the body near the wreckage."

Lord Pembrooke nodded. "No one would be looking for a dead body if no one was missing from the wreckage. We should inform Lord Beckett and ask him to send a team of agents to try to recover the body."

"The carriage accident was almost five years ago," Eliza reminded them.

Mr. Larson acknowledged her comment. "True, but they might have left a clue behind."

"Now that we agree when Lord Camden was replaced, we need to determine for what purpose?" Benedict asked the group.

Jonathon glanced up from the paper he was reading. "What if the imposter intended to infiltrate Parliament and attempt to sway their opinions about the war with France?" He leaned forward and laid his forearm on his knee. "Within a few months of the wreckage, Lord Camden resumed his father's seat in the House of Lords and sided with the Whigs. In fact, he has enough support to become the next Whig leader."

"The Tories are in power and are in favor of the war, but the Whigs' agenda is to stop funding an 'unbeatable war', as they refer to it. They truly believe that Napoléon is an unstoppable force," Benedict stated.

Adrien nodded. "Many of the poor are rallying against the war. With their men leaving to fight, the women and children are left without enough income and are starving. The Whigs are calling for reform."

Eliza shifted her gaze to Lord Pembrooke. "Do you think the imposter's goal is to become Prime Minister? Did you not say that the purpose of your French assignment was to destroy the English government from within?"

Lord Pembrooke shook his head slowly. "Although the imposter holds a prominent appointment within the Whig party, he doesn't have enough power or influence to destroy the government. The House of Lords and House of Commons both hold equal power, and could not be brought down by one imposter. Besides, the Whigs are not in power and will not be for many years to come."

"The French tried to substitute someone for your brother, but failed. What if the French succeeded with other substitutions and have their agents in play within the House of Lords and House of Commons?" Jonathon asked.

Benedict frowned, appearing deep in thought. "How would the French accomplish that?"

"They target the weak, lonely members of Parliament, the reclusive lords," Mr. Stanton said in disgust.

"The lords that have little family," Eliza jumped in.

"The lords that do not socialize within London," Jonathon said, "and are not well known amongst the ton."

"The French agents would target people that would not be missed," Adrien growled, "and are replaceable, like my family."

Mr. Larson organized the papers in his hand. "But there could not be that many lords in such prominent positions."

Standing, Jonathon walked towards the window. "We need to ask Uncle Charles to investigate how many lords, or heirs, have been involved in carriage accidents in the past six years."

Eliza turned in her seat to face Jonathon. "We know that the false Lord Camden has used his position in Parliament to pass along information to the French, and that he was involved in the assassination scheme against Prinny. How do we prove that?"

Jonathon crossed his arms as he looked out the window. "That is where Mr. Wade would have been useful."

"Who is this Mr. Wade you are alluding to?" Adrien questioned.

Jonathon uncrossed his arms and turned to face him, regretting his mention of Mr. Wade. "He was a merchant who bought and sold anything he could make a profit on, including women and English secrets. He would then sell his information to Lord Camden."

"Where is Mr. Wade now?" Lord Pembrooke asked as he sat on the edge of his seat.

"He's dead," Jonathon stated flatly.

Eliza's eyes revealed nothing as she redirected the conversation by saying, "We need solid proof that Lord Camden is an imposter and a French spy."

Adrien stood and poured himself a brandy. He slowly sipped his drink, then lowered the glass. "I could go to the magistrate and open an investigation. I could challenge his claim, forcing him to provide proof of his heritage."

Mr. Larson leaned forward in his seat. "It is your word against an earl. We need evidence, and not just your claim that Lord Camden is an imposter."

Lord Pembrooke wiped his mouth with his hand, looking solemn. "If we know that Lord Camden is an imposter and a French spy, may I propose we simply kill him?"

Eliza smiled brightly at Lord Pembrooke. "I like the way you think, Lord Pembrooke, especially since we know that we are dealing with a French spy and not a lord."

Adrien took another sip of his brandy. "I will do it."

Benedict stood up, and rubbed the back of his neck with his hand. "Killing Lord Camden will not solve the problem. We need to find out how many more French agents have replaced English citizens. Until we know that, we cannot arrest Lord Camden unless we have absolute proof of his guilt."

"I agree with Benedict. This scheme is bigger than just one imposter passing along English secrets," Jonathon said.

Lord Pembrooke shifted in his seat to face Jonathon. "I believe we should petition Lord Beckett to bring *Shadow* in on this assignment."

Benedict walked over and poured himself a drink. "No, that is not necessary. We have five agents," he paused to wink at Eliza, "and a consultant working the case."

Adrien lifted an eyebrow skeptically. "I was under the impression that *Shadow* is responsible for Lady Hannah's protection? At least, that is what Lord Beckett told us," he said, glancing over to Lord Pembrooke. "Where, pray tell, is *Shadow?*"

Jonathon growled. "You do not need to concern yourself with *Shadow's* whereabouts."

Adrien turned to face the group. "I am not a simpleton, Lord Jonathon. I know that *Shadow* is in the room, but I have not discovered who it is."

He pointed at Mr. Larson. "Is it the older, experienced agent?"

Then pointed at Benedict. "Or the young, retired agent turned respectable lord?"

Jonathon stepped closer to Mr. Stanton. "I brought you to Beaumont Castle to help you bring down an imposter that is pretending to be *your* cousin, assuming *your* title, but you dishonor me by insulting my family and my friend?"

Narrowing his eyes, Adrien refused to back down. "My intention was not to insult anyone, but I want to know the truth."

Jonathon glared. "Why do you believe you are entitled to the truth about *Shadow's* true identity?"

Benedict stepped up behind Jonathon and touched his arm. "It is all right, Jonathon. I would be curious if I were in his place, too." Addressing Adrien, he said, "However, *Shadow's* identity is only known to a select few," he paused, "and your assignment does not require this information."

In response, Adrien huffed his displeasure and sat down, brooding silently.

Eliza's voice drew Jonathon's attention. "I believe we have been diverted from our task."

Jonathon nodded and added, "We need to turn Mother against Lord Camden."

Eliza lifted an eyebrow in obvious disbelief. "How do you suggest we accomplish that feat?"

Jonathon's hand swept over the pages. "We have all this circumstantial evidence. I suggest we make it seem more substantial when we meet with her tomorrow."

Lord Pembrooke's brow rose in surprise. "Are you saying your mother, the Duchess of Remington, is a French spy?"

"Yes," Jonathon and Eliza said in unison.

"She is also a horrible mother," Benedict added as he claimed the seat next to his wife.

Laughing wryly, Eliza confirmed, "Yes, yes she is. The worst."

Mr. Larson brought his hand up to his chin. "What if you told her that you have located the real Lord Camden's body and you have proof that the current Lord Camden is an imposter?"

"That could work," Eliza said.

Jonathon raked a hand through his hair. "There is a chance that Mother does not know about this scheme."

Eliza scoffed softly, almost laughing. "Perhaps, but she is still guilty of reading Father's papers from Parliament and passing that information to Mr. Wade and the imposter. Besides, are we to believe it is a grand coincidence that the assassination attempt happened at her annual house party, where she assigned the guest's rooms?"

Sighing, Jonathon admitted reluctantly, "Good point. She really is a lousy mother." Without saying another word, he stood, poured himself a generous glass of brandy and emptied it. Placing his glass on the cart, he frowned. "We should get a few hours of sleep before we ride into town. Uncle Charles said that he was going to bring Mother over at noon."

Nodding, Benedict smiled and offered his wife a hand. "Come along, darling. Let us go to bed."

Smiling to himself, Jonathon watched as Benedict wrapped his arm around Eliza's waist. They strolled out the door, looking completely enamored with each other. He wanted that. He wanted that with Hannah. Now he just had to convince Hannah that he was the man for her.

23

"WHY DID WE HAVE TO TAKE THE CARRIAGE?" JONATHON complained as he stretched his neck from side to side, groaning as the carriage rocked back and forth. He tried to stretch out his legs but was hampered by Eliza and Benedict who were sitting opposite him.

"Diana would have a fit if I were to greet her in a riding habit." Eliza tucked her hand around Benedict's arm, smoothing out her dress with the other.

Benedict smiled down at her. "I think you look beautiful, my love."

Jonathon rested his hands on his legs and looked out the window. The carriage started to slow as they reached the busy streets of London. "This is not a social call, Eliza. I believe Uncle Charles will arrest Mother after this meeting. Heaven knows he has enough proof of her complicity."

Eliza's eyes were fixed on him with calculating curiosity. "How do you want to approach the interrogation?"

"I think we keep asking questions until we discover the truth," Jonathon replied. "And to be honest, I hope she reveals her deceit to us, because if they should question her at Newgate, it will be cruel and painful." He was very aware that other agents often relied on torture to get a suspect to confess, sometimes killing them prematurely.

Shuddering at his words, it appeared that Eliza followed his thinking. "Well, it cannot end well for Mother. She is spying for the French and helped in an assassination attempt against Prinny. Both actions are treasonous."

Benedict put his arm around Eliza's shoulder and pulled her close. "Are you prepared to face her?"

"I am," Eliza confirmed emphatically.

The carriage lurched to a stop in front of Jonathon's townhouse. The footman opened the door and assisted Eliza. Benedict and Jonathon hopped out to greet Mr. Wilde, who was already waiting for them at the main door.

"The Duke of Remington sent over a missive early this morning. It is on your desk, my lord," Mr. Wilde informed them.

Nodding his thanks, Jonathon started towards his study but spun back around. "Lord Beckett and my mother will be visiting soon. Please escort them into my study as soon as they arrive."

Mr. Wilde tilted his head in response. "As you wish, Lord Jonathon."

Knowing the delicacy of that conversation, Jonathon said, "After you direct them to my study, I want the entire household staff to take the rest of the day off, fully paid." If Mr. Wilde was shocked by his words, he did not show it. He just nodded his head in acknowledgement and excused himself.

Jonathon strode into his study and grabbed the missive off the pile of correspondence. As he read the note, Eliza and Benedict waited. He crumpled the paper. "Father is furious at Lord Camden for his treatment of Kate. He plans to arrive tonight with the intention of ruining Lord Camden."

Eliza took a step towards Jonathon. "We need to stop Father. If he comes into town and attacks the man he believes is Lord Camden, he might go into hiding. Worse yet, they might speed up their original plan. Until we know what the plan is, we cannot risk angering the imposter."

Benedict placed his hands on the back of a chair and leaned forward. "I assume the duke will support the divorce."

Jonathon smirked. "If the imposter lives long enough, Father might just take the law into his own hands."

"If I have my way, the man will have a noose around his neck, and Kate will not have to endure a public divorce," Eliza said.

"Although, being married to a condemned traitor might not be much better," Benedict reminded her.

Before either of them could respond, Mr. Wilde walked into the room with Jonathon's mother, Uncle Charles, and two lone agents trailing behind. "The Duchess of Remington and Lord Beckett to see you, my lords." He spun around and walked out, closing the door behind him.

The duchess was a beautiful woman who had aged gracefully. She had a slender face, high cheekbones, and petite frame. Her faded blonde hair was piled high atop her head with a small, jeweled crown. Her burgundy gown had a provocative neckline, complimented by a large, diamond necklace and a feathered reticule hanging from her wrist. She looked as if she were attending an important social gathering rather than an interrogation.

She sat gracefully on an upholstered armed chair, with her nose held high, displeasure in her expression. "Charles has been very vague about why I am here." She cast her brother-in-law a disapproving glance. "Now, will someone please explain why I have been forced to make this unnecessary house call."

Jonathon leaned back against his desk and crossed his arms. Before he could reply, his uncle interjected, "Lord Lansdowne, may I have a moment of your time?"

Benedict's gaze flickered to Eliza, concern evident on his brow, but he nodded. "You may, Lord Beckett."

Jonathon watched as all four agents departed to an adjoining side room, closing the door behind them. This side room was only accessible through his study, and was off-limits to the household staff. It had the added advantage that its occupants would be able to witness everything that was said in his study. He leveled his gaze back to his mother.

The duchess turned her cold, bitter gaze on Eliza. "Does *she* have to be present for this conversation?"

"Yes, she does," he said firmly, smiling supportively at Eliza. "We have heard some troubling news about you, Mother."

The duchess gasped, and her hand flew to her heart. "Oh my, what could you have heard?" Her obviously rehearsed reaction didn't affect Jonathon. He'd expected as much from her.

Eliza managed to keep her expression calm, but rolled her eyes as she moved to sit near Diana. "Unfortunately for you, we know everything."

Her response was venomous. "You know nothing, you ungrateful chit."

Jonathon stifled a smile. That was the mother he was familiar with.

Eliza's outside demeanor remained stoic, but her eyes were analyzing the woman before her. "We know that you have been reading Father's documents from Parliament and passed the information to Mr. Wade and Lord Camden. We want to know why."

With a practiced but insincere smile, the duchess feigned ignorance. "I do not know what you are talking about. I am afraid I am not acquainted with a Mr. Wade."

"No?" Eliza asked innocently, smoothing out her dress. "You should know that Mr. Wade informed me that you two had an..." she hesitated, then continued with an abashed tone, "...intimate relationship."

The duchess jumped up from her seat and advanced towards

Eliza. "How dare you? Are you implying that I have been unfaithful to William?"

"Yes, I am." Eliza dropped the embarrassed lady façade, not flinching at Diana's raised voice.

Stopping in front of Eliza, Diana's nose was flaring, and her chest was heaving. "You have no proof. Besides, William has been living with his strumpet for the past two decades. He has no right to condemn me."

"Father has not condemned you," Jonathon said, keeping his voice calm to lure his mother into a false sense of security. "Eliza was just pointing out that you have maintained an indelicate relationship with Mr. Wade."

Diana shrugged slightly. "I may have met Mr. Wade in passing, but I did not carry on a liaison with him."

"How were you introduced to him?" Eliza pressed.

The duchess set her lips into a tight line. "I do not recall how I met him, but he was kind to me." She gracefully returned to her seat, appearing unrepentant. "I find it is quite lonely at the abbey, and I need constant companionship."

"You were friends with a merchant?" Eliza asked. "I find that hard to believe."

"Oh, I did not know he was a merchant," Diana said with wide eyes. "He was such a kind gentleman that I did not realize he dabbled in trade."

"Mr. Wade did not dabble in trade, Mother. He abducted girls off the streets and sold them to brothels," Eliza said with raw emotion.

Gasping, Diana threw her hand up over her heart again. "That is horrible! I cannot believe Mr. Wade would be involved in something so heinous."

Eliza huffed incredulously. "He organized the entire operation. Not only did he sell girls, but he was also a traitor. He would discover certain secrets and pass them along to a French spy."

Diana shook her head condescendingly. "You have the wrong man, Elizabeth. You always did have such an active imagination. If only you had spent less time reading books, you would have found more time to pursue feminine activities, such as needle-work. Perhaps then you would not make such ludicrous accusations."

Eliza's hand slid down to her right thigh, where Jonathon knew she wore her dagger. "True, I did have an active imagination in my youth. It was far easier to pretend my mother was loving and kind than to admit she had a cold, blackened heart." The intensity in Eliza's eyes conveyed her sadness over her mother's rejection.

Diana's eyes burned with hate as they bore into Eliza. "You are a bastard, and will always be a bastard," she stated smugly.

Shrugging one shoulder, Eliza said, "If you are referring to the fact that Lady Anne is my real mother, I already knew."

Appearing unnerved, Diana hissed under her breath, "When did you find out?"

"Father told me two months ago."

"Have you informed Kate?" Diana asked, appearing anxious about the answer.

Eliza shook her head. "No, not yet."

"Do not tell her," Diana begged. "It would devastate her."

Jonathon uncrossed his arms and placed them on the desk behind him. "I would not concern yourself with Kate's welfare. After all, you forced her to marry Matthew."

The duchess looked at him with shock on her face. "I did no such thing. Matthew loves Kate and she loves him. They wanted to be married."

Eliza gasped loudly. "Now that is preposterous. Matthew has been abusing Kate for years."

"How dare you! Matthew has been nothing but kind to Kate. He worships her!" Diana snapped.

Frowning at his mother's words, Jonathon revealed, "Kate ran away from Matthew and is in hiding."

"Matthew warned me that Kate is prone to fits when she does not get her way..." his mother started.

Eliza spoke over her. "Matthew beat Kate until she lost the babe she was carrying. Kate has scars from years of beatings by her husband."

Diana's face paled. "No, Matthew loves Kate. He promised me he would take care of her," she said weakly.

"He lied," Jonathon confirmed. "Father is on his way to petition Parliament for a divorce based upon attempted murder and multiple accounts of adultery."

"No, no, no," his mother said over and over, shaking her head. "That cannot be."

"Why did you force Kate into a marriage with Matthew?" Eliza pressed.

Diana's eyes drifted towards the window before they snapped back to Eliza. "Matthew wanted to marry you, but I refused. After all, you are nothing special," she said, her voice spiteful. "You were not good enough to be the wife of an earl, so I offered Kate."

Eliza arched an eyebrow in response to Diana's words. "It is ironic that I married a marquess, is it not?"

"I have since suspected that you are with child," Diana said with a flip of her hand. "After all, what other reason could you have to be married with a special license?" she added with a sadistic smile. "It will not take long for Benedict to see through you and move on with a mistress, or two."

Jonathon heard movement in the adjoining room and knew Benedict was outraged by his mother's lewd suggestions. He raised his voice, attempting to hide the noise. "Benedict and Eliza have a love match. It is something I aspire to," he said honestly.

His mother turned slightly to look at him, her eyes clouded over. "I had a love match, but it was snatched away from me."

"Father tried to turn your arranged marriage into a love match, but you refused to try," Jonathon stated.

The duchess shook her head. "It was futile. We were both in love with someone else," she said dejectedly.

"So, you foisted Kate onto Matthew like your father did to you," Eliza pushed.

"It was nothing like what I did for Kate," Diana said, as she jumped up and started pacing. "My father followed me to Gretna Green and dragged me out of bed with my husband, where we had just…" Her eyes grew wide as she stopped pacing.

Straightening, Jonathon shouted in disbelief, "You were married before Father?"

His mother pursed her lips together. After a moment, she spoke, "Yes, I was married, but that did not matter to my father. He ordered me to dress, then escorted me to the carriage. I was threatened and told to never speak of my marriage. He then forced me to marry William."

"Who is Luke's father?" Eliza asked, her eyes betraying her concern.

"I had hoped that Luke was Phillipe's son, but the timing was off." The duchess let out a snort of satisfaction. "Luke and you," she pointed at Jonathon, "are William's children, but Kate is the only legitimate child."

"Phillipe is Kate's father," Eliza said deliberately. "Her father is French?"

Diana stuck up her haughty nose at Eliza as she gracefully lowered herself onto a chair. "Yes. What's more, my grand-mother on my mother's side was French. That is how I met Phillipe. You see, my aunt married a French nobleman and moved to France, but she would spend the summers with us." Her face relaxed at the memory. "Phillipe was her step-son. Gradually, we fell in love and eloped to Gretna Green."

"Did Phillipe follow you back to England?" Jonathon asked.

His mother shook her head. "No, I didn't see Phillipe again until after you were born. I had ordered William to move out of the abbey, since I could no longer tolerate his presence. Although, I cannot say the same for William, but I was faithful to him. Well, I was until he moved his mistress into his estate a few months later," she said bitterly.

"When did Phillipe come back to England?" Eliza pressed.

"Phillipe and I never stopped corresponding, but I didn't see him again until Jonathon turned six months old," Diana revealed. Turning to address Jonathon, she added, "Phillipe used to take you on walks after he moved into the abbey with us. He loved you as his own son."

"Lovely," Jonathon said dryly.

"Everything was blissful until I found out I was pregnant with Kate and had to confess to William," Diana informed them. "At first, William was livid and even threatened me with a divorce, but he approached me a few months later with news of Anne's pregnancy. We decided to compromise and passed you and Kate off as twins."

"How did Phillipe handle the news that Father would raise Kate?" Eliza inquired.

A flash of sorrow showed in Diana's eyes. "He was devastated by the news, and he was furious when William demanded Phillipe leave the abbey." Glancing away, she said sadly, "That was a part of the compromise. The only way to provide Kate with a future was for me to lose mine, again."

Noticing that his mother was softening, Jonathon used that to his advantage. "Is that why you wanted Kate to marry Matthew, because he was French?"

Taken by surprise, Diana's voice had a slight tremor as she replied, "You are mistaken. Matthew is English."

"No, Matthew is a French spy," Eliza chimed in. "We can prove that he is impersonating Lord Camden."

His mother stared at her hands in her lap for a long moment, her face unreadable. "That is absurd."

Jonathon grabbed a chair and placed it near his mother. "We found the real Lord Camden's body near the carriage accident." He hoped the lie would loosen her tongue. "Agents are on their way to arrest Matthew as we speak."

His mother reached for the arms on the chair, gripping them tightly. "But he was so meticulous..." She stopped speaking, her eyes guarded again. "I do not believe you."

Leaning forward in her seat, Eliza asked, "Why are you defending the man that almost killed Kate?"

"Matthew is a good man. He would never intentionally hurt Kate. She must have fallen down the stairs or tripped," Diana rationalized.

Jonathon decided to try a different tactic. "Kate saw you and Matthew in an intimate embrace. Were you aware of that?"

Wincing slightly, Diana muttered, "No, I was not."

"What kind of mother would sleep with her own son-in-law?" Eliza asked in disgust.

The duchess drummed her fingers on the arms of the chair, refusing to make eye contact. "Matthew was persuasive," she said slowly.

"Persuasive?" Eliza said with an arched eyebrow.

For a moment, Diana had the decency to look ashamed, but then her face hardened. "I do not need to explain myself to you," she snapped at Eliza.

One corner of Eliza's mouth turned up, just a little. "True, but you do realize that Father will parade you in front of Parliament during Kate's divorce trial, testifying that you had an affair with Matthew, your own son-in-law."

Diana slowly smoothed out her dress. "It matters not to me," she said.

With a widening smile, Eliza informed her, "Father will have proof of your infidelity and Parliament will grant him a divorce, too. You will lose everything."

Diana's back stiffened as her eyes raged at Eliza. "William has been living with his mistress for over twenty years. He would not dare petition for a divorce."

"Are you certain?" Eliza asked with a raised eyebrow.

"If he did, then I would reveal that I had been married before. Luke and Jonathon would be labeled bastards and inherit nothing," the duchess said triumphantly.

"Hell hath no fury like a woman scorned," Eliza replied sarcastically. "I assume you have proof of your first marriage?"

Narrowing her eyes, Diana countered, "Then I would testify in front of Parliament that you are the bastard child of Lady Anne. You would be ruined."

Brushing off her allegation, Eliza said, "You have no proof. The word of a scorned traitor means very little in polite society."

If looks could kill, Diana would have slaughtered Eliza with her cold, venomous stare. "You are an impertinent one for being a bastard. I tried to care for you when you lived at the abbey, but I soon discovered you were intolerable, much like your father. You have always been too odd for my taste."

For a moment, Eliza returned her mother's stare, keeping her emotions firmly tucked away.

The intensity of her eyes told Jonathon that his sister was now preparing for battle.

"Were you aware that Father asked Uncle Charles to have you followed after he suspected you were reading his notes from Parliament?" Eliza asked directly.

Diana's eyes grew slightly, but otherwise she stayed completely still. "I did nothing wrong. Sometimes I visited William's estates and I may have inadvertently disturbed his papers. No harm done."

"No harm done?" Eliza repeated. "Unfortunately, Uncle

Charles has a different opinion and plans to arrest you after this meeting. He is confident that with the right testimony, you will be convicted as a traitor." Smiling victoriously, she added, "Traitors have historically been drawn and quartered in front of the public."

Jonathon stifled a laugh since he knew Prinny would never draw and quarter a duchess, even a traitorous one. "We can help you, Mother," he said calmly, leaning forward in his chair. "If you confess, Uncle can have your sentence commuted."

The color drained from Diana's face. "I am no traitor. I just passed along information."

"That alone makes you a traitor. But that's not all. You also helped Matthew try to assassinate Prinny at your own annual ball," Eliza pointed out.

His mother shook her head. "Oh, no. That was not my idea. Matthew hired those German assassins. Did you know they killed one of my scullery maids?" Frowning, she added, "That was in poor taste."

"Killing a scullery maid was in poor taste?" Eliza asked, incredulous.

Wearing a perplexed look on her face, the duchess replied, "Of course it was. I had a house full of guests and I was down a scullery maid. They could have waited until after the house party to kill her."

Eliza arose from her seat, shaking her head. "You sicken me. You do not deserve mercy. You've done nothing in your life that could begin to atone for the pain you've caused. We have enough proof to see you executed in a most deserving way." She started to walk towards the side door.

"Wait, Eliza. Do not retrieve Uncle just yet. We should give Mother time to confess." Jonathon ran his hand through his hair, hoping he appeared frantic. "Mother, you need to confess now."

Spinning around, Eliza shouted, "She has never been a mother to me. Why should I help her now?"

Ignoring Eliza, Diana pleaded with Jonathon, her eyes filled with panic. "I know who you truly are, and you can help. You must inform Charles that I was forced to steal your father's notes. Mr. Wade and Matthew threatened to kill me and Kate if I did not provide them with information."

Jonathon's heart fell. He knew his mother was being dishonest with him. "I do not know who you think I am, but I know enough. You are lying to me and I will not tolerate that." He stood up, but was stopped by his mother's hand on his sleeve.

"Wait, please." Her voice was shaky. "Matthew suggested I could read William's documents from Parliament and I would just pass along the information to Aaron. William was a leader in the Tory party and Matthew wanted to know inside information. That is all."

Advancing towards Diana, Eliza pressed, "You also read Father's personal correspondence and reported that information to Matthew, as well, did you not?"

Diana shrugged one shoulder weakly, tilting her head towards Jonathon. "The only letters that Aaron and Matthew wanted to hear about were the letters from Charles to William. For some reason, Mr. Wade was extremely interested in your diplomatic assignments in other countries. He was furious about your meetings with Monsieur LeBlanc and ranted about you and Eliza ruining his business."

"What else, Mother?" Jonathon asked.

The duchess put her hand to her temple. "That is how Matthew and I determined that you were *Shadow*." She looked up, her eyes boring into Jonathon. "He will kill you."

"I can take care of myself. Do not fear for me," Jonathon reassured her.

"How many more French spies have taken over people's lives?" Eliza demanded.

"I do not know…"

Swiping her hand in front of her, Eliza shouted, "Enough lies! How many?"

Diana's eyes grew wide with fear as she shrunk back into her chair. "I do not know, but Matthew has a list. It is," she said, her voice hitching, "it is a complete list of all the French agents."

"Where is the list?" Jonathon demanded.

His mother's eyes filled with tears, something he had never witnessed before. "I do not know," she said weakly, looking down at her lap. "He did not trust me with that information, but I do know that both houses of Parliament have agents in place, and one is a member of Prinny's inner circle."

Placing a hand on her hip, Eliza asked, "Why did you betray your country; your fellowman?"

Diana's eyes whipped up to glare at Eliza. "I did not betray my country. I am French."

"You are English," Eliza replied with a furrowed brow.

"No, I am part French and I side with their cause," Diana confessed. "Phillipe helped me to see the suffering at the hands of our monarchy. It is revolting."

"Yes, I see that you care about the plight of the poor man," Eliza said with contempt as her eyes glanced at Diana's diamond necklace. "Where is Phillipe now?"

The duchess arose from her seat, walked to the drink cart, and poured herself a glass of brandy. She gulped it down, then poured herself another before she turned back around. "Phillipe was killed in battle, two years ago. He was a true patriot." She lifted her chin. "Phillipe approached me about Michel marrying Kate after he assumed Lord Camden's identity. By marrying a daughter of the Duke of Remington, it provided him with immediate power and respectability." Scoffing at Eliza, she added, "At first, Michel was charmed by your face, but he saw that was all you offered. He needed a true lady by his side."

Undeterred by Diana's hateful comments, Eliza folded her arms over her chest. "Michel is Matthew's true name?"

Nodding, she confirmed, "Michel Leroy." She gulped her drink down before turning to place her glass on the tray. Keeping her back to them, she fumbled with her reticule, then spun back with a small pistol pointed at Eliza. "I am not going to trial. I have done nothing wrong," she declared.

Slowly uncrossing her arms, Eliza responded, "You are a traitor."

Diana shook her head quickly, causing her hair to escape from its pins, cascading down her face and back. "No, you do not understand. This is a war that England cannot win. Napoléon will ride triumphantly into London and the plan will be executed flawlessly."

Eliza's gaze flickered toward Jonathon before saying, "Napoléon will not win the war. You have been deceived." She put her hands slowly up in front of her. "We can ask Uncle to give you mercy."

"No, I will not go to Newgate!" Diana shouted as the pistol shook in her hand. "No, I am going to leave, and no one had better follow me."

Taking a step towards his mother, Jonathon tried to reason with her. "There is nowhere for you to go. It is over, Mother." He put his hand out, palm up. "Now, please give me the pistol before you get hurt."

"I am the one with the pistol," Diana said, amused.

Jonathon glanced over at Eliza and saw her hand sliding between the folds in her dress. He knew that her hand was gripping the hilt of her dagger and it was only a matter of time until she dispatched it. However, he did not know if Eliza intended to kill or simply wound his mother.

"Mother, look at me," he said, his tone pleading. "It does not have to end this way."

His mother's eyes crinkled, and her face looked resigned. "I did not know that Michel was abusing Kate. She was supposed to be his wife, his partner. He was supposed to be grooming her," she said in a shrill voice, slowly side-stepping towards the door.

"Grooming her for what?" Jonathon asked.

Diana's free hand reached out for the door handle, without taking her eyes off them. "It matters not. I have every intention of visiting Michel and making him pay."

A loud bang came from the side room, and Diana's eyes flew to the door. Before he could react, Eliza had flung her dagger, embedding it into his mother's right shoulder. Diana screamed as she dropped the pistol. Her hand grasped the dagger's hilt as she collapsed into a heap on the floor, her eyes rolling into the back of her head.

Jonathon crouched down to check his mother's pulse. He pulled the dagger out and pressed his handkerchief over the wound to stop the flow of blood. "She must have fainted."

The door to the adjoining room opened and Benedict and his uncle came storming in, followed by the other agents. Seeing the duchess on the floor, blood soaking into her dress, Uncle Charles crouched down on the other side of her and grimaced. "There will be no trial," he said solemnly. "Your mother will never wake up."

Jonathon wanted to protest, but he knew it was in vain. His mother was a traitor, and not even her title could protect her. Uncle Charles would not risk a public trial, alerting the other perpetrators in the scheme. Besides, with the testimony of the agents who trailed her, Uncle Charles, and the Duke of Remington, her fate was already sealed.

Jonathon removed his hands from the handkerchief covering his mother's wound, knowing he could do no more for her. "I understand." He turned to face his uncle. "I assume you were able to hear everything?"

"Every word," Uncle Charles said as he laid his hand on Jonathon's shoulder. "You might want to leave the room while I let the other agents finish the job."

Eliza crouched down next to him, placing her hand on his back. "It is better this way. Mother will feel no pain, since she is already unconscious."

Uncle Charles signaled the agents to come closer as Jonathon, Eliza, and Benedict quietly left the room, intermittently glancing at Diana's body.

Benedict closed the door and placed his hand on Jonathon's shoulder. "I am sorry it had to end this way."

"So am I," Jonathon said, resigned.

Approaching from his other side, Eliza placed her hand on his arm. "I'm sorry. I truly am."

Jonathon glanced at her curiously. "Will you not mourn her at all?"

Shaking her head, Eliza admitted, "No, I do not believe I will. She was cruel and never showed any true affection towards me. I actually feel relieved that she cannot hurt anyone anymore, especially Kate."

Jonathon felt tears well up in his eyes. "Excuse me, but I need a moment to compose myself." He quickly strode up the stairs to his bedchamber. He sank onto his bed and wept. He wept for the loss of his mother. He wept for the years of torment his mother had inflicted on others. Lastly, he wept for himself, knowing he, too, felt relief that his mother was through hurting anyone.

After some time, he stood and wiped his tears away. Mother may be gone, but she was only a small piece of this puzzle. Now he had to get Matthew, or Michel, or whatever the hell his name was, to confess.

24

EXITING THE CARRIAGE, JONATHON SAW MOVEMENT IN ONE OF the upstairs windows of Beaumont Castle, and he was pleased to see Hannah smiling in his direction. Raising his hand in greeting, he saw her swivel around, vanishing from sight.

Jonathon's heart constricted when she disappeared, and he hoped she was coming to greet him. The carriage ride back from his townhouse had been long and quiet. Neither Eliza nor Benedict spoke much. He longed to see Hannah, to hold her. Only she could give him the comfort he needed. How quickly she had become such an essential part of his life. He never wanted to let her go. However, would she be able to handle his secrets, or would his burdens scare her away?

As Jonathon walked into the entry hall, he saw Hannah quickly gliding down the stairs. He knew his mother would have criticized her for such unladylike speed, but he found it delightful and refreshing.

She greeted him with a bright smile. "Jonathon, you are back."

"I am," he managed to say, despite the intense emotions he felt.

Hannah stopped in front of him, maintaining proper distance, but he found it was not close enough and reached for her hands. Her eyes roamed his face, and a frown touched her lips. She whispered, "I presume that it did not go well?"

Jonathon's attempt to smile failed miserably and she stepped closer. Her face held compassion and empathy.

"No," he said with a slight shake of his head.

"What happened?"

He gripped her hands tighter. "My mother is dead."

Hannah gasped, dropped his hands, and pulled him into an embrace. "I am sorry."

Jonathon's arms surrounded her, hugging her tightly to him, and he placed his cheek on the top of her head. "It was inevitable," he said, closing his eyes.

"Would you like to talk about what happened?" she asked, concern filling her voice.

He frowned, then stated honestly, "I'd rather not." If he told Hannah what happened to his mother, she would hate him. Even though she was a French spy, he still stood by and did nothing as she was killed. It wouldn't matter that it was a more merciful death than hanging. No, Hannah would not understand. How could she?

Hannah stepped out of his arms and reached for his hand, leading him out the entry door. They did not speak as they walked solemnly down to the stream, hand in hand. Arriving at the bench by the stream, he waited for her to sit, then sank down next to her.

She tenderly encompassed his hands and raised them to her lips, pressing a long, lingering kiss on his knuckles. His breath hitched at the compassion, and what he hoped was love, glistening in her eyes.

As she lowered their hands to her lap, she said, "You do not have to say a word, but if you choose to do so, I am ready and willing to help bear your burdens."

Jonathon started to rise, but she kept a firm grip on his hands. He slowly turned his head to gaze at her. "I am not a good person, Hannah. I have done horrible things in the name of my country. You are kind and have no guile. I cannot share my burdens with you, because I do not want to be responsible for corrupting you in any way."

Hannah's eyes slowly roamed his face, her expression revealing nothing. He dreaded every moment that she did not speak because he felt her slipping away from him. As he started to turn his head to avoid her gaze, she placed her hand up and cupped his cheek. The depth of emotion in her words was his undoing. "I find you to be one of the most honorable men I have ever encountered."

"I fear that you have been misled," he tried to quip, but sadness laced his voice.

The corner of Hannah's eyes crinkled slightly as she smiled at him with sincerity and warmth. "No, I fear you have misled yourself. You may believe those horrible things about yourself, but I do not." Her thumb slowly caressed his jawline. "I want to know everything about you, the good and the bad."

He looked away, wary of her encouraging words. "When you hear what I've done, you will grow to hate me, or worse, fear me, and I could not bear that from you."

Hannah's gaze covered his entire face, as if memorizing every detail. After a few moments, her eyes locked with his. "There is nothing you could say that would change the way I feel about you." Leaning in, she pressed her soft lips to his.

As he kissed her, his resolve began to crumble. If he truly wanted her in his life, perhaps he needed to trust her. But what if she grew to hate him? What if she wanted nothing more to do with him?

Leaning back, Hannah's soft voice interrupted his fearful speculations. "Please, trust me."

He heard a hint of a plea in her request, compelling his eyes to find her.

In that moment, Jonathon knew he must tell her everything. Well, almost everything. He could not reveal that Eliza was *Shadow*, because that was his sister's secret.

When he began, he did not start at the meeting with his mother today, but with his childhood at the abbey. He shared how his uncle recruited him as an agent, which eventually led into the story of Mr. Wade who had abducted women and sold them to brothels. He shared details about the last time he met with Lord Camden, and he ended with today's events. He revealed how agents killed his mother to prevent her from suffering a traitor's death. He told Hannah... almost everything.

Hannah never interrupted him, her eyes unreadable as he bared his soul to her. When he was done, he expected to see judgement. Instead, Jonathon saw anger marring her beautiful face. Her cheeks were enflamed, and she looked truly furious. He had anticipated disgust, but not anger. He looked away, wondering what she could be thinking.

Placing a hand on his cheek, Hannah guided his face back to hers. The signs of anger were gone, and her eyes glimmered with unshed tears. "I cannot begin to imagine what you have endured..."

Jonathon interrupted her, his voice gruff. "Trust me, my mother's death was merciful."

Huffing, Hannah shook her head, her lips pressed together in a tight, disapproving line. "I believe her death was too kind for the likes of her. What I wanted to say is that I cannot begin to imagine what you have suffered at the hands of your mother."

Her eyes blazing with fury, she added, "A mother should be kind, loyal, and willing to give her life to save her child. Your mother was mean, cruel, and a French spy. She betrayed her country and her family. I am glad I never met her because if I had, I would have given her a piece of my mind!"

Jonathon raised an eyebrow at her tone, which became more incensed with each point, and her hands which were fisted into balls. It was comforting to realize she cared so deeply for him.

Smiling at Hannah, his protector, he watched as her chest heaved in indignation. He touched the tip of her nose playfully. "I like the thought of you as my protector," he teased.

Hannah's breathing slowed as she granted him a smile, a true, genuine smile that lit up her face. "We can protect each other," she said, leaving no doubt that she meant it.

"Do you hate me, Hannah?" He feared her response, but felt compelled to ask.

Hannah tilted her head. "No, I could never hate you."

"Do you forgive me then?" There was apprehension in his voice, revealing a new, more vulnerable side of himself.

"For what?" She looked genuinely confused. Then realization dawned, and she tenderly drew him close. "My dear, sweet Jonathon," she cooed. "You have done nothing wrong except defend your country and your family. You are exactly what I have always thought you were, a hero."

Jonathon pulled her closer, inhaling her scent of lavender and vanilla. How was he so incredibly lucky to have Hannah in his life? He never wanted to let her go. Would she be receptive to an offer of marriage right now? The honorable thing would be to wait until Lord Camden, or Michel, was in custody, but he did not want to wait any longer.

Releasing her from the embrace, he sought out her hands, engulfing them. He needed to proceed cautiously, hoping that her feelings ran as deep as his. "Hannah," he began slowly, "I may not have been completely honest about my feelings for you."

Hannah's eyes grew guarded, her smile slipping. "Oh?"

He didn't understand her change in demeanor, but forged ahead anyway. "I told you that I have grown to care for you, but in reality…"

"Lord Jonathon," Mr. Larson bellowed from behind him. "Your father has arrived at Beaumont Castle and has requested your immediate presence in the drawing room."

He turned his body towards Mr. Larson. "We will be up in a minute. I have something I need to say to Lady Hannah."

Mr. Larson tilted his head in acknowledgement and retreated a few paces to grant them privacy.

Jonathon turned back and was shocked to see Hannah had moisture in her eyes. Was she upset? Was she happy? He decided to be direct. "What is wrong, Hannah?"

She blinked a few times and he felt her withdrawing from him. "Nothing of importance. We'd better not keep the Duke of Remington waiting." Hannah rose quickly, dropping his hand. Without glancing back, she walked towards Mr. Larson and accepted his extended arm.

Jonathon raked his hand through his hair. What happened? He had never proposed to someone before, but he had not expected a reaction like that. True, he hadn't asked for her hand yet, but he'd been leading up to it.

What should he do now? Would she still welcome a suit from him? Jonathon growled to himself. *Blazes, now I have to ask Benedict for help. Heaven help me!*

Blinking back the tears, Hannah realized what a fool she had been! She had fallen in love with Jonathon, but he did not feel the same. He must have felt sorry for her, knowing that she had feelings for him. He was trying so hard to be kind, always the gentleman.

Mr. Larson raised an eyebrow in question, but did not ask her directly what was wrong. *He's a gentleman, too*, she thought. In response, she smiled tentatively to reassure him that she was all right. He gently patted her hand, conveying his silent support.

Hannah heard Jonathon behind them, but she did not want to look back. He would see the turmoil in her face and know she was upset. He would attempt to make her laugh, but her heart was broken. Jonathon did not love her, nor would he ever.

Mr. Larson escorted her to the drawing room where everyone was assembled. The Duke of Remington and her father were standing huddled next to Eliza and Benedict. The duke was not at all what she had expected. He was tall, distinguished-looking, and obviously a man of rank and power. Yet, there was a sense of warmth about him.

"Father," Jonathon said as he came from behind her, placing a hand on the small of her back. The duke turned to face his son with a smile on his lips. "May I present Lady Hannah, our honored guest." He tilted his head slightly and boldly winked at her.

Lowering her gaze, Hannah's cheeks burned with embarrassment. What was he doing? Everyone must have seen him winking at her. After a moment, she glanced up and noticed the duke was smiling fondly, yet glancing between Jonathon and her with a question in his eyes.

The duke bowed. "Lady Hannah, it is a pleasure to meet you."

"The pleasure is mine, your grace," Hannah replied, dropping into a curtsey.

Shaking his head, Jonathon's father said, "We do not have time for formalities here. Please call me William."

Hannah's eyes widened, knowing she could never call a duke by his first name, but she politely nodded. "Then you must call me Hannah."

Smiling in approval, the duke's eyes crinkled with kindness. "I have heard much about you, Hannah. I am pleased that you and your father are safe and protected here. It's reassuring to know you are out of Lord Camden's reach."

Hannah felt herself relaxing. "Lord and Lady Lansdowne and Lord Jonathon have made me feel most welcome."

Jonathon arched his eyebrow. "I am back to Lord Jonathon?" he asked, bewildered.

"And I better never hear you call me Lady Lansdowne in private again," Eliza censured her. "We are friends, are we not?"

Feeling rebuked, Hannah replied, "I apologize. I did not wish to offend by being too informal."

Benedict raised his drink in her direction. "You are practically family, and family does not make use of titles."

"I am sorry, again," she said with a smile. "I will never call you by your title again, unless we are in public or I am truly vexed by you."

Jonathon smiled his approval of her response, as he offered her his arm. She accepted it, savoring being so close to him. As he began escorting her further into the room, Lord Pembrooke spoke up, "William, now that you have met my daughter, I pray that she may be excused to avoid what we are about to discuss."

"That will not be necessary," Jonathon stated. "I have told Hannah everything and have no desire to keep any more secrets from her."

Her father pursed his lips, wisely avoiding an argument.

Escorting Hannah to the settee, Jonathon claimed the seat next to her, as Benedict sat next to Eliza. Her father, the duke, Adrien, and Mr. Larson moved chairs to create an uneven circle.

The duke's gaze shifted from Jonathon to Eliza. "How was the meeting with your mother?"

As her eyes flickered towards her brother, Eliza replied solemnly, "Diana is dead."

Shock lined the duke's face. "Start from the beginning," he commanded.

Hannah sat back and listened as Eliza and Jonathon took turns sharing the events of the past few weeks. When Eliza mentioned that Hannah's throat had been cut, the duke winced and looked at Jonathon with deep sadness.

Jonathon watched Hannah as they spoke, his concern for her evident on his face. She wanted to wipe his brow and tell him she appreciated his concern, but she couldn't do that now. He had made it abundantly clear that he cared for her only as a friend, and she needed to accept that. She would have to learn to live without him.

When everything was out in the open, no one spoke, and all eyes were on the duke. He was silent, looking at the floor for a long moment. When he spoke, his voice was gruff with emotion. "Given the circumstances, I am glad that Diana did not suffer long." Turning to Eliza, his voice wavered as he asked, "Where is Kate?"

Eliza's eyes filled with worry. "She is up in her bedchamber and is very melancholy. It appears that losing her baby was too much for her."

The duke started to rise, then hesitated. "Do you think she would receive me later?"

"I believe she would." Eliza smiled her approval.

"Does Kate know?" the duke asked, his words hanging.

Jonathon shook his head. "No, we have not told her anything."

"Good, good," the duke mumbled. "Let us not tell her while she is in such a delicate state. Perhaps we should not tell her at all." Glancing up at the ceiling, he sighed deeply. "My intention was to ruin Matthew and petition for a divorce in behalf of Kate, but Charles tells me I am being too hasty."

"I agree with Uncle Charles," Eliza said. "He is planning to arrest Matthew…"

"Can we please just call him Michel now?" Adrien growled, cutting her off.

Eliza acknowledged Adrien's comment. "Uncle is planning to arrest Michel and secretly lock him up in Newgate."

"Is there enough evidence to bring Michel to trial?" her father asked, leaning forward.

Jonathon stifled a laugh. "Once arrested, Michel will never see the light of day again. He had documents in his possession that prove his guilt, a confession from a duchess, and agents who will testify of his deceit. In addition, we have you," he said, pointing at Adrien, "who can cast doubt on his identity."

"Is there any word about my cousin's body?" Adrien asked hopefully.

Mr. Larson shook his head apologetically. "No. The agents are still scouring the area, though."

"Regardless, we now know that Michel has a list detailing all French agents on English soil, and that has become our new focus," Eliza stated. "Michel has served his purpose and Uncle Charles will ensure his cooperation once he is in Newgate."

Adrien spoke up, his voice bitter. "Do you think Lord Beckett would permit me to *help* ensure Michel's cooperation?"

Benedict leaned forward in his seat, assessing Adrien. "Do not let your hatred of Michel cloud your judgement, or you are of no use to us right now."

Hannah watched as Adrien tensed, but he seemed to consider Benedict's wise counsel. She turned to Jonathon and caught him staring at her. He quickly looked away. Turning her head, she saw her father had his arms crossed tightly in front of him, a deep frown on his face, and he appeared to be glowering at Jonathon.

The duke's voice broke through her thoughts, "...we just wait then."

Leaning closer to Jonathon, Hannah whispered, "I am sorry. I was woolgathering. What did I miss?"

Jonathon stifled a chuckle, and whispered back, "You were woolgathering when we were discussing a notorious French spy?"

"Do not laugh at me," she said, playfully nudging his shoulder. "What did I miss?"

Jonathon's smile grew on his face. "If a French spy does not interest you, I do not know what will."

Hannah loved when Jonathon teased her. It made her heart full. "If we were discussing two French spies then I would have been fascinated."

"Oh, I see. We need to find more enemy spies for you," Jonathon teased.

Hannah noticed that his normally groomed hair was tousled, as though he'd been running his hand through it. She desperately wanted to reach up and run her own hand through his soft, brown hair. She clenched her hands in her lap, trying to control the urge. "I believe we are in a room full of spies."

Someone loudly cleared their throat and she sat back, suddenly self-conscious. Apparently, their bantering had been louder than she thought. Or were they sitting too close together? Her cheeks burned with embarrassment. As she looked around the group, she saw that they were all focused on her and Jonathon. Everyone had encouraging smiles on their faces, except for her father. He seemed to be more vexed than before.

Risking a glance at Jonathon, she saw him give her a conspiratorial wink. Her heart warmed at the look in his green eyes, but then she dropped her gaze. She did not understand him at all. One moment, Jonathon was teasing her and showering her with affection, then he would make a comment that would cause her to believe he had no feelings for her.

Lifting her gaze, she saw the duke grace them with an amused smile before continuing. "As I was saying, I will refrain from killing Michel. Once Charles is finished with him, we can claim his body and stage it as an accident." He pointed at Adrien. "And you will take your rightful place as the Earl of Camden."

Nodding, Adrien's eyes held sadness. "I never wanted to inherit the earldom. I would rather have my family back," he said solemnly.

"I understand that sentiment, more than you know," Benedict stated, resignation on his face. Eliza reached for her husband's hand and gave him a sad smile.

Hannah remembered Jonathon telling her that Benedict's stepbrother had murdered his eldest brother, Henry.

The duke slapped his legs and stood up, effectively ending the conversation. "I would like to see Kate now."

Eliza and Hannah both arose, followed by the rest of the gentlemen. "I will take you to her," Eliza said, smiling.

A loud knock echoed around the castle. Everyone turned and waited as Mr. Larson opened the main door. Lord Beckett walked in and took off his top hat, handing it to Mr. Larson. "I am the bearer of unwelcome news," he said. "Lord Camden has escaped."

"Michel," a few members of the group said in unison.

Jonathon stepped closer. "How did Michel elude the agents that were guarding his townhouse?"

Lord Beckett blew a frustrated breath. "I have no idea." He glanced towards the duke. "Once we finished disposing of Diana's body, we went straight to Michel's townhouse. His butler told us that he fled only moments before we arrived, and provided no forwarding address."

"Did you leave agents behind to search for the list?" Eliza asked.

Lord Beckett smirked at his niece. "Do you think I am an amateur?" He chuckled. "I dispatched agents to search his town-house and his country home for the list."

Hannah laughed at Lord Beckett's response, which brought

her to his attention. "You are Lady Hannah, I presume," he said confidently.

She curtsied. "I am, and you are Lord Beckett, I presume," she replied cheekily.

Lord Beckett chuckled. "You are exactly like your mother."

Hannah's eyes grew wide. "You knew my mother?"

Her father suddenly appeared by her side, smiling. "Your mother and Charles had an interesting friendship. They enjoyed teasing each other unmercifully."

Lord Beckett looked fondly at her. "Your mother and my late wife were best of friends," he said almost reverently.

Hannah moved to stand in front of him, noting the sorrow reflecting in his eyes. "I would love to hear stories about my mother and your wife, if it is not too painful."

"It would be my pleasure," Lord Beckett said, his voice hitching. "You are as exquisite as she was."

Hannah smiled gratefully up at him. It had been so long since someone told her stories about her mother. Those stories always helped her feel connected to her. "Thank you," she said.

Lord Beckett watched her for a moment, then returned his focus to the group. "My agents will find Michel immediately and acquire the list."

"Is it safe for Hannah and me to travel home?" her father asked.

"No, you cannot leave." Jonathon's tone was urgent, demanding. All eyes turned to him, but he gazed at her unrepentantly. "It is not safe for Hannah as long as Michel is out there."

Hannah was surprised at Jonathon's tone. He almost seemed frantic about her leaving, but why? He must enjoy their friendship, but she wanted so much more. She needed so much more.

Lord Beckett wiped a smile off his face. "I concur. Once Michel is detained, then you may travel home. Escorted, of course."

"Of course," her father repeated.

The duke stepped forward. "I am sorry for interrupting but I am anxious to see my Kate."

Hannah and her father stayed back as everyone else went to check on Kate. She did not want to intrude on family time, so she would visit Kate before retiring for the night. She frowned. How she wished she could be a part of this family.

❧ 25 ❧

I*T APPEARS THAT* M*ICHEL HAS ESCAPED.* JONATHON SWORE UNDER his breath, tossing his uncle's missive on the table. For the past week, agents had scoured London and the surrounding areas looking for him, with no success. Did Michel flee back to France?

Jonathon poured himself a drink. As he sipped the brandy, he wandered to the window and watched Hannah lift her longbow, nock an arrow, pull, aim, and release. Impressively, she hit the mark perfectly. Lowering the bow, she turned towards Adrien and her father with a wide, bright smile on her face.

His grip on the glass tightened and a wave of frustration washed over him. For the past week, Hannah had gone out of her way to be polite, even cordial, but she avoided being alone with him. If he brushed up against her, she would blush and avert her eyes, not meeting his gaze.

Yesterday, he asked her to walk around the grounds after dinner, but she had sweetly declined, claiming a headache. What had he done wrong? He had been on the verge of proposing. She had seemed to care for him. Was he mistaken? No, he had seen the love in her eyes. She loved him, he knew it, but now she was withdrawing from him.

Jonathon slammed his glass down onto the window sill. It was time he asked for advice, as much as it pained him to admit it. He did not want to lose Hannah.

He left the library to seek out Eliza and Benedict. As he entered the drawing room, he saw them sitting on the sofa, kissing. If he had not been so anxious to receive help, he would have backed up and closed the door, but he did not have the patience to wait.

He cleared his throat loudly as he leaned up against the door frame. Eliza and Benedict both turned towards him, but neither one looked at all embarrassed. "Do you two have any sense of decorum?" Jonathon asked with a smile.

"I enjoy kissing my wife," Benedict replied with a smirk.

Straightening up, Jonathon walked further into the room. "I need help," he admitted.

Benedict nodded. "I wholeheartedly agree. Your clothes look terrible. You need an entirely new wardrobe."

Jonathon looked at him with disbelief. "My wardrobe is of the highest quality." He sat down on the sofa adjacent to them. "That is not why I am here."

Benedict looked him up and down. "Pity."

Eliza laughed at Benedict. "Leave my poor brother alone." Directing her smile at Jonathon, she asked, "Now, what can we do to help you?"

Jonathon rubbed his hand through his hair. "It is Hannah…" He hesitated. "Everything seemed to be going well until last week when I tried to propose, but was interrupted. Now Hannah is avoiding me, and I worry that I may have been too forward."

Benedict removed his arm from Eliza and leaned forward, suddenly serious. "Tell us everything," he commanded.

And so, Jonathon told them everything that had happened

when they were at the stream. He finished with Mr. Larson interrupting them and how Hannah had fled from his presence. When he was finished, he looked up and said, "What did I do wrong?"

"Idiot," Benedict mumbled under his breath.

"I beg your pardon?" Jonathon asked, confused. "Did you just refer to me as an idiot?"

Eliza gave him a condescending smile. "I must agree with my charming husband. You are an idiot."

Jonathon threw his hands up in the air. "Help me, then."

Smiling, Eliza leaned closer. "You told Hannah that you were not honest with your feelings, then you implied that you did not care for her."

Jonathon jumped up from his seat in outrage. "I did no such thing!"

Benedict looked smug. "You did."

Jonathon played back the conversation in his head, suddenly realizing that his words could have been misconstrued. "But surely Hannah must know that I care for her deeply, doesn't she?"

"You did not tell her that," Eliza pointed out. "I believe you led Hannah to arrive at the conclusion that you were not interested in courting her."

"But I kissed her, passionately," Jonathon practically shouted.

Shaking his head, Benedict replied, "Men kiss women all the time with no intention of courting them."

"But, I am a gentleman," Jonathon said, pointing to his chest.

"We know that, but you have confused Hannah," Eliza scolded him. "You need to make this right."

Jonathon dropped back down in the chair. "I cannot seem to get her alone. I fear Lord Pembrooke does not approve of my intentions towards Hannah."

Benedict gave him a pointed look. "So, you need to get into

his good graces. Also, I would be wary of Adrien. He seems to be building a lively friendship with Hannah."

"Hannah is mine," Jonathon growled. He jumped up and started pacing. "I love her," he admitted, stopping in his tracks. "I love her!" It was both exhilarating and frustrating to admit his feelings aloud.

He brought his gaze back to Eliza and Benedict and noticed they were smiling obnoxiously. "Why are you telling us?" Benedict asked, with a flip of his wrist. "Go tell Hannah."

Jonathon's gaze flickered between them and the door. "How will I get her alone?"

With a dramatic eye roll, Eliza reminded him, "You are a spy. Find a way."

"Why does it feel like I am preparing for war?" Jonathon asked anxiously.

Benedict threw his head back and laughed. "Convincing a woman to marry you is harder than boarding a French frigate and fighting to the death."

Eliza playfully slapped her husband's chest. "It is not."

Benedict grabbed Eliza's hand, smiling so tenderly at his wife that Jonathon felt a lump form in his throat. "I loved you from the moment I laid eyes on you, and I would gladly go to the ends of the earth for you."

Melting into his arms, Eliza said, "I love you, too."

Benedict looked at Jonathon, and lifted his brow. "Will you please go now? I need some private time with my wife."

Jonathon shook his head, feigning disgust. "You have a bedchamber, you know."

Benedict's face lit up. "You are correct." With that, he scooped Eliza up in his arms and quickly exited the room.

Jonathon felt a smile grow on his face as he watched his dearest friend and his sister leave the room. Even though they exhibited no social graces, they loved each other. His shoulders slumped, knowing he wanted that with Hannah, but was afraid he would never have it.

He needed a plan. How hard could it be to get Hannah alone, even for a few minutes, to clarify his feelings?

HANNAH SAT AT HER DRESSING TABLE, CLAD IN HER WHITE nightgown. Absentmindedly, she was brushing her long, black hair. Today had been positively heartbreaking as Jonathon repeatedly tried to get her alone. He had asked for her to take a walk with him after dinner, but she claimed a headache. Jonathan then sat down next to her and refused to leave her side.

Closing her eyes, Hannah remembered his smile and how easy it was to converse with him. For a moment, she allowed herself to pretend that Jonathon truly loved her and that he was paying court to her. How wonderful would it be to be married to him? To wake up in his strong, muscular arms, and kissing him as they lay in bed.

She sighed, knowing that Jonathon would never belong to her, even though he had her heart. She frowned into the mirror. Why had she let her imagination wander towards Jonathon again? She needed to banish him from her thoughts. After all, he only thought of her as a friend and nothing more. No good could come of her imagining more.

Hannah placed her brush down onto the dressing table, not bothering to wipe away the tears rolling down her face. The pain of unrequited love was too much for her to bear and she did not want to be strong anymore. She started sobbing and brought her hands to her face.

How would she ever get over Jonathon? Truthfully, she was not sure she wanted to. Hannah sobbed louder as Jonathon's masculine scent reached her nose. Would she ever be released of these memories?

"Hannah, my love." Jonathon's voice came next to her ears. "What is wrong?"

Wanting to banish his imagined presence, Hannah dropped her hands. She almost flew out of her chair when she saw that it was the real Jonathon crouching down next to her. Her eyes grew wide and she looked up to see the door was closed. "What are you doing here?" she asked, her voice hushed.

Jonathon's eyes roamed her face and she knew her eyes and nose must be bright red. "I started to knock, but I heard crying." His eyes shone with compassion. "Why are you crying?"

Hannah plastered on a smile. "Nothing of consequence," she said, attempting to lighten the mood.

Frowning at her response, Jonathon did not say anything. Instead, he stood and offered his hand. Slowly, he escorted her to the settee beside the fireplace. After seating her, he sat down, allowing their knees to touch.

"Now," he said, his eyes roaming her face. "What has caused you such sadness?"

Hannah sniffled and looked down at her lap. She would be mortified if Jonathon ever discovered the depth of her feelings for him. "I believe I have been overwhelmed and..." Her voice trailed off.

Jonathon's hand stilled her knee, which she only now realized had been bouncing up and down. "You are a terrible liar," he said with a smirk. "In the past two months, you escaped men who tried to abduct you, you worked on a farm and milked cows, and you survived having your throat slashed. I highly doubt living at Beaumont Castle has overwhelmed you."

Making the mistake of raising her head, she caught

Jonathon's compassionate gaze. Her lower lip started to tremble, and fresh tears began streaming down her face. Without warning, Jonathon put his arm around her shoulders, drew her closer, and kissed her on the top of her head. "I hate to see you cry, my dear," he murmured.

Hannah rested her head against his shoulder, attempting to control her emotions. Even though he did not care for her, his touch still made her feel safe and protected.

Jonathon placed his cheek on the top of her head. "Now, will you please tell me what has caused you to be so upset?"

Hannah shook her head. "I cannot."

"I see. You are challenging me to extract the information from you," Jonathon teased, trying to make her smile.

"I am not."

"You should know that I am a skilled spy. I'm sure I can deduce what's bothering you."

"I have no doubt," Hannah said, his banter already easing her sorrow.

Jonathon kissed her again on the top of her head. "You were sobbing at your dressing table, which leads me to the conclusion that your hairbrush must have displeased you in some way," he said matter-of-factly.

Hannah laughed. "Your skills of deduction are indeed impressive."

Lifting his head, he turned so he could look at her, but she averted her gaze. She must look a fright. Placing a finger under her chin, Jonathon forced her to look at him. "I have missed your smile."

He leaned forward, and she knew he was going to kiss her. Quickly, Hannah turned her head, causing his lips to meet her cheek. She wanted to kiss him, but since he did not care for her that way, it would be too painful. "I think you should leave."

Hannah tried to stand up, but he reached for her hand,

stalling her. His eyebrows were furrowed as he looked at her. "What have I done to upset you?"

"You have done nothing wrong," she said, attempting to rise again.

Refusing to let her go, he pleaded, "Talk to me."

Hannah could hear the pain in his voice, but she did not feel strong enough to tell him why she'd been crying. She clasped her hands tighter in her lap. What if he laughed at her, or worse? What if he pitied her for her feelings towards him? No, she was not bold enough to voice her feelings.

Jonathon placed his hand on her cheek, guiding her to meet his gaze. She could see moisture filling his eyes as he watched her. "Dare I hope that your tears were for me?"

There was something in his voice that caused her pause, and that something caused her to nod.

Jonathon blinked away his tears. "I love you." His voice was soft and earnest. "This past week, I have watched you withdraw from me and it is slowly killing me." His eyes pleaded with her. "Please tell me what I must do to earn your love, or is it too late?"

Hannah's mouth gaped open. Was her imagination going wild again or did Jonathon just confess his love? Sadly, she did not know. "Can you repeat that?"

Giving her the crooked smile that she so dearly loved, he repeated, "I love you." His free hand cupped her other cheek. "I do not know exactly when I fell in love with you, but I have felt this way for some time. You are beautiful, and clever, and so incredibly brave," he lovingly drawled.

Hannah's eyes welled with tears again. Jonathon would think she was a simpering female, but she could not stop. These were happy tears. "I love you, too."

Jonathon's eyes widened in surprise. "You do? I had hoped you did, but I had started giving up."

"I have loved you for so long," she confessed, her smile

dimming, "but then you told me that you had misled me about your feelings for me."

He groaned as he dropped his hands from her face. "I was attempting to propose to you, but I failed miserably."

Once again, Hannah's mouth dropped open in surprise. "You were proposing?" she asked when she finally found her voice. "I thought you were politely telling me that you did not care for me."

"Please do not tell Benedict and Eliza that they were right." Jonathon's lips twitched in amusement.

Hannah gave him a perplexed look. "What were they right about?"

"Earlier today, I sought them out for help. I could not understand what I had done to upset you," he stated, clearly unsettled by his admission.

"In my defense, I thought you were just toying with my emotions," Hannah admitted as she gripped the lapels on his waistcoat.

Frowning, Jonathon asked, "Why would you think that of me? I thought you knew the depths of my feelings."

"I had thought you might be developing feelings for me, but your words at the stream were ambiguous, to say the least."

"Fair enough," he conceded. His eyes roamed her face. "Please say that you will marry me," he whispered intimately.

Hannah's hands stilled on his chest and she met his gaze. His eyes were filled with love, begging her to take a chance on him. "Ye…" Her words were cut off by his mouth capturing hers.

Jonathon's lips were demanding, but not in a way that frightened her. She felt as if he was branding her as his own. He tilted his head, deepening the kiss in the most wonderful way. A slight moan escaped from the back of her throat and it seemed to encourage him.

His arms wrapped around her, pulling her closer to him as her hands slid behind his neck. At last, she could weave her hands through his hair, and Hannah knew she never wanted this moment to end.

Jonathon broke the kiss as he placed his forehead onto hers. "I love you," he said, almost reverently.

"And I love you," she replied, feeling her heart bursting with happiness.

Jonathon's lips descended again to meet hers, but this time, he kissed her slowly as if savoring every touch. His mouth left hers and started trailing kisses down her neck, but stopped at the top of her nightgown.

"My apologies. I did not mean to take advantage," he said hoarsely, bringing his gaze back up to hers.

She cupped his cheek. "You have no reason to apologize. In fact, I would not mind continuing this encounter," she said, bringing her lips to his.

After a few moments, Jonathon leaned back to gaze into her eyes. "If I do not leave right now, I fear I will drag you to your bed and make love to you." Hannah knew she should be shocked by his scandalous suggestion, but she decided she liked his idea.

Jonathon chuckled huskily. "I believe you are considering that option."

She shrugged. "We are to be married and I do not want to say good night."

Kissing her on the cheek, Jonathon replied, "Nor do I, but I am a gentleman. We will wait until we are married. Then I will sequester you in our bedchamber for weeks."

Hannah giggled. "I will not complain."

Jonathon slowly arose and offered her his hand. He walked her to her bed and waited for her to lay down. He sat next to Hannah and ran his fingers through her hair. "Good night, my love."

"You did better this time."

He stopped and stared at her. "Meaning?"

"This time, I knew you were proposing," she said coyly.

Jonathon grinned, leaned forward, and kissed her. "I will stay with you until you fall asleep. I am not ready to say goodnight, either."

Hannah's eyelids grew heavy and she knew sleep was inevitable. As she drifted into sleep, she hoped that Jonathon really did love her, and that this was not simply part of a wonderful dream.

26

"I think he has gone mad," Adrien teased from his side of the table.

"Maybe he is trying to conjure up Hannah?" Benedict quipped.

"Should we send for a doctor?" Adrien asked, before taking a sip of his tea.

Benedict leaned forward in his seat, his eyes assessing Jonathon. "I do not believe a doctor can cure what ails Jonathon."

Eliza smiled knowingly at her husband. "Leave Jonathon alone," she said, wiping her mouth with a linen napkin.

Jonathon ignored their teasing, and continued staring at the door, waiting for Hannah to walk into the dining room. After she had fallen asleep, he had loitered longer, admiring her. He wanted to whistle a spritely song, since Hannah had agreed to marry him. Maybe he should ride into town and obtain a special license from the archbishop?

"Is he smiling or frowning?" Adrien asked.

"He is smiling," Benedict confirmed. "He is a man in love and we tend to act like fools in the beginning."

"Only in the beginning, dear?" Eliza smiled sweetly.

Adrien threw his napkin on the table. "Maybe I should end his torment and go fetch Hannah for him?"

"Fetch me for what?" Hannah asked as she glided into the room. She was wearing a pale yellow dress and her black hair was piled high up on her head, with small ringlets running along both sides of her face.

Jonathon pushed back his chair and strode over to her, reaching for her hands. He brought both of her hands up to his lips, kissing them tenderly. "You look exquisite this morning."

Hannah's cheeks turned an adorable shade of pink as she met his gaze. "You look quite handsome yourself."

Keeping her ungloved hands near his lips, Jonathon said, "I was worried you would oversleep and miss breaking your fast."

"You must think me quite lazy to sleep the day away," Hannah said with a smile.

His shook his head slightly. "You had an eventful evening last night."

"That I did." Then she whispered softly so only he could hear. "It was a night of my dreams."

"Now, now, Jonathon. You need to let Hannah break her fast before you devour her," Benedict mocked.

Jonathon dropped one of her hands but held the other in his. He escorted her to the buffet and watched as she filled her plate with food. After they sat down, he admired Hannah's long, elegant neck until she turned her head and smiled at him. "On my way down, I stepped in to check on Kate," she informed him, reaching for her fork.

"Oh, how is she faring this morning?" Eliza asked as she picked up her teacup.

Hannah faced Eliza to answer her question. "She has agreed to take a turn around your gardens with me after breakfast."

Eliza smiled with relief. "That is great news. I am worried about her."

Adrien pushed his chair back and looped his arm along the back of the chair. "When will I get to meet this mysterious Kate, or should I say, Lady Camden?"

Jonathon gave him a pointed look. "Do not call her Lady Camden. That is a very sensitive topic for her."

Nodding his understanding, Adrien asked, "Have you told her that she married an imposter?"

"I did," Eliza confirmed. "It did not seem to overly upset her."

"Poor Kate," Hannah murmured.

Striding into the room, Lord Pembrooke announced, "I have decided that Hannah and I will depart as soon as the carriage is packed."

Hannah's head spun towards her father. "We are leaving?"

Lord Pembrooke glanced at Jonathon, narrowing his eyes slightly. "I feel that I can sufficiently protect us back at our country home."

Jonathon tried to rein in the anger he felt rising towards his future father-in-law. "I do not believe that is wise," he said firmly. "Michel still has not been taken into custody and agents have only just broadened their search."

Lord Pembrooke crossed his arms over his chest. "I have been back in England for almost a month, and I have yet to go home. It is time for me to spend time alone with my daughter."

"If you give us some time, we can arrange to have agents escort you home," Eliza reasoned.

Lord Pembrooke tilted his head towards Eliza, acknowledging her words. "I thank you for the kind offer of an escort, but that is not necessary. Would it be possible to borrow a carriage?" he asked Benedict.

Benedict nodded. "Yes, you are welcome to our fastest carriage, and we will send Roger along as the driver."

Jonathon was glad that Roger would be assigned as the driver since he was a former agent. He would be able to help protect

Lord Pembrooke and Hannah. But that was not enough. "I insist that you take along a few footmen, in case you encounter highway robbers."

Lord Pembrooke frowned at him but eventually nodded. "I will agree to a few footmen and a driver, but I do not believe that is necessary. Michel has no reason to pursue us any longer."

Adrien rested his arms on the table, leaning forward. "With all due respect, I believe you may be too hasty in your departure."

Hannah glanced at Jonathon, her expression calm, but her sad eyes betrayed her emotion. She turned back to her father. "Papa, I do not want to leave yet."

Lord Pembrooke's face softened as he looked upon his daughter. "I know, *mi hija*, but it is time for us to go home."

Jonathon arose from his chair and asked, "Sir, may I speak to you for a few moments before you depart?"

Lord Pembrooke nodded and gestured towards the door. Jonathon placed his hand reassuringly on Hannah's shoulder as he walked past her.

Once they were in the drawing room, Lord Pembrooke spoke directly. "What would you like to discuss with me, Lord Jonathon?"

Clearing his throat, Jonathon suddenly felt very nervous. "Before you depart, I beg permission to court your daughter," he asked, meeting Lord Pembrooke's intense gaze.

Lord Pembrooke's eyes twitched, and a tight frown sat on his lips. "Have you asked my daughter's permission yet?" he growled.

He nodded. "I did, sir. She has agreed to marry me." Jonathon hoped that Lord Pembrooke would not ask when the proposal took place. He was certain Hannah's father would not approve of him sneaking into his daughter's bedchamber.

Lord Pembrooke walked over to the window and stared out.

"I saw this coming. In fact, anyone with eyes could see that you two love each other."

Reluctantly, he admitted, "I only confessed my love to Hannah last night."

Lord Pembrooke humphed. "It took you long enough."

Jonathon stifled a groan. "I bungled my first proposal last week, and Benedict informed me that I was a fool."

"Men often are when they are in love." Lord Pembrooke smiled knowingly.

"So, I have been told."

Turning away from the window, Hannah's father leaned back against the sill. "I did not want this life for my daughter."

"What life, sir?"

"The wife of a spy," Lord Pembrooke stated. "Have you considered the ramifications to your family, if you continue as a spy?"

Jonathon lowered himself onto a chair. "I have not."

"Are you prepared to leave your wife's side at a moment's notice, for weeks or even months at a time?"

Jonathon shook his head, knowing he never wanted to leave Hannah's side. "No, I am not."

"And the lies? Are you prepared to keep secrets from your wife, especially secrets that cause regret?"

"I already have a few of those secrets," Jonathon admitted, wincing.

Lord Pembrooke closed his eyes, pain etched on his face. "Don't we all?"

"If Hannah asked me to stop being a spy, then I would not hesitate," Jonathon vowed. "I have acquired a large fortune and inherited lands from my grandmother. We could retire to the country, if she desired."

Lord Pembrooke nodded his approval. "But is that enough?"

"Sir?"

Pushing away from the window sill and taking a step towards

Jonathon, Lord Pembrooke continued. "Working as an agent is in our blood. It drives us to protect our country fiercely and to put our lives at risk, knowing we are a part of a bigger plan."

Jonathon arose, and Lord Pembrooke extended his hand. "I give you permission to court Hannah, but I have one condition."

He held a tight grip and covered Jonathon's hand with his. "Get that French spy bastard and find that list. Once your mission is over, truly consider your options. If you remain a spy, are you willing to bring Hannah into your world of lies and deceit? Or, if you retire as an agent, will you be able to enjoy the boring life of a land-owning aristocrat?"

As Lord Pembrooke released his hand, Jonathon glanced towards the door, hoping Hannah would suddenly materialize. "I believe it would be best if I discussed this with Hannah."

Placing a hand on his shoulder, Lord Pembrooke said, "I will expect to see you at our country home when you have finished with Michel."

Jonathon's heart constricted knowing that Hannah was leaving, even if it was only for a few weeks. "Would you allow me to escort you and Hannah safely home?"

Throwing his head back, Lord Pembrooke laughed in amusement. "Nothing would be worse than being in a confined carriage with an engaged couple in love."

"I am still hoping you will reconsider and stay longer at Beaumont Castle," Jonathon said, attempting to sway him one last time.

Lord Pembrooke faced him, looking tired and worn. "I want to go home, son," he said warmly. "I need time to become reacquainted with my daughter. I have wasted so much time. My little girl has grown into a remarkable woman, and I do not know her at all."

Jonathon could hear the pain in his voice as he spoke about Hannah. It was obvious the years away from Hannah had taken their toll on him, and soon, she would be married and separated from her father again. "When Hannah and I are married, you will always be welcome in our home," he said, hoping to reassure him.

"Thank you," Lord Pembrooke said solemnly.

Jonathon watched as his future father-in-law walked out of the room. He still thought it foolish of Lord Pembrooke to travel unescorted back to his country home. But they would have trained agents acting as footmen, and Roger would ensure that they avoided any unnecessary risks.

Now, Jonathon had a stronger motivation to track down Michel and acquire that list. When that was accomplished, he would need to heavily consider whether he would remain an agent after this assignment. But first, he needed to send a missive to his uncle, alerting him of Lord Pembrooke's rash departure.

WITH HER GLOVED HAND, HANNAH WIPED AT THE TEARS IN HER eyes as she waited. Standing near the front door, she was dressed in a dark grey traveling habit, with her hair in a practical, loose chignon. Physically, she was ready to travel home, but her heart was not ready to leave Jonathon.

Jonathon stood shoulder to shoulder with her, their hands intertwined. They watched the carriage as her trunks were loaded. "You weren't able to convince your father?" he muttered under his breath to her.

She shook her head. "He is adamant we start our journey today."

"I am not ready to say goodbye," Jonathon said, turning to face her.

Hannah smiled weakly up at him. "We are not saying goodbye for long, are we?"

"No, we will be together soon. I promise," he said, his knuckles trailing along her cheek.

"I hope so," Hannah said, closing her eyes.

She had asked if Jonathon could escort them home, but her father insisted that they needed to track down Michel first. Hopefully, they would be in each other's arms in a few weeks. Until then, she would attempt to remember everything she could about Jonathon; his loving eyes, his smile, and his gentle caress.

She opened her eyes to see Jonathon looking at her lips. "Did I tell you that your father granted me permission to court you?" he revealed.

Hannah could not contain her excitement as she squealed, throwing her arms around Jonathon's neck. She could feel him chuckle as she pressed herself tight against him. "I am so happy."

Eliza's voice interrupted them. "I take it that there will be a wedding soon."

Hannah regretfully slid her arms from Jonathon's neck, turning towards Eliza with a wide smile. "Yes, hopefully very soon," she replied, glancing at Jonathon for confirmation.

Leaning closer, he whispered, "If I had my way, I would get a special license and be married by dinner." His breath was warm against her ear as he slowly pressed a tender kiss on her ear lobe.

Benedict chuckled loudly, bringing their attention back to the group. "You do realize that your voice travels, Jonathon." He stood next to his wife and placed his arm around her waist. "I highly doubt Lord Pembrooke would agree to your matrimonial scheme."

Adrien walked closer to the group. "I find Jonathon barely tolerable with Hannah around, and now she is leaving." He stopped near Benedict and smirked. "I fear Jonathon will stare at doorways again until she reappears."

Smiling back at Adrien, she embraced him warmly. "Be nice to my fiancé." She turned her head to look back at Jonathon. "I like the sound of that."

Hannah turned back to Adrien. "I have enjoyed getting to know you these past few weeks. I hope you will travel up for our wedding."

Adrien smiled mischievously, his eyes twinkling. "It is not too late to marry me." He leaned closer to her ear. "Give me ten minutes and you will forget all about Jonathon."

Benedict and Eliza laughed loudly, but Jonathon growled behind her. She swiped playfully at Adrien's chest. "I am afraid I have already given my heart to Jonathon."

Adrien put his hand to his chest, feigning disappointment. "I am too late, then. If only I had met you first."

Jonathon put his arm around Hannah's shoulder and gently pulled her away from Adrien. "Please refrain from flirting with my fiancée," he warned.

Adrien winked at her as he slowly backed away with his hands up in mock surrender. "I will see you soon, Hannah."

Eliza stepped forward and gave her a tight embrace. As she stepped back towards Benedict, she arched an eyebrow. "Do you have your dagger on you?"

Hannah patted the small dagger in the pocket of her traveling habit. "Maggie sewed a pocket in all of my dresses."

Eliza lowered her eyebrow and smiled her approval.

Benedict stepped closer, pulling her into a quick embrace. As he stepped back, a tight frown pulled at his lips. "I am not pleased that your father is taking this risk." He leveled a serious gaze at her. "If you encounter any danger, strike first. The element of surprise will be in your favor."

"Thank you, Benedict," Hannah said, genuinely smiling at her friend. He had become almost like a brother to her over these past weeks and she had grown quite fond of him. "Do not worry about me. My Papa believes that Michel has no reason to come after us now."

Benedict sighed. "We do not feel the same," he said, glancing at Eliza and Jonathon. "Just be alert to your surroundings."

Walking out of Beaumont Castle, her father glanced their way. "Are you ready, *mi hija*?" He acknowledged Benedict, Eliza, and Jonathon with a tilt of his head before he moved towards the carriage.

Hannah was aware that her father and Benedict, Eliza, and Jonathon had been in the library for hours, attempting to sway him to stay, or at least leave his daughter behind. They felt strongly that Michel could strike at any time and they urged him to be cautious. In the end, her father stayed firm about his decision to leave Beaumont Castle.

Jonathon offered his arm and escorted her to the carriage. He leaned forward, kissing her cheek. "I will come as soon as I can."

She nodded with tear-filled eyes, as she felt her heart breaking. "I love you."

Jonathon softly brushed his lips against hers. "I love you, too. Do not forget that."

Her father loudly cleared his throat from the inside of the carriage. Hannah noticed Maggie nervously wringing her hands. Maggie had agreed to continue as her lady's maid permanently, but it looked as though she might be regretting that decision.

"I am sorry you have to ride in the carriage again. I know how much you despise it," Hannah said sympathetically.

"Miss Maggie, would you like to ride up front with me?" Roger asked. "The fresh air might be all that you need."

Maggie smiled weakly up at him. "Thank you. I will do that."

Jonathon assisted Hannah into the carriage and stood in the doorway. Solemnly, he addressed her father. "Roger and the three footmen are former agents and will ensure your safety. There are respectable inns along the main road, and you should arrive at your estate in three days, barring no unforeseen incident."

Lord Pembrooke nodded his head in thanks. "We hope to see you soon, Lord Jonathon."

"If you see any sign of danger, turn around and come back to Beaumont Castle at once," Jonathon said firmly. "Also, there is a spare pistol under your seat, should you require it."

"Thank you," Hannah's father stated.

Jonathon's eyes were filled with sadness. "The moment this is over, I will rush to your side." He opened his mouth but closed it again without uttering another word. She thought she saw his bottom lip trembling as he closed the carriage door.

Twisting in the carriage, Hannah watched him from the window as the carriage rolled away. She watched until she could see Beaumont Castle no more. Turning back, she saw her father had moisture in his eyes. "What is wrong, Papa?"

He sighed longingly. "Your mother used to tell me that whenever I would leave, you would stand outside, rain or shine, until you could no longer see me. Only then could she coax you back inside."

Hannah moved to sit next to her father. "Can you tell me more about Mama? Sometimes I fear my memories of her will fade until they are no more."

Smiling tenderly, he put his arm around her shoulder and she rested against him. "My dear, you take after her in so many ways. Your mother was strong like you are, was fiercely loyal, and had an incredible wit."

"When did you fall in love with Mother?"

For the next few hours, her father told her story after story about their courtship. Hannah found herself laughing aloud at his perspective. He told her about their wedding in Spain and how it differed from an English wedding. He talked about how happy they were to welcome a baby girl, and how he defied tradition by witnessing her delivery.

Hannah was so enthralled by her father's stories that she didn't notice the carriage had increased in speed until they hit a large bump, causing her to fall off the bench. Her father glanced out the window, muttered an expletive under his breath and slammed the window closed. Reaching under the bench, he pulled out a small metal box and placed it on his lap. Opening it, he pulled out a pistol. "I need you to get on the floor, *mi hija*." His tone brooked no argument.

Hannah met her father's gaze and recognized the determined glint in his eye. She slid to the floor. "What is happening out there?"

Before her father responded, she heard muffled shouting, commanding the driver to pull over. In response, the carriage weaved back and forth and her father joined her on the floor. She heard gunfire outside the carriage, and the sound of splintering wood inside the coach.

"I am so sorry," her father murmured. "Whatever happens, I love you." He leaned over and kissed her head. "Stay down."

Hannah could hear more gunfire outside, growing louder with each shot. Suddenly, the carriage veered left and tilted up on two wheels before it slammed back down hard on all four wheels. She screamed, and her father's hold tightened around her arms.

"We just want the girl," a booming voice demanded.

The carriage weaved back and forth sporadically, and Hannah could hear Maggie screaming. The carriage sharply careened to the right and tipped over onto its side, slamming Hannah into her father. As the carriage was dragged for what seemed like eternity, it slowly came to a stop. The eerie silence threatening to consume her.

Hannah reached for her head as she waited for the dizziness to pass. She attempted to push herself up and realized she was laying on top of her father, who appeared to be unconscious. She heard pistols being discharged and she desperately tried to find her father's pistol. She needed to protect herself and her father.

She found it near her father's feet and placed it close to her, then she tried to move her father. A large gash on the side of his head was bleeding profusely. She needed to stop the bleeding. She pulled up her skirt, ripped a large piece of her petticoat, and wrapped it tightly around her father's head. He moaned.

The shouting and gunfire stopped, and the carriage door was wrenched open. Hannah reached for the pistol and pointed it at the door. A grimy face peered down at her, a wide smile on his lips showed his rotting, yellow teeth. He offered his hand to help her out of the carriage. "Up ye go, girlie." Hannah shook her head and leveled her pistol at the man's chest. He laughed mockingly. "A feisty one, I see."

"Leave me be," Hannah commanded.

Without warning, the man lurched forward, grabbing her skirt, and started yanking her towards the top of the carriage. Hannah aimed the pistol at the man's shoulder, shouting, "Stop, or I will shoot."

The man pulled harder and she pulled the trigger. He dropped her skirt and roared with pain, disappearing from her view. Hannah heard another moan from her father. She also heard the man screaming about being shot and ordering someone to kill her.

Shuddering with fear, Hannah tried to cover her father with her skirts. She heard the cocking of a pistol before she saw it being leveled at her. A large man with a tanned, weathered face glared down at her. She gulped down her overwhelming fear.

"Get out of this carriage or everyone still alive will die," he said slowly.

Hannah tried to bargain with him. "If I cooperate, will you promise not to kill anyone?"

His menacing eyes narrowed. "If you cooperate nicely, we will not kill anyone else, assuming no one provokes us."

Hannah hesitated, knowing that this man's word meant nothing. Still, she had to try to save anyone else still alive, and hopefully that included her father. "Agreed," she said, putting her hand out for assistance.

Surprisingly, the man helped her out of the carriage and onto the ground. She took a moment to smooth out her skirt and surreptitiously scan the scene. Five dead bodies were spread out along the road and her trunks were broken open, her dresses and white undergarments flowing around them.

Turning her head, she saw Maggie trying in vain to stifle her sobs. Her dress was ripped, and her hair was flowing down around her shoulders. Roger was kneeling next to her, with his hands behind his head, and an attacker was pointing a pistol at him.

The man she shot had his hand clutching a blood-soaked shoulder. He gave her a glare full of unrestrained hatred. "That wench needs to die. She shot me."

The big, burly man stood looming over her, and for a moment she felt protected. Then, she remembered that this man was trying to abduct her. "Don't be ridiculous. We were paid to bring her to Camden, alive."

"Fine, I won't kill *her*," he spat. He pulled out a pistol from his waistband and walked over towards Maggie, shooting her in the chest without sparing her a moment's hesitation.

Hannah's scream was gut-wrenching. "Maggie! No!" She ran to her friend, dropped to her knees, and cradled Maggie's lifeless body in her arms. Tears flowed down her cheeks as she sobbed loudly.

A loud explosion near her caused her to jump, but she refused to drop her hold on her friend. She looked up and saw the man who had just shot Maggie, dead on the ground a few feet from her, with a large blood stain on his chest.

The big, burly man came over and crouched down next to her. "He should not have killed your friend," he announced. "That ain't right after I promised you."

Hannah's arms tightened around Maggie and she just nodded. What could she say to that?

The man addressed Roger. "I have a message that needs to be delivered to Lord Jonathon Beckett. Can you handle that?" He must have liked Roger's answer because he nodded and stood up. Holding out his hand, he said, "You have had long enough with your friend. She is dead, after all."

The burly man frowned when she did not take his outstretched hand. "If you come now, then I will not kill anyone else." He looked knowingly at the carriage.

Hannah gently lowered Maggie's body onto the ground and closed her eyes. Her lower lip quivered as she allowed the man to help her rise. She sadly turned her head to meet Roger's gaze, and he gave her an encouraging nod. Slowly, she walked towards her remaining three attackers. One of the men came forward with some twine in his hand and roughly tied her wrists together.

The realization of her situation came crashing down around her, and before she could cry out for help, everything went black.

27

JONATHON SIPPED HIS DRINK AS HE STARED OUT THE LIBRARY window. He surveyed the horizon as dusk filled the sky with glorious colors.

He planned to spend the night at Beaumont Castle, return home to his townhouse tomorrow, and report to his uncle soon after. He hoped the other agents would have discovered Michel's whereabouts by then. If fortune smiled on him, Michel would already be in custody, and the work of rounding up the French agents from the list would have begun.

His thoughts wandered to Hannah and their pending nuptials. Once they were married, he truly had no desire to leave Hannah for any length of time, for any reason. Maybe it was time to give up the life of a spy? Could he just walk away from the only profession that he had known?

Taking a sip of his brandy, he considered why he was an agent. When his uncle came to Oxford and asked him to become an agent for the Crown, he'd readily agreed. The idea of adventure excited him. Chuckling to himself, he realized Eliza and he were more alike than he thought.

Being involved with covert operations had given him the

thrill that only came from risking your life for a greater good. After his first few covert assignments, he went on diplomatic campaigns with Eliza and watched as she evolved into *Shadow*. Now that Eliza had Benedict as her partner, he worked alone again, and he felt lonely.

Jonathon put his drink down on the window sill. When he arranged with Uncle Charles to team his sister and his best friend together, he never suspected he would learn how truly lonely his life was. He watched their unusual courtship and saw the depth of love in their eyes. But then he had searched all over the country for Hannah to protect her. The moment he saw her, he felt like his life had a purpose, a new vision. Now, she looked at him with love and tenderness in her eyes and he felt as though his heart would burst with happiness. He had found what he was searching for. He had found Hannah, and he was never going to let her go.

Suddenly, the idea of being a landowner with Hannah by his side, had real appeal. He wanted to be present when Hannah bore their children. He wanted to show them that they were loved beyond measure, something he was never shown by his parents.

Jonathon was pulled from reverie when he noticed multiple riders riding fast towards the castle. His eyes were drawn to a single rider just clearing the cluster of trees. At first, he thought it was a large man, but as the horse drew closer, he saw there were two separate people on top of the horse. The man in front was hunched over and was being supported by the man sitting upright in the saddle. Squinting his eyes, he tried to get a better view of the rider, but the shadows surrounding the men were too dark. He ran down the stairs and out the front door.

Mr. Larson grabbed the bridle of one of the rider's horses. "What happened?" Mr. Larson asked, holding the horse as the rider dismounted.

"Lord Pembrooke was attacked," one of the guards revealed, stepping around his horse.

"What?" Jonathon roared, causing the horses to sidestep away from him. "Where is Lady Hannah?"

"She was taken, my lord," Roger said, his horse rearing to a stop. "Lord Pembrooke is injured, but is still alive." The other two riders helped lower an unconscious Lord Pembrooke off Roger's horse and carefully took him inside.

Roger dismounted and faced Jonathon. "We were ambushed. We were two hours out when a group of five men came out of the woods. They shot the footmen on horseback before we even sensed a threat."

Running his hand through his hair in frustration, Jonathon shouted, "You are all former agents! How did they catch you by surprise?"

Roger furrowed his brow. "We had passed through a thicket, and the attackers used the trees as cover. Once I noticed the riders, I attempted to outmaneuver them with the carriage, but one of the wheels broke, and the carriage flipped onto its side."

Jonathon shouted at an approaching groomsman, "Saddle my horse, now!" He turned back to Roger. "Which way did they go?"

"May I suggest we hear Roger out before we make any rash decisions," Mr. Larson urged.

"I will wait only until my horse is ready," Jonathon conceded.

Mr. Larson glanced at him with compassion, before asking Roger, "How did you escape?"

"I was kept alive to deliver a message to Lord Jonathon," he explained.

As Roger pulled out a note from his pocket, Mr. Larson inquired, "Were there any other survivors?"

"None, sir," Roger confirmed as he extended the note to Jonathon.

Jonathon grabbed the note, ripping it open.

. . .

WILL EXCHANGE HANNAH'S LIFE FOR YOU AND MY WIFE. MEET AT St. Savior's dock, east of Shad Thames, tomorrow at 9 pm. My ship, Bronze Hine, is moored. If you and Kate come alone, Hannah will be released. Tell no one, or she will die a slow, excruciating death. -M

JONATHON CRUMBLED THE NOTE IN HIS HAND AND SPRINTED BACK inside. He skidded to a stop in the entry hall as Eliza and Benedict descended the stairs.

"Lord Pembrooke is unconscious and he is resting in the room he just vacated this morning," Eliza informed him. "I have sent a rider to fetch the doctor, since we have done all that we can do right now."

"When do we ride?" Adrien asked, storming out of the drawing room.

"First, was there a note?" Benedict asked as he approached him.

Jonathon extended him the note as he strode into the drawing room and poured himself a drink. After he swallowed the brandy, he slammed his glass down and turned to see everyone's expectant gaze upon him.

"We will get her back," Benedict said with a dangerous glint in his eyes.

Throwing his hands in the air, Jonathon shouted, "How? I have no problem trading my life for hers, but I refuse to let Kate anywhere near Michel ever again."

"I will do it." A small voice came from outside the door. Everyone turned to see Kate standing at the doorway, her chin set in determination. "It is only fair that I trade my life for Hannah's."

In a few strides, Jonathon closed the distance between them and placed his hands on her shoulders. "No, you will never go near Michel again. We promised you."

Kate looked up at him with disbelieving eyes. "Then how will you save her?"

"Michel has underestimated us, and that will be his downfall," Eliza assured her.

Kate raised an eyebrow in confusion. "No offense, but it appears that you underestimated him. He abducted Hannah."

With a bright, confident smile, Eliza revealed, "Michel did not realize that Hannah is family now." Her voice then shifted to a more angry and dangerous tone. "No one hurts our family and lives to tell about it."

Jonathon felt buoyed by Eliza's words. "She is right, Kate. We will find a way to save her."

Kate's eyes filled with tears. "The Matthew I know is cruel and vicious. He will have no qualms about abusing her. You must save her before he kills her."

Eliza walked over and embraced her sister. "We will find a way, but you have to trust us."

Kate nodded, looking resigned. "I am going up to my bedchamber to lie down again, but my offer still stands."

Jonathon forced a smile on his face. "Don't fret. We will get Hannah back."

Turning, Kate moved slowly back up the stairs. Jonathon hated to see how sad she was and how she moved so unsurely. He wanted his old sister back.

Adrien's eyes were filled with sympathy as they tracked Kate. "Your poor, brave sister."

Frowning, Jonathon replied, "Michel turned my sister into someone I barely recognize."

"It is hard to watch Kate suffer, but I believe the loss of her child has caused her to grieve," Eliza said. "We just need to be patient."

Benedict was standing at the mantel of the fireplace and he crushed the note in his hand. "We need a plan. We cannot trust Michel's word, so we must assume that this is a trap."

Eliza sank down on the sofa. "Why would he ask for Jonathon and Kate, I wonder?"

Adrien shrugged. "Maybe he loves his wife?"

Jonathon guffawed. "No, that is not it. Maybe it is to make her suffer for leaving him?"

Eliza tapped her mouth with her finger. "Michel believes Jonathon is *Shadow*. The French would do anything to capture *Shadow*."

"But Jonathon is not *Shadow*, right?" Adrien asked, glancing between Mr. Larson and Benedict.

Eliza's lips curled on one side. "Exactly. We can use that to our advantage."

"We need to scout the area around St. Savior's dock and see what we are working with," Benedict stated. He smiled at his wife. "It appears we have use for that black clothing again."

"Black clothing?" Adrien asked, confused.

"Do not worry. I have an extra set that will fit you," Benedict told him.

As Mr. Larson started walking out of the room, he said, "I will prepare the carriage."

Resting his hands on the back of the sofa, Jonathon dropped his head in despair. "We need to rescue Hannah tonight." His voice was pleading.

Eliza rose and came around to him, leaning close to avoid being overheard. "I would never want to suggest that you stay behind, but I am afraid your emotions are too raw on this one."

"I am not staying behind," he growled.

"We need you to stop thinking like a fiancé and start thinking like an agent." Eliza's tone brooked no argument. "Getting yourself killed will not help Hannah."

"I am just so," his voice hitched, "frightened."

"We will get her back," Eliza said firmly. "I meant what I said about Hannah being family."

Turning his head to face her, he asked weakly, "What if

Shadow cannot save her?"

Eliza smiled reassuringly. "*Shadow* cannot save her alone, but we can," she said, her hand sweeping the room. "We can save her together, but only if you start acting like the spy I know you are."

Jonathon pushed away from the sofa. "Give me a few minutes to panic as her fiancé, but once I meet you at the carriage, I will be ready."

Eliza nodded at his words. "That should work nicely."

Waiting until everyone left the room, he collapsed onto the sofa. He only had a few minutes before he needed to compose himself. Taking a deep breath, he knew it did not matter if he lived or died, but he would save Hannah. That much he knew.

JONATHON RE-ENTERED THE DRAWING ROOM DRESSED IN A BLACK cotton shirt, black trousers, and Hessian boots. His pistol was tucked into the front waistband of his trousers, and his spare pistol and knife were in their respective boots.

Adrien, also dressed in black, was pacing in the drawing room.

"What is bothering you?" Jonathon asked.

Adrien stopped and glared at him. "Why am I dressed like this?" He tugged at his black shirt.

"To allow us to blend into the shadows," Eliza stated calmly as she entered, dressed in black. She held a black cloth cap in her hand and her hair was twisted tightly against her head.

Adrien arched an eyebrow. "You do not mean to join us at the docks?"

Benedict strode into the room, dressed in black as well, and smiled at Adrien. "You can save your breath. My wife is coming."

"The docks are no place for a lady, much less a marchioness," Adrien sputtered, eyeing Eliza in disbelief. "I understand you consult for the Crown, but this is too dangerous for you."

Eliza frowned as she listened to Adrien. She shook her head and muttered, "Oh dear, we do not have time for this."

Mr. Larson walked into the room, announcing, "The carriage is ready."

Adrien shook his head, bewildered. "Why are we all dressed in black again?"

"Because Eliza requested it." Benedict smiled at his wife.

Eliza smiled appreciatively at her husband, then turned to Adrien. "Once we arrive at the docks, it will be dark, and the only light we will have will be the moon. We need to get as close to Michel's brig as possible without being detected. Furthermore, I need to look for an adequate vantage point for our raid on the brig."

Jonathon spoke up. "Trust us, we have raided multiple ships over the years. Eliza is very proficient at remaining hidden and has often facilitated our safety with her knowledge." He smiled. "As an example, we now dress in black."

Benedict placed his arm around Eliza's waist, before addressing Adrien. "Eliza and I have been discussing something and we believe it is in our best interest to bring you into our confidence." He stopped to be certain he had Adrien's full attention, then continued with a deadly gleam in his eyes. "But, if you betray us then you will have to answer to me."

"And me," Jonathon added, his eyes narrowing at Adrien.

Mr. Larson pulled out his pistol and held it in his hand. "And me."

Adrien stood his ground as everyone threatened him, appearing insulted. "Thank you for your threats," he said sarcastically as he crossed his arms over his chest. "I have no reason to betray you, nor would I ever."

Benedict's lips tightened into a thin line. "My wife's safety is my primary concern, and I might be overprotective."

Jonathon stifled a laugh, turning it into a cough. "Might be?"

Eliza's lips twitched in amusement for a moment, but quickly grew serious. "Adrien, we have grown to trust you these past couple of weeks, but revealing *Shadow's* identity is not something we do lightly."

Adrien's eyes lit up in anticipation and he glanced between Mr. Larson and Benedict. "I knew one of you were *Shadow*."

Shaking his head, Benedict said, "You are wrong." He smiled lovingly down at his wife, and she gave him an encouraging nod. "Eliza is *Shadow*."

Adrien sucked in a breath. "No," he hesitated, obviously not believing. "But you are a woman."

Eliza threw up her hands. "Not again." She marched over to stand toe-to-toe with Adrien. "We do not have time for this. We need to save Hannah, arrest Michel, and retrieve the list, in that order." She poked his chest. "You may ask all the questions you want *after* we finish this mission. Until then, just accept the fact that I am *Shadow*, and I will keep you, and the others, alive."

Spinning around, Eliza marched back to Benedict who shot Adrien a sympathetic look. "It took me awhile to wrap my head around it too, but you do not have the luxury of time. Just accept it. We have a job to do." Benedict offered his arm to Eliza and they headed out towards the carriage.

Mr. Larson walked closer towards Adrien, tucking his pistol back into his waistband. "If you betray my Eliza, I will kill you," he said in a quiet, deadly voice that left no doubt about his intention. "I do not believe in second chances when it comes to those I love." To emphasize his point, he slowly backed out of the room, keeping his eyes trained on Adrien.

Adrien tilted his head at Mr. Larson's retreating figure. "A little overprotective for a butler, is he not?"

Jonathon laughed loudly. "Mr. Larson would be a horrible butler, but that is not his job. His job is to ensure Eliza's protection."

"That would explain his lack of domestic skills," Adrien muttered.

"He runs the household when we are at Beaumont Castle, but Benedict hired him on at Chatswich Manor to continue his protection of Eliza. Besides, he and Eliza are quite fond of each other," Jonathon informed him.

"I have noticed that," Adrien stated. He lowered his voice as he glanced at the door. "Is Eliza really *Shadow*?"

"She really is." Jonathon stepped closer to Adrien. "Remember after you met her in the alley in Florence?" He waited until Adrien nodded before he continued. "After that night, Eliza changed. She asked to become a field agent. Of course, I said no, but she did not back down. Eventually, she became *Shadow*."

Adrien looked thoughtful. "Has she really killed hundreds of men?"

Jonathon frowned at the question. "No, she has not killed that many by her own hand, but she has pinpointed the location of multiple French frigates and American merchant ships, which allowed us to find and sink them."

"Did she really disguise herself as a pirate?"

Laughing, he shook his head. "No, that was most certainly not true."

Adrien shifted in his stance. "I have many questions, but I will keep them to myself for now." He ran his hand over his chin. "The daughter of the Duke of Remington is *Shadow*," he said incredulously. "I cannot fathom it."

Jonathon started walking towards the door. "Wait until you see her in action." He left Adrien in the room, shaking his head in awe.

❧ 28 ❧

HANNAH FELT HERSELF ROCKING BEFORE SHE EVEN OPENED HER eyes. When her eyes slowly opened, she noticed she was inside a dimly lit room and, apparently, on a boat. A tiny window above the bed was shuttered closed, allowing no light from the outside. With her hands tied in front, sitting up was difficult.

With some rolling and wriggling, she managed to slide up enough to rest her back against the wall. She was grateful for the lighted sconce hanging on the wall. It provided enough light for her to see a writing desk on the opposite side of the small, cramped room. A large trunk sat near the bed.

Hannah tried shifting her hands together, attempting to loosen the rope, but to no avail. Knowing she had a small knife in the pocket of her dress, she tried to reach it, but stopped when she heard the door creaking open.

A tall, muscular man with a square jaw and handsome features stood in the doorway. His hair was cut fashionably short, but his jaw had some stubble. He reminded her of Adrien, and it occurred to her that this must be Michel.

"Good, you are awake." He ducked under the door frame and walked over to sit on the trunk. Leaning back against the wall, he watched her for a moment. "I can see why Jonathon is smitten. Even with your disheveled hair and dirty clothes, you are very beautiful. Exotic, even."

Hannah resisted the urge to roll her eyes. "Why am I here?"

Michel smirked. "You are very direct. I appreciate that, but first, introductions are in order."

"I know who you are."

"You do?" he asked, amused.

Hannah nodded. "Your name is Michel and you murdered Lord Camden, then took his place."

He blinked rapidly at her response but then a smile touched his lips. "I should have given you more credit, Lady Hannah." His eyes roamed her body.

She cringed under Michel's intense perusal. "Why did you abduct me? I am nothing to you."

"You are wrong about that." He crossed his arms over his chest. "I am trading your life for Jonathon and Kate."

"No," Hannah gasped. "Why?"

His smile might have been charming on anyone else under other circumstances. He was obviously trying to disarm her. "Because I miss my wife," he said, placing his hand over his heart.

"I find that hard to believe, since you beat her to the point she lost your babe," she snapped at him.

Michel pursed his lips and she realized she might have gone too far. "My wife became insolent, and I abhor that kind of impertinence." His voice held a warning for her.

Hannah swallowed slowly, hoping to hide her growing fear from him. "And Jonathon? What could you possibly want with him?"

Michel's eyes were trained on her and he seemed disappointed in her question. "It appears that Jonathon has not confided his true identity to you."

"Jonathon is not *Shadow*."

Michel started chuckling under his breath. "He has deceived you, my dear. Who else could *Shadow* be? I have tracked the money trail, and it leads to Jonathon."

"What money trail?" she asked, genuinely confused.

"Parliament has awarded *Shadow* multiple lump sums, in the excess of £150,000. The money was transferred to Lord Beckett's account, then it appeared in Lord Jonathon's account."

He sneered. "It is amazing how quickly I obtained the information after I threatened to kill Lord Beckett's solicitors' children."

"If Jonathon is *Shadow,* then he will kill you," Hannah said confidently.

Michel's face grew hard, his eyes spiteful. "You have a great deal of confidence in an English coward. He lurks in the shadows to kill with his longbow."

Bringing her knees up to her chest, she rested her restrained hands on her knees. "*Shadow* is a hero," she responded.

Michel uncrossed his arms and rested his hands on the trunk. "We are at an impasse," he said with a biting tone. "Napoléon wants *Shadow* alive, which is why you are here. You are the bait."

Hannah shrugged one of her shoulders. "Jonathon will not come for me," she said, trying to sound sincere. Sadly, she had no doubt that Jonathon would come for her, even if he meant to trade himself for her.

He perused her body again, lewdly. "I have no doubt he will come for you." Michel moved to sit on the bed next to her.

She tried to shrink back towards the corner, but there wasn't much room to move.

"What you should be concerned about is whether I will enjoy you first or not." He placed his large hand on her knee. Slowly, he started sliding his hand up her thigh and squeezed lightly.

"Please, don't," she whimpered. His touch made her cringe and tears welled in her eyes.

Michel's gaze roamed up to her chest as his hand lifted off her thigh. She was certain he was going to touch her breast, but instead he tipped her chin to look at him. "I will do as you ask, only if you do as I ask. Do we have an understanding?"

Hannah's eyes were wide with fear, and she could only nod. She trembled under his touch, but did not dare move more than her head. She did not want to offend him in any way.

He glanced at her lips and leaned in, as if he intended to kiss her. Instead, he hovered over her lips and his warm breath skimming over her mouth. "I have been told I am a gentle lover."

Hannah willed herself not to move, hoping he would leave her alone. The tears flowed down her cheeks and she realized she was holding her breath.

Michel's lips pressed firmly against hers, forever imprinting the feel of his lips on hers. This was not a gentle, loving kiss like Jonathon's. It was a kiss to demonstrate his power over her. She shuddered against him, which caused him to chuckle.

His lips left her mouth and slowly trailed along her jaw, his tongue darting in and out. "I can feel your body shiver at my touch. I knew you would come around to me," he murmured, his voice low and seductive.

"Please, stop," she begged as she turned her head away.

Leaning slightly back, Michel started fingering the long, black tresses that had fallen around her face. "As you wish, my lady." He dropped her hair and trailed his finger down her forearm. "Assuming you behave."

Hannah closed her eyes. Anything was better than having Michel sitting by her, touching her, scaring her. "I will. I promise," she pleaded weakly. She felt Michel getting off the bed and sighed in relief. Curling herself tightly into a ball, she tried to hide as deeply into the corner as she could.

"If I see you on deck, I will assume you want more of my attention," Michel told her.

Hannah whimpered and refused to look at him. She had

never been so frightened in her life. The loss of her life seemed to pale in comparison to what Michel suggested he would do to her. She had worked so hard these past weeks to learn to protect herself, but it appeared to be all a waste of time. She could no more protect herself against Michel than she could ever stop loving Jonathon.

She started sobbing at her hopeless situation and heard Michel's boots stomping across the floor. When she heard the door close, she tried to calm herself. Soon, her tears turned to hiccuppy sniffles, then she took a few deep, shaky breaths and felt as though she could think again.

Hannah did not dare leave the room, but she knew she should do something to help her dire situation. What could she do? She thought about her knife and remembered she was planning to cut off her restraints before Michel entered the room. No, she should not remove them, but she could weaken them.

She glanced at the door. Did she dare? What if Michel found out? She closed her eyes and thought about what Eliza would do. Well, Eliza would weaken the twine and then calmly leave the ship. No, she was not as brave as Eliza, but she would skim her dagger through the twine.

Please save me, my love, she mouthed, over and over again. She knew Jonathon would come for her, but would it be too late?

LEANING HIS HEAD AGAINST THE BACK OF THE CARRIAGE, Jonathon sighed loudly. The long drive through the streets of London was wearing on his nerves, and he wanted to be out of this blasted carriage.

"I have not been to St. Savior's dock before," Adrien commented, breaking through his thoughts.

Benedict's arm was around Eliza's shoulder. "You are not missing much," he said, glancing out the window. "It reeks like a chamber pot and is in one of the worst sections in London."

The carriage hit a large ditch and they toppled forward. "We are nearing our destination," Eliza confirmed. As the carriage jolted over a rickety wooden bridge, the smell of human excrement was overpowering, causing Eliza to put a handkerchief up to her nose.

Benedict's nose wrinkled, as well. "That is a strong odor, but I believe the clothes that Jonathon wears to the pubs around here are more offensive."

Jonathon balked at his friend's humor. "My clothes are not that bad."

"No?" Eliza asked. "I have seen street urchins shy away from you when you wear those clothes," she teased.

Before Jonathon could respond to their jesting, the carriage jerked to a stop. A moment later, Mr. Larson opened the door and leaned in. "We are two blocks away from where the ship is moored." The men hopped out of the carriage and Benedict reached back to assist Eliza.

The narrow, uneven dirt street had low visibility due to the thick haze that hung over the road. Large holes appeared in the blackened, rotten buildings on both sides of the confined street, and the sounds of babies crying echoed through the night.

As they walked down the nearly empty streets, they avoided the people dressed in rags sleeping in corners and the dead animal carcasses. The closer they got to the River Thames, the more the buildings had collapsed in on themselves, but by the noise coming from within, it was obvious people still resided in these ramshackle homes.

Nearing the end of the street, the River Thames spread out in front of them. Along the river, boats of all sizes were moored along the waterfront. Jonathon looked up and down, trying to decide how they would locate the brig without attracting attention.

Mr. Larson came up from behind, rejoined the group, and cleared his throat. "A lady on the street pointed out the *Bronze Hine* to me. Follow me," he said over his shoulder. They walked close against the buildings towards the waterfront until Mr. Larson put his fist up in the air to indicate they should stop. Leaning closer to the group, he pointed. "May I present to you the *Bronze Hine*."

Jonathon saw a cluster of men talking and laughing near a small gangway. They all had large daggers sticking out of the waistbands of their trousers. The men were boisterous and did not appear to be taking their watch seriously. He counted only five guards and smiled. He could take them. He took a step forward, but a hand on his chest stalled him.

Benedict's eyes held concern. "We cannot jump into this, Jonathon. We need to see what else we are up against."

Turning his attention back to the brig, he saw more mercenaries pacing the main deck. Benedict was right. They could not storm the brig yet.

"Follow me," Eliza said. They kept flush against the buildings until they were about a hundred yards away from the *Bronze Hine*. She pointed at the two-story wooden structure that was parallel to the brig. "That will be an easy place to perch myself until we attack."

Jonathon noticed that the wooden structure that Eliza referred to had soot-blackened exterior walls and a decaying foundation. However, a large, wooden door on the ground floor had a fresh coat of paint. There were two large windows located on the second floor and an old, faded sign between them. The sign read, *Walker & Sons Exotic Imports*.

Benedict gaped at his wife and gestured at the decrepit structure. "You cannot be serious? That building could collapse at any minute."

"I am perfectly serious," Eliza said, crossing her arms over her chest. "I will be within 20 yards of the ships. If necessary, I could kill everyone on the brig, quickly and stealthily."

"It is not that bad, Ben..." Jonathon started but stopped when Benedict's eyes flashed at him, almost daring him to continue.

Benedict placed his hand on the small of her back, obviously worried about his wife. He leaned in, whispering so only she could hear. "Let us keep the killing down to a minimum."

Eliza's eyes flashed with a steely grit. "I know I have struggled with killing so many people as *Shadow*, but Michel made the mistake of abducting Hannah. She is family, and I will do whatever it takes to get her back to us."

Adrien took a couple of steps closer to the ships moored. "It might be simpler to hire a boat to bring us around the other side of the *Bronze Hine*. From there, we should be able to board easily."

Benedict shook his head. "I believe removing the guards protecting the gangway would be the best course of action."

"How many men do you think are on the *Bronze Hine*?" Jonathon asked.

"It is about the same size as the brig that Wade used, and he had fifteen sailors on board," Eliza replied.

"May I propose we attack early tomorrow morning before dawn?" Benedict put his hand up to stop Jonathon, who had opened his mouth to interrupt. "The closer we get to the meeting time, the more those sailors will be on guard."

"Then why not attack now, when they're not expecting it?" Jonathon asked.

"We will need to inform Lord Beckett and get additional agents to help," Mr. Larson answered.

Adrien nodded his head in agreement. "If we wait until just

before dawn, most of the men on board will be tucked in their beds, and only a skeleton crew will be watching guard."

Looping her arm around Benedict's, Eliza ventured, "I propose we stop by Uncle's townhouse and then try to get some sleep at Jonathon's." She smiled at Jonathon. "With any luck, you will have Hannah back in your arms before breakfast."

Jonathon raked his hand through his hair. He glanced helplessly at the river, which had horrible visibility, thanks to the fog. "I do not like it. Too many variables."

"I miss Hannah, too," Eliza hesitated, "but we need to speak with Uncle Charles before we board the brig. We have one shot at saving her life."

"One person I wouldn't mind seeing dead is Michel," Adrien said with a dry laugh.

Shaking his head, Jonathon replied, "Uncle Charles will insist we keep Michel alive for interrogation."

"We shall see," Eliza said with a too-sweet smile.

"Eliza," Benedict said in a warning tone. "We need to find out where that list is before anyone kills Michel."

Eliza arched an eyebrow defiantly. "Either way, tomorrow, Michel will be in Newgate, or dead."

🕊 29 🕊

Jᴏɴᴀᴛʜᴏɴ ʀᴇᴍᴏᴠᴇᴅ ᴛʜᴇ ᴘɪsᴛᴏʟ ғʀᴏᴍ ʜɪs ᴡᴀɪsᴛʙᴀɴᴅ ᴀɴᴅ ʜᴇʟᴅ
it firmly against his thigh. He was leaning against the side of the
building, thirty yards south of the *Bronze Hine*. Benedict stood
on his right and Adrien on his left. They were all in silent
contemplation. After meeting with his uncle last night, four additional agents had been assigned to help rescue Hannah and bring
Michel into custody.

The other agents were scheduled to arrive promptly at four in
the morning. This should be early enough to avoid the early
morning rush of loading and unloading cargo along the St.
Savior's dock.

The moon was bright in the sky and reflected off the river
without a hint of the fog they'd observed earlier. The wail of a
baby was heard for a few minutes, but when it stopped, the only
sound was that of water slapping alongside the brigs.

"Why are we dressed in black again?" Adrien mumbled
under his breath.

"It is to conceal my wife's identity. *Shadow* is known to be
dressed in black, and if she were the only one in black, it would

give her away. Besides," Benedict said, flexing his muscles, "I have been told that I look especially handsome in black."

"No, you do not. Eliza lied to you," Jonathon quipped.

"Do not listen to Jonathon." Adrien leaned forward. "You married a beautiful woman, so you must have done something right."

Benedict tipped his head towards Adrien. "Thank you."

"Where are the other agents?" Jonathon growled for the umpteenth time as he gripped his pistol.

"It is not quite four yet," Benedict said, pulling out his sword and running his finger along the blade. "Be patient."

Jonathon groaned inwardly. Obviously, Benedict did not understand his lack of patience right now. "That is easy for you to say. Your wife is safe…"

"My wife is in a crumbling building, dressed in men's clothing, and is preparing to bring down multiple mercenaries on that ship," Benedict argued, cutting him off. "Do not imply that my wife is safe."

"You are right, of course," Jonathon said, unclenching his jaw. "This must be hard for you, since you and Eliza have retired as agents."

"What? You both were retired? When?" Adrien asked in disbelief.

Benedict chuckled. "We have been retired since our wedding, but things changed once Jonathon showed up with Hannah."

"I am sorry about that," Jonathon said, leaning back against the wall.

Benedict put his sword away and placed his hand on Jonathon's shoulder. "Eliza and I will always support you, and we are glad that you turned to us in a time of need. "

"Thank you. I appreciate that," Jonathon said sincerely, hoping his tone conveyed how much Benedict's words meant to him.

Glancing in the direction of *Walker & Sons Exotic Imports,*

Benedict sighed. "My biggest concern is that Eliza will struggle with the death of these sailors."

"An assassin with a conscience," Adrien commented in disbelief.

"Eliza is not an assassin," Jonathon and Benedict said in unison.

Adrien put his hands up in surrender. "Sorry, I have just heard a lot of stories about *Shadow*. I am still trying to sort out which ones are true."

Four burly-looking men dressed in faded white shirts, tan trousers, and black boots walked towards them. Pistols and swords were sticking out of their trousers and they had a serious stride. Jonathon was pleased they were on their side.

"Lord Jonathon?" one of the men asked as they stopped in front of them.

Jonathon nodded. "First names only from now on."

The man looked pleased by his request. "My name is John." He pointed at the others and said, "Charles, Gavin, David."

Jonathon silently acknowledged the men. "This is Benedict and Adrien," he said, providing the necessary introductions.

John glanced around St. Savior's dock, before asking, "I heard that *Shadow* was helping on this assignment?"

"You are correct," Jonathon confirmed. "*Shadow* is already situated."

"Lord Beckett briefed us when he recruited us earlier, but could you go over the details again," John requested. "We do not want to be caught unprepared."

Together, Jonathon, Benedict, and Adrien outlined the plan that they had agreed upon late last night. Once they were finished, the four men bobbed their heads in unison.

Benedict stepped away from the building. "You ready?" he asked, searching Jonathon's face. "Stay close to the building until the guards on the gangway are dispatched. Then we board, silently and quickly."

Jonathon removed his pistol and kept it pressed against his trousers. "I am ready," he confirmed. He brushed past Benedict. "I will take the lead."

Slowly, single-file, they crept alongside the buildings near St. Savior's dock, using the shadows to conceal them. As they approached the *Bronze Hine,* they noted three tall, husky mercenaries guarding the small, narrow gangway to the brig. On the ship, eight men were seated with their heads leaning back against the wall, their mouths gaping open. It was clear that these men did not anticipate any type of altercation so early in the morning.

Jonathon stopped and leaned flush against the building. "I will give *Shadow* the signal," he informed the group. He handed Benedict his sword and walked out into the street, wanting to appear as if he was bustling off to work. As expected, the men guarding the *Bronze Hine* stared at him, assessing him as he passed them.

The sound of an arrow whizzing past his head caused him to spin around towards the men. In rapid precision, an arrow landed squarely in each man's chest, and one by one, they toppled to the ground, dead. Almost immediately, the agents came out from the building and dragged the fallen men out of sight.

Without hesitation, they boarded the ship with their pistols drawn and sprinted across the gangway. Before the men on the deck were fully awake, they were upon them. Jonathon pistol-whipped one thug who was attempting to stand and knocked him out. A loud cry was given as sailors started rushing towards them.

Jonathon shot his pistol into the stomach of a man charging at him. The roar of multiple pistol shots could be heard, and the acrid smell of gunpowder was strong.

As the first wave of sailors were killed, more rushed up the stairs and onto the main deck, with their weapons in hand. Jonathon tossed his spent pistol onto the deck and drew his sword. He could hear the other agents doing the same before his sole focus became remaining alive.

A tall, lanky sailor aggressively swiped his sword at Jonathon, who jumped back and tripped over a dead body. He fell on his back and prepared for another blow. The sailor stood over him, smirking at Jonathon's misfortune. As he raised his arm to strike again, an arrow flew past him, penetrating his shoulder. Eliza had given him a warning shot rather than killing him outright.

The sailor's eyes grew wide with fright, and he dropped his sword to his side. He started scanning the surrounding buildings. "*Shadow* is with them!" he shouted as he retreated. A few other men followed him, scurrying off the brig.

Jonathon jumped up as another mercenary took the sailor's place. He battled with this attacker until he saw an opportunity to run him through. Once he yanked his sword out of the man's stomach, he turned to find another assailant... and another. He lost count of how many he killed, because the moment he finished with one, he would find another ready to kill him.

Arrows whizzed past his head and he knew that Eliza was taking out many of them, as well. They must have underestimated how many mercenaries were aboard. A steady stream of men continued to flow out from below the main deck. So far, there was no sign of Michel or Hannah, but he would deal with that if he was still alive after this.

He was fighting a particularly skilled swordsman and was tiring fast. The man's offensive attacks were aggressive and pushed him backwards step by step. Unexpectedly, the man slipped, his sword falling to the deck with a loud clatter. The man stared up at him, eyes wide with fear, but he remained on his knees. Jonathon placed his own sword to his throat, preparing to end the fight.

"Drop your weapons," a loud voice boomed from the bridge. "Drop them, or I will kill her." A pistol cocked, echoing loudly.

Jonathon looked towards the bridge and saw Hannah, standing in front of Michel, who was holding a pistol to her temple. Her long, black hair was flowing in the wind as she stood rigid in Michel's arms. Her hands were tied in front of her, but instead of holding them still, she was wringing her hands together.

Making a show of lowering his sword to the deck, Jonathon looked sideways and saw that Benedict, Adrien, John, and David were still standing, breathing heavily, but alive.

Turning his attention back towards Hannah, he saw she was watching him with wide, frightened eyes. When his eyes met hers, she attempted to give him a faint smile. She was trying to be brave.

Jonathon's heart swelled at the sight of her. He wanted to smile at her. He wanted to run to her and let her know everything would be all right. But he did not dare move. So, he did the only thing that he could to comfort her. He winked at his damsel in distress.

HANNAH'S HEART SOARED AT THE SIGHT OF JONATHON WINKING at her. She was sure that his message was that everything would be all right. Michel held her tightly against him, with one hand gripping her upper arm, as his other hand pressed a pistol firmly to the temple of her forehead.

She was attempting to free her hands, without drawing Michel's attention. Earlier she had used her dagger to weaken the twine. She hoped a little jerk would allow her to break through her restraints.

Jonathon, Benedict, Adrien, and two other men, presumably

agents, were being held at knife-point by six vicious-looking sailors. Although the situation was dire, her five rescuers appeared to be completely at ease.

"Where is my wife?" Michel yelled.

Jonathon did not appear to be intimidated by Michel's venomous tone. "Unfortunately, she had a previous engagement and sends her regrets," he quipped.

"I will deal with Kate later," Michel shouted. "I have someone more valuable than my wife. I have the Marquess of Lansdowne." He smirked at Benedict. "I am sure your pretty, little wife will pay a king's ransom to get you back alive."

"Not likely," Benedict said with a smile. "Lately, she has been encouraging me to get out more."

Jonathon turned his head towards Benedict. "A trip to White's might appease Eliza."

"May I join you?" Adrien asked, joining in their banter. "I have not had a night out in ages."

Michel frowned at their interaction, and seemed to focus on Adrien. "Who else did you bring to their death?" he sneered.

Adrien stepped forward. "Adrien Stanton," he announced, performing a dramatic bow.

Michel hissed. "No. You were supposed to be dead."

"And you killed my entire family so you could spy for the French," Adrien retorted with clenched fists.

Michel's grip on Hannah's arm tightened. "Merely casualties of war." He shrugged indifferently, as if murdering an entire family meant nothing to him.

Jonathon casually leaned against the railing of the brig. "What is your plan, Michel? You cannot go back to impersonating Lord Camden. I think you should surrender and hand over the list of French agents that are on English soil."

"You will never find that list. It is on my property," Michel replied smugly.

Jonathon crossed his legs at the ankles as he continued to

lean on the side railing. "What if we just take a walk to Newgate and we can sort this all out?"

Michel laughed bitterly in Hannah's ear. She tried to jerk her head away from him, but he only pressed the pistol harder against her temple.

"You are my ticket to fame and fortune," he shouted at Jonathon. "Napoléon will reward me handsomely for handing him *Shadow*. I will be a hero in France!"

"I give him ten minutes," Benedict said with a glance towards Jonathon and Adrien.

Adrien appeared to consider Benedict's words. "I give him fifteen. He is a little windy."

"What are you fools talking about?" Michel grumbled, momentarily distracted from his tirade.

Jonathon smiled wryly at him. "We are betting on how quickly you will die."

Michel scoffed. "You are surrounded by a group of armed mercenaries and I have a pistol to your beloved's head."

Adrien shook his head dramatically. "I amend my guess to five minutes. I had assumed Michel was smarter than he appears, but I was wrong."

"Enough," Michel shouted, shoving Hannah forward. "I want you all on your knees."

Jonathon glanced over Michel's head. "Did you think we would board your ship without a secondary plan?" He pointed a finger towards Michel. "Lord Beckett is sailing a ship towards you at this very moment, and a bushel of agents will board this brig, capturing you and all these men in the process."

Hannah could feel Michel turn his head to look out at the river. "Impossible," he said, but his voice trembled slightly. "Lord Beckett would never board the ship, risking his nephew's life and that of a marquess."

Jonathon pressed his lips together, appearing to contemplate

Michel's words. "Good point, but at the very least, that ship will block you in, ensuring you will never leave England alive."

Michel muttered an expletive under his breath and was silent for a moment. "No matter, I will trade *Shadow's* life for my safe passage home," he said, his confidence waning.

"Now, that is a solid plan," Jonathon said sarcastically.

Benedict's eyes took on a deadly gleam. "I would not want to be in your shoes at this moment."

"And why is that?" Michel growled.

"You have ignited *Shadow's* wrath by abducting Hannah and beating your wife," Benedict explained deliberately. "You see, *Shadow* does not take kindly to the mistreatment of women."

Michel lowered the pistol from her head. "I do not have time for these games. I know *you* are *Shadow*," he said, directing the pistol at Jonathon.

Jonathon put his hands in front of him in a show of surrender. "I hate to disappoint you, but I am not *Shadow*."

Michel huffed. "Do not insult me. I know you have received payments from Parliament for your work as *Shadow*."

Jonathon threw his hands up in the air. "Is that what we are talking about? The reward money?" He gave Michel a sympathetic glance. "Did you really believe that we would leave a money trail leading directly to *Shadow*?"

Michel's body stiffened behind her, and Hannah used that moment to break her restraints. The twine fell to the floor.

"He did believe that," Adrien piped in, sounding apologetic. "You really *did* believe that England's most beloved spy would be easy to track. Oh, fake cousin…" His voice trailed off.

"Shut up! Just shut up!" Michel shouted at them. His pistol wavered in his hand.

Benedict pointed at the light coming from an approaching ship, a bell chiming in the distance. "Lord Beckett will be here any minute."

Michel turned his head back towards the water and muttered

another expletive. Again, Hannah took advantage of his distraction to slip her hand into the pocket of her dress. She slowly pulled out her dagger before he placed the pistol back to her temple. "You are *Shadow*! You have to be!"

Jonathon shook his head in disappointment. "For a man who impersonated an earl and became a leader in the Whig party, you are quite dim-witted."

"It does not matter what happens to me! This scheme is bigger than all of us. French spies have infiltrated both Houses of Parliament, and one is in position to rid you of your precious Prinny. When Napoleon triumphantly rides into London, key leaders will be in place to continue running the country under French rule," Michel shouted, sounding desperate.

"We will trade your life for the list," Benedict offered. "If you testify against your co-conspirators, you will be spared the noose."

Michel pushed her forward, gripping her arm tightly. "It matters not whether I live or die, but I will kill Hannah first. You stole my wife, and I will rob you of your happiness." He sneered at Jonathon.

Hannah gripped the hilt of her dagger, knowing she needed to stab Michel to free herself. She hesitated. Could she really stab another person?

Suddenly, she saw the six thugs on the main deck, one by one roar in pain. They each tried to reach behind them and two fell to their knees in agony. As they leaned forward, she could see arrows protruding from their backs. *Shadow* was providing a distraction for her.

Hannah thrust her dagger into Michel's thigh and jerked her arm away from his grasp. Michel roared in pain and staggered back. She ran down the stairs of the bridge, straight into Jonathon's waiting arms.

She turned to see Michel pulling the dagger out with his left hand and tossing it to the floor. As his eyes scanned the main deck, venom flew from his eyes when he saw her in Jonathon's arms. Before Hannah even blinked, Jonathon stood in front of her to block her from Michel's view.

"This is your last warning, Michel. Put down your pistol and you can live another day." Jonathon tried to reason with him.

David and John were helping the mercenaries pull out the arrows from their backs. It appeared the men had lost their eagerness to fight. "The game is over," Adrien shouted at Michel. "You are all alone."

Michel's eyes narrowed. "You will not win! English bastards will not be victorious!" He raised his pistol, but before he took aim, an arrow hit his chest, then another, and another. With each arrow, he was pushed further back towards the side of the brig. His pistol clattered to the ground and his glazed eyes wandered over the buildings.

Leaning against the railing, Michel had blood dripping out of his mouth, and five arrows protruded from his chest. He tried to speak, but only managed to gargle blood. Suddenly, he leaned further over the railing and disappeared over the side. A moment later, a loud splash was heard.

Jonathon kept his arm around Hannah and walked her to the ship's railing, looking over. Michel was dead, floating face up. His eyes were open as his body bobbed up and down, completely at the mercy of the river.

Hannah turned and put her face into Jonathon's chest. "You do not need to see that, my love," he murmured, as he kissed the top of her head.

Benedict looked over the railing. "Lord Beckett will not be pleased with this development."

Hannah glanced over at the river, watching a distant light grow brighter. "I thought he was on the approaching ship?"

"That was a strategic lie," Jonathon said, resting his cheek against her head. "There is an approaching ship, but I have no idea who is on it." He snuggled tighter against her.

Together, they turned back to look at the main deck. Hannah saw the bodies strewn all around and mourned their senseless deaths. The man who led her abduction was dead, and his eyes were wide open, staring directly at her.

She shuddered at the image, knowing it could have just as easily been her lying on the deck, dead. Jonathon looked down at her with compassion in his eyes. He leaned over and scooped her up in his arms. She wrapped her arms around him and nuzzled her nose into his neck, breathing in his masculine scent.

As they walked off the brig, Hannah sighed with relief. It was over. Jonathon had rescued her, again!

❧ 30 ❧

JONATHON CAREFULLY CARRIED HANNAH AS THEY WEAVED IN
and out of alleys, until the sight of two black carriages greeted
them. A group of men stood close by, as if waiting for orders.

"I am all for carrying the damsel in distress, but you must
consider Hannah's reputation," Benedict whispered, leaning
close to Jonathon.

Jonathon's grip on her tightened, as if she would float out of
his arms. "I do not give a damn about Hannah's reputation," he
muttered under his breath.

Benedict arched an eyebrow. "That is an interesting thing to
say when you are speaking about your future wife."

Hannah knew Benedict's counsel was wise, and as much as
she wanted to stay in Jonathon's arms, she knew she should
stand on her own two feet. "Benedict is correct." She looked up
at Jonathon. "Please let me down."

Jonathon looked at her, with panic in his eyes. "Never say
that again."

"Say what?" she asked in confusion.

Jonathon gently put her down, leaned in, and whispered, "If

you continue to agree with Benedict, then he will become more insufferable then he already is."

Hannah laughed and swatted playfully at his chest. "You are incorrigible."

"No, he is a bloody fool," Benedict mumbled, but a smile played on his lips.

Jonathon offered Hannah his arm and they approached the assembled men. The group parted, and Lord Beckett stepped out with his hands wide open. "You are safe," he said in relief. As his eyes roamed her face and body, his eyes stopped at the ripped fabric around her bodice. "Did he hurt you...?" His voice trailed off as his face paled.

Hannah shook her head. "No, no, he kissed me but, um, he did not...." She hesitated and could not seem to find the right words. Jonathon's arm slipped around her shoulder and she leaned into him, shuddering at the memory of Michel's lips on hers.

Lord Beckett watched her carefully, then finally said, "I am relieved that you are safe."

Hannah stepped out of Jonathon's arms and embraced Lord Beckett. "Thank you," she replied, with a heart full of gratitude.

As Lord Beckett released her, he gave her a quick smile. Then his face grew serious as he glanced between Benedict and Jonathon. "Where is Michel?"

"He is floating in the River Thames," Jonathon announced.

Lord Beckett's lips pressed into a tight line. "I wanted him alive," he said, in a voice full of rebuke.

"His death was inevitable," Benedict confirmed.

Adrien also chimed in, "He did not give us much of a choice, sir."

Lord Beckett glanced towards the roof of the adjacent building. His eyes shone with worry. "Did *Shadow* kill him?"

Benedict's jaw clenched tightly as he solemnly nodded. "Yes."

"Just Michel?" Lord Beckett asked.

Jonathon shook his head, reluctantly. "No, I would estimate eight."

Lord Beckett muttered a few expletives as he turned his back to them. After a moment, he composed himself and turned back around. "Why so many?"

Adrien stepped forward, looking contrite. "*Shadow* saved our lives. We vastly underestimated how many mercenaries Michel had aboard the *Bronze Hine,* and it became a battlefield. We lost two agents in the fight."

Lord Beckett sighed. "I am afraid to ask about the casualties aboard the ship."

"You will need to send a crew to dispose of the bodies aboard the brig and retrieve Michel," Jonathon informed his uncle.

"Did you at least obtain the list?" Lord Beckett asked hopefully. As they shook their heads, he gave them an exasperated look. "We will discuss this later, after I clean up your mess." He quickly turned and started barking orders to the men standing around the carriage.

Hannah saw two figures dressed in black coming out of the alleyway. One of the men she recognized as Mr. Larson, but the other had a longbow in his hand, with a sleeve of arrows around his shoulder, and a black cloth cap, hanging low on his head. This had to be *Shadow.* He was shorter than she imagined. In fact, he was several inches shorter than Mr. Larson.

Shadow kept his head down as agents streamed past him, seeming oblivious to their blatant perusal of him. As *Shadow* brushed past Benedict, Hannah saw Benedict's fingers discreetly reach out to squeeze *Shadow's* hand. That was odd.

Keeping his head low, *Shadow* approached her, and she felt nervous at the idea of meeting the notorious spy. *Shadow* stopped in front of her and lifted his head, revealing… Eliza.

Hannah's eyes widened in surprise. She was speechless. She opened her mouth to say something, but Eliza put her finger to her lips to indicate she should be silent. She nodded obediently, still in shock at discovering *Shadow's* identity.

Suddenly, everything came rushing back to Hannah and it made perfect sense. The way Eliza handled her attempted abduction, her ability to fence, throw daggers, shoot longbows, Beaumont Castle and why Mr. Larson was tasked to protect her.

Jonathon leaned closer, his warm breath on her ear. "Shocked?"

Hannah smiled at Eliza as she lowered her head and moved to one of the awaiting carriages. "Yes and no," she answered honestly. She noticed that Benedict casually walked over to the carriage that Eliza entered and hopped in. A low thud came from inside, indicating it was time to depart, and the carriage started rolling away.

Adrien walked closer to them. "Is this other carriage for our use?"

Jonathon shrugged at him. "Well, it appears we have one carriage left, but I am not willing to share right now." He placed his arm around Hannah's waist and attempted to escort her to the remaining carriage. "Do you require money to hire a hackney?" he asked over his shoulder.

Hannah refused to budge, despite Jonathon urging her on. "We are not leaving Adrien here," she said firmly.

Jonathon looked down at her and sighed. "You heard the lady. We will give you a ride back into town, but then I must insist you make use of your own carriage from there."

She turned to Adrien with a wide smile. "You are the Earl of Camden now." Her eyes widened as she realized what she'd said. "I am sorry. Well, you have been technically the Earl of Camden for some time now, but Michel... oh dear, I am making a mess out of this," Hannah said, giving him a sympathetic smile.

Adrien's lips twitched at her reaction. "I knew what you meant." He turned to Jonathon with a smug smile. "Just so you know, I have four carriages."

"Just four?" Jonathon huffed.

"I believe four is sufficient," Adrien stated with a flick of his wrist.

"If you say so," Jonathon replied smugly. "And yet, I have not seen one of them."

"I was ordered to go into hiding after I risked my life smuggling documents out of France," Adrien explained.

"It is a shame that you were sloppy and your identity was discovered," Jonathon said, mocking him.

Adrien shrugged. "I suppose, but without me, you would never have had enough proof to go after Michel. So, really, you should thank me for my exemplary spying skills."

Hannah shook her head at Jonathon and Adrien, not waiting to hear Jonathon's response as she climbed into the carriage. They bickered like brothers, but she knew they secretly valued each other's friendship. After all, they came together to risk their lives today to save her and to act as agents of the Crown.

Once they were situated in the carriage, she leaned her head against Jonathon's shoulder and closed her tired eyes. Suddenly, she pulled back slightly and looked up. "Is my father alive?"

Jonathon's arm tightened around her shoulder, pulling her tight against him. "Honestly, I do not know." His voice sounded strained. "He was alive when we left yesterday, but we have not been back to Beaumont Castle since we left to rescue you."

"Are we traveling to the castle or your townhouse tonight?" she asked.

"My townhouse is closer, but we could drive to the castle, if you would prefer," Jonathon murmured into her hair.

"Would you mind?"

"Not at all." Jonathon smiled as he stepped out to inform the driver of their new destination.

A few minutes later, they started their journey back, and although she was worried about her father, sleep immediately overtook her.

Jonathon wiped a hand over his face as he wandered into Eliza's library. He stepped up to the drink cart and poured himself a drink. He gulped it down, then poured himself another. He really should order a bath and take off his soiled clothing, but he needed a moment to think.

He had escorted Hannah to her father's room, and discovered him wide awake, lying in bed, eager to see his daughter. Kate had been sitting next to Lord Pembrooke's bed, but she excused herself once they arrived.

Jonathon did not want to leave Hannah, but he wanted to give her time alone with her father. Hannah had been quiet after she woke up in the carriage. He had attempted to engage her in conversation, but she seemed to withdraw from him.

Closing his eyes, he took a sip, attempting to wipe away any doubt that Hannah may have changed her mind about him. She was probably quiet because she was worried about her father. That must be it. That had to be it.

He tightened his hold on his glass. How he longed to marry Hannah! He never wanted to leave her side again. Would she marry him tomorrow if he obtained a special license today? What if she wanted to wait three weeks for the banns to be read? He did not want to wait that long!

A soft chuckle came from the sofa. Jonathon turned to see Benedict, drink in hand, sitting on the edge of the sofa, watching him closely. "You are frowning," his friend observed.

Sighing, Jonathon leaned up against the wall. "I was trying to think of a way to convince Hannah to marry me tomorrow."

"Why not today?" Benedict teased.

"By the time I ride into London and obtain a special license, it will be almost dusk." Jonathon frowned.

Benedict's eyes never wavered. "What is really bothering you?"

Jonathon furrowed his brows. "Hannah agreed to marry me, but that was before Michel abducted her and tried to kill her."

"And?" Benedict prodded.

Jonathon felt helpless since he could not force Hannah to marry him. "What if," his voice hitched, "she changed her mind? What if being married to a spy is too much for her?"

Benedict eyed him warily. "Did she give you any indication that she changed her mind?"

He shook his head. "No, but she was just rescued from a French spy who had a pistol to her head."

"But she's alive," Benedict countered, attempting to comfort his friend.

"This time," Jonathon said as he looked up at the ceiling. "Last time, she had her throat cut and had to receive four sutures. What if there is a next time? What if Hannah is killed?" He dropped his head down, looking defeated.

Benedict took a sip of his drink, looking thoughtful. "Eliza has been shot, twice now," he said, barely over the rim of his glass. "I worry about the same thing."

"But Eliza chose to be a spy," Jonathon pointed out. "Hannah did not choose this life. It was thrust upon her when Michel tried to abduct her." He took a sip of his drink. "What if Hannah decides she does not want to marry a spy?"

Benedict nodded. "Only Hannah can answer your questions. You should both rest before you have a serious talk with her."

"Is Eliza in bed?"

Benedict turned back towards the fireplace. "I tucked her in, but I needed time to calm my mind after…" His voice trailed off.

Jonathon sat on the opposite end of the sofa. He brought the glass to his lips as he watched the low-burning fire in the hearth.

"How is Eliza faring after killing those men?" He glanced over to see Benedict clenching his jaw.

After a moment, Benedict replied, "Surprisingly well, considering we retired as spies to prevent this from happening again."

Jonathon winced at the truthfulness of Benedict's words. He knew Eliza suffered deeply every time she was forced to take a life. "I am truly sorry for pulling you and Eliza into all of this."

Benedict waved his hand in the air dismissively. "Nonsense. That is what families are about," he said firmly before gulping his drink.

Neither of them spoke for a few minutes, preferring to sit in comfortable silence. What could be said?

Jonathon thought about what Eliza had endured as *Shadow*. He could not ask her to help again. It was too hard on her. In fact, he realized that he wanted to stop working as an agent, too. He did not want to be responsible for putting Hannah's, Eliza's, or anyone else's life in danger again. *Well, he would not mind putting Adrien's life on the line*, he thought, chuckling to himself.

"What are you chuckling about?" Benedict asked, placing the glass on the side table.

Jonathon's lips twitched. He doubted Benedict would be amused by his thought. He did want to talk to Benedict about retiring, though. "I believe it may be time for me to retire as an agent."

Benedict lifted an eyebrow. "Are you in earnest?"

"I believe so," Jonathon replied honestly.

Benedict shook his head in disbelief and brought his hands behind his head. "I never thought I would see the day that you would retire as an agent."

"You did not seem eager to retire either, if I remember correctly," Jonathon said, lowering his glass onto a table.

"True, but it was necessary. Not only did I inherit an earldom at the time, but I wanted to protect Eliza."

"And I want to protect Hannah," Jonathon said fiercely.

Benedict dropped his hands and turned to face him. "Where do you want to go from here?"

Jonathon leaned forward in his seat and placed his elbows on his knees. "Maybe buy some land near Chatswich, build an estate and raise a family."

"Unfortunately, there is no land for sale anywhere near Chatswich Manor," Benedict said, pausing. "But, I would be happy to gift you a parcel of land near our estate as a wedding present."

Lifting his head, Jonathon saw his friend's smug smile. "I would be willing to pay you for the land."

"Not necessary," Benedict said with a wave of his hand, "since I am confident that Eliza will be thrilled to have you and Hannah so close. I would do anything to ensure my wife's happiness, even if I have to endure being in your presence every day."

Jonathon laughed. He considered Benedict his closest friend, and he knew his friend had similar affection towards him. "I would finally be able to teach you how to fence properly, since your skills are so poor," he jested.

Benedict looked amused. "My fencing skills are exemplary, as evidenced by the fact that I killed more men than you did today. Besides, if I was going to ask someone for fencing lessons, I would ask my wife."

"Fair enough." Jonathon laughed, acknowledging the truth. "I am hoping to have a chance to spar with Hannah again."

Benedict chuckled and stood up. "Oh, you will have a chance again. I am sure of it. I think it is time we both get some rest."

Jonathon turned to glance out the window and noticed a few guards roaming the perimeter. He was too anxious to sleep. Suddenly, it dawned on him what he should do. "I believe I will ride into London and obtain a special license."

His friend shook his head and sighed. "You have been up all night, and it seems foolish to ride into London..." He paused and gave Jonathon an exasperated look. "Will anything I say, or do, change your mind?"

"Nothing," Jonathon said as he arose.

Benedict nodded his acceptance. "Well, I tried. I am too tired to even attempt to argue with you."

"Will you inform Hannah of my departure?" Jonathon asked, but then changed his mind. "Wait," he called.

Benedict spun around to look at him.

"Do not tell Hannah *why* I left."

"That is risky, my friend." Benedict frowned.

"It is," Jonathon said as he strode towards Benedict, "and it is a risk I am willing to take."

❧ 31 ❧

PEEKING INTO THE DINING ROOM, HANNAH SAW EVERYONE assembled around the table. Well, everyone except for Jonathon. Why did he leave yesterday so unexpectedly?

The morning before, he had escorted her in to see her father, then he had departed. Benedict told her that he had unfinished business in London. Was it about Michel? Did he go to see his mistress?

Wait, did Jonathon have a mistress?

Hannah shook her head, attempting to rein in her wild, inappropriate imagination. She trusted Jonathon. He must have had something important to do in London.

He had asked her to marry him before she was abducted. What if he changed his mind? What if he went to see a solicitor to determine if he was legally obligated to marry her?

Stop, Hannah! You are being preposterous, she thought.

She must still be exhausted from yesterday's rescue. That would explain her irrational thoughts, wouldn't it?

This morning, she'd taken extra care with her grooming, but that reminded her of her lady's maid. Her heart broke when she thought of Maggie dying over something she had done. She'd given in to the grief, sobbing, desperately wishing that her friend was still alive.

Fortunately, Kate had heard her cries of distress and came in to comfort her. After spending some time crying, Kate had urged her to get dressed, helping her as Maggie would have. It felt wonderful to spend time with Kate, who appeared less grief-stricken, and it had lifted her spirits.

After Kate had excused herself for breakfast, Hannah took her time strolling to the dining room, briefly checking in on her father, who assured her it was all right for her to eat breakfast without him.

Beaumont Castle was not large and it only took a few minutes to reach the dining room. The door was open and she heard the cheerful banter coming from within. Everyone appeared to be in good spirits, which only irritated her. How could everyone be so happy when Jonathon was not with them, with her?

"Are you all right, Lady Hannah?" Mr. Larson asked, standing next to her outside of the dining room.

Putting on a smile she hoped looked genuine, she answered, "Perfectly."

Mr. Larson stifled a laugh. "You are a horrible liar." Glancing briefly into the dining room, he looked back at her knowingly. "Do not fret. He will be back shortly."

"Whom are you speaking about?" she asked, feigning ignorance.

Mr. Larson turned to walk away, muttering, "I am surrounded by love-sick fools."

Hannah watched him leave and decided she should attempt to be social. Lifting her head high and squaring her shoulders, she strolled into the dining room, trying again to smile convincingly. "Good morning, everyone," she said in a falsely cheerful voice.

As she stepped to the buffet table, she noticed Benedict and

Eliza sat at one side of the table reading the newspaper together. Kate and Adrien were on the opposite side of the table in deep conversation. Before she had time to place food onto her plate, everyone turned their attention towards her.

Eliza got up from her seat and came over, giving her a side hug. "I am so glad that you are awake. Have you recovered from your abduction?"

Smiling weakly, she acknowledged, "Physically I have, but I am still saddened by all the people who died because of me.

Eliza's eyes misted over. "I understand, more than you know."

"I know you do, and I am even more grateful for you." She leaned closer to her friend and whispered, "Thank you for saving my life."

Eliza straightened up with a smile. "It was a team effort." She hugged Hannah once more, then returned to her seat next to Benedict.

Hannah placed some food on her plate and took a seat near the middle of the table. As she began eating, she enjoyed watching Adrien as he explained to Kate all about the rescue and how *he* saved the damsel in distress.

At one point, Adrien looked at her and winked, but continued to share a radically different rescue than she had experienced. It was obvious Adrien was trying to make Kate smile. It was working.

Appearing enthralled, Kate occasionally asked a question, to which Adrien would answer with his version of the truth.

Hannah glanced at Eliza and she, too, appeared amused by Adrien's story. Ironically, *Shadow* was not mentioned, but Adrien appeared to have taken on a hundred pirates and lived to tell about it.

"That was quite an interesting tale. Was I even in your story?" Benedict asked with a grin as he lowered the newspaper.

Adrien's eyes danced with merriment. "Yes, you stayed behind to guard the carriages."

Benedict laughed loudly as Eliza reached over to pat his hand. "And what an outstanding job you did, my dear," she teased.

Adrien raised his teacup in salute to Benedict. "That he did, Eliza."

"Didn't Eliza help rescue Hannah, too?" Kate asked Adrien.

Not missing a beat, Adrien replied, "Of course, she did. She supervised Benedict as he guarded the carriages."

Kate smiled at Eliza. "I knew you went with the men last night, and I was worried that you might be hurt. Although, I know you can defend yourself, if necessary."

"It is best to let us men protect you ladies," Adrien stated with a lopsided smile. He then plopped a piece of fruit into his mouth.

Before anyone could reply, Jonathon strode into the room, looking handsome in a dark green waistcoat, tan trousers, and tall black riding boots. He walked over to her, leaned down and whispered, "Are you going to let Adrien get away with saying that?"

Finding herself momentarily distracted by Jonathon's presence, his devilishly handsome appearance, and the feel of his warm breath on her cheek, it took her a moment to find her voice. "I believe I will allow him this small victory," she finally whispered.

"How gracious of you," Jonathon said next to her ear, making her skin tingle. "Are you finished?"

"I am," Hannah replied, placing her white linen napkin on the table and accepting Jonathon's outstretched hand as she rose.

Jonathon placed her hand in the crook of his arm before he addressed Eliza. "Uncle Charles told me that tomorrow it will be widely reported that Mother and Lord Camden died in an apparent highway robbery attack on their way to the abbey."

Frowning, Eliza asked, "Will there not be an investigation?"

Jonathon shook his head. "Uncle informed Prinny of Mother's deceit and how Michel assumed Lord Camden's identity, after slaughtering the entire family." He looked apologetically at Adrien. "Prinny did not want Kate or you to suffer from the gossip that would no doubt follow you for the rest of your lives if the truth came out. So, he gave Uncle Charles the task of covering up their deaths."

"That was most gracious of him," Adrien said as he pushed his plate away.

"Prinny said it was a personal favor to the Beckett family," Jonathon said, informing the group of the great honor that had been bestowed upon them.

Hannah looked up at Jonathon. "Is that why you went to London yesterday?"

Giving her a crooked grin, Jonathon said, "No, I had an entirely different reason, but my uncle caught me this morning as I was leaving my townhouse."

"Then why did you need to go to London?" Hannah wanted to ask him why he left her behind, but pursed her lips together instead. It was not her place to question everything he did.

"If I did not know any better, I would say that you missed me," Jonathon teased. He studied her for a moment before asking, "Did you?"

Tilting her head back, Hannah let her eyes roam his face, as she kept a serious expression on her own. Then, she saw uncertainty on Jonathon's brow. Impulsively, she went up on her tiptoes and pressed her lips into his for a brief kiss. When she was back on her feet, she asked, "What do you think?"

Jonathon just stood there with a foolish smile. However, Adrien could not stay quiet for long and stated the obvious. "It would appear Hannah did, in fact, miss Jonathon."

"Thank you for clarifying that." Jonathon rolled his eyes.

Adrien put two fingers to his forehead and saluted Jonathon. "You are welcome, sir."

Hannah smiled at Adrien, but turned back to gaze at Jonathon. He was watching her with a sense of longing, giving her immense hope that Jonathon still loved her. "Did you miss me?" she asked coyly.

He opened his mouth, but then immediately closed it as he glanced around the table, noticing all the eyes trained on them. "What if we continue this conversation in private?"

Jonathon took Hannah's hand as they left Beaumont Castle, making their way down towards the stream in comforting silence. When they arrived at the bench near the water, he waited as Hannah lowered herself down before claiming the seat next to her. He sat close, but angled his body to ensure he could gaze into her mesmerizing blue eyes.

Slowly, he started tracing circles on the top of her hand with his thumb, enjoying the softness of her skin. He smiled at her, marveling at her beauty and how she was here, holding hands with him. He must have stared at her longer than he intended because he could see her cheeks turning pink. "You asked why I... um... went to London," he stammered. *This was not going well.*

"I did," Hannah replied.

Clearing his throat, he attempted to calm his racing heart. "I went to London to obtain a... something." He hesitated, changing his mind about what he'd intended to say. What if she thought he was too presumptuous?

Hannah raised an eyebrow in question. "Did you obtain that something?"

"I did."

She kept her eyebrow raised, still skeptical. "And can you tell me what you obtained?"

"A special license," he said quickly, then tensed while he waited for her response.

Hannah's whole face relaxed and a wide smile touched her lips. "Why, that is wonderful news."

"It is?"

"Is it not?" she asked, suddenly appearing concerned by his words.

Jonathon put his hand to her cheek, attempting to wipe away any doubt. "When you were abducted, I felt fear such as I have never felt in my life. I panicked. Eliza had to threaten to leave me behind unless I pulled myself together." His thumb caressed her cheekbone. "And when I saw Michel with a pistol to your head," he whispered, his emotions overtaking him.

She covered his hand on her cheek with her own. "I felt the same way when I saw so many men against you on the ship."

His voice was hoarse with emotion. "I can do anything in this world, if you are beside me. Please never leave me again."

"I feel the same way," Hannah said, her eyes full of tenderness.

Tenderly brushing away her tear, Jonathon replied, "I was afraid that you might not want to marry a spy, after what you've just endured."

She smiled lovingly at him. "I fell in love with a spy, so it makes sense that I would be willing to marry a spy."

Knowing she deserved an apology for what she had endured, he furrowed his brow. "I have not protected you very well and..."

Hannah looked exasperated. "You have done an extraordinary job of protecting me, Jonathon."

"Michel abducted you…"

"Because of my father, not you," she stated emphatically. "It was my father's choice to leave Beaumont Castle, not yours."

"Maggie died because…"

Cutting him off again, Hannah said firmly, "Because of Michel, not you."

"You had your throat sliced," Jonathon said, surprised that he finished this thought without Hannah cutting him off.

Hannah placed her fingers to her scarred skin. "Michel sent those two thugs after me, and you ensured that I had protection." She relaxed her shoulders. "You left *Shadow* to protect me."

Removing his hand from her cheek, he reached out, encompassing her ungloved hands into his. The longing of his heart was stilled, and he was blissfully happy. "I love you, Hannah. I had no idea how empty my life was until you captured a piece of my heart, altering my course completely." He fought against his rising emotions, trembling under the strain. "I need you. You make my life worth living."

"Oh, Jonathon," Hannah said, her eyes full of tenderness. "I love you, too."

He leaned forward until his lips hovered over hers. "I do not deserve you, I know that. But my selfish heart will not allow me to set you free."

Her warm breath fanned over his lips as she said, "I do not wish to be set free."

Ever so gently, he pressed his lips against hers, knowing Hannah would forever hold his heart. She melted against him, her lips softened against his mouth. He deepened the kiss, wishing that he could stay in this moment forever, but he knew he needed to ask one more question. Reluctantly, he broke off the kiss, resting his forehead against hers. "I asked you this question before, but so much has happened since that night." He hesitated, before saying, "Will you marry me and make me the happiest of men?"

A brilliant smile graced Hannah's lips. "Yes, I will marry you. I love you unconditionally and without reservation."

Feeling his heart swell with joy, he swiftly kissed her before leaning back. "I feel the same, even though I was a fool about you learning to defend yourself. I have never been so grateful to be proven wrong."

Hannah reached into her pocket to bring out her dagger. Her smile faltering. "I am ashamed. I spent weeks learning to defend myself, but when the moment came to use this against Michel, I hesitated. If *Shadow* had not provided me with a distraction, I might not have had the nerve to stab him in the thigh."

"My dear, brave Hannah. You were stoic, and I was so proud of you," he said as he pulled her into an embrace.

Her hands slid around his waist. "You were?"

Jonathon kissed the top of her head. "I was." He kissed her head again. "I still am." He felt her smile on his chest, as she tightened her hold on him.

"You know, I was right about something," she murmured.

He rested his cheek on the top of her head. "And what was that?"

"When we first met, I said, 'Only one man can save me now'."

He smiled slightly, remembering her disheveled state at the time. "And did I save you?" he asked.

"You most certainly did." She shifted so her face was tilted up towards him, her eyes full of love, peering deep into his soul. "You will always be my hero."

Contentment shone in his eyes, as love radiated from his heart. "And you, my love, will always be my favorite damsel in distress."

EPILOGUE

Hannah burrowed closer to Jonathon as she tried to sleep in the bouncy carriage. His arm was draped over her shoulder as he gazed out the small window. As much as she wanted to give up on the prospect of sleep, she enjoyed being tucked protectively in his arms.

This past month had been an enchanting blur. She loved spending time with her husband, which was something that she would never tire of saying. She sighed contentedly. How was she so lucky to marry her true love?

They were married the day after Jonathon secured the special license. Then, they traveled to Luke's estate in Scotland for a honeymoon. Hannah enjoyed becoming acquainted with Jonathon's older brother, Lord Downshire, and his charming stud farm, Downshire Farms. For so long she had been alone, and now she had a husband and an extended family. *What a marvelous blessing!*

Jonathon had surprised her on their wedding tour, explaining that he had retired as an agent of the Crown to become a full-time, land-owning aristocrat and devoted husband. Benedict had granted them a sizable parcel of land near Chatswich Manor and construction had already begun on their new estate. Until their home was ready, they would stay as guests at Chatswich Manor, while Benedict and Eliza stayed in London for the Season.

The carriage started slowing down as it veered to the right. Hannah lifted her head to glance out the window. "Are we already at Chatswich Manor?"

"No, my dearest," Jonathon said, kissing the top of her head. "I asked the driver to take a detour on our drive back, so I could show you something."

"Oh," Hannah murmured.

Effortlessly, Jonathon pulled her onto his lap and she looped her arms around his neck. "I promise you will enjoy this surprise."

"You have already spoiled me enough, my dashing husband," Hannah said playfully.

Jonathon arched an eyebrow. "Dashing, am I?"

Leaning in, she kissed him. "Yes," she said, her lips hovering over his. "And charming," she said, kissing him again, but this time she turned it into a passionate, all-consuming kiss.

After many wonderful moments, Jonathon rested his forehead against hers, breathing hard. "I find I rather enjoy being married to you."

Hannah's face broke out into a smile. "Do you now?"

"I am still in awe that you agreed to marry me…" Jonathon's voice trailed off as the carriage rolled to a stop.

"Where are we?" Hannah asked as she tried to glance out the window.

Jonathon closed the drape over the small window. "No peeking." He gently placed her next to him on the bench and hopped out of the carriage. He spun around and assisted her as she stepped out.

Hannah surveyed the surrounding area, noting the large, gated pastures, filled with beautiful horses, spanning both sides of a narrow dirt road that led up to a stately home. A massive red barn was adjacent to the estate and multiple paddocks of assorted sizes were systematically placed next to the barn.

Standing behind her, Jonathon placed his arms around her waist, pulling her close to him. For a few moments, neither of them spoke as they watched the horses graze on the rich, fertile grass. He leaned closer to her ear. "I invested in this stud farm. Does this please you?"

Hannah leaned back against him. "Everything you do pleases me."

"Everything?" he asked, chuckling in her ear.

Turning in his arms, Hannah tilted her head up so she could gaze at the dark green eyes that she had grown to love. "Honestly, the sight of these horses makes me a little melancholy," she said, hoping she did not offend her new husband.

"And why is that, my love?" he asked, his arms tightening around her waist.

Her eyes misted with tears. "It reminds me of Lucy. It was her dream to own a stud farm with Samuel."

Jonathon's eyes were filled with compassion. "I suspected as much."

Hannah managed to smile, for her husband's sake. "But, this does please me, if it pleases you."

His face softened at her words. "Oh, Hannah." He brought up his hand to cup her cheek. "Do you honestly think I would forget about Lucy and her family? They saved your life, effectively saving mine."

"I do not understand."

"Samuel owns the farm, and I am only a silent partner." He smiled.

Hannah's eyes grew wide. "You did this for Samuel and Lucy?"

He shook his head, his words laced with love. "No, I did this for *you*."

As she threw her arms around his neck, he laughed joyously

in response. "If I had known you would be this happy, I would have bought you several stud farms."

"Hannah!" Lucy shouted from the doorway of the estate.

"Lucy!" Hannah shrieked as she turned around. She picked up her skirts in a most unladylike fashion to run towards her friend. They met halfway and embraced warmly. After a few moments, Hannah dropped her arms around Lucy. "Did you and Samuel finally get married?"

Lucy enthusiastically nodded. "We wed at the parish after the banns were read."

"I am so pleased." Hannah glanced over Lucy's shoulder. "Where is Samuel?"

Beaming, Lucy replied, "Samuel is in the stable. He will be out shortly. I was in the kitchen when I saw your fancy carriage pull up." She leaned closer. "You married the son of a duke?"

Hannah's lips curled in amusement for a moment before she longingly glanced over her shoulder at Jonathon. "I did. After he rescued me, I found I could not live without him," she said dramatically.

Jonathon closed the distance between them, wrapping his arm around her shoulders. "It is a burden that I must bear," he said, winking at Lucy.

Lucy giggled. "Yes, I see. What a horrible burden for you, my lord."

"No 'my lord' from you," he said emphatically. "Please call me Jonathon. After all, we are as close as family."

Lucy's eyes grew wide, obviously surprised by his request. "As you wish... Jonathon," she said slowly.

Jonathon laughed amusedly. "You might want to practice saying my name since I expect we will be spending a lot of time together."

"How far are we away from Chatswich Manor?" Hannah asked, curiously.

"Two hours by carriage," Jonathon replied.

"How delightful," she said, as she smiled at Lucy. "How are your parents?"

"They sold their sheep farm and moved in with us," Lucy said, scanning the stately home. "There was plenty of room and... Jonathon," her eyes skirting to him, almost as if she wanted to confirm it was still all right to say his given name, "... provided a few servants to help with the cooking and cleaning."

"And Lord Jonathon set up this stud farm to be fully operational and profitable from the beginning," Samuel said, walking up wearing dusty trousers, a white shirt, and black boots.

Jonathon arched an eyebrow. "I have asked you repeatedly to call me Jonathon. We are almost brothers," he stated.

Samuel nodded in response. "You have been most generous. We will never be able to repay all the kindness that you have bestowed upon me," he placed his arm around his wife, "and Lucy."

Jonathon shook his head. "You are wrong there." He glanced down at Hannah. "I am in your debt. If Lucy and her family had not saved Hannah from the ravine, and you had not protected her from those men in the village, then Hannah would not be standing here as my wife."

He extended his hand towards Samuel. "It is I who could never repay you for your kindness."

After shaking Samuel's hand, Jonathon slipped his arm back around Hannah's shoulders. "Shall we go inside so I can be introduced to your parents? I want to personally thank Mrs. Dawson for not allowing Mr. Dawson to smear horse dung all over Hannah. If she had smelt like manure, I doubt I would have let her kiss me."

Hannah's mouth dropped open. "I did no such thing."

"No?" Jonathon shrugged nonchalantly. "I seem to recall you being somewhat forward." He again winked at Lucy to let her know he was teasing his wife.

"Come on, you two," Lucy said, smiling. "I can't wait to hear all about your courtship."

"It was a peculiar courtship," Hannah said, glancing at her husband.

Jonathon smiled at her tenderly, his eyes full of love. "Yes, it certainly was. It was perfect."

COMING SOON

To Love
a Spy

"His greatest mission was to mend
her shattered heart."

by

Laura Beers

ABOUT THE AUTHOR

Laura Beers spent most of her childhood with a nose stuck in a book, dreaming of becoming an author. She attended Brigham Young University, eventually earning a Bachelor of Science degree in Construction Management.

Many years later, and with loving encouragement from her family, Laura decided to start writing again. Besides being a full-time homemaker to her three kids, she loves waterskiing, hiking, and drinking Dr. Pepper. Currently, Laura Beers resides in South Carolina.

Made in the USA
Middletown, DE
12 November 2022

14760071R00186